Contents

Chapter One

LOUISE 1985

My favorite grandchild, Lulu, came to see me today. I know one ought not to have favorites, but I cannot help it. She is the child of my son, the youngest of my children. He arrived long after I had thought our family was complete, at the beginning of the last war, when my husband and I were middle-aged. As one can imagine, his impending arrival caused an enormous upheaval. Harriet, the eldest of my three daughters, was eighteen, and acted as though I had become pregnant solely to embarrass her in front of all her friends. Sheila and Carrie, thirteen and fourteen respectively, took it in their stride, though there were blushes and giggles when it dawned on them in what activities their parents had been engaged. And although Harriet sulked for many months, and showed no interest in her baby brother when he arrived, she now dotes on him, his wife, and their three children, Lulu being the eldest.

Her name is actually Louise, named for me, but when she was three, the minister's wife asked her what her name was, and all that came out was "Lou-Lou". So she became Lulu. She was an enchanting child, as her father before her had been, and she still is today. The mop of golden curls, now darkened to the color of liquid honey, is cut to surround her face like a halo, and her brown eyes are a startlingly dark contrast against the creamy skin of her face. She emphasizes them, of course, with mascara and eyeliner, but uses only

7

a hint of pearly pink color on her mouth. Her skin is blemish-free, soft, and fragrant when she rests her cheek against mine.

"I want my skin to be as nice as yours is when I am your age. Look, Gran! You have hardly a wrinkle, and your skin is soft as a baby's."

I remember passing a mirror, once, and being startled by the reflection. *Who is that old woman?* I wondered for a split second, and then laughed at my foolishness. I am eighty-eight now, and although my skin may not be quite as soft as a baby's, and I have more than a few wrinkles, I have to admit I do not look my age. Is that vanity? I have always creamed my face every night, and never have worn make-up—maybe the slightest touch of powder on a warm day to keep my nose from getting shiny.

I live alone in the small house in Point Grey that my husband and I bought when he retired twenty-five years ago. He died eleven years later, just before our fifty-first wedding anniversary. The family had organized an enormous party for our golden wedding the year before, and friends and relations from all over came to celebrate with us. Our attendants were there, my husband's sister and her husband from Ontario, my sister Norah, her husband and several members of their family from Prince Edward Island, and the whole family here in the Vancouver area. Lulu was only five at the time and adorable in her party dress. She insisted on sitting on my lap and feeding me pieces of wedding cake. She still remembers it.

Harriet worries about my being alone, and every once in a while threatens to move in with me. More realistically, she would probably have me move in with her. It would not work. I am independent and enjoy my own routine, which varies from day to day. She would have me organized to the minute. I turn the volume on my record player up to fill the house with music. It would drive her mad. She has never married, having lost her 'beau', as she called him, in the final days of the last war. Whether they would have wed is a moot point; the fact is, she has remained single, and ever since her retirement at fifty she has devoted all her spare time to good works, church committees, and volunteering for charity fund-raisers. She is a worthy woman, but I find her exceedingly dull.

I have a wonderful cleaning woman, who comes in once a week and travels through my house like a whirlwind, leaving it shining. Her husband is a gardener, and he keeps my small yard in pristine condition, plants my bulbs in the fall, mows the lawn, cleans my gutters, and prunes the bigger shrubs. I weed and prune my small shrubs and enjoy setting out the annuals in the spring. I have been so fortunate that I am not troubled by arthritis in my hands and knees. Friends my age have difficulty opening doors, and certainly can't get down on their hands and knees in the garden as I do. Twice a year my gardener and his wife collaborate and wash my windows inside and out until they sparkle, and if I need other workmen, he will interview them first, ruthlessly asking questions and demanding references. Lulu's father David and his wife Petra have always come by for a visit at least once a week, bringing the children with them, and my married daughters come when they can. Sheila's husband and I have never cared much for each other, so her sister Carrie will usually pick her up. Both girls live away up the valley, and are getting older. Freeway driving is not for them. But they telephone frequently, and if I'm not home they leave long, chatty messages.

I am happy here, with my books and music and my garden. I am coping all right alone. If I fall downstairs and break a hip, or become so forgetful that I leave the stove on and set fire to the house, or wander off and get lost, that will be the time to move into a retirement home, but definitely not Harriet's. Lulu insists that her Aunt Harriet will probably be in the home before me!

Lulu chattered for a long time today about fairly trivial things: a movie that she had seen with her girlfriend Jaime, how she spotted a pileated woodpecker in the woods beyond her home. Lulu is an avid bird-watcher, and attends the local naturalist society meetings. She talked about her brothers and how they were doing in high school, and how Johnny, the younger, had broken the record in high jump. She told me her mother has decided to stop tinting her hair and is dismayed as to how much grey has grown in. She showed me the postcard from her fiancé Bruce, who is away at university in the East.

She is only twenty, and in my opinion rather young to become engaged. I thought that she should get a university education, have

9

a career, and do a bit of traveling before settling down. However, she says she wants to write, and can do that and have babies at the same time. She and Bruce will travel together later on. They haven't set a date yet, but it will be a year or so before Bruce is finished his studies and joins a firm. He has achieved a chartered accountancy, and is presently working on his MBA. Like my daughter Harriet, he is worthy, but rather uninteresting. Mind you, it is quite possible that there is no man in the world good enough for my darling Lulu.

Lulu sat in silence for a long time, twisting Bruce's diamond round and round her finger, seemingly entranced by the sparkling gem. We were out in the garden enjoying this unusually warm April day. On the West Coast April can be as hot at times as July, the spring flowers bloom in profusion, and the trees are all in leaf. In contrast, Ottawa, where I grew up, can be still chilly, with patches of snow remaining in shady spots, and the tulip bulbs barely showing their pale green fingers to the sky. I waited patiently for her to speak, my eyes closed, savoring the feel of the sun's rays on my face, and listening to a white-crowned sparrow singing in the tree beside my back door. Lulu told me its name one day last year, and gave me her field glasses to look at it. She pointed out the white stripes on its head, and told me to listen to its song. We watched when it flew down and began to hop about, looking for food. Presently she went into my kitchen and refilled the empty bird feeder she had bought me for my birthday. It wasn't long before there were a crowd of gregarious house finches clustered about the feeder cheerfully squabbling and jostling for the best position. I remember her pleasure in watching their frenetic activities. One flew to the top of the tree and began his warbling song.

"Isn't it a lovely song, Gran?"

"Yes, it is," I answered. "It's as though he's singing a hymn of praise to the Creator."

I remember how she smiled at that. "Yes, you're right, but I think the white-crowned sparrow is still my favorite."

She wasn't hearing the song today, I thought, as I opened my eyes and watched her twist the ring endlessly. Finally she looked up at me and said, "Gran, I met a man last week, and I don't know what to do."

Her dark brown eyes were distressed, and her fingers twiddled the ring even faster.

"You are attracted to him."

"Oh, Gran, yes! But I promised to marry Bruce. How can that be?"

I smiled. "My darling child, it's quite possible to be attracted to more than one man at a time. It's chemistry. It doesn't mean you're in love."

"But I thought I was in love with Bruce. How can I look at another man and wonder . . ." She broke off, blushing.

"And wonder how it would feel to be in his arms making love to him?" I asked, with a little smile.

She looked at me in surprise. "How did you know that?"

"I may be old, but I haven't forgotten some things," I said.

She put her hands up to her cheeks. "I haven't talked about him to anyone, not even Mother," she confessed.

"Will I do?" I asked.

"Oh, Gran . . . ."

My mind wandered for a moment, and a face appeared in my mind's eye. Such a young face, looking so handsome in his uniform. Blue eyes gazing into mine, one hand firmly in the small of my back, and the other holding mine as we moved slowly to the music . . . was it April then, too?

"His name is Denby, Denby Chalmers. He says he hates his name, but I think it's rather nice . . . Gran, are you listening?"

"Yes, dear, his name is Denby. A nice, old-fashioned name. Probably his mother's maiden name."

Lulu nodded. "He teaches, and is also a photographer, mostly a wildlife photographer, but he does people, too." She paused, blushed guiltily, and looked down at her ring again. "He was the guest speaker at the Naturalists' Club meeting last week. He spoke to us, and then showed these wonderful slides." She sat there, hands clasped in her lap, no longer fidgeting with Bruce's ring. Her eyes shone at the memory. "There were birds and sea life, marvelous shots of shore birds, and views of the ocean and beach. He's really very talented."

She paused, and gazed at me, her broad forehead wrinkling with worry. I reached over and patted her hand encouragingly. "Tell me all about it, dear," I said softly.

Chapter Two

LULU AND DENBY

The meeting was over, and now all that could be heard was the clatter of coffee cups and the buzz of conversation. Lulu remained sitting in the corner, and watched the guest speaker fold up his projection screen and put away his slides. It had been a marvelous show and several members came and clustered around him asking questions and making flattering comments. Hannah Jacobs, the Club secretary, who had also introduced the speaker, waved her coffee cup at Lulu.

"Come and have some coffee," she called. As Lulu joined her, she added, "Wasn't Denby splendid? Shall I introduce you?"

"You've known him a long time, haven't you," Lulu remarked.

"Yes. He has a sister who is much older that he. She and I have been friends forever; in fact, I remember when Denby was born. We were eleven, and not quite out of the doll stage yet, and Denby was a real live doll for us to play with. He was a darling." She laughed. "Gosh, that makes me feel old." She led the way to the group surrounding the speaker, which was now dispersing. His eyes lit up at the sight of his sister's friend.

"How did I do, Hannah?" he asked. "Everyone seemed to liked it, but I never know if they're just being kind."

"It was very good," she told him seriously. "I want to introduce a former student of mine, Lulu Ferris. She's a keen bird-watcher, and I've been trying to persuade her to come on the executive. We need young blood. Lulu, this is Denby Chalmers, though you know that, don't you."

She bustled away to the counter where the coffee was being served, picking her way amongst the groups of chatting members.

Lulu put her hand out shyly and smiled at him. "I really enjoyed your talk, but the slides were wonderful. I especially liked that shot of shore and sky, with the flock of gulls squabbling over whatever it was they had found on the beach."

Warm amber eyes behind large glasses smiled back at her. "That's my favorite, too. Are you having coffee? Oh, here's Hannah, struggling with three mugs. Thanks," he said, relieving the older woman of her burden. Hannah smiled at them both and moved away to another group of people.

"Have you known Hannah long?" he asked conversationally, sipping his coffee.

"She taught me English and Science in grade eleven. A couple of years ago she invited me to come to a meeting of this club. I've been a member ever since."

"Do you go on the field trips?"

"Usually just the birding ones."

"I'm going to be leading the one on Sunday, as Peter Morrison is ill," he said. "Were you planning on coming?"

Lulu nodded. "Hannah asked me to go with her."

They talked a short while longer, about what Lulu couldn't remember. She was watching his long sensitive fingers wrapped around his mug of coffee. She liked the way his hair waved softly away from his face and curled down onto his shoulders. His hair was exactly the color of polished chestnuts. His eyebrows were bushy, and they moved as he talked. He wore a casual denim shirt tucked into dark grey corduroy trousers, and an unbuttoned navy knitted vest. She detected the faintest odor of lemon scented aftershave. Afterwards, walking home along the well-lit street, she remembered

14

his mouth and the curve of his smile. That night his face filled her dreams.

The next day she thought about him, and wondered how she could have been attracted so suddenly to another man, especially one who was so different from Bruce, both in looks and manner. Bruce had a solid, compact frame, short, reddish hair, and broad hands with rather stubby fingers. His handsome features were classic, his mouth was usually set in a straight line. Sometimes he didn't understand her jokes, and she found herself explaining the punch line. It wasn't as though he was unintelligent, for he passed his exams with excellent marks, but there were times when she wished he appreciated her humor, and didn't regard her attempts to make him laugh with the patience and perseverance of an adult humoring a child. He would explain things to her as a teacher lecturing a student, which annoyed her somewhat, which would then make her feel guilty. They shared a love of music, and that made up for a lot of things. Two months ago, the evening before he went off to his spring term, they had sat close beside each other on the sofa at his parents' place listening to a symphony by Dvorak. When it came to an end, she sighed with pleasure. He pulled her closer to him and kissed her. Bruce's kisses were very satisfactory. They always left her breathless and wanting more. That night his kisses were more demanding than ever and he whispered that they had the house to themselves for at least a couple of hours. Would she come upstairs to his room? Just for cuddling, no more.

"We're cuddling here, aren't we?" she said sensibly.

Bruce kissed her again. "But, sweetheart, I want to lie beside you." Lulu slid away, got up, and put on another tape. She would have enjoyed that, too, but she was afraid of where it might lead them.

"You've always wanted a virgin on your wedding night, haven't you," she said.

"Well, yes, but if it happens before we get married it doesn't matter, does it?"

Lulu wasn't ready for 'it' to happen just yet. She knew half her friends at school had already slept with their boyfriends, for they

15

discussed it quite openly. Something had always seemed to hold her back, and when Bruce, whom she had known and admired all her life, last year suddenly decided that she was for him, she was glad that she had not taken that step.

"It's only a year and a half, Bruce. We can wait, can't we?"

Even as she said this, she was tempted to go upstairs with him. But no, she wanted her white wedding dress to mean something, and she would wait. In the middle of her attempting to explain this, he kissed her again and told her how beautiful she was and how difficult it was for him to keep on holding back. He took her home then, and she felt that somehow it was her fault for tempting him.

Now she thought of Denby and wondered if he had a wife or a girlfriend. He wasn't wearing a ring; she had noticed that. He was considerably older than she was, and when they had bade each other good night she called him 'Mr. Chalmers'.

"You make me feel old," he said, with a rueful smile, "and I'm only thirty-four. Please call me Denby."

She blushed and said, "Goodnight, Denby. I'll see you Sunday morning." Sunday morning was teeming with rain, and she stared out her bedroom window with acute disappointment. On top of this, Hannah telephoned to say that she had a streaming cold, and was going to stay in bed all day and drink gallons of hot lemonade.

"You go anyway, Lulu. A little rain won't discourage many folks. And besides, Denby will be disappointed."

She didn't think Denby Chalmers would miss her if she failed to turn up, but she got out her rain gear and her plastic covering for her binoculars and notebook, and sallied forth. When her father dropped her off at the meeting point, she told him she was sure that someone would drive her home in the afternoon.

"Call me if you need a ride, chicken," he said, kissing her cheek. There were only four others besides herself and Denby, and she could see how disappointed he was with the weather and the turnout.

"We'll see lots of birds," he said comfortingly.

"We'll just get wet seeing them," somebody said with a laugh.

And they did get wet; Lulu's binoculars misted up, and she dropped her notebook in the ditch, spoiling a month's recording of birds. Finally at eleven o'clock, the foursome, who had come together, decided to pack it in.

"Shall we go as well?" he asked her. They had driven together from the meeting point.

She was still smarting over her ruined notebook. What a klutz he must think she was. He probably couldn't wait to get rid of her. When she hesitated, he said. "Look, I think it's brightening up. Let's give it until noon, and then I shall take you to lunch. How's that?"

"I packed a lunch," she began.

"So did I, but I don't feel like a peanut butter sandwich and potato chips," he replied, with a grin. "I know a place in the village that makes the most wonderful minestrone soup, just what we need on a day like this. Come on, Lulu, just another hour. We haven't identified a semipalmated plover yet." Lulu found herself rather breathless, as though she'd been running. She nodded wordlessly, and they waved goodbye to the others, then turned and went back along the path to the shore. An hour later, as they returned to the parking lot, the sun came out and shone brilliantly. Drops of water on the new young leaves looked like shining jewels, and the waves in the bay sparkled and danced. They hadn't spotted the plover, but they had enjoyed each other's company. Denby learned that Lulu was the eldest of three, and that her brothers, Peter and Johnny, were in high school. Her parents were both physicians, and shared a family practice. Lulu discovered that Denby taught environmental studies and biology at the community college where she was taking a creative writing course. He was astonished, and wondered aloud why their paths hadn't crossed at school. Lulu explained rather diffidently that her course was only two hours twice a week, and that was her total time spent in that building.

"I want to be a writer," she went on, shyly, "and I try to spend every morning at my typewriter. I'd like to write children's books."

He looked at her with great interest. "Are you taking the course from Maxine Hamilton?"

"Yes."

"She's very good."

"Oh, do you think so, too?" she asked eagerly. "She's so encouraging." True to his promise, Denby took her to a small café in the village and there they had a large bowl of thick, satisfying soup, accompanied by thick slices of warm home made bread. This was followed by a pot of tea and oatmeal cookies. Lulu sat back and sighed with satisfaction.

"That was delicious!" she exclaimed. "Much better than what I packed. Thank you!" And she smiled at him across the table.

Denby took off his glasses and polished them vigorously.

"Lulu," he said slowly, "I'd like to take pictures of you, if you would let me."

He saw her expression and smiled, shaking his head. "I don't mean those kind of pictures! You didn't really think I meant those kind of pictures?"

Lulu's face was scarlet with embarrassment.

"No! I mean, for a split second . . ."

"I should have phrased it better. I would like to take portraits of you. Preferably outside, in the late afternoon when the light is good."

Lulu hesitated. "You know I'm engaged . . . ."

He nodded. "I've noticed your ring. It is lovely. Is it old?"

She nodded. "It was Bruce's grandmother's. His mother inherited it, and gave it to him when he told her he wanted to marry me."

"Would your fiancé mind my taking pictures of you?"

"I don't know. I don't think so."

"More important, would you feel comfortable?"

Lulu decided that she would. He was a relaxing person to be with. She told him this, and then added, "I'm sorry for thinking that you . . ."

He smiled and touched her hand briefly. "Put it out of your mind. You have a face I'd love to paint, if I could paint. So if you'd let me take some photographs, I'd be delighted."

"When?"

"Fridays I am always free by two o'clock. If it's a nice day, I'll call you, and then pick you up soon after. Would that be all right?"

18

Lulu found herself breathless again. She nodded. She wondered what she'd tell her parents. Would they think it queer that a man wanted to take her portrait?

When Denby dropped her off later, she came in with shining eyes and a smiling face. Her mother looked up from her dinner preparations.

"I thought you'd be home early, it was such a terrible day," she said, with a smile.

"We went for lunch afterwards," explained Lulu, and when her mother mentioned to her father later that 'they had all gone to lunch', Lulu didn't inform them that it had been just she and Denby Chalmers. She wondered afterwards why she hadn't told the whole truth. She didn't know for sure that Denby was going to photograph her on Friday; it might be raining. And if she had thought for a second that Denby's intentions weren't honorable, might not her parents think the same?

Friday afternoon was perfect. She was spared explanations to her mother by the fact that it was her afternoon to visit patients in the hospital, so Lulu left a note for her brothers saying she was going to Stanley Park. She never knew when the boys would be home; besides, they were old enough to look after themselves.

Denby spent the better part of two hours taking photographs both of Lulu and views in the park. She found it an interesting experience posing in various ways, and offering different expressions for the camera as Denby demanded. He was entirely professional, in fact he was almost off hand with her, though he put her at her ease at first telling amusing stories, and commenting on the birds he had spotted that week. At the end of the session he produced a notebook for her.

"As a thank you, and to replace the one that got ruined on Sunday," he told her seriously.

Lulu was delighted with it; it was especially designed for recording bird sightings, with an index, checklist, and some illustrations.

"You didn't have to," she began.

"I know," he said simply. "I saw it yesterday and I thought of you." She blushed with pleasure.

19

"When shall I bring you the photos?" he asked, back to business. "I'll start developing them right away."

Lulu had been thinking about this, and wondering what her parents would say if he came to her house.

"I'm going to be visiting my grandmother on Sunday," she said slowly. "Why don't you drop by there later on in the afternoon? Gran would love to see them, too."

It was five o'clock and the sun was almost set when he dropped her off. No one was home yet, so she found the note she had left and screwed it up, tossing it in the wastebasket. Then she phoned her grandmother and asked if she could come to visit Sunday afternoon. She didn't mention Denby.

Am I being sneaky? She asked herself. She hadn't told any lies, but she had omitted information her parents would have found interesting, and perhaps questionable. Would she tell Bruce? And, most important, what would Gran say?

Chapter Three

LOUISE

"You've invited Denby here this afternoon?" I asked, as Lulu finished her narrative.

Her fingers began to play with Bruce's ring again, and she nodded. She glanced at her watch.

"He'll be here soon. Do you mind, Gran?"

"Not at all, darling. I want to meet this young man who has made such an impression on you."

She colored. "Oh, Gran . . ."

"Why don't you go inside and make tea for us? Then you can answer the door when Denby arrives. There are muffins, which I made today. You'll find them in the blue crock on the counter."

Since it was Easter, I had gone to church, having been picked up and brought back by neighbors who attend regularly. I used up the last package of frozen blueberries from last summer and made Lulu's favorite recipe, knowing she was coming for a visit. I still like to bake, though it takes me a little longer than it used to.

"Are you sure it's still warm enough for you out here?" she asked anxiously, pausing on her way indoors.

"I'm quite comfortable," I assured her, and closed my eyes.

I must have dozed off, for I dreamed I was standing on the edge of a lake, looking at strings of lights on the far shore. Music was wafting on the breeze to me, and I could see people dancing. Then, as dreams do, it changed, and I was one of the dancers, moving to the music in the arms of a man in uniform. Was it Johnnie or Jeremy? I couldn't look up to see. The music was familiar, too. Then I was awake, and the sound of voices was nearby. I sat up and saw Lulu and a tall young man coming across the lawn to my chair. He was carrying a large tray with the tea things on it, and Lulu had my tartan shawl that I bought years ago in Scotland.

"Gran, this is Denby Chalmers. Denby, my grandmother Mrs. Ferris." Denby put the tray down on the table nearby, stooped, and shook my hand.

"It's a pleasure to make your acquaintance," he said. His voice was pleasant and deep, and his eyes smiled at me.

They sat down, and Lulu poured the tea. I gazed at Denby and saw a young man whose face, though serious in repose, lit up when he smiled. His mouth reminded me of Johnnie's, sensitive, but humorous. He had large hands with long fingers. He was slim and well dressed, but wore his dark red hair rather long. He wore glasses, but his eyes were entirely visible. I have always been able to read people very well, and can usually tell when someone is insincere. Denby's eyes smiled into mine naturally; he was polite and interested in what I had to say, and he didn't attempt to charm or flatter me. He treated Lulu as he would one of his students, but didn't talk down to her at all. We discussed bird watching, photography, touched on local politics and world affairs. He asked me about my family, and I'm afraid I boasted about all my grandchildren, Lulu included. My darling girl blushed when I mentioned her accomplishments, but continued to sit (metaphorically, of course) at his feet and worship. I don't know whether Denby even noticed, or was he used to his female students hero-worshipping him? I felt a momentary pang of sympathy for Bruce.

He showed me the photographs that he had taken of Lulu, and they were excellent. There were a few of Lulu as an accessory to a scene, but most of them were of her. He had captured her personality beautifully. There was one of her looking back at him, with the light behind her. It was quite wonderful, and I asked him if I could have a copy. He smiled and nodded in approval, as though I had passed a test.

"That one is the best, but my personal favorite is this one," he remarked, showing me one of her smiling wickedly at the camera. "She had just told me a joke, and I was laughing so hard I could scarcely hold the camera still."

"You managed all right," I said. I glanced at Lulu and she was gazing at Denby with her heart in her eyes. Denby was still studying the photograph, and wasn't aware of her glance. When he looked up, she averted her gaze, eyes demurely downcast. I mentally shook my head. *Oh dear*, I thought, *problems ahead.*

The sun was getting low when Denby suggested a few photographs of Lulu and me. He retrieved his camera and equipment from the kitchen, then proceeded to order both of us to do this and that. By now Lulu was quite comfortable being his subject, and she was relaxed and smiling as she posed for him. He took a few of me by myself, and then asked Lulu to sit by me and asked us to look at each other.

"Oh, this will be good! This will be very good," he muttered as he clicked away. Finally he apologized for tiring me, and suggested that it was growing cool, and the light was going, so we should go indoors. Lulu picked up the tea tray and started back to the house, while Denby helped me to my feet. It's most annoying how stiff I become after sitting in one position for a while. I straightened myself up, he offered me his arm, and we started across the lawn.

"Are you a married man, Mr. Chalmers?" I asked.

He glanced at me in surprise. "No, I'm not," he replied. He paused. "I was engaged once, but it didn't work out." He said no more, except to ask me to please call him Denby, and I didn't probe.

In the kitchen, Lulu was busy washing teacups and putting away the muffins. She looked up and smiled at us as we came in.

"How did you get here, Lou, would you like me to drop you off on my way?"

Lulu glanced at me, and I could see that she was torn, desiring to go with him, while at the same time wanting to talk to me about him.

"It's not really necessary, Gran's coming to our house for Easter dinner later, and Aunt Harriet is picking her up, isn't that right, Gran?"

"Harriet is coming by at five-thirty," I replied. "I'm going to have a bath and change my clothes, so if you want to go now, that's fine. We can talk later on."

Lulu glanced at Denby and blushed. "If it's not taking you out of your way . . . ."

"Of course it is, but it will be a pleasure," he said, smiling. He took my hand. "It was also a pleasure meeting you, Mrs. Ferris. I'll come over with the photo proofs when I've developed them, and I'll bring that one of Lou that you admired."

Lulu kissed me and said she'd see me later. Denby thanked me again for the tea, and they both went out. I watched from the front room window, and saw him open the car door for her. The sun had gone down, and evening was drawing in. It was that time of day when the lights have come on, and windows glow golden, but there is still light in the sky. I saw a painting once that reminded me of this time of day. I've forgotten the artist and where I saw it, but I remember the title. It was called 'Empire of Light' and I liked it very much. There was a house with a streetlight illuminating the front windows, but the house itself and the trees surrounding it were a dark silhouette. Above, the sky was light blue and filled with puffy white clouds. I remember I stood and gazed at it for a long time, thinking, *how beautiful!* and wishing I had a hundred thousand dollars and that I could buy it. In a sense I do own it, for it is still in my mind's eye, and I can take it out and admire it any time I want.

I went into the bathroom and turned on the water. I like a hot bath with scented water. Soon after my husband died Harriet insisted I have installed a handle on the wall to assist me getting in and out of the bathtub. It is useful and I am glad she suggested it, but it serves to remind me of my advancing years. I took off my clothes, and put them carefully away, my underwear into the laundry basket. I put on my silk kimono that my husband brought back from Japan fifty years ago. It is black with a huge scarlet dragon on the back, and I have worn it back and forth from my bath for all these years. The silk still glows and the dragon has not faded. I have always loved the very sensual feel of silk on my bare skin. Harriet would be shocked if she knew that I still could enjoy that sort of thing. She would be shocked if she knew how much I still miss my husband, and not just his companionship. We had a very satisfactory sexual relationship right up until the day he died. As I lay in the steaming water, soaping myself with bath gel, I thought of the times when we would bathe together, as a prelude to loving. My body was younger then, my skin taut, my face unlined, and my breasts firm and high. They sag a little now, no matter how much firming cream I use. Getting old is not my cup of tea, but it is inevitable, of course. My mind is still with me, and my memories keen. So what if I can't remember what I had for dinner last night; that doesn't matter at all.

It took a little effort to get out of my bath, but I eventually climbed out and toweled myself off with one of my lovely bath sheets that Lulu gave me last Christmas. They are a beautiful shade of blue that matches my bathroom, and they are thick and soft. They are so big I can wrap myself in them. After drying myself, I rubbed perfumed body lotion all over, then put on my kimono and slippers and padded back to my bedroom, where I considered what I should wear to David and Petra's home. I checked the time, and saw that Harriet would be here soon, so I dressed, combed my hair, and put on some lipstick. I thought of Harriet, and I suddenly felt sorry for her. Had she ever made love to a man, I wondered. I didn't think she had had a boyfriend since her fiancé died forty years ago. I suppose her life has been satisfying to her. It never would have been for me. I feel blessed. I have loved two men, (and been loved back), borne four children, enjoyed wife and motherhood. Ridiculous, though, that my daughter Harriet is sixty-three. It seems only yesterday that I was that age, looking forward to my husband retiring. In fact, we bought this house on my birthday, and my husband, with a gallant gesture, gave it to me!

I hope that Harriet won't trouble me this evening with her fears and doubts of my living alone. If she does, I'll have to ask Carrie to speak to her. Carrie is the only one who stands up to Harriet. It isn't in Sheila's nature to disagree with anyone, let alone her eldest sister, and David is too much younger than she. Harriet was grown up when he was born, as I've said, and he's always been rather in awe of her. Though I think she would listen to him if he took my side in this issue. I shall have to gently bring the subject up one of these days.

Harriet fussed, as I was afraid she'd do. Lulu, to my surprise, took my part rather vociferously when my daughter announced to David that it was time their mother moved in with her. Petra kept quiet until Harriet asked for her opinion, and Petra replied cautiously she thought I was coping well, as far as she could see, and what did I think? I said I was happy in my little house. Harriet stated rather forcefully that I was too old to be on my own.

"Aunt Harriet," Lulu said, growing rather pink, "I think Gran is just fine in her little house. She's got lots of help, and she's happy there, aren't you, Gran."

Harriet is a tall, commanding woman; in past days she would have been called handsome. Her hair is getting quite gray, and she finally succumbed to wearing reading glasses a number of years ago. She says her distance vision is as good as it ever was. Unfortunately, emotion makes her face red. She has always had this tendency. I can remember her as a small child, purple with rage because we wouldn't return week-old Carrie to the hospital. Her nose was out of joint for some time, and when Sheila was born less than fourteen months later, she was downright nasty. The two babies kept me very busy, and I expect Harriet felt pushed aside. Her father was good to her, though, and the two formed a close relationship that lasted for over fifty years.

She glared at Lulu, and her face grew quite pink.

"I scarcely think that you are qualified to make those kind of judgments," she said icily.

Aunt and niece regarded each other, and I suddenly saw a resemblance between them, and not just the pink faces.

"I visit Gran a lot, and she is just fine in her house. She's not senile, or anything."

"She could fall and break a leg or a hip and lie there for hours."

"Mother phones her every day."

"Look," I said, "I really don't like sitting here listening to you two discuss me as though I weren't here."

"It seems like such a waste for us to be maintaining separate establishments, when we could easily share," Harriet protested.

"My dear Harriet, are you willing to give up all your things and move in with me?" I saw her expression and nodded. "Of course you're not. So why should you expect me to give away all my lovely possessions, some of which are the only things I have left of your father, and move in with you? When I am ready, I will consider one of those retirement villas where meals are prepared for you, and a nurse is in attendance."

I was quite pleased with my courage to stand up to Harriet. Perhaps it was David's encouraging face in the background, or Petra's smile, or Lulu's pink cheeks. Harriet backed off then, muttering that she only had my best interests at heart.

"I know you do, dear," I said, hoping to mollify her.

No more was said, and when Harriet arose to take her leave I went with her meekly, even though Lulu offered to drive me home later, if I wished. Of course Lulu and I hadn't had a chance to chat about Denby.

"Come visit me after class this week sometime," I told her, when Harriet went out to turn the car around and bring it close to the front door. "I'm playing bridge on Thursday, that's the only afternoon that I'll be out," I added, consulting my little daybook. I kissed her cheek and whispered in her ear. "I think he's a dear."

She blushed and glanced at her parents who were standing nearby. "I'll come tomorrow and bring lunch," she whispered in return.

"Thank you all for dinner," I said. "Petra, dear, you outdid yourself. You know, David was awfully lucky to find you." And I meant it. I am very fond of Petra. She and David balance their careers in medicine and child raising very nicely.

Chapter Four

LOUISE REMEMBERS

Harriet drove me home in silence; I could feel waves of emotion still emanating from her. She was still upset at my refusal to allow her to take over my life: which is what would happen if I moved into her suite. She has a very nice flat in Kerrisdale, an older section of Vancouver filled with upper middle class families and well-heeled retirees. She is handy to shops and the library and the community center. She walks everywhere. It is true, her location is perfect, even better than my own, and though I can walk to Safeway and the bank, it is uphill returning, so I usually get my groceries delivered. It is fairly flat where Harriet lives, and I actually prefer the shops there as well, though I would never admit it to her. If I did, there would be no peace until I had sold my house and furniture and moved across town to her.

Harriet helped me into the house, and checked everywhere to make certain that it was safe. I don't know who she thinks is going to be in an old lady's house at nine o'clock of a Sunday night. She is always showing me newspaper stories of senior citizens being mugged in the streets, or their homes invaded and the owners being found tied up hand and foot with their valuables gone. Or perhaps an elderly woman has fallen and broken her hip, and has lain on the floor for two days before anyone found her. Or worst case scenario, her body discovered by the neighbors when the milk began to collect on the doorstep. My bones are fine, either Petra or Harriet phones every day, and I don't open my door to strangers.

"Would you like a cup of tea?" I asked politely when Harriet had finished her tour of the house.

"That would be nice," she answered. "Petra insists on making coffee, and I just can't drink it at nights now. You'd think she'd offer me at least hot water," she grumbled, taking the kettle from my hands and filling it with water at the sink.

I hung up my coat in the hall, and returned to the kitchen. Harriet was peering into my blue crock.

"Blueberry muffins!" she said. "Mother, did you make these?"

"Of course I did. Remember the berries you brought me last August and helped me freeze? These are the last of them. Why didn't you just ask Petra for hot water or tea?"

"If you have to ask, it must be a bother," she replied stiffly.

Out of her sight I rolled my eyes, but said nothing. She removed her coat and flung it over the back of a chair, a habit of hers I have obviously failed to break. That's another reason living with Harriet would be uncomfortable. She may organize her time well, but she is an untidy housekeeper. She's lived alone all her life, and has had to please only herself. A couple of years after my husband died she and I went on a cruise to Alaska. I enjoyed the scenery, but rooming with Harriet was not easy. I found myself picking up after her in order to simply sit down. When I mentioned it she sulked for hours. No, I will definitely stay where I am.

Harriet brought the teapot over to the table and we sat down. We sipped in silence for a moment.

"Mother, why is it that you have always resented me?" she asked.

I stared at her in astonishment. "What on earth are you talking about?"

"Mother, you've always preferred Carrie and Sheila, you must confess that. And when David arrived, you shut us all out."

I reached over and touched her hand. "Harriet," I said softly. "You're wrong. I love you girls all the same. I always have. David, well, he was special, you understand that now, don't you? He was so

29

unexpected, and it took all my energy caring for him when he was tiny. I'm dreadfully sorry if you felt excluded." Her expression was bleak, her lips a firm uncompromising line, her cheeks pink with emotion. "Tell me why you felt that way," I begged.

She said nothing, sitting there stiff and unrelenting, her tea untasted. I was appalled. I had no idea that she had been so unhappy. Was she lonely, too? Was that why she wanted us to live together?

"I should go," she said finally. "Thank you for the tea."

She cleared our cups from the table, but instead of putting them in the dishwasher, she dumped them in the sink. Then she gathered up her coat, kissed me on the cheek, and went out the front door. I almost called her back to ask her again to tell me why she felt as she did, but she was in the car and starting it up before I could get the words out. I went inside slowly, pondering my eldest daughter.

What a bundle of unresolved resentments she is! As a contrast, Carrie and Sheila are close together in age, and have always been pals. There has never been any rivalry between them. They are still the best of friends, in spite of Sheila's husband. Toby Williams is a bit of an old fraud, talks a lot, but says nothing substantial. I'm not sure why he doesn't like me; perhaps he knows I see through him. He's good to Sheila, though, so I put up with his vagaries and his little fictions for her sake. They have two nice children who are well into their thirties, neither married, and tolerate their father with unexpected patience, and don't argue when he utters a completely inane statement. Carrie's husband, Tom McNabb, has just retired from engineering, and I know he shares my feelings about his brother-in-law. However, he also puts up with Toby, in fact some times he leads him on disgracefully. Toby never knows when his leg is being pulled. Carrie and Tom have two children also, and the cousins are all good friends, though I have a feeling that there is more than friendship between Sheila's daughter Stephanie and Carrie's son Paul. No doubt the young people will sort out their own affairs. Though they are hardly children. Carrie's daughter Lynn was married a few years ago, and she's about to produce my first great-grandchild. Carrie says it's high time she was made a grandmother. Most of her friends have been grandmothers for ages. I am very fond of Carrie.

She will be a very good grandmother. For the most part, my family is very satisfactory.

Except Harriet.

Later, as I lay sleepless in bed, I thought about my eldest daughter and her accusation that I had always resented her. Surely that was completely false. My mind flashed back more than sixty-three years. I saw myself standing in front of the mirror in my bedroom, my hands on my swollen stomach, actively resenting the child within, and angry at life's bad timing of events. But I had gotten over it, hadn't I? I remember how thrilled I was when they placed a red-face, screaming Harriet in my arms, and what a rush of emotion I felt when I put her to my breast and she immediately began to suckle fiercely. Harriet has gone through life fiercely wanting things, I thought, but not always getting them. Then my mind went to Lulu and her problem. I think she'll have to hear about my younger days. How surprised she'll be when I tell her I was in a very similar situation to hers when I was eighteen.

"You were engaged at eighteen?" I can hear her asking in surprise. "And you think I'm too young."

I will tell her things were different then, and they were. Also, there was a war on. Ah, yes, whenever we needed an excuse to do something different we would say, "Well, you know, there's a war on!"

And it was the war to end all wars, and that made it almost a holy war. But I know now that wars never really solve anything. You destroy one monster, and another pops up to replace him. Wars cause untold misery and suffering, change the face of the earth, and to what end? Women all over the world mourning lost sons, husbands, and lovers. Most of the returned men with whom I was acquainted never talked about their experiences. All they wanted to do was to get on with life.

I have a wall of framed photographs in the little room that was my husband's study. My parents, both sets of grandparents, and many others. The largest is a group photograph of us children taken on our verandah when I was ten. We had just moved from the country into Ottawa. Gerald, the oldest, is twenty, and is suitably solemn as befits the elder son. He stands between my two older sisters—Norah Rose, two years younger than he, and Gladys, who would have been fourteen at the time. My brother Frank, who was just a little over a year older than I am, is seated beside me on the step, trying hard not to break into giggles. Five-year-old Val, christened Percival for my maternal grandfather, is next to me. I have a mop of wild curls that my mother struggled in vain to tame, and Frank is covered with freckles. Like Carrie and Sheila after us, Frank and I were always the greatest friends until the day he died. There was a baby between Norah and Gladys who died when it was a year or two old. Mama said once that when you lose a child it's like losing a piece of your heart. And it never really heals.

I didn't realize it until I was older, but we were so very fortunate to be born into our family. When you're a child you take things for granted, your parents are your parents, and that's the way it is. My father and mother were William and Rose Laurier. We weren't related to our illustrious prime minister, nor were we Quebecois or even Acadian, but Huguenots, French Protestants who fled religious persecution in the 1700's and came to America. During the American Revolution one of my ancestors brought his family to Canada, and settled in the Ottawa Valley. Lauriers related to us are still scattered throughout eastern Ontario. I'm the only one left in my family now. Norah died ten years ago, and Val last year at age eighty-two. Norah's children and grandchildren mostly live in Prince Edward Island, and I seemed to have lost touch with most of them. Val never married. Gerald had only daughters, so there are no Lauriers in our line left.

They say you should choose your parents well. Mama and Papa were wonderful parents. We were well off. Not rich, but comfortable. Times were good when I was young, and we never wanted for anything. My father was a partner in a law firm in Perth with James Ferris, and we lived in the country outside the town in a large house surrounded by an orchard. While my father was outgoing and gregarious, my mother was a gentle soul, but she was not without an inner core of steel. She could sing beautifully and play the piano. She had a smile that lit up any room she was in, and a laugh that made you smile with her. Sundays she played the piano for the Sunday school in the small Anglican church, which was a mile down the tree-lined lane from our house. She read to us at bedtime and sang lullabies. My father adored her. We all adored her.

The Ferris family was our close friends. Mr. and Mrs. Ferris had three children, Jeremy, who was Norah's age, Susie, who was Frank's age, and Michael who was the same age as Val. So all we children fitted in as a group and family get-togethers were always amusing and entertaining. Sometimes the older four, Gerald, Norah, Gladys and Jeremy would go off together and do the things that teenagers do, and Jeremy would flirt with both my sisters. There would be many blushes and giggles, especially from Gladdie. Frank, Susie, and I were usually left to mind Michael and Val, but we didn't mind. With the three of us, it was never 'two's company, three's a crowd.' We played our own games, and if the older ones included us, that was fine, too.

When I was ten we moved to Ottawa. Papa left the law firm and went to work for a Member of Parliament. We lived in a large brick house on the Canal; there was an enormous garden, which made Mama happy, as well as a conservatory where she grew her tropical plants. There was also a big music room where she kept the piano, and where she would hold musical *soirees* once or twice a month. On other occasions Mama would organize dances for Gerald, Norah, Gladdie, and their friends. As Frank and I got older we were included as well. She taught Gladdie and me to play the piano. Gladdie was quite talented; I struggled.

And Dorcas! She was as much a part of our family as anyone. I hadn't thought of her in years until this morning when the Scripture reading from Acts mentioned her namesake. She came to work for us when Gladdie was born, I think, and stayed with us forever. She also adored Mama.

Another picture on my wall is one of Norah with the twins, Sarah and Ben. Norah married a widower, and the twins were his, though I think Norah loved them as much as her own that she eventually had. Sarah is the only one of that family who still keeps in touch on a regular basis. Heavens, she must be seventy-seven now! Her children and grandchildren have always called me Aunt Louise.

33

Sarah sends me photographs every Christmas of her growing clan. I remember the first time I saw her, hanging out of the big black automobile, waving at me. The summer that Norah and I went to Prince Edward Island. The summer that war broke out in Europe . . . .

All the faces out of the past that appear to me, as I lie sleepless! When Lulu comes to visit me this week I shall show her the photographs again, and tell her how, when I was about her age, I, too, had to make a decision of the heart. She will ask me if I made the right one; I can't answer that. Sometimes circumstances make decisions for you. I know that my life would have been entirely different. It is quite possible that Lulu wouldn't exist. When I tell her that she'll assure me that I did indeed choose correctly!

Chapter Five

1914

Seventeen-year-old Louise Laurier and her brother Frank were poring over the atlas spread out on the large kitchen table. His freckled face was pale with concentration as he moved a stubby forefinger along a border.

"Here it is, Louise," he said. "Sarajevo. It's the capital of Herzegovina."

"I see," she said.

"Those crazy Balkans countries have been fighting for years," remarked Frank. "Now this has really torn it."

Louise went back to studying the newspaper story that had sparked her search in her old school atlas. "'The Archduke of Austria,'" she read, "'and his wife have been assassinated by an agent of the Black Hand, a Serbian terrorist group. Austria is threatening to invade Serbia if she isn't given the right to investigate the incident on Serbian soil.'" She gazed anxiously at her brother. "It's just a European problem, isn't it, Frank?"

Frank grinned. "We hope so, though if England gets involved, maybe Canada will, too."

"Oh, no, Canada would never go to war over some little incident in Eastern Europe," protested Louise. "Surely we've outgrown that sort of thing."

"Don't be too sure. And if we do, Gerry and I will have to join up."

Dorcas Fraser, the Lauriers' indispensable maid of all work, banged down on the table a bottle of silver polish and glared at the two young people. "Now don't you two go bothering your mother with that sort of talk," she ordered grimly. "She's still not well. War," she muttered. "It's wicked talk." She gathered up the newspaper and spread it out in front of her. She bustled into the dining room and brought back the silver tea service, and began to polish briskly. "Frank, you put that atlas away, and watch out for the egg man, please. I want to make a nice soufflé for supper tonight. I think your mother would enjoy it. Louise will help me with this silver, won't you," she added, fixing the girl with a fierce stare.

Louise smiled and put on the other pair of soft cotton gloves her mother and Dorcas always used when they polished the silver. She actually enjoyed doing this chore. It was always a pleasure to make the pieces bright and shining.

"You've been with us for a long time, haven't you, Dorcas," she remarked, smiling at the older woman, her hands busy.

Dorcas' face softened. She was a tall, gaunt woman whose Scots accent was still present in her speech. She had dark hair that was turning gray, and sparkling black eyes. She glanced affectionately at the youngest daughter and nodded.

"Och, yes. Your sister Gladys was yet to be born, and your dear mother was so ill. She hadna recovered from the death of wee Constance." She sighed gustily.

"What happened to the baby?" asked Louise curiously. "Mama never talks about it."

"Your mother woke up in the morning and the bairn was dead in her crib," Dorcas said sadly. "It was a dreadful shock for her. Eleven months old and beginning to walk, such a lovely child. They thought your mother would lose the bairn she was carrying, but the Lord didn't see fit to take it. Your sister Gladys was born six months later, big and healthy and strong. I remember her first cry. It was though she was angry to have to come into this big, cold, world." Dorcas shook her head.

Louise blushed a little, but she was pleased that Dorcas thought her old enough to discuss these kinds of subjects. She remembered her mother explaining 'things' to her three years ago when she was fourteen, though with two older sisters, Louise wasn't entirely ignorant of the facts of life and the problems of emerging womanhood. She distinctly remembered her mother before Val was born and asking Norah why Mama was so fat. Thirteen-year-old Norah had quickly shushed her, but Mama had explained that she was carrying her little brother or sister under her heart, and, inviting Louise to climb upon the bed beside her, she held the child's hands to her.

"Do you feel him moving, Louise?" she asked softly.

"Oh, yes, Mama! Norah, come feel our little brother kicking inside Mama! Isn't it wonderful?"

Louise remembered how Norah had blushed and shook her head. She put her hands behind her and backed out of their mother's bedroom. Louise had snuggled up to Mama and once more cautiously felt the mound of her mother's stomach. There it was again—faint kicks against her small hand.

Her mother put her arms around her and cuddled her little daughter.

"It's a small miracle, Louise," she told her softly. Louise had never forgotten that moment.

Now she regarded Dorcas seriously. "Is Mama not well yet?"

Mrs. Laurier had had an operation three months ago, and had not yet quite 'picked up', as Dorcas would say.

Dorcas reassured her. "Your dear mother will be quite well again. The doctor says she should get away from the heat and humidity, to the Island, I think. Sea air would be splendid for her."

Dorcas had lived in Prince Edward Island for twenty years before she had come to Ontario, and to her 'the Island' was the only place in the world.

"Will you be going with them?" Louise asked anxiously.

"Wouldn't I love to, but who would look after the likes of you?"

"I'll miss Mama. Will they be away the whole summer?"

"I think your dear father will come home once or twice. They'll be staying with your Aunt Bernice, of course, and your Mama will be just fine."

Bernice Laurier was her father's sister, and lived in a rural area on the south shore. She was what they called 'a maiden lady of uncertain years', being the eldest in Papa's family. She had visited them once or twice before they moved into Ottawa, and Louise remembered being terrified of her. Gerry had told her Aunt Bernice was a witch when she was at home, and if she weren't careful the old lady would put a spell on her. She had believed utterly in Aunt Bernice's witchhood for a long time. Louise smiled to herself. What a gullible child she had been!

As she polished Mama's big silver teapot she thought about her older sisters. Norah was the elder, and was tall and pretty, with long fair hair swept up, sparkling blue eyes, and a curving mouth with a tiny dent on the upper lip. Dorcas said that when Norah had been born a fairy had placed a finger there. A young man had recently told Norah that she had the most kissable lips he had ever seen. She had been teaching for several years at a school near Perth, not far from where they used to live, and was boarding in the town. She loved her little school, and had children from grades one to eight. The Ferris family lived nearby and she saw them frequently. Jeremy had recently returned from Engineering school and was working for the Town of Perth, and he had escorted her to several evening affairs, as well as meals at the Ferris'. The last time Norah had been home to visit she had indignantly reported how someone on the school board had queried her relationship with Jeremy Ferris.

"Do you know, they think that the only male I should be out with in public is my brother or my father? Can you imagine that? It's 1914, for heaven's sake! We're not wearing button boots and bustles any more. I told them that I had grown up with Jeremy and he was just like a brother to me, anyway. Thank goodness Mr. Ferris is also on the board. He soon put the odious man straight."

"Don't you like Jeremy?" Louise asked, trying to sound casual.

Norah smiled. "Of course I like him. But if you mean do I feel romantic about him, the answer is no. It's hard to feel sentimental about a young man whom you've known since he was in short pants and whose skinned elbows and knees you've doctored with iodine. I was such a tomboy! Mama despaired that I'd ever be a proper young lady. Besides, I think there's someone else in the family who fancies him." And she glanced meaningly across the room at her sister Gladys.

Gladys was four years younger than Norah, having just had her twenty-first birthday that spring. She called herself a strawberry blonde, but as Norah had once said privately to her friend Barbara, it was just plain sandy red! She had the pale skin of the redhead, and freckles, which she hated. She was forever trying to bleach them with lemon juice, or cover them with cream. She wasn't pretty like Norah, but she had a beautiful figure—a full curving bust (which she emphasized with frothy fronted blouses) a narrow waistline, and slim legs. She wore the latest fashion, the shorter skirts, which showed off her shapely ankles and a hint of calf. Norah had hesitated to follow suit because of the old-fashioned school board members, but she had a new outfit hanging in her closet, and was just waiting for Mrs. Topping to appear in the shorter skirt. That worthy woman was the wife of the member who had voiced remarks about her and Jeremy. Gladys, on the other hand, hadn't showed the slightest inclination to go to college, and had a job as companion to an elderly lady who didn't seem to mind if she displayed her legs to all and sundry. Gladys played the piano and sang for her, answered her letters, read to her, and accompanied her employer to various functions. She lived with Mrs. Marchbanks, and came home on weekends when they weren't traveling. Louise thought she had the most glamorous job in the world, but Norah said she wouldn't want to be at the beck and call of an old woman, resented by the woman's family, who probably thought that the girl was scheming to cut them all out of their relative's will.

That weekend the whole family was together at home, and the European conflict was the topic of conversation around the dinner table.

"Mrs. Marchbanks has canceled her European tour," complained Gladdie. "She's worried about the problem in Serbia. Surely that's a long way from Paris. I was so looking forward to seeing the Eiffel Tower. It's not fair."

"It could lead to more problems," Gerald said quietly, glancing at his mother, who was looking quite distressed.

"I think she's wise to stay home."

"You're glad I'm not going," continued Gladdie sulkily. "You're all just jealous because you haven't had the chance to go abroad."

"What's the matter with seeing Canada?" asked Norah. Changing the subject, she said, "Mama, Louise mentioned that you and Papa are going to Prince Edward Island for the summer."

"Yes, the doctor has ordered sea air, and your Aunt Bernice has kindly invited us to stay as long as we want. She has a small farm on the south shore, so it will be quiet and relaxing for us. The only trouble is that Papa is having some trouble getting away when we had planned to go."

Louise had a sudden idea. "Why don't you get Dorcas to go with you?" she suggested. "I know she's longing to go back there, but feels she has to stay with us. Norah will be home, now that school is out." She glanced at her elder sister. "It's really only just Val that needs looking after. Frankie and I can look after ourselves, and Gladdie is at Mrs. Marchbanks' during the week . . ."

"What do you think, Norah?" Mama asked.

"We'll be fine," Norah said. "It's a great idea. I can do the cooking, and we all can look after our own rooms."

Dorcas was against the idea at first, but finally agreed to accompany her mistress down to the Island and return in two weeks. "That's as long as I can stay away," she stated firmly. "The dear knows what state the house and garden will be in when I get back. I'll make up a list of chores for everyone, and I'll also speak to Harvey White." Harvey was the man of all work who did all the rough stuff in the garden. "He'll never listen to anyone but me," she continued.

"I'll be home for a week," Gerald said. "Then I'm back to work." Gerald had been with the Central Railway since he had been nineteen.

His parents had been disappointed that he hadn't gone to university for a degree, but he was happy in his job, which took him

40

back and forth across the province as a brakeman on the train. He was unofficially engaged to a young woman named Rhoda Cameron. It was what Mama called 'an understanding', and she had urged them to make it official and set a date. Now the rumblings of war were frightening the girl's mother and Rhoda had begged for more time. Gerald wasn't in any rush to get married. He had a savings account at the bank, and was putting a little bit by every month, so they could find a nice place to live. As much as he loved his family, he wasn't in favor of living with his parents after he and Rhoda were wed.

Gerald arose from the dinner table, kissed his mother's cheek and announced that he was going to see Rhoda tonight. It was a nuisance, but the very week that he had off her parents were taking her and her young brother to Toronto, so he wouldn't be seeing her for some time. He went through to the kitchen where Dorcas was stacking dishes.

"I think Louise had a good idea, your taking Mama to Prince Edward Island," he said to her seriously. "I've suggested that when you return Norah and Louise should travel down with Papa, if he can get away by then. They deserve a little holiday, too. You'll have Val all to yourself."

It was a known fact that Dorcas' favorite was Val, now twelve, and the baby of the family. She had looked after him when he was a baby until Mama was quite well, and everyone knew she spoiled him dreadfully.

Dorcas smiled at the eldest of the family. It was nice to have him home, but it was time he got married, she thought, though she didn't think Miss Cameron was good enough for him.

"I'll be late, Dorcas," he said, as he went out the door into the early evening. "Leave a light on for me."

Chapter Six

LOUISE AND NORAH

Three weeks later, their father having wound up his business obligations, Louise and Norah traveled with him to Prince Edward Island by train. Dorcas had returned to her charges, well satisfied with her visit to the Island. Mrs. Laurier had settled into her sister-in-law's home, and was enjoying the fresh air of the countryside.

"Miss Laurier has a little farm, so there are fresh eggs and milk and cream. It's no' so bad there." For Dorcas, that expression was the height of praise. "It's a lovely old house, and very comfortable. You two will share a room," she added. "It's a nice room, upstairs, and you can see the sea from the window. You'll like your aunt's place."

Praise from Dorcas was rare indeed! The sisters exchanged glances. Aunt Bernice had obviously found favor in Dorcas' eyes.

The journey for Louise was an adventure. She had been to Montreal with Mama once, not very long after they had moved into the city, but she could hardly remember anything about the trip.

Dorcas packed them a box lunch, and they had their meal as the train rumbled along the riverside. Louise's eyes were glued to the window looking at the scenery when she wasn't observing her fellow passengers. Norah sedately read her book, and Papa slept. They spent the night on the train, too, in bunks that seemed to come out of the wall. Louise had the lower berth and lay awake for a long time after

42

Norah had gone to sleep. The rhythm of the train was lulling, but she was too excited to sleep. She peered out her window, but could see nothing in the darkness. *'Clickety clack, clickety clack, running along the railroad track'* kept going around and around in her head. Finally she slept.

The next afternoon found them on the ferry crossing the Straits of Northumberland. Aunt Bernice would be meeting them at the ferry terminal, so they had left the train on the mainland, taking their luggage with them on to the ferry as foot passengers. A nice porter, well tipped by Papa, had transferred their bags from the train to the ferry, and now they were aboard! Louise spent the whole time outside on the deck, watching the sea birds, smiling at the antics of two obstreperous little boys who wouldn't pay any attention to their distracted mother, but raced up and down the deck, laughing and shrieking.

I would be doing the same thing, she thought, if I wasn't seventeen and grown up. She longed to join them and let the excitement that was bubbling inside her out with a shout of joy. Norah and Papa would be mortified if she did a thing like that, so she contented herself with smiling sympathetically at their mother as she chased them ineffectively, and secretly championing them in their cause to elude that worthy woman.

Aunt Bernice was waiting for them with a horse and buggy when they arrived on the island.

"We're still pretty old-fashioned here," she said, as she helped them put their luggage in the back and assisted them into the seats. "I suppose there are hundreds of automobiles in Ottawa, now."

"Quite a few," said Louise, smiling at her aunt, and wondering why she had ever thought she was a witch. Why, she had a wonderful smile, and was as friendly as can be!

It was a long drive to the farm, but Louise enjoyed every minute of it. The red road that wound along close to the sea for several miles, and then turned inland fascinated her. Once they passed a man changing his flat tire on his automobile. Two ladies sat in the back seat, looking most uncomfortable. Louise wanted to call out, "Get a horse!", but knew her father and Norah would be scandalized. She giggled to herself, imagining the expressions on all their faces if she hadn't controlled herself.

At length they drove through a small village. A man in a doorway waved at them, and Aunt Bernice raised her whip to him.

"This is Fairlea, our village," said Aunt Bernice. "We're almost home. It's only a mile to the Kidd farm. We're just before that, on the way to the sea."

'On the way to the sea.' What a lovely phrase! Louise looked around her. There were some shops, a small church, and a hall, set back in amongst some trees. A number of homes could be seen, and as they turned up the road out of the hamlet they passed a schoolhouse, its yard empty of children now that summer was here.

"There's the school," Aunt Bernice told Norah. "It's so sad, the school-teacher died recently. He was such a nice young man. He grew up here, too. His father owns the hardware store in the village. That was the gentleman that waved at us," she added.

"What happened to him?" asked Norah.

"Well, there was talk," Bernice said. "He and the Kidds, our neighbors, you know, were friends, and he and Mrs. Kidd went out for a boat ride in the bay. Nobody knows what happened, but the boat somehow overturned, and they both drowned."

"How awful!" exclaimed Norah.

"Now, I don't think there was anything wrong between them, but there was a lot of gossip," their aunt continued. "Harry Kidd has become a complete recluse since his wife died, and those poor children of his are just running wild. They're at the grandmother's in Charlottetown at the moment. You can see their farmhouse from my place. There are just the two men there, Mr. Kidd and his hired man. Neither of them will give you the time of day. I took food over to him, and he was barely civil to me. Well, well," she sighed. "It must have been a terrible shock. She was young and pretty and liked to have a good time. Perhaps her husband was too old and dull for her, I don't know."

"The school children must be very upset, as well," said Norah, her heart going out to them. "When did it happen?"

"About three months ago. It was a lovely warm spring day, and John Crocker (the schoolteacher) apparently met the Kidd family, who were picnicking on the beach, and invited them to go with him in his boat. Mr. Kidd declined, but his wife wanted to go, so she went with him. Isn't it a blessing she didn't take the children?"

"How old are they?"

"They're about five or six: twins, a boy and a girl. Mr. Kidd had packed up the picnic things and was taking the children home when the accident happened. When they didn't come home, he took his horse and rode down to the bay, but apparently saw nothing. They had just vanished. He rode up to the Crockers' home, but of course Mr. and Mrs. Crocker hadn't seen their son since he had gone out earlier. I don't think it was particularly windy that day, so the waves weren't high. Nobody really knows what happened. Their bodies were washed ashore about a week later, away down at Finlay Harbour." She took her handkerchief out of her pocket and blew her nose. "It was very sad."

She clicked her tongue at the horse, and they turned into a long drive that led up to a house built on a small ridge surrounded by trees. There was a stable, a barn, and a hen house.

"I have a French Canadian hired man, and a girl that helps me in the dairy and in the house. Mary is a hard worker, and Pierre is quite reliable for a Frenchman. I've got five cows, and we make our own butter. Jimmy Foreman, the grocer in the village, buys most of it. Folks say it's very good."

She led them into the house, where a familiar figure rose from the sofa by the window where she had been resting. It was Mama, looking cheerful and rested. She and Papa greeted each other rapturously. She hugged Norah and Louise in turn, exclaiming how much she had missed everybody, and inquiring about the others at home.

"Val has sent you a present," Norah said, rummaging in her handbag. "I don't know what it is, but he made it himself."

"Gladdie has been feeling sorry for herself because Mrs. Marchbanks canceled her European trip, but now she is talking about going out West on the train, so Gladdie is more cheerful," said

45

Louise. "And Frankie has been hired as the grocers' assistant down at Mr. Mackie's store! He's so excited!" Mama smiled at her daughters. She had missed her family, and was very glad to see Louise and Norah. She sighed. Louise was becoming an attractive young woman. Soon all her children would be grown. She might even be a grandmother if Gerald and Rhoda would hurry up and get married.

"Shall I show you our room, darling?" she now said to Papa. "Let me help you unpack. We have a balcony, would you believe, where we can sit in the morning and drink our tea! Come and see." So saying, she took his hand. Papa smiled, stooped and picked up his case, and eagerly followed her upstairs.

Aunt Bernice led the way after them and showed Norah and Louise their room, on the south side of the house overlooking the garden. Sure enough, there was a glimpse of blue through the trees.

"There's a path through the trees that leads down to the water," she told them. "It's a nice walk, about half a mile. You can see Mr. Kidd's house away over there through the trees. Actually, the roof you see is his barn."

"Does the path lead down to the beach where it happened?" faltered Louise.

"Well, it comes out on the easterly headland of the bay," replied her aunt. "The boat launch is toward the other end of the bay, another mile up the coast."

She left them then. Louise continued to peer out the window and think of the two young people who had lost their lives in that blue water. Mr. Kidd sounded like a grumpy old man, the way Aunt Bernice had spoken of him. Perhaps his young wife *had* fallen in love with the handsome schoolteacher. What a price she had paid!

Presently she turned and surveyed Aunt Bernice's guest room. It was roomy and pleasant with the two casement windows making it fresh and airy. The big double bed was a four-poster with a canopy and drapes. Two chamber pots were tucked away under the bed, but there was also a bathroom and toilet down the hall; Aunt Bernice had pointed it out to them on their way to the room. An old fashioned washstand stood in the corner, with an oval mirror over it. The bowl and pitcher was a beautiful robin's egg blue. A huge wardrobe stood between the windows, and there was ample room for them to hang up all the clothes they had brought.

"Me for a sponge bath," announced Norah, "and then I'm going to lie down with my book. I know we've been sitting for days, it seems, but I'm very tired."

So saying, she took the pitcher and headed to the bathroom to find some hot water. Louise merely changed out of her traveling outfit and put on a summer dress. Then she went out to explore.

Chapter Seven

LOUISE'S ADVENTURES

It was a fine July day, the sun warm on Louise's bare head as she strolled through her aunt's back garden and out into the grassy meadow. Wildflowers nodded, a solitary blackbird sang from a tree, and from the distance gulls called their plaintive cries. From the stile at the far side of the meadow a well-beaten path led into the woods at the top of the ridge. When she emerged from the trees after about ten minutes she saw that the land dropped sharply away to a red, rocky headland less than a half-mile away. There was a cool breeze here, so she stopped and took a deep breath of the salty air. How fresh it was after the humidity of Ottawa, and the stuffy train car!

She followed the path down the slope between sand dunes where the long grass waved in the breeze and there she found a large flat rock, and flung herself down. The sun had deliciously warmed it. She was perhaps thirty feet above the water.

Now I know how a lizard must feel, she thought sleepily.

Presently she arose and continued the path that led down to the beach. The tide was out and a large expanse of damp sand stretched before her, red and shining in the sun. Not a soul could be seen. With a laugh, she picked up her skirts and ran as fast as she could close to the water's edge. How she wished Frankie were here to share this spot with her! Finally she stopped, puffing with the exertion, turned and started back. At the foot of the hill a large shaggy dog of doubtful parentage met her, one ear pricked up as he regarded her quizzically. He barked at her, but his tail was wagging furiously, so Louise, who liked dogs, took it for a greeting.

"Hallo, there," she said in a friendly way, and waited for the dog to approach. He sniffed at her hand, decided she was acceptable, and allowed her to stroke his head.

"Where have you sprung from?" she asked him, "and what's your name?" The dog gave a sharp bark, wagged his tail, and then trotted to the water's edge, where he found a small piece of driftwood. He brought it to Louise and dropped it at her feet.

"Oh, so you want to play fetch," she remarked, picking it up.

She tossed the stick out into the water and the dog jumped in eagerly and retrieved it. He returned to her, and the game resumed until Louise was thoroughly tired of it. She jogged back along the beach, throwing the stick as far as she could, and the dog obligingly fetched it, and chased her with it. By this time Louise was hungry and thirsty, so shaking her head at him, she turned and started up the path to the top of the ridge. The dog overtook her hopefully, stick firmly clenched between his teeth, but Louise would not relent. He undoubtedly accepted her refusal, for he dropped the stick in resignation, and went ahead of her up the path, pausing once to shake the water from his coat. She strode after him into the trees, and discovered to her surprise that she had taken a different path, for when the trees thinned out she found herself some distance west of her aunt's property in another field. The big red-roofed barn that she had noted from her bedroom window was merely a hundred yards off, and in the barnyard a man was pitch forking hay through the wide doors of the building. Her new friend scampered ahead of her to the man. Louise hesitated, and then came forward in a friendly way.

"You must be Mr. Kidd," she said, smiling. "I'm so sorry to trespass, but I followed your dog up from the beach and must have taken a wrong path."

The man was perhaps forty-five or fifty, a straw hat pulled firmly down on his head. He glared at her.

"Here, Charley," he growled. "You're wet and dirty! Now get!"

"I'm sorry, but it's my fault he's dirty. He wanted to play fetch." She held out her hand. "I'm Louise Laurier, and I'm staying with my Aunt Bernice Laurier over there." She nodded her head in the direction of the Laurier farm.

He said something unintelligible, ignoring her outstretched hand. Louise let her hand drop, and backed away. He was still glaring at her, one hand on his hip, the other holding the pitchfork.

"Aunt Bernice told us about Mrs. Kidd," she faltered. "We are all so sorry . . ."

He ignored her, muttering something she didn't catch, and turned back to his work. Louise, feeling thoroughly snubbed, turned without another word and hurried away. The dog Charley followed her to the edge of the field.

"We're both in trouble with your master," she whispered, and gave his flanks a swift slap. "I think we'd both better go home."

She found her way through the trees, and so down to the road, and started up the road past the Kidd farmhouse to her aunt's home next door. As she was nearing the Kidd driveway an automobile approached from the direction of the village, a cloud of red dust in its wake. She caught a glimpse of an elderly woman and two children in the back seat. One, a small girl, was hanging out the window, and waved at Louise in a friendly way. She watched the vehicle disappear into the driveway, and then went quietly and thoughtfully home, where she found her sister still reading in their room.

"You've been gone ages," Norah declared, putting down her book. "I was just going to go downstairs to see if I could help Aunt Bernice with supper."

Louise washed her hands at the washstand, and looked at herself in the mirror. Her hair was in wild disarray from being blown by the wind, but her eyes sparkled and her cheeks were pink.

"Such adventures I've been having, Norah!" She climbed onto the bed, crossing her legs tomboyishly. Reaching for her sister's hairbrush, she began repairing the ravages the wind had done to her hair. "I went down to the beach where, you know, 'it' happened," she began. "I played with a dog named Charley, and I met HIM.

You know, Mr. Kidd." She glanced at her sister with dancing eyes. "I followed the dog home and found myself in his barnyard."

She had Norah's complete attention. "What's he like?"

"He's quite old," Louise told her. "Not as old as Papa, but nearly, I should say. And rude! He growled at me quite unnecessarily. I was only trying to be neighborly and polite. And he was quite cross at me for letting the dog go into the water." She tossed her head. "It's no wonder Mrs. Kidd went off with the schoolteacher!"

"Hush, Louise, you mustn't say a thing like that. Aunt Bernice is sure that there was nothing wrong with their friendship."

"Well, maybe. But you haven't met Mr. Kidd. Oh, yes, and I saw a car go by with an elderly woman and two small children. Do you suppose his children are home from visiting their grandmother?"

Norah gazed at her sister. "Maybe Aunt Bernice will know. You've certainly been having an interesting time, haven't you, and we've only been here a few hours." She slid off the bed. "I guess we had better go down and see if we can be of any help."

Aunt Bernice and a girl who she introduced as Mary were in the kitchen preparing supper. A savory stew bubbled away on the back of the stove, its enticing aroma filling the room. Their aunt showed them where the silver and linen were kept, and together Louise and Norah laid the table in the dining room, after which Norah went out and picked some flowers and made an attractive centerpiece. Presently they all sat down, and after giving thanks for a safe journey and good food, they proceeded to enjoy their meal. Louise regaled them with her adventures on her walk, lightly passing over her encounter with Mr. Kidd, not liking to make negative remarks about Aunt Bernice's neighbor. She then told her aunt about the automobile that had turned in next door.

"Do you think it was the Kidd children?" she asked.

Aunt Bernice smiled. "I have heard that they were returning soon. You'll find out tomorrow. Mr. Kidd's mother always takes them to church on Sundays when they're here."

"That's them," whispered Louise ungrammatically to Norah the next morning as they sat in church. She nodded at the trio across the aisle. An elderly woman dressed in black from head to toe sat quietly, flanked by two small children. Norah couldn't see the boy, but the girl was fair-haired, with two bright blue intelligent eyes, which were gazing around the church. Her dress was of drab brown cotton and on her head was a straw hat with a black velvet ribbon on the crown. She saw that Norah and Louise were looking her way, and she smiled at them.

Louise waggled her fingers at her and smiled back.

After church the old lady hurried her charges away. There was no sign of Mr. Kidd.

"Yes, those are the Kidd children," confirmed Aunt Bernice as they drove home after the service. "The lady is their grandmother, who lives in Charlottetown. They've been staying with her since the accident. Harry Kidd hasn't seen the inside of this church since his wife's funeral. The elder Mrs. Kidd is planning to stay for the rest of the summer, so Mrs. Crocker was telling me a little while ago."

Norah's heart had gone out to the two motherless youngsters. It was too bad if their father was a bad-tempered person; however, Norah was ready to give him the benefit of the doubt. Not only had he lost his wife in a sudden and terrible way, but also Louise, with her youthful intolerance, tended to be a harsh judge. Perhaps he wasn't as unpleasant as she had made out.

That first week of their visit, the two sisters were persuaded to help Mary with the milking. For two city dwellers, it was a new experience. Norah had grown up in the country, but not on a farm, and neither had ever milked a cow or churned butter. Mary, who was probably about Norah's age, was an expert at both. She showed them what to do, and supervised them with much amusement. The cows were placid and good-natured, standing stolidly while the girls made their fumbling attempts. Norah caught on fairly quickly, and was delighted to see the streams of milk flowing into the bucket. Louise was awkward, but stayed with it, and after several attempts managed to fill the pail with the warm milk.

Mary praised the cows for their patience as much as she praised her students for their success.

"What a girl, Clover!" she exclaimed, as Norah finished milking her. "Isn't she a dear? She also wants watching, you know. She loves Mr. Kidd's cornfield. I've chased her out of there three times already this summer." She regarded the girls with pleasure. "You've done very well, I must say. Bring the buckets and follow me. Next is a lesson in churning butter."

The next day Norah's hands were so stiff she could scarcely button her dress, and her back and shoulder muscles screamed in agony. Louise, similarly afflicted, groaned and refused to get out of bed.

"Come on, we can't let them know what sad specimens of womanhood we are," Norah said, massaging her hands and flexing her fingers. "Ouch! I'm feeling muscles I didn't know I had," she added with a laugh.

"How does Mary do it, day after day," muttered Louise. "Gosh, I can't even hold the blanket to make the bed."

Aunt Bernice gave them liniment for their aches and pains, and told them that Mary had been impressed with their efforts.

"We'll make dairy farmers out of you before you go back home."

"Not likely," said Louise quietly as she helped with the dishes after breakfast. "I never thought I'd be glad to get my hands into hot dishwater," she added with a grin.

Chapter Eight

NORAH

Later that week Aunt Bernice drove Mama and Papa to Charlottetown to spend a week with Aunt Mercy and Uncle Robert Lesley. Aunt Mercy was Papa and Aunt Bernice's younger sister. She had immigrated to the Island with her elder sister twenty years ago along with their young brother Simon. Uncle Simon had returned to Ontario, not liking farming life, Aunt Mercy had met Robert Lesley, married him and had gone to live in the capital city, leaving their small farm in Aunt Bernice's capable hands.

Mama and Papa were planning to stay for a week, and then return to Fairlea with the Lesleys. Mary and the hired man were left in charge of the farm, while Norah and Louise were to run the house for a week.

"We'll be fine," Norah assured Mama, kissing her fondly. "You enjoy your visit with Aunt Mercy, and we'll look forward to seeing her and meeting Uncle Robert next week. We'll expect you all for supper on Friday. Louise and I will enjoy planning a fancy meal to impress them."

The next two days passed pleasantly, though it was very quiet with just themselves in the house. Mary was busy in the dairy, and the hired man Pierre in the fields. They saw them at suppertime, Norah and Louise joining them for the evening meal in the kitchen.

54

"It's silly to set two tables, and you eat in here alone just because you work for my aunt," declared Norah. "Besides, Canada is a democracy."

Sunday evening Pierre and Mary decided to walk to the vespers service at the little Catholic Church a mile and a half on the other side of the Kidd farm.

"We're going to talk to Father Lacombe about me taking instruction," Mary confided to Norah and Louise. "We'll have the banns put up by the end of the summer." And she blushed.

Norah smiled and congratulated her. She had thought there might be romance in the air.

After they had gone, Mary having left instructions as to when to go out to the meadow and bring the cows in, the girls tidied the kitchen and while Norah sat down on the verandah swing with her book, Louise went out for a walk. Norah read for a while, then her eyes grew heavy, and the next thing she knew was Louise shaking her.

"Norah! Norah! Wake up! That darn Clover has gotten into Mr. Kidd's corn patch!"

Norah sat up with a start, not quite knowing where she was. "Come help me get her out before that awful Mr. Kidd sees her!" Norah was now wide-awake. She followed her sister around to the back and sure enough, there was Aunt Bernice's red cow munching contentedly in the cornfield next door. The corn, young and tender, would be ready to pick in a few weeks. Mr. Kidd would be furious!

"Hurry! Get that stick! We shall have to climb over the fence!"

"How on earth did she get out of our pasture?" panted Norah, clambering over the wooden fence.

"There was a break in the fence up by the chestnut tree, but I thought Pierre had mended it," replied Louise. "Hey, Clover! Get out of there!" And she struck the cow with the stick.

Clover, not surprisingly, did not like this sort of treatment, and gave a loud bellow.

They managed, after a few minutes of shouting and prodding with the stick, to persuade Clover to vacate the corn patch. They were driving her up along the fence towards the chestnut tree when they heard a yell and saw a man striding purposefully across the meadow from the red-roofed barn. Norah stopped, and looked at Louise.

"Oh, golly! Is that Mr. Kidd? Now we're in for it."

Louise squinted at the figure hurrying toward them. "No, that's not him. It must be his hired man."

"What the devil do you two think you're doing?" he said crossly, as he reached the pair.

He was a man of medium height, and it passed through Louise's mind that he was considerably younger than Mr. Kidd, and nicer looking, too, if it weren't for the unpleasant expression on his face! He was clean-shaven, with a thin, brown face, and bright blue eyes that were now snapping with anger.

Norah was regarding the man with an apologetic air. "I'm sorry, Mr., er, er. But Clover had gotten into Mr. Kidd's corn and we were just trying to get her out."

He looked at her with an amazed expression. "That cow happens to be mine!"

Norah drew herself up. "Pardon me, but I think I know my aunt's cow."

"Nonsense!" he exclaimed with derision. "You city people can't tell one animal from another, can you." He came up to her, snatched the stick out of her hand and tossed it away. "And I don't like my cow being hit!" He took her by the arm and rather roughly dragged her several yards along the fence where there was a clear view into Aunt Bernice's pasture next door. "Look, you silly female, count 'em, for heaven's sake. One, two, three, four, five! I believe Miss Laurier has only five cows? And there's your damn Clover—though why anyone would give a cow such a silly name."

Norah looked with dismay, and sure enough, there was Clover amongst her sisters grazing contentedly.

She looked at Mr. Kidd's hired man, then back at Louise, who had her hand up to her mouth, eyes big as saucers.

Norah drew herself up with her last shred of dignity. "It was an honest mistake, and there's no need to leave bruises on me," she said coldly. "Mr. Kidd won't be best pleased to find that you've been manhandling his neighbor's guests."

56

Mr. Kidd's hired man regarded her quizzically, and his grin, even if it was sardonic, transformed his face.

"No, I suppose not," he said easily, dropping her arm.

Norah found herself gazing into his extraordinary eyes with a feeling that she might drown. Her heart beating rapidly, she backed away, and found herself against the fence.

"Don't worry, Miss Laurier, I won't eat you," he said, smile fading.

Norah felt her cheeks grow warm.

"I'm sorry we made a mistake ... ."

"It was all my fault," put in Louise. "I told her it was Clover."

The man turned on his heel without acknowledging the offered apologies, walked over to the cow without a word, and gave her a slap. "Come on now, get away from here," he told her. "You'd better be careful where you stray. The next time you might get stolen."

The cow turned obediently and headed away, the man following. "Well!" said Louise, when he was out of earshot. "I'd say he's as rude as his employer!"

Norah said nothing, but climbed over the fence and marched across the pasture toward the small herd.

"Let's get those infuriating animals into the barn and start the milking. I've had enough of cows for one day!"

The next day Norah went riding. She enjoyed the activity, and when the family lived in the country had taken lessons at a neighboring farm. She was eighteen when the Lauriers had moved into the city, had gone to Normal School, and then had begun teaching nearly five years ago. Jeremy Ferris had encouraged her, and she had recently taken it up again. Aunt Bernice had two horses, and both were suitable for young ladies, but she didn't have a sidesaddle. In some ways her aunt was a modern woman, for she wore trousers when she rode. Norah had recently acquired a pair of trousers herself, and was annoyed that she had not brought them.

"You can't ride astride with a dress on," objected Louise.

Norah was still smarting from yesterday's encounter with the Kidd hired man, though why that should make her want to defy convention she didn't know. His thin brown face and bright blue eyes were in her mind's eye when she retorted, "Just watch me. I'll ride down to the bay. No one will see me there. There hasn't been one person bathing there since we came."

"Maybe they're still thinking about the accident," Louise said. They were in their room, and she went over to the mirror and began to pin up her hair. "While you're out, I shall have a nice bath. May I borrow your bath salts, please?"

Norah took a large bottle out of her drawer and handed it to her sister.

"It will be delightfully cool riding in a skirt," she remarked.

Louise was a bit shocked. "I certainly hope nobody sees you."

Norah pulled on her trim boots and laced them up deftly. "Nobody but Pierre, and he doesn't count."

Pierre was in the stable saddling a mare called Ginger, and glanced doubtfully at her dress, but said nothing. He helped her into the saddle, and Norah primly pulled her skirt down over her knees, and gave the horse a kick. She clattered out of the yard, down the driveway and on to the road that led to the village. She turned right and trotted by the Kidd farm. She heard voices coming from the front of the house and saw a small boy running across the lawn to the trees.

"Dad, Dad, catch me!"

She heard a deep male laugh, and thought that Mr. Kidd couldn't be as bad as Louise had made him out to be. He had a nice laugh and was playing with his son. As she rode by she kept her face forward, and only caught a glimpse of his back out of the corner of her eye. Then the trees hid the front garden of the Kidd house, and she was riding past open fields. A narrow track turned right toward the sea about a half-mile past the farmhouse, so she headed her mount that way, and soon came out on top of the ridge, and was looking down at the waters of the next bay. She guided Ginger down the slope and along the beach toward the headland. The tide was out, and there was room to go around the point without going in the water. Ginger seemed quite used to the waves sliding in at her feet, tossed her head only a few times, and presently they were on the other side and the long stretch of beach that Louise had walked on was before her. She gave the horse a sharp kick and they galloped along the shore, the wind streaming through her hair and blowing her skirt up to her waist, exposing her bare thighs. She laughed out loud with exhilaration. Behind her she heard a dog barking, so she slowed down, turned Ginger around and watched a dog scampering down the hillside, a child close behind. From Louise's description, she decided it must be the dog Charley, and the child one of the Kidd twins. She rode slowly toward them, and the child waved her hand. At that moment she tripped and fell headlong on the shingle. Charley barked, and Norah urged Ginger into a trot, and she reached the child in a moment or so. She was getting to her feet stoically. Louise jumped down.

"Are you all right?" she asked anxiously.

The child was examining her knees under her dress, and said, her eyes filling, "I've skinned my knees."

"Here, let's go over to the grass and sit down. I'll take a look."

Norah comforted the child, took a handkerchief, dampened it in seawater and gently cleaned the scrape.

"Sea water is good for cuts and scrapes," she told the child. "There! It stings a little, doesn't it."

The little girl nodded solemnly.

"You're one of the Kidd children, aren't you. I'm Norah. Should you be down here all by yourself? Does your daddy know where you are?"

"I'm Sarah Kidd," she announced. "Charley is with me, the tide's out, so it's okay."

"What are you doing down here?" persisted Norah.

Sarah was silent for a moment, and then said. "I was looking for my mother. She went away, and I thought I'd look where I saw her last."

Norah frowned. "Have you asked your father about this?" she asked slowly.

"Daddy said Mummy went away and isn't coming back." He eyes filled with tears again. "I thought if I could find her, I might ask her to come back. Benjy and I miss her so. Do you know where she is?"

Norah was appalled, and found herself furiously angry with the child's father. Maybe Louise was right about him . . .

"What does your Grandmother say?"

"She says she's in Heaven, but I don't know where that is. Do you, Miss?"

Norah's arm tightened around the child. "No, I don't, Sarah. Nobody does."

"Not even the minister? I was going to ask him after church last Sunday, but Granny hurried us away."

Norah was silent, wondering what to say. "Do you know where she is, Miss?"

"No, dear."

"Daddy says Miss Bernice is your auntie. Is that right?"

"Yes. My sister Louise and I are visiting her with my parents. They went up to Charlottetown a few days ago. There's just Louise and me at the house right now."

This was a safe topic, but Sarah had a one-track mind.

"Has Miss Bernice seen Mummy?"

"I don't think so, dear. I think you should talk to your Daddy and your Granny about this."

"Daddy won't talk about her. I overheard Granny saying to Daddy, 'You should explain to the children about Lucille.' My mother's name is Lucille. So I know Daddy knows what happened to her, he just won't say."

"You keep on asking, Sarah," Norah said firmly.

"Do you know what happened to her?"

Norah was silent.

"You do, don't you! Tell me!" she demanded.

"I only have been here for a couple of weeks," Norah said lamely. "I only know what Aunt Bernice said about her."

"Oh, tell me, Miss, please do! I do so want to find her."

"Let's go and talk to your Daddy...."

"No! He said he didn't want me to talk about her with strangers, but you're not a stranger, are you? I saw you in church with Miss Bernice, and the other lady, she's your sister, isn't she."

Norah didn't know what to say. How could a father not tell his children their mother had died?

"Sarah, I think you should ask your father what happened. Tell him he must tell you."

Sarah's eyes widened at Norah's grave tones, and looked up at her. "Is she dead, Miss? Is that what being in Heaven means?"

Norah nodded solemnly. "Aunt Bernice told me she fell out of a boat in the sea and drowned."

"Drownded dead?"

"Yes, dear, I am so sorry."

Sarah got to her feet. "There's no point in looking for her, is there," she said sadly.

"Would you like a ride back home on Ginger?"

"Oh, yes, thank you, Miss!"

Norah lifted Sarah up and gently settled her in front of the saddle, and then she found a large rock, climbed on top of it, and mounted the horse. They trotted up the beach, and retraced their path around the headland. The tide had turned, and Ginger had to wade through six inches of water, but she didn't seem to mind. The dog Charley was waiting for them on the other side, and led the way up the trail, tail wagging. They reached the top of the hill, and Norah suddenly felt Sarah's shoulder heaving. The child was weeping silently, tears running down her face. Norah found it far more unsettling than if the child had sobbed noisily. She pulled the horse to a stop, and put her arms around the child in front of her, laying her cheek on the top of her head.

"It's all right to cry, Sarah," she said softly.

Sarah leaned back against Norah, gave a couple of muffled sobs, and then wiped her face with the skirt of her dress. Norah would have given Sarah her handkerchief, but it was a sodden lump in her pocket. Presently Norah urged Ginger forward, and they trotted back to the road and along to the gates of the Kidd Farm. Sarah wriggled out of Norah's arms and slid off the horse.

"Would you like me to come and talk to your Papa?"

"No, thank you," she said politely. "Thank you for bringing me home."

Troubled, Norah watched the child hurry up the drive to the house, the dog at her heels.

61

Chapter Nine

NORAH AND HARRY

Norah and Louise discussed her experience with Sarah Kidd over their cups of tea after supper that night.

"Those poor children!" Louise said, shaking her head. "I can just see Mr. Kidd neglecting them. He was such a grouch when I met him, quite by chance. You'd think I trespassed on his property on purpose." Louise had not forgotten how she had met the unpleasant man on their first day at Aunt Bernice's.

"And yet," Norah remembered, "I heard him laughing quite pleasantly and playing with young Benjy, as his sister called him." She again pondered her conversation with Sarah. "What would you have said, Louise? I just couldn't go on lying to the child. Imagine a father not telling his children their mother had died! It's absolutely shameful, don't you think?"

She was still musing on the injustice of it all the next morning as she helped Mary with the milking. As she milked Clover, however, her thoughts turned toward the hired man, and their encounter of two evenings before. She remembered how his blue eyes mocked her as he counted the cows in Aunt Bernice's pasture. She could still feel his hand around her arm. It had hurt, but she hadn't minded, somehow. She had wanted to hurt him back. Just recalling his face made her heart beat a little faster. What on earth was the matter with her? She tried to erase him from her mind, but he persisted. Her hands slowed her rhythmic squeezing and she laid her hot face against the cow's flanks. Clover moved uneasily. So large did he loom in her thoughts that she imagined she could hear his voice as well....

"Where the hell is she? The older one?"

Her head snapped back as the barn door flew open and he stood there silhouetted against the light, feet apart and hands firmly on his hips. She stared up at him, her mouth open in surprise.

"What on earth...?"

He reached down and grabbed her wrist, dragging her to her feet. "What right did you have to speak to my daughter of her mother? What right?" He was furious. The blue eyes that had gently mocked her two days ago were as hard and cold as steel.

She could only stare at him in bewilderment.

"You saw Sarah on the beach and spoke of her mother. Didn't you? Didn't you?" His hand tightened around her wrist, and he bent toward her, his face a few inches from her.

"Are you Mr. Kidd?" she gasped. "I thought...."

"I really don't care what made you jump to the conclusion that I was the hired man. I care that my children cried themselves to sleep last night, all because you took it upon yourself to tell Sarah—"

"The child was searching for her mother down on the beach! What kind of father would not tell his children that their mother had died?"

"That's no business of yours," he said furiously.

"I told her to talk to you, but she kept asking me, Mr. Kidd. It's been three months since the accident! You've been depriving your children of the chance to grieve properly and come to terms with their loss. Don't you know you could harm them irreparably?"

Harry Kidd looked at her and sneered. "What do you know of bringing up children—an old maid like you?"

Norah's face flushed with mingled anger and embarrassment. "Please take your hands off me," she said coldly. "I've been teaching school for five years, and I think I know a little about children."

Harry dropped his hand from her wrist, and Norah strode out of the barn.

He followed her.

"God save me from schoolteachers," he said unpleasantly.

She whirled on him. "Is this how you treat everybody who disagrees with you?" she asked. "Is this how you talked to your wife? If it is, it's no wonder she preferred the company of—"

She broke off, appalled at what she was implying, and put her hand up to her mouth.

The color receded from his face and for a moment he looked as though he had been slapped. Then the blood rushed back and he took a step toward her. Out if the corner of her eye she could see Mary standing nearby, eyes wide with alarm.

"What have you heard?" he demanded in a low voice. "What lies have they been telling you?"

"Nothing," she said. "I've heard nothing. Aunt Bernice said there was talk, but . . ."

"Be good enough to mind your own business from now on, Miss Laurier," he said, wheeling and striding away. In a moment he had disappeared into the trees that divided the two properties.

Mary rushed over to her. "Did he hurt you, Miss Norah?' she asked anxiously.

"No, he didn't," she said. She was staring after Harry Kidd, her heart beating rapidly. She had been angry with him, and she knew her words had hurt him, but somehow it didn't give her any satisfaction.

"Mary," she said slowly, "has there been a lot of gossip about Mrs. Kidd's death?"

Mary thought for a moment. "People talked at first, but it died down soon after." She shook her head. "I've heard Mr. Kidd has an awful temper, but I've never seen him on the rampage before. Don't worry, Miss," she added, as Norah made a gesture. "I won't talk about this. Not even to Pierre. Let me tell you, if Pierre spoke to me like that I'd send him on his way so fast his head would spin." She patted Norah's shoulder sympathetically. "I'll finish up the milking, you go and lie down. You're still upset, I can tell."

Norah thanked her and went upstairs to her room. As she thought of the encounter, her anger returned. Odious man! What nerve he had to come over here and lecture her! She had been trying to be kind to the child, and all he could do was berate her... She flung herself on the bed, and found that she was in tears. Damn him!

Louise came in a short while later.

"Norah, Mary said that Mr. Kidd came over and that you two had words! What happened?"

Norah was suddenly irrationally annoyed with her sister. "The man you thought was Mr. Kidd must be his hired man," she said. "That was Harry Kidd that came over the other afternoon when we thought Clover was in his corn. How could you have made such a mistake? I felt such a fool . . ."

Louise sat down in surprise. "Are you sure?" she asked, rather foolishly.

"Of course I'm sure," Norah replied, wiping her eyes. "He's a horrid, horrid man, and I never want to lay eyes on him again!"

Louise was rearranging her ideas. "I guess I just assumed, when Mr. Kidd, no, I mean the hired man, didn't put me right. Oh, Norah, I'm so sorry!"

Norah's irritation vanished at the sight of her sister's contrite face.

"It wasn't your fault," she said, putting her arms around her. "Let's not talk about this, shall we? I'd rather Mama and Papa and Aunt Bernice didn't know what a fool I am."

"You're not a fool. It's him that's the fool," she added ungrammatically. "Don't worry, we'll be going home in a couple of weeks, and you need never think about him again."

"I can't wait," Norah said fiercely.

The next day they were busy preparing for their parent's return along with the others on the following day. The house was dusted and swept, the beds in the other guest room aired, and the table in the dining room set for seven with Aunt Bernice's best china. Norah baked a cake and made two pies, while Louise boiled a ham, covered it and set it to cool in the pantry, and cooked vegetables for a salad. In the morning when it was still cool they walked to the village and bought bread and cheese at the grocer's. On the way home they discussed what still had to be done. Louise offered to prepare greens for a salad if Norah would do the devilled eggs.

"I can never make them neatly. The halves are never the same size, and I make such a mess with the filling," she confessed. They walked for a while in silence, and then Louise went on,

"Have we met Aunt Mercy and Uncle Robert before?"

Norah thought for a moment. "Aunt Mercy came to visit us with Aunt Bernice years ago. I think it must have been before she was married. You must have been pretty young, because it was a few years before we moved to town. She was small and dark and vivacious and always laughing. I remember she wanted me to call her just 'Mercy' because having a niece so grown up made her feel old. I thought she was wonderful."

"Oh, I didn't realize Aunt Mercy was there as well. I remember Aunt Bernice, because I was terrified of her. Gerald told me she was a witch and would put a spell on me if I misbehaved."

Norah chuckled. "Gerald could really be a devil when he wanted to. I supposed you believed him."

"Well, of course," smiled Louise. "It was almost like Papa speaking, and I knew that Papa was second only to God!"

Norah threw back her head and laughed heartily at the foibles of children. After they had finished their chores and eaten a late lunch, Norah, restless, went for a walk down to the bay. Two families with their children and dogs were bathing there, so she sat on the flat rock on the headland and closed her eyes. She thought of little Sarah, and the conversation they had had not far away from where she was sitting. What else could she have said to the child? When the little girl asked if her mother was dead, should she have lied and said she didn't know? She was concerned for both the children, even though their father had made it clear that it was none of her business. She shivered at the memory of how cold and hard his eyes had become. There was a moment when she thought that he was going to strike her. She told herself that she should despise him, but she somehow couldn't, because deep down in her heart she sensed that he was suffering terribly.

"It's still no excuse for the way he spoke to me," she said aloud, as she got to her feet and started up the path. Ah well, Louise was right. In two weeks they'd be going home and she need not even have to think about him again.

Uncle Robert's big touring sedan drove up to the house just before five o'clock. Papa looked very grave, and Mama hugged Louise and Norah very hard.

"What is it, Mama?" asked Louise. "What's wrong?"

"You haven't heard yet, then. It's War, my dear. Britain has declared war on Germany, and Canada will follow suit immediately. Papa has decided to go straight back to Ottawa. The office will need him."

Papa worked for the fledgling Department of External Affairs.

"I'm going back with him," Mama continued, "but I want you and Norah to stay for the original scheduled time."

"Oh, Mama, I want to go back with you and Papa! What if Frankie should want to join up?"

Mama's face went white. "Don't even think of such a thing! He's only eighteen, for heaven's sake!"

"Besides," put in Aunt Mercy, "I thought that you and Norah could come back to Charlottetown with Robert and me and stay for a week before going home." She held out a slim gloved hand. "I'm Mercy, my dear. I don't suppose you remember me." She turned to Norah and kissed her affectionately. "You're all grown up now and teaching school! How lovely to see you after all these years! You haven't met Robert, of course.... Robert, dear, these lovely young ladies are Norah and Louise, and of course you know that. Don't you feel old and decrepit to have such grown-up nieces?"

Robert Lesley was a tall, distinguished gentleman, with a well-trimmed beard and mustache. He doffed his hat gallantly and bowed to the two girls. Aunt Bernice led the way into the house, her sister and brother-in-law following, Mercy chattering gaily. It seemed she was determined to temper the gloom with bright conversation. Mama, her arms around the waists of her daughters, went inside, Papa immediately behind, carrying their bags.

"I want you to rest before supper, my love," he said anxiously. "Travel is so tiring. You must gain your strength before we go home."

67

"When were you planning to leave, Papa?" asked Norah. She watched Louise take her mother's arm and start up the stairs.

"I can't see getting away before Monday," he replied, taking off his suit coat and hanging it on the hook in the entrance alcove. He led the way upstairs. "Bernice has a dinner party planned for Sunday evening. She has invited the minister and his wife and the doctor and his wife. I believe Mercy is acquainted with the doctor's wife."

"I'd like to go back immediately," she said quietly.

"Haven't you enjoyed yourself, my pet?"

"Oh, yes, Papa, it's just—"

"I know, you're worried about your brothers. I am too. Frank is far to young to join the army, and Gerald is too sensible! They'll do what they think is right, though," he sighed. "You know young Ferris, of course you do. He came to me a few weeks ago, after the trouble began in Europe, and asked me to recommend him for officer's training. I was happy to write a letter of recommendation."

"Jeremy's joined the army?" Louise, at the top of the stairs had over heard and was gazing anxiously down the stairs as her father and sister came up.

"Why, yes, my dear. He'll make splendid officer material. So would Gerald, of course, but I don't think he's interested."

"Let's go down and help Aunt Bernice get the supper on the table," urged Louise. "And let's not mention the War, please!"

After supper Mercy suggested a game of Hearts "to take our minds off things" and she busied herself clearing the dining room table. Norah stayed in the kitchen and helped Mary clear up. Aunt Bernice was appreciative of Norah's help.

"Thank you for preparing supper, my dear," she said with a smile. "Are you going to join us in a game of cards?"

"No, thank you, I don't think so," Norah replied, as she dried and polished the silverware. "If you don't mind, I'm going to take my book to the verandah and enjoy the evening sun."

Chapter Ten

NORAH AND HARRY

Norah, sitting on the verandah a little while later, could hear Mercy's merry voice as the six played their game of Hearts.

"Aha! You're stuck with Her Majesty, Robert! That's how many points, Louise?"

There was much laughter and nonsense. Even Mama was enjoying herself, thoughts of war put aside for the moment. Norah didn't feel like playing games. She was restless and couldn't concentrate on her book. From the swing she could see the roof of the Kidd farmhouse through the trees, and smoke arising from the chimney. She tried to analyze her feelings about the day before yesterday when Mr. Kidd had strode over and called her down. She had lain in bed the night before, Louise sleeping peacefully at her side, while the confrontation between her and Mr. Kidd replayed itself over and over in her mind. Why on earth had she blurted out that remark about Mrs. Kidd? Well, she had stopped herself in mid-sentence, but the inference had been there, and she grew cold when she remembered how hard his face had become. She shouldn't have said it, even though he had goaded her into it, making that remark about her being an old maid and praying to be saved from teachers. Teachers! Oh, mercy, and Mr. Crocker had been a teacher, too, hadn't he! Her face grew warm. She would be so glad to get away, whether to

Charlottetown or home! She didn't ever want to see him again. But those poor children . . .

She heard footsteps, looked up, and to her surprise saw the object of her thoughts striding across the front lawn. She jumped to her feet awkwardly, her book tumbling to the floor. He stopped at the bottom of the steps and looked up at her. He was dressed in a suit of clothes and a collar and tie, and his hair was combed carefully back. He was looking as awkward as she felt.

"Miss Laurier, I'm sorry to intrude. I didn't realize you had company," he said politely, gesturing at Uncle Robert's sedan.

"Everyone is occupied at the moment. Did you want to see Aunt Bernice?"

He gazed at her steadily. "No. I wanted to speak with you." Norah's eyebrows flew up before she could stop them.

"For heaven's sake, I'm not going to eat you," he said irritably, sounding more like himself.

Norah found herself smiling for no particular reason. "I shouldn't think so. Besides, my uncle and Papa are only a dozen steps away. Please come up and sit down."

Harry Kidd came up the steps and on to the verandah. He took a seat in the large straight-backed chair. There was a long, awkward silence.

He cleared his throat and frowned. "Miss Laurier," he said stiffly. "I have come to apologize for my behavior this past week. I had no right to speak to you as I did. My only excuse is that I have been troubled in my mind since my wife died."

Norah looked into his blue eyes and thought he was sincere. She took a deep breath.

"Mr. Kidd, I also need to apologize to you. I had no right to question your integrity or to comment on your relationship with Mrs. Kidd."

"I goaded you into it, didn't I," he remarked in a more normal tone.

"Well, you did, but that's no excuse," she replied warmly. "Especially when my aunt stated she was sure there was nothing wrong with the friendship between Mr. Crocker and your wife."

"Miss Laurier said that?"

"Yes. And I have not yet expressed my condolences to you."

"Well, I've hardly given you a chance, have I?"

"It was unkind of you not to put me right about who you were when you came over about the cow. That, by the way, was an honest case of mistaken identity."

Mr. Kidd's blue eyes twinkled, and Norah was astonished how it changed his expression. "Who, the cow or me?"

Norah found herself laughing. "Well, both of you. The day we arrived my sister strayed into your barnyard by mistake and assumed the gentleman she met was Mr. Kidd. He didn't correct her, and scolded her for letting the dog go in the water."

"Jed's a trifle deaf, but he won't admit it. Also, his dentures don't fit him well, and he inclines to mumble. I suppose you think we're a couple of curmudgeons."

"Well . . ."

"I wasn't very gracious to your aunt, either, when she brought casseroles of food over to us after Lucille died. I should apologize to her, too." He moved uneasily. "Miss Laurier, you were kind to my daughter, and I paid you back with abuse. I am truly sorry."

Norah was wondering what had made him change so suddenly. "Your apology is accepted if you will accept mine."

"Done!" he said. "Miss Laurier, my children are very important to me. My mother has been looking after them since the—accident because I just didn't feel capable. Sarah thinks you're quite wonderful, you know."

Norah blushed with pleasure. "She's a darling." Up until now she would have said he didn't deserve her. "I would love to meet Benjamin, too."

"Would you?" he asked eagerly. "I came to ask a favor of you as well. Sarah and Ben say I can't read their stories very well. I don't make the voices different as their mother did. Would you come and read them at bedtime some evening?" Norah mentally shook her head. The first time they had met he practically bodily threw her off his land, and the second time he berated her for telling Sarah the

71

truth. Now he was eating humble pie and asking her to read to his children!

"Unfortunately, I am planning to return home with my parents on Monday," she said, and was amazed at the disappointment she felt. "And tomorrow night Aunt Bernice has invited guests for supper."

"Could you come this evening, or Sunday?"

"You mean now, this minute?"

He stood up, and then remembering his manners, sat down again. "Could you possibly?"

Norah's sense of humor came to her rescue. "Since you ask so nicely, I will. I'll just let the others know where I'm going."

She went into the house and put her head into the dining room where the rest of the family was gathered.

"Mr. Kidd is here," she said, "and has asked me to read to his children. I don't know how long I'll be, an hour, perhaps?"

Louise was gazing at her with her mouth open.

"That's nice, dear," said Aunt Bernice. "I do hope he's coming out of his shell. Poor man," she said in a low voice to the others. "His wife died in a boating accident this past spring. Two young children. So sad."

Her mouth still agape, Louise watched her sister turn and go out. She heard the screen door on to the front verandah close, and heard a deep male voice. She jumped up and went out, peering through the open door. She saw Norah and Mr. Kidd walking across the lawn toward the house next door, which was mostly hidden by the thick grove of trees between the two properties. She returned to the dining room.

"When did you make Mr. Kidd's acquaintance?" asked an unperturbed Aunt Bernice, who was dealing out the next hand.

"Just the other day. We thought it was Clover who had gotten into Mr. Kidd's cornfield, but it turned out to be one of his cows. He rushed over and was quite rude. Actually, we were under the impression that he was Mr. Kidd's hired man . . ." Louise stopped, remembering that Norah hadn't wanted her to discuss the two encounters with Aunt Bernice's neighbor. "Norah met little Sarah on the beach the next day," she added. "I think they took a shine to each other."

The game continued, but Louise had difficulty concentrating on her cards. Norah had professed intense dislike for Mr. Kidd, now here she was going to his house! What if he had unsavory designs on her? She had recently read a novel in which the heroine, governess to the children of a rich man, barely escaped with her virtue intact. She knew Mama would have disapproved of the book had she known of it, but it was an exciting and intriguing story, and Louise could hardly put it down. Reading to his children could just be a ruse . . . but no, wasn't his mother there as well?

"Louise, you're not paying attention. You discarded on the last play, and now you're following suit."

"Oh, sorry. I was just thinking about Norah. The other day she didn't seem to like Mr. Kidd . . ."

"He has his brusque ways, but I think he's basically a decent man," remarked Aunt Bernice. "His wife was very gay, but she looked after her children well."

Maybe Norah wasn't in danger after all . . .

It was after nine o'clock when Norah returned from next door. Now that it was past the middle of August daylight was fading fast, and Louise had lit a lamp. She was already in bed, though the others were still down in the kitchen having tea. Norah had paused to say goodnight to her elders, and had climbed the stairs knowing that Louise would be waiting up for her.

"I suppose you're wanting an explanation," she said, as she came into the bedroom.

"Well, yesterday you never wanted to see him again."

Norah smiled. "True. But I think we've misjudged him, Louise. He came to apologize, and he did so very politely and sincerely. He explained that the children liked someone to read to them at bedtime, and he wasn't very good at 'making the different voices', as Sarah would say. His mother was there. Her eyes are bad, she says, and she can't read at night. She seems like a very nice woman, and is very fond of her grandchildren."

73

"What did you do?"

"Well," answered Norah, "we played with the children for awhile, then I read two stories, their grandmother tucked them in, and we had tea when Mr. Kidd was through with getting the cows to the barn."

Louise was sitting up in bed, arms clasped around her knees. "What's his house like?"

"Very much like this one, as a matter of fact. Apparently the same builder erected both of them about fifty years ago when this farm was first split up. Two sisters inherited the property from their parents, and wanted to live near each other, so their husbands had the houses built. Twenty years ago both couples decided to sell and move away. Aunt Bernice and Uncle Simon and Aunt Mercy bought this half of the farm, while a Mr. Carpenter bought the other half. Six years ago Mr. and Mrs. Kidd bought the farm next door from Mr Carpenter. Mrs. Kidd, Senior, told me all this over a cup of tea."

"Did she talk about her daughter-in-law, and the accident?"

Norah shook her head. "All she said was that the children preferred to be here than in the city. They were coming to accept that their mother was gone." Norah began to get undressed. "The children are sweet. Ben doesn't look like his sister at all, but they're real pals, just like you and Frankie."

"Are you going to go back?"

"I don't know. I invited Mrs. Kidd and the children for tea on Sunday afternoon. I told Aunt Bernice, and she is quite pleased."

Norah washed her face, creamed it thoroughly, and got into bed. "Do you like Mr. Kidd?"

"I don't dislike him any more," replied Norah seriously. "But I think the children are wonderful. They're both very bright."

It was Louise's turn to lie awake and consider these new developments. Was it just the teacher coming out in Norah, was she drawn to the father because of the children? Or was it the other way around? Louise had to admit that there was something attractive about Mr. Kidd. He was old, of course, but not as old as the hired man she took to be Mr. Kidd at first. Louise cheeks grew warm at the memory of their talking at cross-purposes. Or had the man deliberately misled her? Mr. Kidd certainly had when they were trying to get what they thought was Clover out of his corn. He had been laughing at them all the time, quite likely thinking what little fools they were. What on earth had made Norah change her mind so quickly? And what of the children? How did they feel about another woman in their father's life? Louise turned over and punched at her pillow. This was all nonsense, of course! She was imagining a budding romance where there was nothing but Norah's pity for two motherless children. Mr. Kidd for a brother-in-law? Saints deliver us, as Dorcas would say.

Chapter Eleven

SARAH

Sarah Kidd woke up early the next morning. She lay in bed, cuddling her rag doll Cornelia, and thought about the grown-ups in her life and how puzzling they could be. Daddy was very unhappy, she concluded. Though he had talked to her at last about Mummy, and Sarah felt a little better about that. Deep in her heart, she *had* known that her mother had died. Granny Kidd had come to be with them for a while, and had agreed to stay home with Ben and her when Daddy went to the church to 'say good-bye' to Mummy. Granny kept telling her that Mummy was in Heaven, and Great Aunt Sophie kept wiping away a tear saying how sad it was that Sarah and Ben had lost their mother at so young an age, until in Sarah's mind it was her mother who had gotten lost and had somehow found her way to Heaven, wherever *that* was. After that she and Ben had gone to Charlottetown with Granny and stayed in her grandparents' big square house in Merridew Gardens. Two weeks ago Daddy had come into the city for a couple of days. Granny said with a sniff that he had come to "join up." Join up what, Sarah wondered, and had a mental picture of people holding hands in a circle. She heard Daddy and Granny talking softly when they didn't know Sarah was cuddled down with Cornelia in the big leather chair by the fireplace, only a few steps away.

"What's a man like you wanting to join up for? What about the farm and your two children? It's been over three months, Harry, it's time they went home with you where they belong. I'd be willing to stay until the end of summer, if you like, until you can get some help in the house."

"Mother, it's something I have to do. If war comes, they're going to need every able body . . ."

"Join up!" Granny snorted. "More likely you'll be joining Lucille in Heaven, and then what will Ben and Sarah do?"

Daddy had gone away looking grim and determined, but returned shocked and angry.

"They wouldn't have me!" he exclaimed to Granny, and they went into the parlor and shut the door on a curious Sarah.

The next day Granny packed several suitcases and they all drove back to Fairlea in Daddy's new car. He and Mummy had bought it so that they could take trips around the Island. He was going to teach Mummy how to drive, but that never happened, of course, nor had they taken any trips. Sarah was glad to be home again, though it seemed very strange without Mummy. She missed her especially at bedtime. Mummy would read to them and then tuck them in. The twins had adjoining rooms and they would take turns as to whose room the reading would take place. After their prayers were heard, and the lights turned off, Ben and Sarah would talk to each other quietly through the partially open doorway before drifting off to sleep.

When Sarah returned she had been glad to see familiar things around her: her favorite trees, the barn, stables, and of course, the animals. She liked to hunt for the eggs that the hens would cunningly lay outside the chicken coop. Sarah, however, always seemed to know where they were. Mummy always said she was very perceptive, whatever that was. After being away from home for over three months, Sarah and Ben had to explore their domain again, and make sure all was well. Ben wouldn't come with her to the beach, though they had frequently played there before, so she and the dog Charley, who was her best friend after Benjamin, ventured down at low tide a few days later. It was then she had the notion of finding her lost mother, and it was there she met Miss Laurier. She had seen both the ladies in church with Miss Bernice, had thought they both looked friendly and kind, but she was especially drawn to the older lady, who had a nice face. She was so sympathetic, bathed her scraped knee, and comforted her when they talked about Mummy. "I'm Norah," she had said, and Sarah privately thought of her as Norah, though she politely called her Miss to her face. It was when she saw Norah's sad face when she said her mother was in heaven that Sarah realized once and for all that her mother had died, finally connecting the 'Heaven' of Sunday school to the one that Granny mentioned. Heaven was where Jesus was, and Mummy was safe in His arms like the hymn said. When she went home she told Ben about meeting Miss Norah and what she had said, Benjy like a fountain had burst into tears, and wouldn't stop. Sarah cried, too, not because of her mother (she knew that Mummy was safe) but because her brother was so upset. Daddy was very angry when he finally was able to discover what had happened. It seemed that Sarah had broken two cardinal rules: going down to the seaside on her own, and speaking to a stranger.

"Charley was with me, Daddy, and she isn't a stranger, I knew who she was. She was nice to me, Daddy, and bathed my knee that I scraped."

"She had no business talking to you about your mother. What does she know about it?"

Sarah was always fair. "I asked her, and she said she didn't know, only what Miss Bernice had said."

"Why didn't you come to me?"

"Daddy, I have! And you wouldn't talk about it."

Daddy's face had softened, and he admitted that she was right. "Come up on my knee, Sugar," he said. "You, too, Ben. Look, old son, I can't hear myself think with you howling like that." He handed Ben his large handkerchief and helped him blow his nose. Ben gave a couple of gulps, swallowed his sobs, and climbed on Daddy's other knee. He talked to them quietly about Mummy and the accident with the boat. Most of it went over Sarah's head, but she was happy being in Daddy's arms, savoring the faint lemony scent of the soap he used, and feeling his strong arms around her.

Later, when they were both in bed she heard Ben crying again, so she crawled in beside him to comfort her twin. When he finally sobbed himself to sleep she crept over to the window and knelt on the window seat.

"Dear Jesus," she prayed, "please look after my mother. And make Daddy and Ben happy again. Amen."

She crept into her own bed between the cool sheets and immediately fell asleep.

The next day she was up early and, seeing that Ben was still sleeping, went downstairs. She went outside in the cool morning in time to see her father come out of the barn. She heard the clink of the cowbells as Jed was leading the cows out to the meadow. They had finished the milking, Granny was in the kitchen making porridge and boiling eggs, so breakfast would be soon. She expected her father to come immediately up to the house, but instead she saw him walking purposefully down the path to the grove of oak trees that bordered the two properties. There was a stile there and the path led to the Laurier farmhouse. She was about to follow him when her grandmother called her.

"Breakfast is almost ready, Sarah. Will you go up and see if Ben is up?" Sarah went slowly upstairs and woke her brother, then returned to the back porch where she peered out through the screen door.

"What are you doing, Sarah?" inquired Granny presently as she brought milk out of the cooler and took it back into the kitchen.

"Waiting for Daddy. He went over to Miss Laurier's." "You must be mistaken, Sarah. He's still milking, isn't he?"

"They finished ages ago, Granny. Here's Jed coming back from the pasture."

Mrs. Kidd looked out, and indeed there was Jed, washing at the pump and toweling his head. She looked perplexedly across the back garden to the barnyard watching the hired man. There was no sign of her son, and the cows were certainly in the near meadow, for she could see the small herd moving about as they grazed. A few moments later Sarah's father emerged from the oak grove, and both grandmother and granddaughter could see by the way he moved that he was still angry. Sarah scuttled away and stopped in the next room as her father slammed the screen door and entered the kitchen.

"Well, I told her exactly what I thought of her interfering in our lives," he said shortly, but there was little satisfaction in his voice.

"Harry! Have you been having words with Miss Laurier?"

"Miss Norah Laurier, and yes I have, mother. She is the most arrogant woman I've ever met. Thank God she's only here on a visit. Interfering busybody!"

"Harry, don't you think she was just trying to be kind to the child yesterday? Sarah thinks she's quite wonderful."

There was a pause. "I told her to stay out of our lives. She was extremely rude."

"Well, that's natural. You march over there into her yard and call her down. I'd be rude, too."

"She had no business talking to Sarah about Lucille," he said defensively.

"I've been telling you for weeks to talk to the children about their mother. I'm surprised this sort of thing hasn't happened sooner!"

"Mother, I thought you'd be on my side ...."

"Breakfast is ready. Go wash. I'll call the children."

Sarah retreated to the stairs and met Ben on his way down.

"Daddy had words with Miss Norah," she whispered.

Ben shrugged. He didn't care about the lady next door. He had awakened to realize that his mother was gone forever. His pillow was still damp with the tears he had shed in the night.

"But she's nice, Ben. I'll bet she can read better than Granny or Daddy." Daddy was a most unsatisfactory reader. He didn't make the voices different from each other as Mummy always had. And Granny read with no expression whatsoever. Mummy had made the stories come to life. Sarah sighed and followed Ben into the kitchen.

"Granny, why is Daddy mad at Miss Norah?" The twins had been tucked into bed, and Granny had told them a story. Ben had asked for the one about David and Goliath. He said when he grew up he'd be a giant and kill the enemy with slingshots. He was already secretly practicing behind the barn.

Granny paused and thought a moment.

"I think he's more angry at himself than at Miss Laurier," she said surprisingly.

"Because he shouldn't be mad at her. I tried to tell him how kind she was to me down on the shore. See my knee?" Sarah stuck one sunburned leg out of the covers and displayed her injury. "She bathed it with sea water—she used her hanky, Granny—and she let me ride on her horse in front of her." Sarah was remembering how comforting Norah's arms were around her, and how it felt when she put her cheek down on the top of Sarah's head. "And I kept asking her about Mummy, you know. I knew she wouldn't tell me lies."

"I think your daddy's mistaken about Miss Laurier," agreed Granny. "I'm acquainted with Miss Bernice Laurier, and I respect her. Though I haven't met her nieces, I've seen them in church, and they appear to be very nice young ladies. Don't bother him about it, though, children, and he'll get over it. One thing about him, he may have a temper, but he doesn't often hold a grudge."

All the next morning Sarah and Ben played at being Indians stalking their prey. Their 'prey' in this case was Norah and Louise, who were busy tidying the house and preparing for their relatives' return on Friday. The sisters were in and out of the house, and not once did they suspect that their every move was being monitored from the bushes along the fence, the big oak tree at the rear of the house, and from the barn loft.

Not only did the children know every inch of their own farm, but also the neighboring property as well. Mary spotted them once or twice, smiled to herself, but said not a word.

"Poor little motherless chicks," she thought to herself. "Let them have their fun."

Had she known the twins had seen Pierre kissing her in the barn a few times, she might not have been so indulgent. However, it was harmless amusement for Sarah and Ben, and they had a strict code of silence about what they observed.

The following day their quarry walked to the village, which was beyond their allowed play area, so instead they visited Mary and watched her do the milking.

"Where's Miss Norah?" inquired Sarah, who was sitting on the other milking stool, fascinated with Mary's capable hands as she milked the cow.

"Miss Norah and Miss Louise have gone to the village. Miss Bernice will be back on Friday with Mr. and Mrs. Laurier and Mr. and Mrs. Lesley," replied Mary.

"Who are Mr. and Mrs. Lesley?"

"Mrs. Lesley is Miss Bernice's and Mr. Laurier's sister," explained Mary. "They live in Charlottetown."

"So does my Granny," said Sarah. "We stayed at my Granny's after Mummy got drownded."

Mary saw Ben's eyes fill with tears at the mention of his mother.

"I don't blame you for feeling sad about your mother," she said, reaching out and stroking his head. She got up from her stool and lifted the big shiny pail filled with milk. "Come on into the dairy with me," she invited. "But you must sit quietly and just watch me. We must keep the dairy spick and span." Later she took the two children up to the kitchen for a drink of lemonade.

"I was very sad when my father died," she remarked as she poured out the drinks for the children. "And so was my mother. She's feeling pretty lonely these days, now that my brother and sister have both gotten married and are away up Island. Maybe you'd like to visit her one day. I live at home with her and I walk here to work every morning."

"Is it very far?" asked Ben.

"A little far for you to walk," admitted Mary. "Do you know where the road forks just a little past the bridge? One fork goes down to the sea and the other into the hills. My house is in the hills, about two miles up that road."

"Maybe Miss Norah would take us on her horse," suggested Ben, brightening. "She gave Sarah a ride home from the beach when she fell and scraped her knee."

"Did she now?"

Sarah displayed a brown leg and presented her injuries to Mary.

"It's healing fine," Mary said, examining the knee. She looked at the clock on the wall. "It's after eleven-thirty, children. Your Granny will be looking for you for your dinner." And she shooed the children home with a gentle smile.

Sarah felt as though she had made another friend.

The next afternoon Sarah and Ben were sitting on the fence when Miss Bernice and the others returned in the big touring car. From a distance they saw Norah and Louise come out and greet their parents. Mr. Laurier was big and tall, much bigger than Daddy, and Mrs. Laurier was pretty, like Miss Norah. The other lady was Miss Bernice's sister. She was small and dark and vivacious. Sarah could hear her peals of tinkling laughter. Mr. Lesley was also tall, but thin, and had a small beard.

Daddy came home from the village later to tell Granny that Canada was going to war. He didn't say much, but ate his supper in silence and went out to finish the chores. Sarah was very surprised, therefore, an hour or so later when he reappeared with Miss Norah!

"I've asked her to come and read to you at bedtime," he said gruffly.

Granny said nothing, but greeted Miss Norah warmly.

Miss Norah played Snap! and Old Maid with them, and after Granny had tucked them into bed she read a story about Peter Rabbit and Benjamin Bunny, one of Ben's favorites. Sarah had to admit she read almost as well as Mummy, and told her so. Miss Norah blushed with pleasure, then she kissed them goodnight.

Ben asked her if she would take them on her horse to visit Mary's mother, and the two children told her about their visit with Mary and how lonely Mary's mother was.

"We'll talk about it another day," promised Norah.

"Will you come again?" pleaded Sarah.

"I can't come tomorrow night, as Aunt Bernice is having company for supper," replied Norah. "Perhaps you'd like to come to tea on Sunday afternoon? I'll ask your Grandmother, too," she added.

Then she wished them goodnight and went quietly away.

Now Sarah lay in bed remembering all the happenings before and since she had met Norah on the beach. She had thought that Daddy hadn't liked Norah at all—"Interfering busybody," she had heard him say to Granny—but he had asked her to come and read to them, and he had been quite polite to her. And Sarah noticed that he had changed his shirt after supper. What on earth did that mean? Anyway, she wouldn't worry about that, for she and Ben and Granny were going to have tea with Miss Norah and Miss Bernice on Sunday! Perhaps Granny would let her wear her new white dress with the purple embroidered flowers on the collar and pockets. She hadn't worn it yet, and wasn't this a 'special occasion'? She'd get up now and ask Granny if she could! She peeked into Ben's room, but he was still sleeping. She quickly pulled on her play clothes, brushed her hair until all the tangles smoothed out, and trotted downstairs to the kitchen.

Chapter Twelve

HARRY

For over four months Harry Kidd had been living in a sort of fog. The mist had descended upon him the day his wife disappeared, and although he went through the correct motions—identifying his wife's body a week later, attending the funeral, doing the daily chores, reading the newspapers with growing concern over the crisis in Europe, even volunteering for service in the army—it had all taken place as if he were surrounded by a protective blanket. He came out of the fog temporarily with the shock of having been rejected by the army, but that hadn't lasted long. His mother had been very supportive. She had hurried down from Charlottetown, planned the funeral for him and accompanied him to the church while his father's sister Sophie stayed with the twins. He wasn't having them come to the church and see their mother lying in her coffin. When he was five years old his grandmother died, and he still recalled with horror the sight of her lying there and someone prodding him from behind.

"Kiss your grandmother goodbye, Harry."

He had screamed in terror as whoever it was forced him to bend over the body and touch the cold cheek with his lips. He was carried out in hysterics and had to endure the disapproval of his family for making a scene. It was one of his earliest memories.

85

He didn't want his children to remember their mother that way, so he refused to let them come to the funeral. His mother and aunt took the twins back to Charlottetown with them a few days later and they had been with them until he had brought them home last week after that abortive attempt to join up.

He hadn't realized how much he had missed them, and he had promised his mother he would sit down with them and talk about their mother.

He hadn't counted on Sarah's meeting Norah Laurier! He was appalled to realize that the children didn't believe their mother was dead, and furious that an outsider had spelled it out to Sarah so bluntly. That night he had taken them both on his knee and talked about Lucille. Sarah had cried, too, but Harry knew she didn't blame Miss Laurier. In fact, she was filled with admiration for her!

He had actually met both Miss Lauriers the previous day when he caught sight of the visitors from the neighboring farm in his cornfield, attempting to drive one of his cows back into Miss Bernice's property. He very naturally hollered at them, and she annoyed him by contradicting him over whose cow it was. She further annoyed him by assuming him to be the hired man, drawing haughtily away from him and regarding him with scorn. 'High and mighty city girl,' he thought to himself, with a mental snort. It amused him in a sardonic way not to correct her mistake. She was fairly tall, and their eyes were almost level with each other. He preferred small women (Lucille had been only five feet tall) but as he gazed at her he noticed the high cheekbones, flushed with pink, long-lashed gray eyes, and the gentle swell of her bosom. Tendrils of her fair hair were escaping from the combs holding it back, and for a moment he wanted to reach over and remove them, letting her hair tumble onto her shoulders. To his astonishment, dismay, and shame, he felt the stirrings of desire. He turned quickly, and to cover his confusion he made some inane remark to the cow as he drove her back to the meadow. Harry couldn't believe that he could look upon another woman that way—Lucille had been his whole world.

So when the next day Sarah told him what this woman had said to her, all he wanted to do was to strike back at her. Which he did, in

Miss Bernice's barnyard the next morning, and found himself being called down by Norah. Her accusation of his being a bad husband and father cut him to the quick. She had no right to judge him! But her words stayed with him, and as he went about his work the next two days, he considered them.

He had fallen in love with Lucille ten years ago when she had been sixteen and he twenty-six. Her parents were both dead, and her grandmother had brought her up. He was visiting his elderly cousins in Summerside, and they introduced him to Lucille at a church picnic. She was dark and pretty and full of life, and he was immediately captivated. He courted her for three years, and when he was able to buy the farm near Fairlea, the old lady gave her consent for them to marry. The twins arrived eighteen months later, and Harry was overjoyed. He worked hard for his family and they were very happy.

Weren't they?

If there was any trouble between Lucille and him, it was over his quick and sometimes violent temper, and his capacity for jumping to conclusions. "That's how I get my exercise," he'd say lightly, whenever Lucille accused him of it.

His friend John Crocker admired Lucille greatly. Lucille seemed to sparkle more when the young schoolteacher was near, and Harry found himself being eaten up with jealousy. Was she bored with her husband after six years of marriage? He accused her of flirting once, and they quarreled terribly. She was very angry with him and they didn't speak to each other all day. He remembered how she lay on her side of the bed, stiff and unresponsive, and when he reached for her, she slid out of bed and silently left their bedroom to sleep in the guest room. He humbly begged her pardon the next day, and they kissed and made up, but she was rather cool for some time.

They had an early spring this year, and May was particularly warm. The mayflowers in the woods were in bloom, and even the June lilies were in bud. That dreadful Sunday the children clamored for a picnic on the shore, so Lucille packed the baskets and they drove to the dunes, which were just a mile or so from the farmhouse. The white-capped waves fairly sparkled in the sun. They ate their lunch on the sand, and then Sarah and Ben raced up and down the beach. They were packing up the picnic baskets when John appeared, inviting them for a sail. The wind was just perfect, he said, and there was room for all of them.

"Oh, Mummy, may we?" asked Sarah.

Harry and Lucille had gone out with John in his boat once the previous summer. Harry had not enjoyed it. Lucille, however, loved it, and talked about nothing else for weeks. Harry had felt sick and disoriented while in the boat; Lucille was pink cheeked and exhilarated. The memory of this embarrassed Harry, and consequently he gruffly refused.

"For heaven's sake, Harry, the children would enjoy it. I know I would," exclaimed Lucy, frowning.

"Go if you wish, but the children and I are going home. It'll be milking time soon."

"Oh, Daddy," complained Sarah. "Don't you want to go, Benjy?"

"Well, sort of," her twin replied slowly, "but it goes up and down too much."

"Will you come with us, then, Sarah?" asked John.

The little girl hesitated, and then answered politely, "No, thank you, not without Benjy."

Harry sometimes still woke up in the middle of the night drenched in sweat because in his dream Sarah had gone with her mother.

When six o'clock came and went with no sign of Lucille and John, Harry saddled his grey gelding and went in search of them. He was angry. Had Lucille and John planned this? Up in the sheltered meadow he hadn't realized how much the wind had arisen, and when he reached the sands he began to be anxious for their safety. No one was on the beach; no one was on the water. But surely John was an expert sailor! He galloped up and down the beach several times, then turned and rode into the village. He must have looked like a madman as he pounded at the Crockers' door, demanding to see John. He didn't remember what he said; he recalled only their white, frightened faces staring at him, and their mouths forming identical circles of bewilderment. He and the children spent a dreadful night huddled beneath the covers of his bed.

Harry paused, shaking off the memories. He had been wrong not to talk to his children about how their mother died. He had been wrong to direct his anger toward Norah Laurier instead of at himself. He had overheard his mother last night tell Sarah that her father didn't really hate Norah; he was really angry at himself. He had to admit that she was correct. What could he do to right the situation?

That evening, without thinking about what he would say, he marched over to the farmhouse next door and apologized. He expected Norah to give him short shrift, so no one was more surprised than he to find her at his side walking back to his house calmly discussing children's books! The twins were delighted, his mother took to her at once, and they were going to tea to Miss Bernice's on Sunday. He didn't know quite what had happened, but for the first time since the accident the day seemed brighter and the sky a little bluer.

Sunday afternoon his mother took Sarah and Ben to the Laurier farm for afternoon tea. Sarah wanted to take the shortcut over the stile on the other side of the grove of oak trees, but Granny pointed out that she had her best dress on, and besides, it was more polite to come in the front way. So the three walked down their driveway to the road, along the dusty red footpath to the big gate in the stone wall, and up the long winding drive to Miss Laurier's farmhouse. A half hour later the telephone rang, and it was Bernice Laurier.

"I've been scolding my niece for not including you in the invitation," she said, with a smile in her voice. "Also, my brother and brother-in-law would love to see that big black automobile of yours. Do come."

Harry didn't have a ready excuse, as chores were done, and he was relaxing with yesterday's newspaper. He changed his clothes, got into his vehicle, and drove it the short distance next door. Bernice came out to meet him, and shook his hand. Harry regarded her for a few moments. She was smiling at him in a friendly way, and he suddenly felt deeply ashamed of himself. Last May, soon after Lucille and John had been discovered drowned, Miss Laurier had called on him, bringing food and sympathy. He had accepted the food with poor grace, and shut his front door in her face, cutting off her words of condolence.

89

"Miss Laurier, I believe I owe you an apology for my behavior after Lucy—died. I fear I was very churlish when you visited me."

Bernice nodded, and put her head on one side. "Mr. Kidd, you had been through a ghastly time, and I made allowances for you. Your apology is accepted. Think no more about it, but come in and have a cup of tea."

She led the way into the sitting room where Norah's mother was pouring tea. Mrs. Laurier looked up with a sweet smile and asked him if he took milk and sugar.

"Just milk, thank you," Harry replied, and accepted the cup and saucer.

"How nice to meet the father of those lovely children," Mrs. Laurier said. "Norah has taken them out for a walk to see the afternoon milking. They've apparently made the acquaintance of Mary, who does most of the milking, I understand."

Harry found himself chatting to Norah's mother as though they were old friends, and presently Mrs. Lesley, who was conversing with Louise and his mother, spoke up.

"Mr. Kidd, may I call you Harry?—Do call me Mercy, please—Mr. and Mrs. is so formal, I think—I find that your mother and we live not far apart in Charlottetown!" She turned to Mrs. Laurier. "Rose, you remember that delightful square we pointed out on one of our drives. It is completely enclosed, and the families living around it have keys to the gates? It must be like having your own private park," she added, a trifle enviously.

"It is pleasant," admitted Mrs. Kidd. "When the children were staying with me, it was a wonderful place for them to play. Mind you, they needed supervision, as there is a large pond with a fountain." She smiled at Harry. "I never told you this, dear, but once Sarah went for a swim in there before I could stop her."

Mercy turned to Harry. "Mrs. Kidd tells me that you will be driving her back to Charlottetown in a week or two. You must bring her round for tea before you return home," she said gaily.

Harry's mother demurred. "Oh no, you and Mr. Lesley must come to Merridew Gardens and have lunch with me and my sister-in-law, who lives with me. And if Louise decides to go with you tomorrow you must, of course, bring her too. Are you on the telephone? Then I will ring you up as soon as I get home. There, that's settled. Now we should let these poor gentlemen go outside and inspect Harry's new automobile. I must say, it's a much more comfortable way to travel than by carriage."

"Don't you go to Summerside and catch the train there?"

"Actually it's just as fast to drive directly to Charlottetown," Harry commented, rising. With a smile at Louise, who was sitting quietly in the corner next to Mercy, he led Robert Lesley and William Laurier outside.

Out in the yard, Robert lit a cigarette, and the men strolled over to Harry's automobile, shiny black with silver trim.

"It's called a McLaughlin," explained its proud owner. "A five passenger Touring Car, made in Oshawa, Ontario!"

They duly admired it, looking under the hood and making intelligent noises about its innards. Harry pointed out the diamond tufted leather upholstery, and the canvas top to which isinglass curtains could be attached during inclement weather.

"The piece de resistance, of course, is the self-starter—no cranking!" He demonstrated, and the vehicle came to life with a grumbling, grinding sound. The men took turns seating themselves behind the steering wheel and peering through the plate glass windshield.

"Most impressive," declared Mr Laurier, and when Harry switched off the starter they began to drift back to the house. Harry looked up to see the twins running toward them from the direction of the milking shed, Norah behind them. Her hair was pulled back casually into one long braid down past her shoulders, and she was wearing a summer dress in an attractive blue-green.

"Daddy, Daddy!" shouted Ben. "Norah's going to take us to visit Mary's mother, and I'm to ride on the horse with her."

"Miss Bernice says I can ride her pony—if you'll let me—do say yes, Daddy." Sarah was starry-eyed at the thought of riding all by herself.

Harry smiled at his children and caught their hands. "You mean Miss Laurier, don't you?"

"She said we could call her Norah," Sarah informed him.

"I thought you were going back to Ottawa tomorrow," he said, gazing at the young woman as she approached.

"I changed my mind. The children talked me out of it."

Harry was astonished how light-hearted he suddenly felt. He looked down at the happy faces of the twins and smothered the guilty feeling that arose.

"We've been watching Mary milk Clover; Clover's ever so sweet. The other day we watched Mary churning butter. She let us taste the cream. Daddy, can I ride the pony, please?"

"Let's talk about it tonight, shall we? I think I'd like another cup of tea and one of Miss Bernice's scones."

The twins ran ahead, and Harry and Norah were left to come in together. "Will you come and read to them tonight?"

"Yes."

"I don't like them calling you by your Christian name," he said frowning. "It's not polite."

"'Miss Laurier' is so formal. All my friends call me Norah."

"But they're children—they should respect you. Don't your students call you Miss?"

"Yes, of course, but Sarah and Ben aren't my students."

"I can't go on calling you Miss Laurier, then, can I."

"It would be silly."

"You can't go on calling me Mr. Kidd, either."

"It would be even sillier."

"Norah. Thank you for being a friend to my children."

Norah looked at him steadily. "They're delightful children, and they love you."

Harry found himself blushing, something he hadn't done in years. "They're all I have left," he said, in some confusion. "Shall we have that cup of tea with your family?"

They went inside then, to hear the children regaling their elders about cows and horses and how they were going to ride to Mary's mother's house.

92

"Mary says her mother needs company now that all her children live somewhere else. Well, all except Mary, but she and Pierre are getting married soon, did you know that?" confided Sarah.

"I'm sorry." began Harry.

"Don't apologize, Mr. Kidd," said Bernice firmly. "It's lovely to see them coming out of their shell."

Ben overheard this. "I'm a chick," he said. "Peep, peep, and I are hatching!"

He pretended to flap his 'wings'. Mercy laughed, and patted her lap. "Does the new chick want a nest to sit on?"

Ben blushed, but got up on the sofa beside Norah's aunt, and she laughingly fed him crumbs of her sister's scones. Mrs. Kidd arose.

"I think it's about time we took the chicks home," she said, smiling at her grandson. "Thank Miss Laurier for the nice tea, now."

Sarah and Ben remembered their manners, and said their thank-yous and goodbyes. Harry finished his tea, shook hands all around, and followed his mother and his children. He held Norah's hand a trifle longer than was necessary.

"Until later, then," he said to her. "About the same time as the other night?"

She went to the door with him, then turned and faced the others.

"I gather you'll be staying on, Norah," smiled Bernice.

Norah's cheeks grew pink. "If that's agreeable to you, Aunt Bernice."

"You know you're always welcome, my dear."

Norah's parents were regarding their daughter thoughtfully. Mrs. Laurier opened her mouth to say something, and then closed it again.

"We're friends, Mama," Norah said. "And I like the children."

Chapter Thirteen

NORAH AND THE TWINS

"Norah, are you falling in love with Mr. Kidd?"

Louise was in bed, and Norah was brushing her long fair hair at the dressing table. Her arm paused in midair, and then resumed its slow strokes.

"You made me lose count. No, I am not falling in love, Louise. I'm just trying to be a friend to Sarah and Ben."

"And their father, too? I think he likes you, Norah."

Norah, her face growing warm, was glad the light was fading so Louise couldn't see her blush.

"You're imagining things. His wife has been dead only a few months."

"Well, I think *he's* come out of his shell in the last week," Louise remarked.

"He actually smiled today."

Norah said nothing. Whatever she said Louise would take the wrong way.

"What did you do tonight?"

"The same as last time. Read to the children, tucked them in, had a cup of tea with their Granny."

It was a small fib. Tonight Harry had walked her home, and they took the long way down the driveway to the road and along the footpath to Aunt Bernice's gate. They had talked about books and travel and the war. Harry had told her bitterly how he'd gone to join up and they wouldn't accept him. It was a combination of his age, which was thirty-six, and his heart sounds.

"I've always had an irregular beat," he said to her, "and I tried to explain it to them, but they wouldn't listen, but told me to see my physician. Dr Black, my doctor in Charlottetown, said it wasn't a problem, and so does Jerry McPhee, the man I see here. I was so angry, Norah."

"I understand your feelings, Harry, but it doesn't make you any less of a man," she responded quietly. She was unprepared for the rush of an emotion that swept through her when she realized that Harry would be safe. Thank goodness for irregular heartbeats! "And besides, you have an important job here, running a farm and raising your children."

"You're quite right," he said, taking her arm. "My mother said exactly the same thing. Have you been talking to her?"

She knew by the tone of his voice that he was teasing, so she just chuckled and shook her head.

Harry hadn't asked her not to say anything about their conversation to anyone, but she decided to keep it to herself. If anyone queried his not volunteering she would certainly defend him. She got into bed beside Louise and lay quietly, thinking about what he had said.

"What are you going to do tomorrow?" asked Louise, interrupting her thoughts.

"Seeing you off, I guess. What time are you all leaving?"

"After breakfast, I think, around ten o'clock. We're driving straight to the train station and putting Mama and Papa aboard, and then going to Aunt Mercy's. I do wish you'd come, Norah."

"I'll come a day or two before we have to leave. Aunt Bernice said she'd drive me to Summerside and I can take the train to Charlottetown there."

"I still think you're falling in love," she muttered turning over.

95

Norah said nothing. She didn't know herself how she felt. The only thing she was sure of was that it was too soon for Harry to consider her anything else than a friend.

It was rather quiet after Mama and Papa, Louise, Mercy and Robert had gone. Mama had left one trunk to be sent on later, when Louise and Norah came home. There had been no room for it in Robert's automobile. There were suitcases strapped to the back and the top of the car, as well as squeezed into where the passengers sat. Norah wondered how they all fitted in.

"You're like sardines in a tin," she smiled, as Uncle Robert started the motor. "You'll need a can opener when you stop."

She and Aunt Bernice waved them goodbye, and a few minutes later two small figures emerged from the oak grove next door and climbed over the stile. They were brandishing a pair of white tea cloths.

"We saw them go!" panted Ben.

"We waved them goodbye!" Sarah told them. "Louise waved at us and smiled."

"Now can I ride the pony?" asked Ben.

"I get to ride the pony," his sister declared. "You get to ride with Norah on the big horse."

Bernice and Norah exchanged glances.

"First, there will be riding lessons for you both," she insisted. "Sarah, will your Granny mind if you wear a pair of Ben's trousers? Aunt Bernice doesn't have a side saddle to fit the pony."

Sarah thought it a novel idea to wear trousers, so the two of them turned and trotted home again, and returned a half hour later dressed exactly alike.

"Now, we're really twins," Ben said. "Sarah looks like a boy."

Sarah took his teasing in a good-natured fashion; besides, she was more interested in learning to ride a pony. She took Norah's hand, and the three of them walked toward the horse stables behind the barn. There they made the acquaintance of Robin, Aunt Bernice's elderly pony. He was a dear, gentle animal, who loved the children. They fed him bits of carrot, and petted his nose and stroked his flanks. Bernice had told Norah that he had belonged to friends of hers over Summerside way, and they had intended to put him down because of his age.

"One look at me with those big brown eyes, and I immediately took him off their hands and brought him home," she confessed the night before. "He doesn't cost much to feed, and he's company for the others. Ginger treats him as though he's a young colt."

The twins were enchanted with the small horse, and they could scarcely wait to ride him. Norah showed them how to saddle the horse, and a riding lesson for each ensued. Sarah was a natural, and took to being astride a pony as though she'd been born in the saddle. Ben was a little timid, but Norah thought that with a little encouragement, he'd be fine.

Mrs. Hastie, Mary's mother, lived about two and a half miles away up a winding road that led through birch woods, by a small lake, and into the rolling hill country. She lived in a medium sized cottage painted white. The front door and the trim around all the windows were painted red, the roof was moss covered, and there were two large stone chimneys, one at each end of the house. The windows sparkled in the sunshine; Mrs. Hastie had washed them that very morning. Three tall chestnut trees guarded her home. Norah thought that in the spring their blossoms would be very beautiful.

Mary had told them that her mother expected them for lunch, so they had started off from home at eleven o'clock, Sarah on Robin the pony, and Norah on Ginger, with Ben sitting in front of her. It was a fine warm day, and they enjoyed their ride. Sarah urged Robin to a trot a few times, and Norah, who was riding carefully because of Ben, had to call her back.

"What would I tell your father if you fell and hurt yourself?" she scolded. Mary was aware that Mr. Kidd was looking for a permanent housekeeper, for she knew that Mrs. Kidd couldn't stay with them forever.

"Mother is worried that she'll be in the way when Pierre and I get married," she had confided in Norah.

"You know we're planning to live there. Perhaps her living at the Kidds' would be the very thing. I have mentioned it casually to her, so she's likely been thinking about it. Ask her, Miss Norah."

Mrs. Hastie was a small plump woman in her sixties, her hair still coal black. She had a round smiling face and a pair of the kindest eyes imaginable. She was on the front steps to welcome them, and she showed them where they could tether the horses so they could have a drink and eat the grass.

"We mustn't have our lunch without making sure they have theirs," she said, admiring Robin.

"I rode him all the way by myself," announced Sarah proudly.

"Well done," said Mrs. Hastie.

"It's too bad Miss Bernice doesn't have two ponies," went on Sarah, "then Ben could ride, too."

Ben was lifted down from Ginger's back, shook hands gravely with his hostess and said how do you do, just as Norah had instructed. Sarah followed suit, and then they went in and washed their hands in Mrs. Hastie's enormous bathroom.

"Mmm, the soap smells nice," Sarah remarked, as she dried her hands on the fluffy white towel.

"I think it's sandalwood," Norah said, inhaling the scent. "That's a tree that grows in India."

"It stinks," said Ben, wrinkling his nose.

"Don't say stinks, dear, say 'I don't like its smell'."

"I don't like its smell," he repeated.

"Here's some plain soap. Use that," suggested Norah.

"That's the biggest bathtub I've ever seen," commented Sarah, who had only seen two others in her life.

Sarah repeated her observation to Mrs. Hastie, and their hostess told them that Mr. Hastie had been very tall, had built the bathroom himself and ordered the bathtub specially.

"He loved to soak himself before going to bed," she said with a sigh. "Many a bath he's taken in that tub over the years."

"Is Mr. Hastie in heaven with Mummy?" asked Sarah.

"Why, yes he is," Mrs. Hastie answered heartily. "He died last year. I do miss him. He grew the most wonderful vegetables."

Norah saw Ben's eyes fill with tears at the mention of his mother, so she quickly changed the subject, and asked Mrs. Hastie if they could see the rest of the house. Mrs. Hastie was happy to oblige, and took them on a tour.

They were able to peek into Mary's room. Mrs. Hastie said, though, that when Mary got married she would give her daughter the main bedroom where she and Mr. Hastie had slept for nearly thirty-six years.

"It's much bigger than Mary's. A man needs more space," she said. "I like Pierre," Ben ventured. "Do you like Pierre, Mrs. Hastie?"

"Yes, I do. He's a hard worker, and he's very fond of Mary."

"Do you have other children?" asked Norah, as they made their way to the kitchen for lunch.

"Why, yes, I'll show you photographs after lunch."

After their meal of delectable cold chicken, a cold vegetable salad, and homemade bread and butter ("This is Miss Bernice's butter," she told them.), they went into the sitting room where Mrs. Hastie showed them many photographs, of her children, her husband, and a picture of the house when the chestnut trees were very small.

"That must be a very long time ago," Sarah said thoughtfully.

"Long before you were born. In fact Mary wasn't even born yet."

Presently the children went out to explore, and Norah and Mrs. Hastie were left alone. It was then that Norah brought up the subject of a housekeeper for the Kidds.

"I've been thinking about it, Miss Laurier," Mrs. Hastie said, "and I should like to see the house. Can you tell me, would there be a room where I could have some of my bits and pieces for a sitting room? It wouldn't be proper for me to sit in the parlor with Mr. Kidd." She paused. "Those poor motherless darlings. They need someone to look after them. Not that their Granny hasn't, but she can't stay there forever, can she."

"Not really. Her elderly sister-in-law lives with her in Charlottetown, and she needs looking after."

"And newlyweds need to be alone," Mrs. Hastie went on, gazing earnestly at Norah.

"Shall I tell Mrs. Kidd that you are interested?"

"I'll write a little note, and if you would take it to her, I'd be most obliged." Mrs. Hastie heaved herself to her feet and went across to her desk. She sat down and wrote for a few moments, and sealed the note in the envelope. She wrote "Mrs. Kidd" on it, and handed it to Norah. "I've just told her I was interested, and if she'd like to interview me, I am at her disposal," she said. "I could go to my other daughter's for a time, but I think a job like that would be good, don't you agree?"

"I think they'll be very fortunate if you go and work for them," Norah said sincerely.

"I think they're very lucky to have you as a friend, Miss Laurier."

"Couldn't you call me Norah, Mrs. Hastie?"

Mrs. Hastie hesitated, and then said, "No, Miss, I don't think so."

"Why ever not, Mrs. Hastie? I'm your daughter's age."

Mrs. Hastie's eyes twinkled. "You think about it, Miss Laurier. Now perhaps we had better find those twins."

The next day, Harry drove his mother over to see Mrs. Hastie, and Mrs. Hastie accompanied them back to look the house over. As Harry said to Norah later that evening after the twins had been put to bed, he had been hard pressed to decide who was interviewing whom! In any case, Mrs. Hastie and Mrs. Kidd were delighted with each other, and Harry said that he could easily convert the room next to the kitchen that Lucille had used for her sewing and ironing into a small sitting room for their new housekeeper. She would sleep in the little bedroom at the top of the stairs, which was across from the twins' rooms, and next to the bathroom. He mentioned that he already had been thinking about installing a second bathroom, and had spoken to Jim Dobbs, the plumber from Summerside. He'd get on to that immediately. Mrs. Hastie nodded her approval. She didn't approve of everyone using the same bathroom. Mr. Hastie had been very handy; he had installed a second bathroom in their house himself so the children didn't have to come downstairs. She had enjoyed the privacy of having the main bedroom and bathroom on the ground floor, the way she and her husband had planned.

The twins were very excited. "Your mother is coming to look after us," they told Mary the next day.

"I know," replied Mary, who was busy churning butter at the time. "She's very pleased. You'll have to mind your P's and Q's, though. My mother was very strict with us."

"What are our peas and kews?" Ben asked Norah later, and Norah explained.

"It means to remember your manners and do what Mrs. Hastie tells you. I am sure that she and your father will discuss that sort of thing."

"She'll be like a second Granny," Sarah nodded. "I love Mrs. Hastie, don't you, Norah?"

"Yes, I do," agreed Norah.

"I love Norah," said Ben stoutly, and ducked his head with embarrassment.

"Well, of course we do," Sarah agreed quickly, not wanting to hurt Norah's feelings.

Norah's heart swelled within her. She stooped and gathered the two children to her. "And I love you both."

"Will you stay with us, too, Norah?" asked Ben.

"Oh, darlings, I can't. Remember I told you I teach school? It begins soon, and I will have to go home."

Ben's eyes filled.

"You'll have Daddy, and Mrs. Hastie, and Mary, and my Aunt Bernice. I'll write to you, I promise."

"A proper letter with a stamp and everything?" asked Ben, sniffing.

"A proper letter through the post office," she promised.

"Will your Aunt Bernice let us ride Robin when you've gone?' asked Sarah.

"I'm sure she will, Sarah, and I'm also sure your father will make sure that happens. I'll talk to him."

"He's going to take Granny home tomorrow. He said when he got back he would take us to Summerside for lunch on Sunday."

"He wants you to come, too," added Ben.

"Well, of course Norah is coming with us! Oh, do you promise to write?"

"I promise, Sarah, cross my heart." And Norah solemnly made a cross on her bosom.

"I don't see why you can't teach here," said Ben, who had been thinking. "They need a teacher."

"But my school needs me."

"I know," suggested Sarah. "You could marry Daddy, and we'd have you forever!"

"We already have a Mummy," objected Ben.

"She's in heaven, Ben, you know that, don't you? Now, don't cry." His sister frowned at him.

Ben nodded, eyes filling.

"Wouldn't you like Norah to be with us for always?"

He nodded again.

"Well, she has to marry Daddy, then."

Norah wasn't sure how to halt this conversation. It was almost as though they had forgotten she was there.

"I don't believe your Daddy is thinking about marrying anybody," she said carefully. "And that's entirely his business. I want to be your friend, is that all right?"

"Don't you want to get married, Norah?"

"Someday, if I find the right man."

"But I think Daddy is wonderful!" exclaimed Sarah.

"Your Daddy and I are friends."

This seemed to satisfy Sarah for the moment, and Norah heaved a sigh of relief. Goodness, she hoped that Sarah wouldn't be discussing this with anyone else, but she didn't know how to tell her this without putting undue emphasis on it.

The next day Mrs. Kidd departed with Harry, and Norah took this opportunity to let Mrs. Hastie get better acquainted with Sarah and Ben. They insisted Norah come over at bedtime, however, and Mrs. Hastie seemed to encourage it. They both read to the children, and the next day Sarah told her that Mrs. Hastie read almost, but not quite, as well as Norah. She had told this to Mrs. Hastie as well, and that good woman had merely chuckled and said that it was a compliment.

On Sunday, true to his promise, Harry took Norah and the children to Summerside for lunch at the hotel. Norah wore her best hat, and an attractive dress with a matching coat. Harry put on a collar and tie and wore his best suit of clothes. The children dressed up and rode in the back seat, chattering all the way.

"Norah," he said quietly as they went into the hotel, "I want to thank you for being a friend to my children. I haven't heard them laugh and chatter like this since—since their mother died."

"I haven't done much, Harry. They're adjusting very well, I think."

"Yes, you have," he said, touching her hand briefly.

Norah was astonished at her reaction when their hands had touched. I think it's time I went home, she thought to herself.

"My mother had Mr. and Mrs. Lesley and your sister for lunch yesterday," he said. "Louise and I went for a walk in the garden. It's quite beautiful, all fenced in, with flower beds and paths and a fountain in the middle of it."

"Was Louise enjoying her stay with Mercy and Robert?"

"Very much. We mostly talked about you."

Norah found herself blushing. At that moment the twins joined them, Sarah taking her father's hand, and Ben taking hers. It was as though they were a family. Norah suddenly remembered Mrs. Hastie's remark about not calling her by her first name, and her little smile. Did she think that Norah wanted to marry Harry Kidd? Norah's face burned, and she had a feeling that things were moving too quickly. Perhaps she had been unwise to accompany them today.

That evening after the children had gone to bed, Harry walked Norah home, and they stood at the gate in silence for a time.

"Norah," he began, "I told you a little about how Lucille died, didn't I."

"Just that she and your friend John Crocker went for a boat ride and they both drowned."

"I thought, at first, you know, that she and John—well, liked each other too much. We had a dreadful quarrel the week before about him."

"Harry, you don't have to tell me this—"

103

"Yes; I do. That's why I got so angry when you made that remark about how I treated people—"

"Oh, Harry," cried Norah, distressed, "I feel terrible about what I implied that day!"

"I know, Norah," he said, taking her hand. "You were speaking the truth, you know. The one trouble between Lucille and myself was my quick temper, and my habit for jumping to conclusions. That day when they didn't return, I thought all sorts of terrible thoughts, and I went to John's parents and said the most awful things to them. You know, I couldn't even go to John's funeral, and we had been friends! And I've never apologized to Mr. and Mrs. Crocker, either. I'm a poor sort of man, Norah."

"Why don't you go and apologize to them, Harry?" she asked quietly.

"You know how something gets harder and harder the more you put it off."

"But it's bothering you, isn't it."

"Yes, it is."

"Go now and do it."

"Just like that?"

"Just like that. It's only eight o'clock."

Harry burst out laughing.

"I'll wait for you on the verandah," went on Norah, smiling at him. Harry went home and saddled his grey, and as the sound of the horse's hooves faded in the direction of the village, Norah picked up her book, and then put it down again. Her thoughts went back to earlier in the day, and her concerns that if Mrs. Hastie, who lived off the beaten track, was speculating on the possible relationship between herself and Harry Kidd, were others closer to home gossiping about her? Perhaps it was time to end her visit. She'd go to Charlottetown and stay with Mercy and Robert for the few days that were left of the month, and then she and Louise would take the train to Ottawa.

The decision made, she picked up her book and read until the light faded. It was nearly nine-thirty when Harry returned. He must have ridden home and unsaddled his horse, for she happened to look up and see him emerge from the oak grove and come over the stile.

He was smiling broadly as he came up the steps to the verandah where Norah was standing. He grabbed her hands and did a little dance.

"I did it, Norah!" he exclaimed boyishly. "Mr. and Mrs. Crocker were so kind about the whole business. We had a long talk, and they'd forgiven me months ago. She said I should forgive myself, now. Thank you for making me go!" And he gathered her in his arms and hugged her affectionately.

Norah's heart was hammering away. He grew still for a moment, and gazed at her tenderly.

"Oh, Norah . . ."

"You see, it wasn't so difficult," she began, gently trying to extricate herself from his embrace.

"Norah, Norah, could we—could you—"

"Harry," she said breathlessly, "it's too soon. You're still dealing with your loss, and the children—"

"They love you, Norah!"

"As a friend, Harry. I've promised to write to them when I go home. Could we write to each other as friends, too?"

He stepped back, still regarding her intently. "Is that what you want?"

"That's the way it should be, Harry, don't you see?"

He smiled then and nodded. "You're right, we should be sensible. But Norah, do you think...."

Norah shook her head. "I don't know what to think, Harry. Let's just wait and see."

Chapter Fourteen

LOUISE AND NORAH GO HOME

Louise and Norah sat in silence on the train as it chugged and swayed through the New Brunswick countryside. Norah was gazing out the window lost in thought, and Louise was pondering her eldest sister.

Norah had left Fairlea and come to Charlottetown three days ago on the day train from Summerside. Mama's trunk accompanied her, and Norah's big suitcase. A telegram from Ottawa had arrived the same day saying all was well except that Gerald had gone to join the army. She thought that Louise and Norah should come home as soon as possible. Uncle Robert had arranged passage on the train and had driven them to the station this morning.

Norah had talked brightly about the twins, and how clever and sweet they were, and how she had begun to give them riding lessons. She went on at length how the banns for Mary and Pierre were going up next Sunday at the tiny Catholic church in Morrisville, the small village on the sea road east of the farm, and that the date set for the wedding was October 15. Mary was to have her first communion in a few weeks when her religious instruction came to a close. She mentioned that Mrs. Hastie was now installed as the Kidds' housekeeper, and she had furnished the room off the kitchen

106

for herself as an office and sitting room. The children loved Mrs. Hastie, Norah said, and they were very excited to be starting school in two weeks. She described Aunt Bernice's painful boil on her neck, and how the doctor had to come and lance it; how Clover had gotten into the cornfield next door, much to Mary's disgust. Not once did she mention Harry Kidd by name. When she referred to him it was as 'the children's father', or 'Mr. Kidd'. He insisted on driving her to Summerside; he would have taken her all the way to Charlottetown, but Norah had refused.

"But why, Norah?" asked Louise. "It would so much more comfortable in that big automobile of his than struggling with your bags on the train."

Norah shrugged, and didn't really give an answer.

"You know his mother invited Aunt Mercy and Uncle Robert and me to lunch last week while he was still there. We went for a walk in the gardens, did he tell you that?"

Norah nodded.

"Mrs. Kidd gave us a big key to open the gate. We strolled and had a lovely talk. I mean, Mr. Kidd did most of the talking, and it was mostly about you and the twins. He even asked me to call him Harry. I was wrong about him, Norah. He likes you very much."

Norah sighed. "I know." She was silent for a few minutes, and Louise, glancing at her, was horrified to see a tear trickling down her cheek.

"Norah! What's wrong? Did you and Harry—Mr. Kidd—quarrel?" She shook her head, and struggled to find her handkerchief.

Louise gazed anxiously at her sister, not sure of what to say. Louise had always gone to Norah for comfort when Mama wasn't available; now here their roles were reversed.

"Can you tell me about it, Norah? You know I can keep a confidence."

Norah reached out and took Louise's hand. "I'm so afraid I've made myself cheap."

Louise squeezed her hand. "You, cheap? Not a bit of it," she said indignantly, then gazed around at the other passengers, but nobody was paying them the slightest bit of attention. "Tell me what has happened," she demanded, now sure that something had occurred between Norah and Harry.

Norah wiped her eyes, and repeated what Mrs. Hastie had said to her, and her interpretation of it.

Louise wanted to laugh, but she realized that Norah was worried, and the remark had been weighing on her mind.

"Oh, Norah, you don't think folks have been gossiping about you?"

"I thought if Mrs. Hastie thinks I'm possibly the next Mrs. Kidd, what do other people think?"

"I think you've made a mountain out of a molehill. Aunt Bernice would know if there was talk, wouldn't she?"

"They mightn't say anything to her, after all I'm her niece."

"I don't believe anyone's gossiping about you and Mr. Kidd," declared Louise loyally.

"I would die if I harmed Harry and the children," Norah said, her voice breaking.

"Oh, Norah, you *are* in love with him, aren't you."

"I don't know what I feel. I told him it was too soon after he lost his wife … we're going to write as friends. I've promised to write to the twins, too."

"Has he kissed you? There, I've no business asking you that! You don't have to answer."

A dreamy smile curved her sister's mouth, and she put her hands to her lips.

"Yes, he did, the night before I came up to Mercy and Robert's." And taking her younger sister's hand, told her in a low voice.

Norah had said her goodbyes to the twins; they had cried, and she reminded them of her promise to write.

"You must write me back," she told them, "and tell me all the things that you're doing: school, and new friends, all that sort of thing. Aunt Bernice has said you may ride Robin, and your Daddy agrees. I've talked to him," she said in a whisper, as their eyes lit up.

She kissed them both, and then went downstairs, where Mrs. Hastie had made tea for Norah and Harry.

"There, Miss, you enjoy your tea. I must say," she sighed, "we will miss you, Miss Laurier, dear."

Harry and she had walked back to Aunt Bernice's, and it was there in the shadow of the verandah he had kissed her, in spite of Norah's protests that they were to be just friends. Harry had laughed shortly and told her he wanted to give her something to remember him by. The next day he drove her to the Summerside train station, and they had shaken hands decorously in public, but his eyes told her he was remembering last night's kiss.

Louise snuggled up to Norah and tucked her hand in her arm.

"Cave man tactics, huh?" she whispered, smiling.

"Well, he is forceful, isn't he." Norah was smiling again, but then grew sober. "You think I'm being silly, worrying about gossip, don't you."

"No, darling, not silly. You could never be silly. I think you're being unduly sensitive. You like Mrs. Hastie, don't you?"

"Oh, yes, and I am sure she likes me, and I don't think she'd gossip, in fact I'm sure she wouldn't."

"Then forget about all those mythical people who are talking about you. It's my experience that people don't care a darn about other people."

Norah smiled. "You've put me in my place, haven't you, little sister! You're right—I've been overly sensitive. Thank you for listening to me, Lou." She put her head back and closed her eyes, then opened them again. "I really ought to be ashamed of myself! Here I am whimpering about my own selfish affairs while Mama and Papa must be going crazy with Gerald joining the army. I wonder when he'll be sent overseas? Oh, Lou, I can't bear the thought of his being wounded or killed!"

Louise squeezed her sister's hand. "And Frankie—he'll want to join up, too, won't he. Surely Mama and Papa will forbid it!"

"Frankie's eighteen, Lou. Mama and Papa can't stop him if he wants to go."

"Jeremy Ferris is being commissioned," Louise said. "I guess they'll need engineers overseas." She tried to sound casual, but her voice trembled a little.

109

Norah didn't notice. "He'll make a fine officer!" she declared proudly. She sighed. "It seems so long ago that we were all playing together. Gerry and Jeremy were such pals when we were growing up. You were too young to remember that. Gladdie was the one who tagged along after us until she was big enough to join the group."

"Do you suppose Jeremy will be sent overseas right away?"

"I don't know, I believe Papa mentioned that his training course lasts for some months." Norah glanced sharply at Louise, but could read nothing in her face. "Louise, are you fond of Jeremy?"

Louise blushed, started to deny it, and then remembered how Norah had confided in her. "I've always thought he was quite, quite wonderful," she said simply.

"Jeremy's a nice young man," conceded Norah, "but not worth breaking your heart over."

"How can he break my heart if he doesn't know I exist?"

The train chugged on, and each of them was lost in her own thoughts of lovers, brothers and Canada at war.

The following afternoon the train steamed into Ottawa Station, the passengers beginning to yawn and stretch, and to gather their belongings together. Louise peered anxiously out the window, wondering if Papa had taken time from his busy day to meet them. Norah had been writing a letter to the twins, and now she folded the paper, put it in an envelope, and addressed it: *Miss Sarah and Master Ben Kidd, Arbutus Farm, Fairlea, P.E.I.*

"I didn't know Mr. Kidd's farm had a name," Louise remarked, as she read the envelope.

"Apparently that was the farm's original name when Aunt Bernice's and Harry's properties were one. The trailing arbutus is supposed to be very lovely there in the spring."

"Aunt Bernice's farm doesn't have a name, does it?"

"I think her address is simply 'Laurier Farm', Fairlea," answered her sister. "Do you have a stamp? I could mail it here at the station."

"I'm not sure . . ." She dived into her handbag and triumphantly produced a single stamp. "My last one!"

The two struggled down from the car to the platform, found a porter, and gave him their baggage tickets. As the man hurried away to find their luggage, they heard their names called, and looked up to see Gerald making his way along the crowded platform. He was waving cheerfully at them. Norah ran to meet him, and they embraced affectionately. He put his other arm around Louise.

"It's good to see you two. What a crowd! What about your luggage?"

"The porter is fetching it," said Louise. "He'll need an enormous tip, Gerald. Mama's trunk is with us."

"I have a cab waiting. Will there be room for it?"

They managed to put the trunk into the cab's rear, and the suitcases in the back seat, so it was a tight squeeze for the girls. Gerald sat up front with the driver.

"I thought you might be in uniform by now," said Louise brightly. "Mama and Papa sent a telegram to Aunt Mercy's, you know."

Gerald gave them an odd look over his shoulder. "I'll tell you about that when we get home," he said, and his voice had an edge to it.

Louise and Norah exchanged puzzled glances, but said no more. Mama and Dorcas were at the front door with welcoming embraces. Val was also there, and he helped them with the smaller pieces of luggage. The cab driver helped Gerald bring the trunk in, and Dorcas directed that they take it down to her room. She'd unpack for Mrs. Laurier, she said, and check to make sure none of her clothes needed to be mended. Gerald slipped the cabby an extra tip as he went out the door.

Louise thought it seemed strange to be having a bedroom all to herself again, after sharing with Norah at Aunt Bernice's. She had missed her sister when she had gone to Charlottetown with Aunt Mercy and Uncle Robert, though she had enjoyed their company, for they had gone out of their way to entertain her, and show her the sights. Aunt Mercy had sighed and remarked once how lovely it would have been to have a daughter; her sister-in-law Rose was so fortunate to have three! However, she supposed it was too late to consider that now, now that she was nearing forty. Louise unpacked her suitcase, carefully hanging up the clean clothes in her big wardrobe as she had been taught, and gathering up the soiled and crumpled things to be washed or pressed. She wondered what Gerald was going to tell them, and voiced her thought to Norah, whom she met at the top of the stairs, several articles of clothing over her arm.

"He seemed a trifle annoyed, didn't he," Norah remarked, as they went downstairs and out to the laundry room.

They found him reading in the sitting room, and he looked up as they came in.

"Tell me about your time on the Island," he invited, putting down his book. "Mama certainly enjoyed her visit with Bernice and Mercy." His eyes twinkled. "How did you find the witch, Lou?"

Louise made a face at him. "You were awful to tell me those fibs," she said.

"Hard to resist when you were so gullible," he retorted.

"Aunt Bernice is really nice, and so is Aunt Mercy," went on Louise, ignoring the interruption. "She and Uncle Robert were very good to me when I stayed with them the last two weeks." She glanced at Norah. "Norah made friends with the children next door to Aunt Bernice. She was giving them riding lessons, weren't you, Norah."

"Yes, such sweet, bright children. They loved Bernice's pony." "Nice parents, too?"

"He's a widower. Their mother was drowned in a boating accident in May," Norah explained to her brother. "Harry—Mr. Kidd—is bringing them up alone now."

Louise went on. "Mary works for Aunt Bernice, and her mother is Mr. Kidd's new housekeeper. The senior Mrs. Kidd lives in Charlottetown, and she invited Aunt Mercy and Uncle Robert and myself for lunch after she got back home. She had been staying with her son, and Norah invited them to tea."

Gerald smiled at this rather incoherent explanation.

Norah hastened to explain about Bernice's neighbor, and his mother who had been staying with him and the children until they could get permanent help.

"Now tell us your news," she urged, wanting to steer the subject away from Harry Kidd.

Gerald scowled.

"The news is, I'm not fit to be in the Canadian Army," he told them disgustedly. "My eczema has flared up, and the doctor took one look at me and said that I couldn't be in the trenches with skin like that."

"Oh, Gerald, how utterly devastating!" exclaimed Louise.

Norah made sympathetic noises.

Gerald got up and paced the floor, hands in his pocket. "What's even worse, when I went back to work and told them about it, the boss said if you're no good for the army you're not good enough for Central Railway, thank you, here's your notice, pick up your pay and be on your way."

"What!" exclaimed Norah. "How utterly unfair!" She put out a sympathetic hand to him. "What did Mama and Papa say?"

"Papa is furious, and Mama is relieved, and trying to hide it," he said, with a wry smile. "Pop would have contacted the president of Central Railways himself, but I persuaded him not to do so. If they don't want me, I don't want to work for them."

"But you've worked for them for eight years!" Norah protested. "You'd think they'd have some loyalty to their employees."

"I got a job yesterday as a motorman on the streetcar," he went on, and added coldly, "The railway can go to Hell."

"Maybe Rhoda and you could get married now," said Louise, casting about for a ray of light. She was shocked. Gerald never swore.

Gerald shrugged. "Rhoda's been rather cool lately, and I haven't seen her for a week. I don't know what she'll say."

"What a time you've been having!" Norah exclaimed.

Gerald shrugged. "Life deals out bad luck," he said shortly. "Tell me," he said, "what did you think of P.E.I? Is farming a good life?"

"Aunt Bernice seems to be happy there. Fairlea is just a small village, and everyone knows everybody else. All the people I met, though, were friendly and kind. There's a Presbyterian church in Fairlea, and a tiny Catholic church a few miles down the road in an even smaller village. And the red roads! You liked the red roads, didn't you, Louise!"

"I did indeed. The countryside is very pretty, and Charlottetown is a nice little city. Not nearly as big as Ottawa, of course, but they have streetcars and automobiles there, too."

"By the way, Jeremy's got a week's leave. He's at home at the moment. I expect you'll see him when you go back to Perth, Norah. He came for dinner Sunday night on his way home—Gladdie happened to be here this past weekend, and I heard her making all sorts of plans with him."

"Is he in uniform?" asked Norah interestedly.

"Oh, yes. He's a Lieutenant, you know, and involved in the recruiting at Valcartier Camp."

"Does he know when he'll be sent overseas?"

"Not right away, he says, though I think he's itching to get a shot at the Hun. No, he'll be busy with the new recruits. They've been pouring in all summer, you know."

Louise had been listening avidly to this exchange. "Are he and Gladdie sweethearts?" she now asked, trying to sound casual.

Gerald looked surprised. "I don't know! They seem to get along very well. I know Gladdie has always admired him, hasn't she."

Norah glanced at Louise and said easily, "I'll call him at the Ferris' Friday when I get to Mrs. Talbot's." Mrs. Talbot ran the boarding house in Perth where she had lived for five years during the school season. She turned her head as the front door slammed followed by the clatter of footsteps. "That must be Frank!"

Frank greeted his sisters enthusiastically, especially Louise, with whom he was the closest.

"The job is fine," he said when the girls asked him how the grocery business was. "I take orders over the telephone and do deliveries. I'm just putting in time, though until my nineteenth birthday. I promised Mama I would wait until then before I enlisted."

"Oh, Frankie, must you?" wailed Louise.

"Yes, I must, now that old Gerry isn't fit. I'd be as sick as mud if it were me. Gosh, Lou, you should see Jeremy! I must say, he looks absolutely splendid in his uniform. I can hardly wait until spring. I've told Mr. Mackie that I shall be giving my notice then, and he said he'd be sorry to lose me. What do you think about that?"

"That's terrific, Frankie," said Norah, "but I hope you don't go on like this about joining the army in front of Mama and Dorcas."

"Well, I try not to, but it's hard, when every other fellow I know is talking about enlisting. Jeremy says they'll probably be sending the first contingent over in a month or so. He thinks he'll be here until the spring. Maybe we'll go over together! Wouldn't that be splendid!"

Later, Louise lay in bed, wide-eyed and sleepless. She wondered what sorts of plans Gladdie and Jeremy had been making last Sunday. She could imagine them sitting in the corner, his dark head close to her sandy curls, she smiling up at him. Gladdie wasn't beautiful, but she had a certain charm about her. Once Louise had overheard Dorcas saying, "Miss Gladys did have that 'come-hither' look in her eyes." Dorcas' voice had been half-critical and half-admiring. Louise wasn't sure what it exactly was, but she had observed her sister flirting with young men in the past, and had seen how they had reacted. Louise didn't have a soft, curvy figure like Gladdie, nor was she adept at small talk like her elder sister. She had listened to the ball of conversation being tossed back and forth between Gladdie and various young men, and had wished that she could converse like that. There were a half dozen of them who would have gladly squired Gladdie around the town, so why did she have to care about Jeremy? Louise sighed. She was quite aware that Jeremy thought of her merely as Norah and Gladdie's little sister.

However, she had no business feeling sorry for herself when Gerald had been having such a bad time. While she regarded Frank as a chum, she had always put Gerald up on a pedestal with Mama and Papa. He was her adored eldest brother and could do no wrong. She hated to see him suffering. While he appeared to be taking rejection by the army philosophically, she was sure that losing his job had hurt him deeply. She had never before seen that cold, hard look in his eyes when he had spoken of his former employer. To be sure, he had gone out and immediately got a new job, but she didn't think working as a motorman on the streetcars for the City of Ottawa would be a satisfying career for him. Perhaps he'd go to university now, as Papa had wanted him to do ten years ago. No, Gerald would be the first to say that he was too old to be a student.

Louise turned over in bed. Well, that was Gerald's problem. And what of Rhoda? Gerald had been quite off-hand about her. Had they quarreled? Deep down, Louise knew her heart wouldn't be broken if Gerald and Rhoda didn't get married. She wasn't quite sure why, but she had never been overly fond of Rhoda. Perhaps it was the way she expected Gerald to be at her beck and call at all times. Or the way Louise had heard her once speak of her own parents so deprecatingly. Another time she had been visiting here at the house and had treated Dorcas no better than a servant. Louise had wanted to slap her face. However, if she was her beloved Gerald's choice, she was prepared to try and love Rhoda for his sake. Louise sighed again. She must get to sleep. She closed her eyes tightly and Frankie's cheerful countenance appeared in her mind's eye. She was fond of Frankie, and wished he didn't want to go overseas. Louise was quite sure that a war wasn't the adventure that Frankie thought it was. If women had the vote, she thought resentfully, there'd be no wars in the world. We'd see to that!

She got up for a drink of water, and listened as she heard footsteps coming up the stairs. It was probably Norah coming to bed at last. She and Gerald had still been talking quietly in the little sitting room when Louise had said goodnight at ten o'clock. Yes, there was the creaky board outside of Norah's room next door. Norah always laughed and said she'd never be able to sneak in late with that board waking up the whole house. She heard a murmur of voices, and then Gerald's raised a little saying, "Thanks, Norah, you're a brick of a sister. Sleep well." Then Norah's door closing, Gerald's footsteps past Louise's room to the end of the hall, then silence. Louise thought of going next door and talking to Norah, and then changed her mind. She got back into bed, turned over, and her last thought was that Gerald's voice sounded fairly cheerful when he said goodnight to Norah. Then she slept.

Chapter Fifteen

FAMILY AFFAIRS

The war still seemed far away and unreal, even though thousands of men were assembling at Valcartier Camp, preparing to be a part of the first Canadian Expeditionary Force. The various routines of the family members once more fell into place: Norah went back to Perth to her school, Gladys went to Toronto with Mrs. Marchbanks, Frank and Gerald continued at their jobs, and Val went back to school, protesting that if Frankie was to be a soldier, so would he. Dorcas told him he mustn't even think of that—think how she and his dear mother would feel! Besides, he was only twelve—("Nearly thirteen, Dorcas," he objected.)—And the war would be over long before he was old enough to join the army.

Louise was at home, now, and rather at loose ends. She wasn't academically inclined as Norah was, nor talented musically and socially as Gladys was, and under normal circumstances she would have been sent to a finishing school in Europe. With a war on, of course that was impossible.

Papa and Mama mentioned several fine schools for young ladies in southern Ontario and one in New York State, but Louise begged not to be sent away from home.

"I want to be useful!" she declared. "After all, there's a war on!" Mama suggested hospital work, and, shuddering at the thought,

Louise bravely signed up as a ward maid at the local hospital. She spent her days mopping floors, emptying bedpans, disinfecting walls and beds under the grim supervision of an elderly dragon of an English nursing sister. Miss Love had been visiting relatives in Ottawa, and having being advised not to return to England for the time being, she volunteered her services turning young, inexperienced girls into competent ward maids.

"If ever there was someone who didn't live up to her name," she muttered under her breath to Lizzie Porter, with whom she had been partnered. Lizzie grinned and gave her the thumbs up signal. Lizzie, a fifteen-year-old who had dropped out of school, and at whose grammar Norah would have raised both eyebrows, was none-the-less cheerful and hard working, and Louise liked her. For two weeks the girls slaved in the wards, learning routines and skills. At this time Miss Love recommended them for ward work, which was essentially a volunteer position. They would receive a small stipend, enough to cover their midday meal and carfare. Miss Love took Louise aside one day and asked her if she had ever considered nursing as a profession.

"Why, no," Louise answered, surprised. "I can't bear the sight of blood." Miss Love said dryly that it was a myth that nurses encountered gallons of blood in their daily routine, except perhaps in the operating theatre. Most nursing, she went on, was routine, and laborious. As a ward maid, she was providing a welcome service for the nurses, who could concentrate on their patients, rather than be concerned with the tasks of housekeeping. A clean, neat, ward was safer and promoted good health. Good basic cleaning techniques were vital. Believe it or not, in the past sick people avoided hospitals because they often became sicker in them. Modern scientific knowledge of germs and how they were spread had made an incredible difference. She regarded Louise seriously. It was her opinion, however, that Miss Laurier's talents were wasted in being a ward maid, important a job as it was. Miss Love remarked that Miss Laurier was intelligent, a quick learner, and appeared to like people. She understood that McGill College in Montreal had an excellent nursing program. Miss Laurier should think about this. Meanwhile, keep up the good work she and Miss Porter were doing. She was proud of her two students.

Louise went away, surprised and humbled at compliments from the dragon. She had never thought herself to be particularly intelligent, and not once had she considered that looking after sick people would be a satisfying career. However, she had observed the nurses on the ward, and she found them for the most part not only to be dedicated to their work, but also to be enjoying it, difficult as it sometimes was. She thought about it seriously over the next few days, and thought that she'd wait until Norah came home for one of her weekends. Norah would give her good advice. In the meantime she went to the hospital each day, and worked very hard. They had been given two uniforms apiece, made out of strong, serviceable muslin, of a rather drab gray. 'Drudge gray,' Lizzie called it, but the uniform's saving grace was a crisp, white apron of thick cotton, that Dorcas starched for her every day. A hair net confined Louise's unruly curls, and on her feet were sensible laced shoes of black leather, similar to the ones that the nurses wore.

Norah came home Saturday at noon, and to Louise's surprise and pleasure Jeremy was in tow. He greeted Louise with a bow and a flourish.

"Here she is, all grown up!" he exclaimed, kissing her cheek. "Norah tells me you're skivvying in the hospital."

Louise's cheeks were pink with the excitement of seeing her hero. However, she had been working at a job for a month now, and had acquired a certain confidence.

"I'm not just a skivvy," she replied, with spirit. "I'm a ward maid, doing an important job, relieving the nurses from housekeeping chores. It's war work!" Jeremy's eyes twinkled, and Louise knew he was amused at her protestations.

"Keep up the good work, then," he said, and tucking her hand into the crook of his elbow, he led her to the sofa in the sitting room. "Tell me all about it. My father's in hospital," he went on. "That's mainly why I'm here. You must be doing a good job, for he says he's getting excellent care."

"He's in my hospital?" asked Louise. "Is he very ill?"

"He was complaining of chest pain, and Dr Thibault didn't like the look of him," Jeremy told her, "but it seems to be a false alarm.

119

I rushed to the hospital last night, and found him sitting up in bed wanting his pipe. He's on the second floor. You might pop in and see him, Louise. The doctor wants to keep him in for a few days, just to make sure."

"I certainly will."

"Norah and I went to see him on our way here this morning, and he enjoyed the company. He's mainly bored. My mother can't get into town to see him, as she's got a bad cold. Susie is looking after her. You should go and visit my sister sometime, Lou. She'd love to see you."

"Gladdie will be sorry she missed you," remarked Norah as they sat down to lunch a little while later. "She's still in Toronto with Mrs. Marchbanks. Mama says they expect them back next week."

"I probably won't be available before Christmas, now," Jeremy replied. "As you know, the first of the Expeditionary Force sailed for England two weeks ago, but I am going to be swamped with work."

"Frankie is determined to join up in March," Norah said.

"We'll need every able bodied man," he said. "However—let's not talk of war, and let me enjoy the company of you beautiful ladies."

Jeremy stayed for a while after lunch, and then went away, but not before kissing both Norah and Louise on the cheeks, and holding Louise's hand a trifle longer than she thought might have been necessary.

"Such a nice young man," Mama said, after he went out the door. "I thought, once, Norah, that you and Jeremy might make a match of it."

Norah laughed. "Oh, no, Mama, I've always thought of Jeremy as just another older brother."

"I thought it was tactful of him not to be in uniform," remarked Gerald, who was preparing himself for his afternoon shift on the streetcar. "I suppose he thought I'd be upset."

"Wouldn't it be wonderful if he were my commanding officer?" Frankie mused.

Louise went upstairs to her room and gazed into the mirror. Jeremy Ferris had kissed her not once, but twice! To be sure, they were only brotherly pecks on the cheek, but he didn't squeeze her hand as he left? She vowed not to wash her face until at least tomorrow. And he had listened to her when she mentioned that Miss Love had suggested she train to be a nurse. Perhaps he hadn't been so amused at her after all!

"Do you think that's what you'd like to do?" he had asked.

"I don't know," she answered. "I know I don't want to be a ward maid all my life, but at the moment I feel I'm being useful."

"One of the chaps I know at Camp has a sister who had taken a patient to France, and was caught there when the war broke out. She is still there, working in a Red Cross hospital. Her family has received several letters about her experiences. What a fine, brave, girl!"

Louise made up her mind right then and there that as soon as she was eighteen she would take nurse's training. It would be three years, and the war would surely be over by then, but she would give anything to have Jeremy be half as proud of her as he was of that nurse he had never met.

Gladdie returned several days later, and came home on a few days leave from Mrs. Marchbanks. She was crestfallen to discover Jeremy had been in town on the weekend.

"Is Mr. Ferris still in hospital? I must go and visit him."

Louise informed her that Jeremy's father had gone home the previous day. On Monday after her shift was over she removed her hair net that had flattened her curls, patted them into place, smoothed her apron, and went into Mr. Ferris' ward. Shyly, she introduced herself. He seemed delighted to see her, and kept telling her that he never would have recognized her.

"You're all grown up now, and working, too! But," he added, frowning a little, "does your mother approve of what you're doing? Cleaning in a hospital really doesn't seem to be a proper job for a young lady."

Louise went into her spiel about taking the housekeeping load off the nursing staff, and being useful in wartime.

"I'm seriously thinking of taking up nursing as a profession," she went on. "But I won't be eighteen until April."

"The nurses have looked after me very well." He smiled at her. "I wouldn't mind you coming in and holding my hand anytime."

Louise blushed. Was he flirting with her?

She was remembering this as she talked to Gladdie. She told her sister about visiting Mr. Ferris, but not his remarks about wanting to hold her hand. He had been teasing, of course. Jeremy hadn't been teasing her, when he listened so thoughtfully to her plans, and made serious comments in return. She also didn't mention to Gladdie that Jeremy had kissed her hello and goodbye. There was no reason not to; after all, he had kissed Norah that way, as well, but Louise didn't want to share that information with anyone, especially Gladdie.

Her sister was prattling away. "Mrs. Marchbanks is going to Montreal next month. Is Valcartier close to Montreal? If I write to Jeremy, perhaps he could come into the city for a day or so. Did he ask about me, Louise?" Louise thought about it, and realized he hadn't. Of course, Norah had told him that Gladdie was in Toronto. Perhaps he knew already, if he and Gladdie were corresponding.

"He and Norah traveled in from Perth together, and I'm sure he asked Norah about you," Louise said comfortingly.

The days and weeks passed quickly for Louise. While the weather was still good she walked the fifteen blocks to and from Memorial Hospital. On very cold days she took the streetcar, which let her off right in front of the hospital. She would come home physically exhausted, eat supper, and fall into bed at eight o'clock. Gradually, however, her body got used to the routine, her muscles hardened, and her energy increased. She found that she was enjoying the hard work. Nobody except Gladdie seemed surprised that she was slaving away on a hospital ward with a mop and a pail. After all, there was a war on!

One December afternoon Louise was preparing to go home after her shift. She was in the small change room that had been made available to non-medical staff, and just about to remove her shoes when she heard her name. She looked up to see Sister Love in the doorway, and in nurse's uniform! She was wearing the cap and veil of her English nursing school, which Louise had always thought most refined and elegant.

"May I have a word with you, Miss Laurier, before you go home?" Louise nodded and smiling, stopped untying her shoelaces and retied them. She got to her feet and followed the elderly nurse across the corridor into a small office whose window overlooked the garden in the area formed by the U-shaped building. She looked around wonderingly, and seated herself opposite the gray haired Englishwoman, who hesitated a moment, then spoke.

"You may or may not be aware that Memorial Hospital is starting a nursing school. The program was to be in place last September, but has been delayed for a number of reasons, one of which is that the Director of Nurses had been ill. It is now scheduled to begin on January fifteen. I was wondering, Miss Laurier, if you had given any thought to my suggestion that you train to be a nurse, and if so would you consider applying here." She looked around with a smile. "I've been persuaded to take on the job as Director of Nurses until Miss Ramage is well enough to take over. This is my new abode."

Louise clasped her hands eagerly. "Oh, Miss Love, how exciting! I have thought a lot about it and I've decided that it is what I want to do, but I'm not eighteen until April. Wouldn't I be too young?"

Miss Love considered this. "I don't think you're too young, and the fact that your birthday isn't for a few months could very easily be overlooked." She handed Louise an envelope. "Go home and discuss this with your parents, and if you decide to apply, fill out the forms and bring them back to me. There is a place for them to sign as well." She stood up. "Do you have time for a short visit to the school?" She turned in her chair. "It is in the building across the quadrangle, and is connected to the hospital. It's the nurse's residence as well. We have room for fifteen students a year for the next three years. Four of the big bedrooms are taken up by staff who have opted to live here."

Louise smiled and nodded. "Oh, yes, I'd be most interested! I'd have to live in the residence, then? One of the reasons I was hesitating was because I really didn't want to leave home at the moment."

Miss Love nodded. "One of the requirements is residence living, but I think you'll find, at least for the first six months, that you would have weekends off and be able to go home on Friday and return Sunday evening." She stood up. "Shall we go along, then?"

Around the dinner table that evening Louise described her tour of the new nursing school.

"It's quite nice," she told them. "There are forty bedrooms, some are big enough for doubles, but right now we shall all have rooms to ourselves. There are four graduate nurses living there, so we will have to share the sitting room with them. I don't know how they're going to like that. They have their own kitchen and bathroom at their end, though, and we have our own kitchenette where we can make toast and such when we come off shift. There's a piano in the lounge. There's a classroom, with desks and black-boards, just like in school, a library, and another big room that Miss Love calls the clinical laboratory. It's fitted up like a hospital ward, and there's a life-sized doll we will practice on."

"Why are there so many bedrooms, if there will only be fifteen of you?" asked Val curiously.

"There'll be fifteen more coming in the fall, and fifteen more the following year. That's forty-five, plus the graduate nurses that live there. Some will have to share rooms."

Mama looked worried. "Are you sure this is what you want?" she asked. "But Mama, you suggested it, didn't you? Look, Miss Love says that you and Papa can call on her and tour the school, and she'll answer any questions you have. She gave me the application forms. See where you have to sign it as well? I can't apply without your permission."

She had the determined expression on her face that Dorcas used to call 'mulish'.

Her three brothers had differing reactions. Gerald, surprisingly, was skeptical.

"You'll never make it," he declared. "It's hard work, and not very nice at times, I understand."

Frankie hugged her and told her she was a brick. "You can come overseas as soon as you're finished, just like that girl Jeremy told us about."

Val wondered aloud if she would be his nurse when he got his tonsils out. He'd had a series of sore throats throughout the fall, and the doctor had been talking about surgery. Mama had been resisting the idea, but Val liked the thought. One of his friends had had his tonsils out, and he had been given dishes and dishes of ice cream to eat. Val loved ice cream.

"What about your ward maid job?" asked Papa.

"That will be finished, of course. I have a notion, though, that the student nurses will be doing that kind of work as well as learning about nursing."

Louise wished that she could talk to Norah, but there had been a bad snowstorm two nights before, the worst of which had just missed Ottawa. Six inches fell at the capital, but according to the morning paper, Perth and the surrounding district were completely snowed in. The telephone lines were down, and they weren't even sure whether Norah would make it home for Christmas. Gladdie was now in Montreal with Mrs Marchbanks and her family, and would be spending Christmas there. Louise wondered whether her sister had gotten in touch with Jeremy.

Two days before Christmas telephone service had been restored, and they were able to get in touch with Norah.

"The roads are still impassable," she told them, over a crackling line. "Mr. and Mrs. Ferris have invited me to their home for Christmas. They surprised me this morning by stopping here with the sleigh, taking me to church with them, and back home for luncheon."

"Will Jeremy get home for Christmas?" asked Louise casually.

"Well, they hope so, as I believe the trains are running, but it's still uncertain. I shall enjoy becoming reacquainted with Susie and Michael. May I tell them your plans about nursing?"

"Oh, yes, do! When I visited Mr. Ferris in the hospital I actually mentioned that I was thinking about it. Susie will be interested, too. Will you give them all my very best regards?"

"No Norah for Christmas!" sighed Mama later.

"It don't seem right," agreed Dorcas.

Louise agreed. Norah always filled Val's stocking Christmas Eve, and last year they had done it together. Now it would be up to her, unless Val thought it too childish, and she didn't think he'd feel that way. She'd consult with Dorcas, who'd be only too happy to accommodate Louise in order to please her favorite.

125

"Who'll do my stocking?" the twelve-year-old demanded, when he discovered that his eldest sister would be away.

"Aren't you a bit old for Christmas stockings?" chaffed Louise.

"Of course not. Who's going to fill it?"

"Why, Santa Claus, of course, same as every year," replied Louise with a straight face.

"Oh, Lou ... ."

Val saw she was teasing him, and subsided. Louise ruffled his hair affectionately, then went away thoughtfully, and thought how rather topsy-turvy life was right now. A far away war that would be sure to affect her personally, if Jeremy and Frank went overseas; Christmas without Norah and Gladdie; Norah interested in a Prince Edward Island farmer; she pining over Gladdie's young man. Well, not really pining over him, just dreaming about him every day, and *was* he Gladdie's beau? Louise went slowly to her room and stretched out on the bed, her hands behind her head. She knew that Gladdie would like him to be ... oh well, there wasn't a chance that Jeremy thought of her as anything except Gladdie and Norah's little sister. She was sorry, in a way, that Norah couldn't be romantic about him. She could bear his being married to her oldest sister, but never to Gladdie!

Chapter Sixteen

A NEW YEAR

The New Year was seen in rather somberly. The whole country seemed to be holding its collective breath, waiting for something to happen in Europe involving its young men. There were reports in the papers of fighting in France, but as far as they knew, their boys were still in England. Frank champed at the bit, waiting for his birthday in March, while Louise studied her lists of articles needed when she entered the school of nursing in two weeks, and tried to forget Gladdie's triumphant face when she returned from Montreal. She had seen Jeremy, she said, and they had had such a marvelous time! She had taken him to a party that friends of Mrs. Marchbanks had held in their mansion in Westmount. There was an orchestra, a champagne supper at midnight, and they had danced all night, after which he had taken her to breakfast, *tête-à-tête*, at a small café in downtown Montreal. He had looked so handsome in his uniform, and she had been the very first to know of his promotion to Captain! Oh, how they had celebrated! She didn't actually say that they were practically engaged, but hinted at it, her mouth curving in a coy smile. Louise, despairing, endured her tinkling laughter all day, and her playing on the piano and singing, 'If You Were the Only Girl in the World'. She of course sang, "if you were the only boy in the world

127

and I were the only girl", accompanied by *arpeggios* and *glissandos* until Louise thought she would scream.

Louise checked her list. For Christmas, Mama and Papa had given her a beautiful watch with a second hand that she would pin to her uniform. It was encased in gold, with a white face and gold numbers, and on the back was engraved the initials *LFL-1914.*

"But it's upside down!" exclaimed Val, as the gift was passed around and admired.

"No, see, when I pin it to my front and look at it, it's right side up," Louise told him, demonstrating. She was very pleased. Mama and Papa must have rushed out and ordered it as soon as she had made her decision and handed in her application.

Susie Ferris had sent her a gift of a pair of bandage scissors and a note with Norah when Louise's sister finally came home a week after Christmas. To Louise's delight, Jeremy's sister had also applied to enter the school, and had been accepted! Now she wouldn't mind if she had to share a room in residence if it could be with Susie.

She had been fitted for shoes and stockings, both black. The hospital would supply the uniforms, and Louise was unsure what they would be like. Anything would be better than 'drudge grey'! She looked at her wardrobe and decided what clothes she would pack for her off-duty times, though she hesitated over her winter coat. She had two, one a year old, and one a hand-me-down from Gladdie. The newer one was plain and serviceable, but Gladdie's had fur collars and cuffs and a muff to match. She said the color wasn't right for her, but Louise loved it. It was a deep red, the color of Dorcas' cranberry wine, and there was a jaunty tam o'shanter in the same color. Louise always felt gorgeous in it. She had been wearing it the day Jeremy had come to lunch and he had admired it. The red coat was duly laid out. Cotton nightgowns and undergarments that would wash easily, warm boots for walking in the snow, and the white scarf she had crocheted herself. Louise eschewed the fashion of whalebone corsets, hating the confined feeling. Gladdie, on the other hand, laced herself in until her waist was like a wasp's, and her ample bosom bulged over the top. Louise examined herself in the mirror.

She wished she had a figure like Gladdie's, but she wasn't prepared to be squeezed within an inch of her life.

She dragged her big suitcase out from under the bed and began to put things carefully into it. Downstairs the piano was silent, and a few minutes later Gladdie appeared at the door to Louise's room.

"Packing already? You've got weeks before you go," she remarked, coming in uninvited. She spotted the red coat hanging on its hanger, the crocheted scarf draped over its shoulder.

"There's my coat! I wondered what had happened to it!" She put it on, gave a little twirl, and looked at Louise accusingly. "You've been wearing it! My lovely red coat!"

Louise's mouth had fallen open in surprise. "You gave it to me! You said it didn't suit you!"

"I most certainly did not! Where did you get that idea? Where's the matching hat?"

"Gladdie, you did! Last year you said you wouldn't be wearing it anymore, you said it was a mistake!"

"Don't be so silly, of course I didn't. I love this coat. Oh, you are so gorgeous," she murmured, turning up the collar and stroking her cheeks with the fur. "Anyhow, I'm taking it back now." She noticed the scarf for the first time. It had been crocheted with soft white wool, and was long, and edged with a silky fringe. "This is nice," she remarked. "It'll go well with the coat."

Louise grabbed it out of her hand. "No you won't. That's mine. I made it myself."

"If you're going to be like that," Gladdie said sulkily. "Where's the matching hat, then?"

Louise silently handed her the tam, and as Gladdie turned to go, Louise reached into her wardrobe drawer and pulled out the fur muff.

"Here!" she said, "You forgot this, didn't you." And she angrily threw the muff at her sister.

"There's no need to be snippy with me. You've got a perfectly good winter coat, I've seen you wearing it." And Gladdie flounced out, garments over her arm.

129

Louise slammed the door and flung herself down on the bed, close to tears. The unfairness of it! For Gladdie to walk off with the coat she had so carelessly given away a year ago. And to lie about it! How she wished Norah were here. She'd sort Gladdie soon enough. She rejected the temptation to talk to Mama. It would worry her that her daughters were quarreling. She had enough on her plate with all the newspaper stories about the war, and Frankie barely concealing his eagerness to enlist. No, she'd just have to put up with Gladdie.

"I hate her," she said out loud through gritted teeth.

A late February snowstorm had added to the three feet that covered the Perth area, and Norah was once more snowed in. For the first time in three days the postman was able to get through, and he brought a veritable treasure trove of mail for her. She noted with pleasure that there were two fat letters from Prince Edward Island. She had not heard from Harry in several weeks, nor from the children, and she had wondered whether they had forgotten her. She had missed the newsy epistles from the Kidd family. The last time she received a letter from them was the middle of January, a long letter describing their Christmas. The snow storm which had prevented Norah from going home to Ottawa had struck the Maritimes the day after, and Harry had to cancel travel plans to Charlottetown where they had intended to spend Christmas with his mother.

The children didn't mind at all, he had written. *I harnessed the horses to the sleigh and we drove to Pierre and Mary's to make sure they were all right because Mrs. Hastie was fussing. We found them holed up in their cottage, snug as two bugs, and if they didn't appreciate unexpected visitors, they didn't let on. I had a feeling they were enjoying an extension of their honeymoon! I passed on a message from your Aunt Bernice for them to come and spend Christmas Day with her and Mrs. Hastie, and since we weren't able to go to my mother's in Charlottetown, we all gathered at Bernice's for Christmas dinner. Even Jed came, his sciatica notwithstanding. We had a merry time exchanging gifts, and the twins sledded on the top meadow. We haven't heard them laugh so much since Lucy died. We had turkey with all the trimmings, and we ate until we could hardly move. I wished you were there so that we could have gone for a long walk in the snow.*

There was much more, and concluded with many thanks for the parcel she had sent. She had made Christmas stockings for the three of them, and stuffed them with an assortment of small gifts, candy and fruit. Dorcas had made a large batch of fruitcake in the fall, and she had given Norah a portion. Norah wrapped this and included it in the parcel. Along with the stockings, she selected two books for the twins, and a hand-knitted scarf of rich red wool for their father. She worried a little about the scarf. Was it too personal a gift? But Harry had seemed delighted, and the children were enchanted with the stockings and the books.

Norah had planned to be home for Christmas with the family, but the snowstorm had kept her in Perth, and on the Sunday two days before Christmas, visitors had surprised her. Mr. and Mrs. Ferris, along with Susie and Michael, stopped by on their way to church. Norah was preparing to walk through the snow to the service, but it was a pleasant ride in the sleigh, harness bells jingling, and the horses snorting their steamy breath. Mrs. Ferris insisted on her coming back to have dinner with them, and when they discovered that she'd be alone for the holidays, they invited her to spend Christmas Day with them. It had been a different sort of Christmas not to be with her own family, but the Ferrises, old friends that they were, made her feel very welcome and most comfortable. It was then that she mentioned to Susie that Louise had made up her mind definitely to train to be a nurse.

Susie was an attractive girl, small and compact, but with an athlete's wiry body. She was an excellent skater, and in summer she swam and played tennis. She had dark brown hair that curled naturally, and brown eyes fringed by thick lashes. Two young men were currently vying for her attention, but she wasn't the least interested in them. When she smiled, two dimples appeared in her cheeks. She was smiling now.

"I've been thinking about that very thing for quite a while now," she said excitedly, "so when Father came home and told me he'd been talking to Louise, and she was thinking about it, too, I wrote away to

131

the hospital to ask them how I might go about it, and the Director, Miss Love, sent me an application form. I haven't heard yet, but I feel quite confident. What fun to be with Louise again! We used to be such good friends when we were children."

Her eyes sparkled with enthusiasm, and her dark curls bounced as she nodded her head.

"I even ordered two pairs of bandage scissors, and planned to send one to Louise for Christmas, but they haven't come yet. Do you know if she has already bought them?"

Norah shook her head. "Give them to her anyway, she'll be really pleased."

"May I send it with you when you go home to Ottawa?" "By all means."

Susie sobered a little. "Jeremy told us that Frank is planning to enlist as soon as he has his nineteenth birthday. Louise must be worried; they've always been such chums."

"He would have gone as soon as war was declared, but Mama made him promise to wait until he was nineteen."

They sat down to a huge repast, and afterwards Mrs. Ferris played the piano and they sang carols.

"We need your sister Gladys here to play for us," remarked Mrs. Ferris, as she stumbled over the notes. "Did she pursue a musical career? I always thought she was very talented as a young girl."

"Not really. She's a secretary and companion to a rich old lady in town. She often plays when they entertain, though."

"I thought she might have gone on and become a concert pianist."

"Gladdie doesn't have enough staying power," replied Norah shortly. "And I'm not sure she has that much talent."

Mrs. Ferris raised her eyebrows, but continued on with the carol, 'Silent Night.'

"This is Jeremy's favorite," she said. "What a pity he couldn't be here! I have a feeling it'll be a long time before he's home for Christmas."

She stopped and put her hands in her lap, her face suddenly sad and serious. Susie stooped and put her cheek against her mother's.

132

"We said we wouldn't mention the war. He'll be all right, though, just you wait and see."

Mr. Ferris smiled. "And we have Norah instead of Jeremy. She's very much prettier!"

They all laughed at his attempt at a joke, and Mrs. Ferris continued with a jolly tune instead of Jeremy's carol.

Norah sat in her room at her boarding house, and gazed unseeingly out the window where the snow was now falling again, remembering Christmas Day with the Ferrises. She had had a nice time, and it was next best to being at home. After all, she had known the Ferris family forever. She looked at her other letters. One was from Louise, and the other from her friend Barbara. Barbara had recently gone out West, and was presently in British Columbia teaching in a small town called Fort Langley.

She read Barbara's first. Her friend described her life there, her first Christmas so far away from home, and then went on to relate the news that she was engaged to be married to a policeman, and was getting married next summer! The wedding would be held in Fort Langley, and her parents were making a holiday of it, and traveling out by train in July. Barbara wanted nobody but Norah for a bridesmaid. Would she consider the trip west?

Norah put the letter down and retrieved her atlas of Canada from her bookcase. There was Fort Langley, a tiny dot just east of the city of Vancouver. She put the atlas away and again gazed out the window. What wonderful news! Could she do it? Could she travel all the way out to Vancouver by train? She had been thinking that it was time for her to find a new place to live. Mrs. Talbot was a good, kind, person, but a boardinghouse was after all just a boardinghouse and not the same as a real home. She had money saved, enough to pay the rent of a decent house. Did she want to stay in Perth? A trip out west might be the very thing, though the direction her thoughts often went was, of course, east. Well, she thought, as she ripped open Louise's letter, it was something to think about seriously.

Louise's letter was filled with life as a student nurse, and the first six weeks had gone splendidly. Most of the time had been spent in the classroom, and they had just finished examinations in Nursing

133

Arts, Anatomy and Physiology, and Common Diseases of the Body. She and Susie thought they had done fairly well. They were to have a long weekend off, then on Monday they were to start on the wards.

Miss Abbott is our instructor in Nursing Arts, and she will accompany us on to the wards, she wrote. *And I thought Miss Love was a dragon when I was a ward maid. She doesn't hold a candle to Miss Abbott. Miss A. can be just awful to you. So far, I've escaped her acid tongue. 'Miss Ferris,' she said scathingly to Susie the other day, 'do you really think a patient would be comfortable in that bed?' And she ripped it apart and made Susie remake it from the bottom. Suppose she does that on the ward? I'd die of embarrassment!*

Last weekend Jeremy came to call. I was wishing you were here instead of Gladdie!

He sat and chatted to us all. Frankie was all questions about Valcartier Camp, and what he should expect. It's only three weeks until his birthday, and he can't wait to join up. Mama is overly cheerful and smiles too much. It would be better if she looked sad and cried; because I'm sure that's how she's feeling. Jeremy took Gladdie back to Miss Marchbanks' house and we haven't heard from him since. Ah well.

I am enjoying Susie's friendship very much, Norah. Isn't it queer that we were thinking of taking nurses' training at the same time unbeknownst to each other? We're such good friends and tell each other everything. Well, almost everything. The only thing I haven't shared with her is my being fond of her brother. I don't think she'd give me away on purpose, but I'd die if Jeremy knew how I feel about him. And it would be ten times worse if Gladdie knew!

At this point Louise had started to write something, then blacked it out with thick lines of ink, and went on to write of something else. Norah peered at the line, but no words were visible. She had noticed the last time the three sisters were at home that there was coolness between the other two, and she had wondered at the time if there had been a quarrel. Gladdie had always been prone to take umbrage at imagined slights, but it didn't sound if the two had discussed Jeremy. Wasn't it odd that Jeremy could cause her two sisters' hearts to beat more quickly, but didn't affect hers one iota! Speaking of rapidly beating hearts... she smiled and picked up the letters from Harry and compared postmarks. One had been mailed on January 26, and it had a second postmark on it. It looked as though it had gone to Winnipeg by mistake, and then been sent back to Perth. She opened it, glancing at the date, which was January 25. First she read the note from the children with pleasure. Ben's printing had improved immensely. She must remember to comment on that when she replied. Sarah's neat script was quite amazing. It was almost writing, and it was hard to believe that a six year old could write like that. She enclosed a drawing of 'The View from my Window', and Norah was astonished. The child had talent! It was just a sketch done with crayons, but she had got the shape of the barn right, and the blue shadows on the snow. Harry's letter was only two pages, telling her some of the problems he had encountered (one of his cows had died), his birthday celebrations that day (and had he told her his middle name was Robert after the poet with whom he shared a birthday? And when was hers?) Norah hadn't known his birth date. The subject had never arisen. They had known each other for barely three weeks before she had gone home.

His social life, he said, was improving. He had been seeing quite a lot of the Crockers, and he had made friends with the doctor and his wife.

Norah remembered the doctor and his wife. Aunt Bernice had had them, along with the minister and his wife, to dinner, when Mercy and Robert were visiting. She hadn't really got acquainted with them, but she thought they were a pleasant couple. She finished reading the letter, and then opened the second one. This one was even shorter, expressing his concern that perhaps she was ill because he hadn't heard from her in the last few weeks, or was she just busy at school? He enclosed more drawings by Sarah. Ben was down with bronchitis, and he was a little concerned—the doctor had gone away frowning this morning. Norah put down the letter and put her hand to her breast, her heart fluttering in anxiety. If something should happen to that delightful child! He had dated the letter February 21, over a week ago. She decided to put in a telephone call to Aunt Bernice that weekend when she got home. She would know how the children were. In the meantime she sat down and wrote a long letter to Harry, explaining that one of his letters had taken a long detour, and that they had arrived together. Then she penned a get-well note to Ben, complimenting him on his fine printing, and wrote a short letter to Sarah, saying how beautiful her drawings were. She bundled up in her boots and warm coat, and trudged through the snow to the Post Office, where she mailed them.

The sun had come out, and the sky was a brilliant blue. In spite of her concern for Ben, her spirits had lifted. Her friend Barbara was getting married and she wanted Norah for her bridesmaid; her sister Louise was enjoying her training, and she had heard from Harry at last! She conjured up a memory of him as he had said goodbye at the train station in Summerside. His blue eyes had smiled at her, and he had held her hand. For a moment she thought he was going to kiss her again, but he merely touched her cheek, and said his farewells. She watched through the window as the train pulled out of the station. His shoulders had slumped a little, but he squared them, lifted his hand and waved, then turned and strode away.

Norah walked briskly back to Mrs. Talbot's boarding house, humming a tune, and waving cheerfully to a neighbor who was also out for a walk. She expected that school would start again tomorrow, and she had lessons to prepare. Life would be perfect if it wasn't for that unspeakable war across the Atlantic Ocean. She thought about Jeremy, who, by his own admission, would probably be sent to France in the spring, and of Louise and Gladdie, who were both fond of him. And what of Frankie, her little brother with the freckled face and the open, honest countenance who was determined to 'do his duty'? And her own students—she couldn't bear the thought that boys like Reggie Peters and Michael Johnson, now only sixteen, but idealistic and patriotic, could in a couple of years be fighting in Europe. She didn't think she was unpatriotic, but she couldn't see why Canadian boys had to go overseas and risk their lives—and to what end? Norah had heard that it was a war to end all wars, but she had her doubts about that.

Chapter Seventeen

LOUISE AND JEREMY

"Miss Laurier, Miss Ferris, your brothers are here to see you." Miss Love emerged from her office as Louise and Susie came off duty.

The entrance to the corridor connecting the residence to the hospital was just beyond her office, and she had been on the look out for the girls. She smiled at them.

"They came to my office a little while ago, and asked if they might take you home tonight. I said that was fine. They're waiting in the residence lounge."

Both girls flushed with pleasure and excitement.

"Jeremy and Frank?" asked Louise.

Miss Love smiled again. "Captain Ferris and Private Laurier." She looked keenly at Louise. "I believe it is your birthday tomorrow. Many happy returns, Miss Laurier."

"Thank you, Miss Love." Louise's heart had begun to beat a little faster. "Run along then, my dears," Miss Love said, unbending a little. "Enjoy your weekend."

Barely containing themselves, they nonetheless walked sedately down the corridor past the doors leading to the laboratories and utility rooms until they reached the corner where it turned right to lead to the nurses' residence. Who knew if Miss Love was still standing outside her door watching them? As soon as they were out of sight they sprinted hand in hand giggling with excitement. It was Friday, and Susie was spending the weekend with the Lauriers. Moreover, it was Louise's birthday tomorrow, there was a party planned, and Jeremy and Frank had been able to obtain leave!

The two young men in uniform rose to their feet as Louise and Susie appeared in the doorway of the nurses' lounge. Frank gave his sister an affectionate hug. They looked at each other admiringly. It was the first time they had seen each other in uniform.

"Gosh. Lou, you look just wonderful!" he exclaimed, gazing at the blue and white clad student.

"You look pretty fine yourself," she returned, smiling at him. It had taken awhile, but she was now used to the idea of Frank being in the army. He had enlisted five weeks ago on his birthday. Mama had cried, and said she was proud of him, and Papa looked grim and hugged him, a rare gesture on his part.

Susie kissed her brother, and was smiling at Frank and Louise. Jeremy extended his hand to Louise.

"Frank is right. The uniform suits you," he said, and there was admiration in his voice.

Louise blushed and found herself tongue-tied.

"Just wait until we get our caps in June," Susie interjected.

"Will you still be here, or do you know?" asked Louise, recovering her poise.

"I don't know," Jeremy said. "Susie was telling me there is a ceremony. I hope we'll be able to attend."

"I guess we shouldn't be standing around in our uniforms like this," said Susie. "We'll go up and change and meet you down here in fifteen minutes."

"You get ready in fifteen minutes?" asked her brother in mock amazement.

"Just watch our dust," returned Susie with spirit. She dazzled Frank with a smile and took Louise's arm as two of their classmates came in, curious to see who Louise and Susie were entertaining.

Susie introduced them. "Miss Howard, Miss Craven, my brother Captain Ferris and Louise's brother Private Laurier. Come on, Louise; let's go upstairs. Mollie and June will keep them occupied."

There was envy and admiration in the eyes of June Howard and Mollie Craven fifteen minutes later as she and Susie sailed out on the arms of Jeremy and Frank. Louise would have preferred to sit in the front seat of the car with Jeremy, but Frank had ushered the girls into the back seat along with Susie's weekend case, and jumped in the front seat himself. The situation became even more less than perfect as Jeremy made a right turn instead of the left turn toward the Laurier home, and said casually that he had promised to pick Gladdie up this afternoon and take her home as well. When they arrived at Mrs. Marchbanks' house, Frank got out and went up to the front door. A black and white clad maid who gestured for him to come in opened it.

"Your sister is never on time," Jeremy remarked.

Louise wondered miserably how often Jeremy had waited for Gladdie outside this house.

Five minutes later the door opened and Gladdie emerged, Frank behind her carrying a suitcase. Gladdie was wearing a brand new outfit in the latest shade of pale green, a navy cape flung carelessly over her shoulders, and a navy and green hat perched on her reddish curls. She looked stunning. With a brilliant smile, she opened the door to the front seat and got in, leaning across to Jeremy to give him a kiss. He smiled at her indulgently.

"Be careful of that hat," he warned, as Frank reluctantly got in the back seat beside Louise.

"Gladdie, you'll have to take your suitcase in the front," he said. "There's no room here." The suitcase was digging into Louise's leg.

"There's no room here, either," she answered. "Hold it on your lap."

Jeremy eased the car into gear and they moved off down the road.

"You're staying with us, of course," stated Gladdie to Jeremy.

Louise had been longing to ask that very question, but shyness had kept her silent.

139

"'Fraid not, Glad, just Susie. I have to pick up my parents and Michael at the train station later on this afternoon, and we're all staying at that little inn down the way from your house. Do you know if Norah will be with them, Louise?"

"I think so."

"No need for your father to meet her at the station, then. I'll drop her off at your house on our way to the hotel. We'll practically be going right by. Susie, will you be coming with me and having supper with us?"

"Would it be all right if Louise joined us?"

"Sure. Then I might as well collect you both when I drop Norah off." Gladdie smiled at Jeremy, and waited for an invitation from him. Jeremy said nothing, but concentrated on his driving. When they got home, Gladdie sailed into the house without a word, leaving Frank to bring in her suitcase. Jeremy raised his eyebrows, waved goodbye to the other three, and drove off. Louise mentally hugged herself. She would be having supper with Jeremy and his parents. No matter if it was Susie who offered the invitation. And he hadn't asked Gladdie!

Louise's eighteenth birthday dawned mild and sunny for the sixteenth of April. She thought she had barely slept a wink all night, so excited was she. The evening before had been lovely, though it didn't have a perfect start. When Jeremy brought Norah home from the train Gladdie was there at the front door to invite him in, and to spirit him off to the conservatory where they were in deep conversation when Susie tracked him down. She put her head in the doorway and informed him that she and Louise were ready to go, and was he?

"I must go, Glad," he said. "I'll see you tomorrow afternoon."

"What did Gladdie want?" inquired Susie curiously as they joined Louise in the front hall.

"Nothing much," he answered evasively, and led the way out to the car. Norah called her thanks to him from the stairs, and when Gladdie appeared opened her mouth to ask her if there was a problem, then after one look at her sister's face shut it again. Gladdie hurried upstairs, brushing by her without a word, and went to her room, slamming the door behind her.

Louise dined with the Ferris family in the hotel dining room where they were staying. There were potted palms and snowy white linen, and the headwaiter wore tails. It was all very elegant to a student nurse whose meals normally were received on trays while standing in line. Mr. Ferris greeted her effusively, taking her hand and winking slyly at her saying he had got to hold her hand, after all! She blushed, but surprised herself by coming back with a remark that he should let her know when he was going to be in hospital next, that she'd arrange for him to be her patient. Mr. Ferris took her into dinner and pulled the chair out for her. He sat down next to her saying that it wasn't fair for Jeremy to always have the pretty girls. Instead of wondering who else Jeremy had brought home to dinner in the past, she grinned impishly and said soothingly for him not to mind, she was sure he'd make a much better patient than Jeremy.

"I always knew Louise was an intelligent girl," he said to the table in general, smiling fatuously at her.

Susie got into the act then, and there was a lively discussion as to what made a good patient. Jeremy was watching the girls from across the table.

"You're enjoying your training, then?" he asked Louise, as the waiter handed round the menus.

"Oh, Jeremy, yes! So far, anyway! It's wonderful to be on the wards at last, isn't it, Susie, to be actually caring for the patients."

"I think a small glass of wine for the young ladies is in order," Mr. Ferris told the waiter, and they toasted Louise's birthday.

"Is it to be a big party tomorrow?" asked Mrs. Ferris.

"Mama said she'd invited twenty people, that's not including ourselves. She and Dorcas have been baking and cooking up a storm all week, I believe." Her eyes danced. "She has two aunts that don't speak to each other, but she always has to include them in a family gathering. They don't fight. They just ignore each other."

"Fancy!" said Mrs. Ferris. "Are they sisters? Has it been going on a long time?"

141

"Yes. They're her father's sisters, and they've lived across the lane from each other for forty years. Neither will move because the other one would think that she'd won. Their back gardens face each other, so if Aunt Sylvia comes outside, and Aunt Matilda is in her yard, they'll both go back indoors. Isn't it silly?"

"It's very sad," Mrs. Ferris said firmly. "I always wanted a sister to share things with, and I'm sorry I didn't have another daughter so Susie would have a sister. She's enjoying your friendship, you know, dear," she added in a low voice.

"I don't know what started it," Louise said thoughtfully, her mind still on the aunts. "It's always been that way."

"Probably a man involved," said Mr. Ferris sagely. "Women always fight over men."

"Oh, Dad. They do nothing of the kind!" Susie was indignant. "Men aren't worth fighting over."

"I like that!" said Jeremy with a smile.

Gladdie popped into Louise's mind at that moment, and she glanced at Jeremy. He was gazing at her with an unreadable expression on his face.

Afterwards Jeremy brought the girls back to Louise's home, and they found Norah and Mama knitting in the sitting room. Norah was making mittens for the twins, and Mama had offered to help. The two were knitting and chattering away.

"All is ready for tomorrow," smiled Mama, looking up as the girls came in. "All I want is for you to arrange the flowers tomorrow, Louise. You are the best at it. I splurged on tulips and last week I brought in forsythia to force into bloom. It is all in the conservatory."

"I'd love to," she answered. "By the way, Mr. Ferris gave us a small glass of wine tonight. I liked it. May I have some tomorrow, please?"

Not waiting for an answer, she kissed both of them on the cheek, and bid them goodnight.

Now she turned over and stretched, then crept out of bed, so as not to disturb Susie, who was still sleeping. She decided that she'd have her bath early, before anyone got up. Soon she was soaking happily with Norah's bath salts, and planning her morning. Do the flowers; press her new dress that was Mama and Papa's present to her.

"Now that there's a war on, we must be more careful, so I've decided that birthday presents will be practical and useful," Mama had said a few weeks ago when they went shopping for a dress. Louise was careful and noted prices, and didn't choose the most expensive. It would have to do for several seasons, so she chose a style that would carry her through. She was not really aware how very flattering it was, but she only thought it made her look older.

"Happy birthday, my pet," said Dorcas, when Louise came into the kitchen a little later. "Your dear Mama has said we must not spend too much on birthday presents, so I am giving you something that belonged to my dear sister Rachel. I've told you about Rachel, haven't I."

Rachel had been her adored elder sister, and she had died young. Dorcas had several things that had been Rachel's, and they were all her treasures. She went to her room and returned with a small parcel.

"May I open it?"

Dorcas nodded, and Louise opened the box to discover the choker of pearls that Dorcas had often showed them when they were growing up. She never wore it, as it was too small for her. Louise gasped with surprise. It was Louise's favorite piece, and she often admired it.

"Oh, Dorcas! How lovely! Are you sure you want to give it to me?" And she gazed anxiously at the older woman.

Dorcas was pleased with Louise reaction, and nodded. "I can't have them forever, so I thought you should enjoy having this now."

"Oh, thank you!" And she kissed her warmly on the cheek. "It will be perfect to wear with my new dress! You are kind, Dorcas, dear."

"Run along now and put it away safe. I don't want you coming to me weeping and telling me you lost it."

Louise grinned. She knew Dorcas hadn't thought for a moment that she might lose it; however she kissed Dorcas again, and took it upstairs. By this time, Susie was up and dressed, and the two girls admired the pearls as they lay gleaming on their velvet bed.

143

"See how well they go with my dress," she said, holding the jewelry up to the garment.

Susie said that they were perfect together, and then brought out a parcel from her bag. "Happy Birthday," she said.

Louise unwrapped it to reveal two beautiful combs trimmed with pearls. "Your hair always looks so nice when you put it up with combs," she said. "And honestly, I didn't know that Dorcas was giving you the pearls!"

Louise laughed delightedly and held the combs up against her hair.

"They're perfect!" she declared and kissed Susie affectionately.

"You'll be gorgeous tonight," her friend told her.

And indeed she was. Susie helped her dress her hair, and caught her dark curls back with the combs. The new dress was flattering, making her waist appear slimmer, her bosom fuller, and accentuating her slender neck. The pearls lay on her throat, glimmering whitely.

"You look so grown up," said Mama, when she saw her daughter decked out for her party.

"Mama, I am. I'm eighteen!"

Mama sighed.

The guests began arriving at seven o'clock. The lights that Papa had put up in the conservatory flickered and danced in the spring breeze. The huge spray of golden forsythia stood on the hall table in Mama's tall Chinese vase, and the spring bulbs, which she had carefully cultivated in the conservatory, had opened their blooms and were a splash of color on the dining room table. The huge silver punch bowl which Dorcas had polished within an inch of its life reposed itself on the sideboard, filled to the brim with a tangy fruit drink, surrounded by two dozen silver punch glasses. Trays of savories were laid out on the table. Later on there would be a splendid buffet, with hot and cold dishes, followed by a magnificent trifle.

Louise had invited several friends from school that still lived in the neighborhood, the minister and his wife who had known Louise since they had moved into the city, assorted extended family members, including her mother's warring aunts, and of course the whole Ferris family whom she had known since she was tiny. Two of the young men were in uniform, and they and Frank were soon in the corner, discussing their chances of going overseas. Gladdie had agreed to play the piano for the first part of the evening while Mama and Louise greeted their guests at the front door. Mr. and Mrs. Ferris, with Jeremy and Michael, were among the last to arrive. Mr. Ferris first took Mama's hand and smiled at her affectionately.

"Rose, it's been too long since we've seen you. How well you look! You must be proud of your youngest daughter. How lovely she looks and what a splendid nurse she'll make!" He amused Louise by raising her hand gallantly to his lips and murmuring, "When can I hold your hand, my dear?"

Louise blushed, and looked past him to see Jeremy gazing at her admiringly. She scarcely noticed Mrs. Ferris kissing her on the cheek and wishing her many happy returns, for he came forward, taking both of her hands in his and them to his lips.

"How beautiful you look," he whispered.

Louise thrilled from head to toe.

The next part of the evening was a blur. The young men flocked around Louise, everyone danced, even Papa did a turn with Mama's aunts, and when Gladdie declared that it was her turn to dance, Mama played a lively polka, and Gladdie, flushed and smiling, whirled around the room with Jeremy. When they went into supper at ten o'clock, Gladdie managed to find a seat on the stairs next to Jeremy. Mr. Ferris was entertaining Louise in the sitting room and she didn't notice; however, she was having such a good time she probably wouldn't have minded. Susie and Frank found a secluded corner where they chatted enthusiastically, heads together, and their plates lying untouched in their laps.

Later on Gladdie was persuaded to play again.

"Do play for us, Gladdie. You're such a terrific pianist," Jeremy coaxed.

"How about 'There's a Long, Long Trail'?"

As Gladdie began to play, Jeremy took Louise by the hand on to the dance floor and soon there were four or five other couples dancing. Several more were grouped around the piano singing along. Jeremy skillfully steered Louise through the french doors into the conservatory. He paused, closed the doors behind them, and took Louise's hand, leading her to the small stone bench by the little indoor fountain. The room was in darkness, and was illuminated only by the torches in the garden. When they were out of sight of the drawing room, Jeremy stopped, and looked down at her. Louise felt suddenly shy.

"Doesn't the garden look wonderful with Papa's lights?" she said, turning and looking out the windows.

"Louise."

She looked up at him questioningly. He put his finger on her mouth and said, "Hush." Then he stooped and kissed her gently on the lips. He drew back for a moment, then cupped her face in his hands and kissed her again, this time firmly and lingeringly. In all of Louise's dreams she had never envisaged this. In one daydream he came back from the war wounded, and she nursed him back to health; in another Gladdie was unfaithful to him, and he had turned to Louise for comfort.

"Jeremy . . ."

"Hush, my dear," he said softly, and gathered her to him. She trembled in his arms, and he laid her cheek against hers.

"Will you marry me, Louise?"

She was momentarily speechless. "Jeremy, I thought it was Gladdie you came to see."

He laughed a little. "Oh, Louise, my funny darling, it's always been you. Didn't you know I've been waiting for you to grow up?"

She shook her head. "But Gladdie is fond of you . . . ."

"She knows it's never been serious. She's fun to be with, but it's you I want for my wife."

Louise's legs were suddenly weak, and she sat down. Jeremy smiled down at her. "You haven't answered me. And I thought you cared for me a little." Louise shook her head in amazement. It really was true. Jeremy loved her, and not Gladdie!

"Oh, Jeremy, of course I'll marry you! Whenever you want!"

He sat down and retrieved a small container from his uniform pocket. Opening it, he produced a ring, an exquisite circlet of pearls. He drew it onto the third finger of her left hand. Then he took her in his arms and kissed her again, and this time she responded by putting her hands on the back of his neck and drawing his face down to hers.

Presently she whispered, "We should go back."

He nodded; they stood up, and started back, one arm about her waist.

"Student nurses can't get married," he remarked.

"Oh! You're right! What shall we do? Get married secretly?"

He laughed, and then grew serious. "No, darling, I wouldn't marry you secretly and then rush off overseas. What if I should be killed and leave you with a child?"

Louise blushed. He was right, of course. She would have to quit nursing, and there would be such talk. Better to wait and have a splendid wedding when he returned.

"But of course I shan't be killed," he went on. "I just know it. We'll get married when this terrible war is over. I'll come back to you, I promise! Now let's go tell the others."

Norah had been enjoying the party. She had danced with everybody, including Jeremy, and during one turn around the floor he remarked to her how beautiful her little sister had become. She had glanced at him sharply, and he smiled and said, "Yes, I mean Louise. I've quite fallen for her, you know, Norah." So she wasn't surprised when she saw Jeremy spirit Louise away and into the conservatory. She was standing by the piano, this time singing, 'If You Were the Only Girl in the World' to Gladdie's tinkling accompaniment, when she spotted them returning to the drawing room. Jeremy had one arm possessively around her waist. Louise was glowing with happiness. They went to where Mama and Papa were standing watching the dancers, and said a few words, Louise holding up her left hand to them. Norah saw something gleaming on her finger. Papa kissed Louise affectionately and shook Jeremy's hand, then clapped his hands loudly.

"Friends!" he called. "May I have your attention? Jeremy wants to make an announcement."

Norah was watching Gladdie whose fingers now faltered on the keys. She spun the piano stool quickly around in surprise. Norah saw her face go slack with astonishment as Jeremy drew Louise forward,

147

arm still encircling her waist, and announced their engagement. Gladdie's mouth formed an unattractive circle, and her eyes widened, then narrowed. In the rush of congratulations to the couple, no one but Norah saw her slip away.

Norah found her way through the well wishers and hugged Louise fondly.

She then kissed Jeremy firmly on the lips, something she had never done before.

"I'm glad we're to be brother and sister, Jerry," she said, reverting to the old diminutive.

Jeremy hugged her in return. "I'm the happiest man in the world," he declared.

Norah then slipped away upstairs to find Gladdie. She knocked on the door of her room.

"Go away," came her muffled voice from within.

"Gladdie, it's me, Norah. May I talk to you?"

Norah didn't wait for an answer but opened the door and walked in. She found her sister hunched in her big upholstered chair, staring out the window. She had not shed tears, but the expression on her face was a mixture of anger and astonishment.

"Gladdie . . ."

"I can't believe it. That chit of a girl has stolen Jeremy from me. I can't believe it. I won't believe it!"

"Gladdie, did Jeremy ever make you think it was you he wanted to marry?"

Gladdie turned and glared at her sister. "Well, we've been on—affectionate terms," she said.

"What does that mean? He's kissed you once or twice? You should know by now that Jeremy is a bit of a flirt," Norah said seriously.

"I know he was in love with me. I know it. How could he ask her to marry him? How could he?"

"Gladdie, you'll have to come down and speak to them . . ."

"I won't. Tell them I've got a headache. And I'm going back to Mrs. Marchbanks' first thing in the morning. I won't stay in the same house with that brat. Little hussy! I wonder what she's done to make him forget me?"

"Gladdie! What are you insinuating—"

"A girl that works as a skivvy, then goes into nursing—I've heard nurses have loose morals."

"Gladdie! I'll forget you've said such a thing. I know you're upset." Norah was shocked.

Gladdie glared at her again. "Just go away and leave me alone." Norah went slowly downstairs where Papa was filling wine glasses and passing the drinks around for a toast. Mama saw Norah and raised her eyebrows at her questioningly.

"Gladdie's gone to bed with a headache," she said simply.

"Is she very upset?"

"Yes."

Mama pressed her lips firmly together and turned to join in the toast. Norah found a glass pressed into her and, and soon everyone was sipping wine and laughing and talking. Later, Norah heard Louise and Susie talking excitedly into the night. And in the morning Gladdie was true to her word. She was up and gone before anyone came down to breakfast.

Chapter Eighteen

NORAH AND HARRY

Norah found herself pouring out her heart to Harry.

Louise is still walking on air, she wrote one day early in June, *even though her fiancé is gone overseas. We said goodbye to Jeremy and Frankie last week. Have you heard of Lieutenant-Colonel John MacRae, Harry? He composed a wonderful poem called 'In Flanders Fields' just before he was killed in battle. It was published only a short while ago, but it already has made him famous. What a wonderful thing the transatlantic cable is! I read the poem and wept. Frankie was absolutely thrilled with it. 'We're taking up the quarrel with the foe,' he told me. 'We won't fail Colonel MacRae.' So many boys have died already, Harry.*

I'm worried about Gladdie, too. She hasn't been home for a visit since Louise's birthday party. I went to see her at Mrs. Marchbanks' the other day when I was in town. She was polite but very distant. She says she will live there permanently from now on. Mama is very upset. Papa is bewildered. I don't think he has an inkling that both his daughters are in love with Jeremy Ferris. Dorcas says nothing. Mama put an announcement of their engagement in the Perth newspaper as well as the Ottawa edition, and now people in Perth are gossiping about me. The talk is that Jeremy and I were courting, and he dropped me for my youngest sister! Can you believe that? I thought I had convinced the school trustees last year that he was just a family friend. Just because he squired me around a few times when he was home visiting his parents... I already have been thinking about moving and teaching elsewhere, perhaps renting a small cottage instead of boarding. There are teaching positions open in other towns, and I think I am ready for a change. I'm not really running away, Harry....

You will meet my brother Gerald very soon! Perhaps Bernice has already mentioned this. She wrote Gerald last month, and asked him if he would consider coming to Fairlea and help her run her farm. I never dreamed that Gerald would even consider it. I knew he wasn't really happy with his job, but I've never thought of him as a farmer. However, he says he'd rather work on a farm than make munitions for the war effort. He's just as cynical about this war as I am. I guess I should be grateful for people like Jeremy and Frank who are willing to go to war for king and country, but all I can think about is their getting maimed or killed. And for what purpose? Louise feels much the same as I do, though she's still proud of her brave fiancé and brother.

The only good tidings I have to report is that I am definitely going west next month for Barbara's wedding. I told you about Barbara, didn't I, my friend who is teaching in British Columbia. She met a handsome Mountie (her words) and is marrying him in July and wants me to be her maid of honor. We met and became good friends in high school after we moved back to the city, and then we went to college together. I think I shall stay for two or three weeks, stopping at Banff on the way home. I've always wanted to see the Rockies.

So all the Laurier sisters are traveling this summer. Louise is accompanying the Ferris family to Winnipeg in July. According to Louise, Mr. Ferris has a brother who lives in Winnipeg, and apparently they've been estranged for many years. His nephew got in touch with him recently to say his father was ill and wanted to see him. So the whole family is traveling out there in July when Susie and Louise have their summer holiday. I think I may be leaving about the same time. Gladdie is going south to the States with Mrs. Marchbanks—Washington, DC, I think.

I started off telling you about Gerald, and didn't finish. He will be arriving at Bernice's in a week, will stay for a few weeks, and if he decides to give it a try, come home and wind up his affairs here. His fiancée, Rhoda, wrote him a letter from Toronto breaking their engagement. I thought he'd be heartbroken, but he's quite philosophical about it. He has

151

not had a happy year—rejection by the army, losing his job, and now his fiancée. Perhaps a new life in a new place is just he needs. I hope you and he will become friends. I'm very fond of Gerald.

This letter has been one long moan, and for that I apologize. Though isn't that what friends are for? We still are friends, aren't we?

Give my love to the children and tell them I will write to them soon. Norah.

Harry Kidd sat on the back porch enjoying the afternoon rays of the sun reading Norah's letter. He leaned back in his chair, the letter in his lap, and was lost in thought for a long time. It was only when Mrs. Hastie came and called him for supper that he roused himself, went upstairs and put the letter carefully away.

Then he washed his hands and went down to eat.

"Norah sends her love," he told the twins. "She says she'll be writing to you soon."

"Dad," said Sarah, "are you going to marry her someday?" Harry hesitated, and glanced at Mrs. Hastie, who was busy at the stove serving the vegetables. She turned and placed the bowls on the table.

"Mr Kidd," she said frankly, "you can speak in front of me. I would never repeat anything I heard in this house."

Harry looked into the honest face that was regarding him affectionately, and he believed her. She opened the oven door, retrieved the roast beef, placed the platter in front of him and handed him the carving knife and fork, then sat down. Harry always insisted she eat with them. ("Only when you don't have company," she had answered.)

He carved the roast in silence, and handed the meat around. Mrs. Hastie served the vegetables. Ben didn't want rutabaga, but she insisted.

"Come on, now, you must try it. I put butter and cream and brown sugar in it," she coaxed.

Sarah regarded her father solemnly waiting for an answer.

"I don't know," he answered finally. "I hope so. How do you feel about it?"

"Oh, I love her! I do hope she wants to marry you. So does Ben, don't you, Ben?"

"Would I have to call her 'Mother'?"

"I am sure she would want you to call her whatever makes you feel comfortable," Harry said.

"Would Mrs. Hastie have to go away?" Ben persisted.

"Not a bit of it," his father declared. "Why, we couldn't do without Mrs. Hastie, could we?"

Mrs. Hastie beamed. "I hope it works out, Mr. Kidd. Miss Laurier is a nice young lady."

"Norah's brother is coming to help Miss Bernice on the farm," Harry told them. "His name is Gerald, and you'll be meeting him soon."

"He'd be sort of an uncle, won't he?" asked Sarah. "What fun! We don't have any aunts or uncles, do we? Well, except for Aunt Sophie, and she's your aunt, isn't she."

"Why don't we?" asked Ben, absentmindedly eating his rutabagas.

"Because neither your mother nor I had any brothers or sisters," he explained.

"Would Miss Bernice be a sort of aunt then?" Sarah inquired. "She's Norah's aunt, isn't she."

"Yes, she's Norah's aunt. And so is Mrs. Lesley in Charlottetown. Children, would you like to visit your grandmother for a few weeks next month?"

"I guess so," said Sarah doubtfully. "Will you be coming, too?"

"No. Mr. Gerald Laurier will be visiting his aunt for a few weeks, and then will be going back to Ottawa. Perhaps I will go with him."

"You could visit Norah while you are there," suggested Ben helpfully.

"The very thing!" Harry said, smiling. "What a good idea."

Gerald arrived two days later, and he and Bernice paid the Kidd farm a visit soon after. He had a parcel for the twins. Harry strode down from the barn and the two men shook hands. They looked each other up and down, each assessing the other. Gerald was the taller of the two, with a thick thatch of light brown hair and a pair of keen hazel eyes. Harry had thought he would be rather pale and pallid, having lived in the city, but he was mistaken in this, for Gerald liked sports, and kept himself lean and fit by exercising regularly. Gerald saw a wiry man, perhaps half a dozen or more years older than he, skin tanned from being out of doors, hair the color of polished mahogany, and two very bright blue eyes under thick brows. The brows dominated the thin face, but Gerald liked his looks. So this was Norah's friend! He wondered how she really felt about him.

They walked around the property.

"The two farms were originally one," Harry explained, "but were split and sold separately. I've been telling your aunt that they should really be run together. You could raise more stock if the meadow down by the road was drained and planted with hay. My barn, here, is the original one. It's constructed of stone, and is as sound as when it was built fifty years ago."

"I know next to nothing about farming," confessed Gerald. "I shall be just a laborer at first, while I learn. I hope that Bernice will be patient with me."

"I have some books you could read," suggested Harry, "and I'll answer any questions you have. Don't think anything is too trivial to ask about."

He was pleased that Gerald would be staying. He realized he had missed the company of a male friend. He and John Crocker had been such good friends.... Harry shivered. Someone walking over his grave, as his father used to say.

"Norah mentioned that you would be returning to Ottawa to move properly," he now said. "Would you mind if I went back with you?"

Gerald looked at him keenly. "Will you be wanting to see Norah?"

"Yes. I want to see her before she goes off to her friend's wedding."

"Oh, yes. Barbara Collins. They've been good friends for ten years. She's marrying a policeman, I believe."

Harry couldn't have cared less whom she was marring, only that by marrying she was dragging Norah five thousand miles away. Norah was planning to resign her position in Perth. What if she should decide to stay out West?

"It would be good to have your company," Gerald went on warmly. He had decided that this man was good enough for his sister. If she decided to marry him, she would be living next door, and Gerald thought that it would be splendid. He was fond of his sister Norah.

"You would certainly be welcome to stay with us while you are in Ottawa," Gerald said.

Harry hesitated. "It probably would be better if I went to a hotel," he demurred.

Gerald thrust his hands in his pocket. Harry was probably right. What if Norah decided she didn't care for the fellow? It would be rather awkward for them both.

"There's a small inn on the canal not too far from where we live. Louise's prospective in-laws stayed there when they came for her birthday party in April. They said it was very comfortable."

Having made up his mind to go and find out how he and Norah felt about each other, Harry put all thoughts of her aside for the time being. He would telephone her when they decided when they were to leave. He smiled. Gerald was amazed how the smile transformed the man's face.

"Good. It's settled, then. Now, down to business."

Norah's school year was over. She had bade her students goodbye, and the younger ones who would be returning in the fall were mourning the fact that she would not be there. They had put their heads and their pennies together and bought her a gift of a china cup and saucer in a pattern of forget-me-nots.

"That's so you won't forget us, Teacher," they said, as Norah unwrapped it and was admiring it. She held it up to the light and showed them how they could see the shadow of her hand behind it.

"It's translucent," she said, and explained the meaning of the word to them. "It's a lovely gift, and I shan't forget any of you."

She had given her notice to Mrs. Talbot, and had begun to pack her trunks, but before she left she visited two women with whom she had become friends during the five years she had been teaching in Perth.

155

One tactlessly brought up the fact that there had been gossip over Norah's sister becoming engaged to Jeremy Ferris.

"It annoys me that everyone takes for granted that it is always the man that drops the woman," she remarked over a cup of tea. "I've told them I am sure you refused him and he then took up with your sister." Norah found herself extremely annoyed with her friend.

"There has never been a romance between Jeremy Ferris and me," she replied shortly.

Her friend looked skeptical and changed the subject. Norah went away knowing that her friend thought she had been just saving face.

"It's not as if you can't come back and visit us," said the other one as they sat in her back garden seeking a breeze. It was a hot, sticky day. "Ottawa isn't that far away."

Norah wasn't sure that she would be returning for visits. Her second friend had been more tactful than the first, but her solicitous manner made Norah feel that soon she might pat her back kindly and declare that all men were cads.

She went back to Mrs. Talbot's in a black mood that was aggravated by the heat and the airless condition of her room. How had she put up with these cramped conditions for five years? she thought irritably, as she finished her packing. She had to pay extra for a delivery wagon to pick up her luggage and take it to the train station. How on earth had she managed to accumulate all this stuff? She sat on the train, her book lying in her lap unread, unreasonably annoyed at Jeremy and Louise, and relieved that she had she had seen the last of the gossipy, petty town.

She came home to an almost empty house, as Val and Louise had gone to spend a couple of weeks at Ottey Lake where the Ferris family had a cottage.

"They'll be back before you leave on your trip," Dorcas told her. "Young Michael has decided he doesn't want to go to Winnipeg with the family, so he's coming here to spend the rest of the summer with Val. It won't be so quiet then."

"Have you heard from Gerald?" she asked.

156

"Only that he's decided to take Miss Bernice Laurier's offer up and learn to farm. He'll also be here before you leave. He's not quite sure when he'll arrive."

"I had hoped to be traveling with Barbara's parents, but they've already gone. Barbara has rented a cottage on a nearby lake for them, and they plan to spend the summer seeing British Columbia. I confess I am a little nervous traveling all that way alone. I don't have to go all the way to Vancouver, though, as the train stops at Fort Langley."

Mama and Papa had heard from Frank; he had arrived safely in England, but didn't know when they would be sent across the Channel. They didn't mention Gladdie, who had gone away with Mrs. Marchbanks to Washington, DC, for two weeks, but Dorcas told Norah that she had come to visit her parents the preceding week.

"Oh, that's good! I was afraid—"

"No, it wasn't good, Norah," interrupted Dorcas. "She said some things about Louise that I can't repeat, and accused your mother and father of encouraging her to take Jeremy away from her. She was quite—how shall I say?—irrational about it."

Norah shook her head and wondered if there was anything she could have said to Gladdie that would have made a difference.

Louise and Val came home a week later from the lake, bringing young Michael Ferris with them. It was amazing how full the house felt with two thirteen year olds clattering up and down the stairs, snacking at all hours in the kitchen, sprawling with their long legs akimbo on the sofa in the sitting room reading 'Boys' Own' books, and discussing the war in loud, enthusiastic voices.

"Dorcas caters to them disgracefully," Louise remarked to Norah as the sisters discussed their summer plans. "She lets them raid the ice box any time—they'll eat us out of house and home."

"I'm sure they were doing the same to the Ferrises," Norah responded with a smile. "Let me show you my dress."

"Your bridesmaid dress! How I wish it was for my wedding!"

"Have you heard from Jeremy?"

"Oh, yes! Two letters already! I have them tied up with a blue velvet ribbon," she confided, "and tucked away in my jewelry box."

Norah brought out her dress, which she had made herself. It was of a soft blue fabric, an ankle length skirt cut on the bias so it swirled with every step, and the bodice with the wide fashionable collar. There was a broad brimmed straw hat swathed with matching tulle.

"The hat is an extravagance," she confessed, "but the blue net matches my dress perfectly. I stilled my conscience by saying that I would wear it every summer, and trim it differently." She put it on.

"It does suit you, Norah, your being so tall. I do hope Barbara has lots of photographs taken. You'll look so glamorous. Don't you wish Harry could see you?"

"Do I look so different from the milkmaid he so callously berated?" Norah asked, with pretended coyness.

"He couldn't help falling in love with you straight away," declared Louise loyally, kissing her sister on the cheek.

Louise watched her sister hang up her dress in the wardrobe and put the hat back in the hatbox, carefully tucking the tissue around it. She took a deep breath.

"Norah, have you talked to Gladdie lately?"

Norah glanced at her sharply, and seeing the troubled expression on her face, shook her head. "I went to see her, oh, about six weeks ago when I was in town, but I haven't seen her since."

"Did she talk to you? How did you find her?"

"She was polite, but distant," said Norah, after a moment.

"Norah, she hasn't spoken to me since—my birthday. Was she very upset about Jeremy and me?"

"Yes, she was. She had no idea that he was serious about you." Norah didn't think she would tell Louise about Gladdie's outburst with Mama and Papa.

"Norah, she hates me!"

"Oh, surely, Lou, no. She'll get used to the idea . . ."

"Norah, remember the red coat and hat that she bought two winters ago and decided she didn't like?"

"Yes, didn't she give it to you?"

"Yes, she did. But at Christmas time when she came home from being in Montreal she waltzed into my room and took it back!"

158

"You mean she changed her mind?"

"She said she wondered where it had gotten to, and took it back. She practically accused me of stealing from her."

"I've never seen her wear it."

"I know. Norah, she just didn't want me to have it."

"But why?"

"I don't know. Jeremy admired it once, I can't remember if she was there or not."

Norah pondered. "She must have been jealous of you back then. I wonder if Jeremy said something to her."

"I didn't say anything about the coat to anyone. I was so angry with her. I loved the coat, it made me feel beautiful."

"I know what you mean," Norah said sympathetically. "That's the way I feel about my blue dress. I'd be very upset if something happened to it."

Louise stood up and took Norah's hand. "I want to show you something in my room." Her face was pale. "I haven't told a soul about it."

Norah followed her sister into her bedroom next door, and watched while Louise went into her wardrobe and brought out a bundle of red.

"I found this on my bed when I came home from the hospital three weeks ago."

"It's Gladdie's red coat!"

"Yes. At first I thought she had returned it as a good will gesture—but look, Norah!"

She held the garment up, and Norah could see that it had been hacked and slashed beyond repair. It was in tatters—even the fur trim had been damaged. Great rents were in the lining and the collar and cuffs were hanging in shreds. Louise was regarding the garment again, lips trembling. Ignoring the sick feeling in the pit of her stomach, Norah took the ruined coat out of her sister's hands, dropped it on the bed, and took Louise in her arms.

Louise burst into tears.

"I've tried to forget about it, but I can't! Oh, Norah, why would she do such a thing?"

159

"What a shocking experience, dear!" murmured Norah, patting her back. She could visualize Gladdie angrily hacking at the garment, and the thought chilled her. Dorcas had called her 'irrational'. It probably was a good thing that Louise was going away with the Ferrises.

"Louise, do you trust me to look after this?"

Louise blew her nose. "Are you going to talk to Gladdie?"

"I don't know. I'm not going to tell Mama and Papa, though. They would be very upset, and I don't think they could do anything. Do you mind if I confide in Dorcas? Will you leave it to us?"

Louise nodded doubtfully, regarding her sister with round eyes. Norah drew her down on the bed beside her, and took her gently by the shoulders.

"Look, Louise, I want you to try and put this out of your mind. I didn't say forget it; just don't dwell on it. When you think of it, firmly and deliberately put the thought away." She gave the younger girl a warm hug. "Dorcas and I will not let Gladdie hurt you, do you understand?" She drew back and looked her sister in the eye. Louise nodded, and closed her eyes.

"It's just that I felt so sick when I found it . . . ."

"I don't blame you. I feel the same way myself. I want you to enjoy your trip with Susie and her parents, and then concentrate on your nursing. All right?"

Louise gave a half smile. "Yes. Thank you, Norah. Oh, I'm so glad I told you."

"'A trouble shared is a trouble halved'," she quoted, and gatheredup the remains of the coat. "I'll get rid of this. Just put it out of your mind, Lou. We needn't talk about this again."

Norah took the coat to her room, found a paper sack, put the ruined garment in it, and took it downstairs to the kitchen. Dorcas was in her room next to the kitchen reading.

"Do you have a few minutes, Dorcas?" she asked.

"Of course, Norah. I was just finishing my chapter before I start supper."

"I'll help you with supper, Dorcas. I want to talk to you."

Dorcas put the book down. "What's wrong, Norah?"

160

Norah closed the door behind her and sat down beside the older woman. "Louise just showed me this—" And she drew the red coat out of the bag. "This was on her bed when she came home three weeks ago. Was that about the time that Gladdie was here?" And she repeated to Dorcas what Louise had told her.

Dorcas put her lips firmly together and slowly shook her head. "I was afraid she'd do something."

"Do you think this is just malice or is she—unbalanced?"

Dorcas pondered this. "I don't know, lassie. I've been wondering if something was on Louise's mind. I just assumed she's been worrying about Frankie and Jeremy." She took the coat, put it back in the bag, and thrust it out of sight in her cupboard by her bed. "It was right for you to come to me, and not to your Mama. This would upset her no end." She got up. "Now you let me think on this problem, and perhaps I can come up with a plan of action. Will you set the table for me? And then I need you to peel some taties."

The telephone rang that same evening while they were still sitting around the dining room table. It was Val's turn to help clear the table, and he was coming back from the kitchen when the bell jangled. The telephone was located in the hallway between the kitchen and dining room, and he grabbed the receiver as he went by.

"Hullo? Regent 101 ... yes ... yes, she's here. Norah!" he yelled. "It's for you! Charlottetown calling!"

Norah jumped to her feet in surprise. Val thrust the receiver into her hand. "Do you know a Mr. Kidd?" he hissed.

Norah's face flamed. "Yes, of course, Val," she said. "Hello?" she spoke into the mouthpiece. "Yes, it's me," she went on ungrammatically. "I'm fine, how are you and the children ... I can hardly hear you .... Oh! That will be just fine ... yes; I'll do that ... yes ... that's right. Yes, please ... Gerald? You sound so far away .... Everything's fine here, yes, we'll look forward to seeing you. Yes, I'll tell them. Bye bye."

She replaced the receiver in its hook and turned to the family. "That was Mr. Harry Kidd and Gerald," she said unnecessarily. Her cheeks were still flushed. "They're traveling up to Ottawa together, leaving tomorrow."

"Did you ask him to stay here?" asked Mama.

161

"I didn't get a chance. He wants me to make a reservation at the inn where the Ferrises stayed. And they'll be on the Friday afternoon train, Papa. Gerald wants to know if you can pick them up."

Norah found that her heart was thumping rapidly, and that her cheeks still felt warm. She busied herself helping Val stack plates, and brought in the dessert and coffee. Later when she and Louise were alone in the sitting room, she said, "All I could think to say was 'fine'. A million other adjectives, and all I could say was 'fine'. He'll think I'm such an idiot."

"Do you think he's coming to propose?"

"Oh, Louise, I don't know! I don't even know how I feel about him!"

"You'll know when you see him," said Louise comfortingly.

"What if he takes one look at me and finds that he doesn't care?"

"Norah! Don't be such an idiot!"

Norah laughed and kissed her sister's cheek affectionately. "You're right! I am being an idiot. But it's so sudden—and I'm going away next week to Barbara's wedding—when are you and the Ferrises leaving, by the way?"

"Next Wednesday—don't tell me we're on the same train."

"What fun! And I was a bit nervous traveling by myself. Now I'll have friends until Winnipeg."

Norah chastised herself many times in the next two days for her nervousness, her apprehension, and for not knowing her own heart. She and Harry had been writing to each other for nearly a year now, and although she hadn't seen him since last September, she would have thought she was getting to know him through his letters. She decided suddenly that long distant relationships were easier in a way. You wrote letters, and you received letters. You could think through what you wanted to say, and then write it. Face to face conversations were more difficult. It was easy to express oneself in writing, she thought ruefully. She tossed and turned until the thin fingers of dawn crept into her room, then she slept.

Papa and the boys went to the station that afternoon to meet the train. Norah nervously bathed and dressed, the knot of apprehension that had been forming all day in her midsection so large it seemed almost hard for her to swallow. She looked at herself in the mirror, and saw a pale, worried reflection of herself. She tried to smile, but her face seemed to resemble a grinning skull.

"This is ridiculous," she said out loud. "Where's my sense of humor? It won't be the end of the world if I discover that I don't love him, or vice versa."

She put on her brightest dress, sat down, and tried to read her newest book from the library. When she heard the murmur of voices downstairs, she went down. Gerald was there, large and smiling, his voice booming happily in a way she hadn't heard for months. He gave Norah a huge bear hug.

"We dropped Harry off at the hotel," he told her. "He wanted to clean up. He's coming for dinner, but he said he'd walk. I should think he'd be here in an hour or so."

She wasn't sure if she felt disappointment or relief.

"You look just fine!" she exclaimed. "You're pleased about becoming a farmer?"

"Norah, I think it's the best decision I've ever made. Isn't Aunt Bernice just grand?"

"And isn't the Island lovely?"

By this time, Mama and Louise had come in from the garden, Dorcas was in the doorway, smiling at him, and everybody was talking at once. Norah slipped away upstairs to her room, tidied her hair, then went halfway down the stairs to the landing and pushed open the french doors that led on to a balcony at the front of the house. She often sat there at the end of a hot day to catch the evening breeze. It also afforded a good view down the street in the direction from which Harry would be coming. It was a quiet afternoon, with little traffic of any sort on their street. Presently she saw the figure of a man in the distance, striding purposefully her way. It was Harry. There was no mistaking that walk. She remembered the first time she had seen him, coming across the field to the corn patch to rescue his cow from the two city women next door. Only she and Louise had thought he was the hired man, and while he had been rude, she also had been rather haughty with him. And his blue eyes ... .

163

As Harry neared the house, he disappeared behind the hedge, and a moment later she saw him standing in the gateway. The house was perhaps fifty feet from the street, a lilac hedge separating the lawn from the pavement. The gate had a trellis over it on which wistaria grew. In the spring their front yard was a mass of purple and white. There were three steps down from the street to the front walk that was bordered by tulips and daffodils in the spring, and then in the summer by flowering annuals. Her mother had put in scarlet salvia this year. Harry paused in the gateway for a moment, his shoulders sagging a little. Then he straightened up with a gesture she remembered from last summer. Why, she thought, he's as nervous as I am! And in that moment the knot of anxiety dissolved away, and her heart lifted at seeing him. As he came down the steps Norah stood up and leaned over the railing.

"Harry!" she called.

He looked up, their eyes met, and they both smiled in unison. "I'll be right down!"

She turned, went through the doors, and down the stairs to the front hall.

When she opened the front door he was standing there, still smiling.

"Norah! It's wonderful to see you," he began, taking her hands in his. Norah was about to suggest they go quickly into the garden, but footsteps in the hall stopped her, and Val's smiling face appeared in the doorway to the small sitting room at the front of the house. He obviously had been watching for Harry as well.

"He's here!" he called. "Norah's lover is here!"

Unexpectedly, Norah chuckled as her eyes met Harry's twinkling blue ones. He whispered, "If only it were so!" and she blushed becomingly.

"We can go for a walk after supper," she said. "Come and meet everybody. On second thought, I guess you've met them all except Dorcas."

Harry followed her down the hall to the big parlor at the back that the family used as a sitting room. He shook hands with Norah's parents, and wished Louise well on her engagement. Dorcas was there, and offered him her bony hand in a firm grip. Her keen eyes looked him over.

"This is Dorcas, without whom our home would fall apart," said Mama with a smile. "This is Mr. Harry Kidd, Dorcas, Bernice's next door neighbor."

"We didn't have the pleasure of meeting when I was visiting the Island last summer," said Dorcas. "I am pleased to make your acquaintance."

"I'm afraid I wasn't a very friendly person last summer," Harry admitted. "I apologize."

Dorcas merely nodded, and remarked that she hoped he liked pot roast. "It will be on the table in ten minutes," she announced. "Louise, will you give me a hand?"

Mama sat Harry on her right, and chatted with him through dinner. Every so often he would glance across at Norah, and smile slowly. She thought her heart would melt away.

After the meal Mama rose and remarked that she would like to show Harry her orchids, and proceeded to whisk him away to the solarium. Norah helped clear the table, and began to rinse the dishes at the sink.

"Now you run along and take that young man for a walk," Dorcas commanded "Be firm with your Mama, now, or she'll have him in there all evening."

Norah smiled gratefully, washed her hands, and took off her apron. Then she went through the parlor into the conservatory where Mama was lecturing Harry on orchid growing. He was looking interested, and asking intelligent questions, but he didn't object when Norah announced she was stealing him away from her mother to go for a walk.

"Have I been boring you, Mr. Kidd?" asked Mama.

"Not at all, Mrs. Laurier," he said sincerely. "A good walk will be nice, though."

Mama smiled. "We'll have coffee in the parlor later on," she said. Norah took Harry's hand and led him out from the conservatory into the back garden.

"There's a pleasant walk along the canal," she said.

Once they were out of sight of the house, Harry stopped. They were alone. "Norah," he said softly, and she went eagerly into his arms. His kiss was warm and tender, and she responded enthusiastically. After a while they disentangled themselves and began to stroll slowly, arms entwined.

"This feels so right," she said softly, her head leaning against his shoulder.

Harry thought he had never felt so happy in his life.

"When will you marry me, Norah?"

"Whenever you want."

He stopped and took her in his arms again, much to the amusement of two boys who suddenly appeared from around the curve of the path walking their dogs. Neither Harry nor Norah cared a wit.

"Shall we go back and tell the others?" he asked.

"Not just yet," said Norah shamelessly. His arms tightened around her. The boys gave a whoop and began to run the opposite direction, the dogs scrambling after them, barking furiously. Norah and Harry gazed after them, looked at each other and laughed.

"Shall we call the twins tonight?" she asked, as they continued their walk hand in hand.

"I have strict orders from Sarah to do just that," he said. "She wants you for her new mama. In fact, she said, 'I'm going to call Norah Mama 'cause that's what she calls *her* mother.' Ben doesn't know what he wants to call you. I don't think he's ready to give anyone his mother's title."

"And they shouldn't!" declared Norah warmly. "Ben should call me what makes him feel the most comfortable."

Harry squeezed her hand, and said in a low voice, "I love you, Norah. I told them that's exactly what you'd say."

"Let's go back and tell the others, and make that telephone call! I want to talk to my new family!"

Harry and Norah talked to his mother and the children while Papa decanted the wine, and soon they were all drinking the happy couple's health in the small front room. Even the boys were allowed a sip, and then were chased off to bed.

166

Norah and Harry were sitting close together on the sofa, their shoulders touching, and between them their fingers interlaced. Harry was softly stroking her palm with his thumb. To Norah it was the loveliest feeling in the world.

The twins had been so excited. Sarah referred to her as 'Mama' already, but Ben asked her wistfully what he should call her.

"Whatever you feel comfortable with, darling," she told him. "Take all the time you want to make up your mind. If you want to go on calling me Norah, that's all right with me."

Mrs. Kidd told her how pleased she was, and asked if she could call Norah's aunt and uncle who lived not too far away. Harry told her they'd let them know their plans, and they rang off. They then tried to get Bernice on the telephone, but they couldn't get through. Harry said he'd send a telegram the next day.

"Her last words to me when she saw us off was, 'Don't hurry back, Harry.'"

Norah was jolted back to the present by her mother gently asking, "What do you think, Norah?"

Norah hadn't been listening, of course. All she was aware of was Harry next to her, and the soft, delicious pressure of his fingers in her palm.

"We're talking about dates, dear," said Mama. "When do you get back from Barbara's wedding?"

"Oh, let me see." She straightened up and thought a moment. Harry did not relinquish possession of her hand. "August 12, I think."

Norah listened with growing dismay at the plans her mother was making.

Church, guests, reception....

"Couldn't we just get married here with the family? I want Louise to be my bridesmaid, that's all—who's to be your best man, Harry?"

"I'd like it simple, too," Harry said eagerly. "Gerald, would you stand up with me?"

"I'd be honored."

"Who would you invite?" inquired Louise. "We can't leave out the awful aunts, and what about Mrs. Kidd and the twins?"

"'Awful aunts'?"

"Rose has two aunts who have been quarreling for years," Papa frowned at Louise as he explained to Harry. "They'd never give us any peace if one was invited and not the other. Only Aunt Matilda was at Louise's birthday, because Aunt Sylvia was away, but I can't see having them if there's only a few guests . . . ."

"I won't have them," said Norah unexpectedly.

"Why don't you elope?" Louise asked. "Just go along to the rectory next week and then catch the train to British Columbia. I'm sure Barbara won't mind your being her matron of honor."

Harry sat up straight. "Your sister is a genius," he told Norah. "She and Gerald could meet us there . . ."

"But what about your mother and the twins?"

"Darling Norah, they're expecting me to bring you home as my wife."

"Mama and Papa, do you mind horribly? It would save a lot of trouble . . ."

"Aunt Sylvia and Matilda would be bound to ask me if I knew that you were getting married, and I don't want to tell lies," said Mama firmly.

Harry was looking thoughtful. "You could tell them truthfully that we didn't tell you when we were getting married. You needn't— um—let on that Louise accidentally spilled the beans, and you happened to be having tea with the Rector's wife at the same time. Um, he does have a wife?"

Mama's eyes twinkled. "Yes, Reverend Wentworth has a very nice wife, we're quite good friends, and I could have her 'accidentally spill the beans' instead of Louise. Matilda can't call down the Rector's wife."

Harry turned to Norah. "Would you like a honeymoon in British Columbia?"

Norah's eyes were shining. "It's the very solution!" She jumped up and embraced her mother. "You don't mind if I don't have a proper wedding?"

"My dear, let me quote you girls—'There's a war on'—and besides, I want you to be happy, and I think you will be happiest marrying Harry immediately."

Papa smiled and hugged her fondly, then said to Mama, "Shall we leave the planning to the children, and wait to hear from Mrs. Wentworth?"

Norah and Harry were married quietly in the Rectory at noon on Tuesday. They saw the Rector on Saturday, and on Sunday after church Mrs. Wentworth took Mama and Papa aside and with a conspiratorial twinkle in her eye asked them for morning coffee on Tuesday at eleven thirty. Not a word was said about weddings.

Tuesday was a fine, warm day, not too humid, so Mama and Papa decided to walk the dozen blocks to the Rectory while Val and Michael stayed behind to help Dorcas with the lunch that would be served afterwards. Norah put on the blue dress that she would be wearing as Barbara's matron of honor. She carefully coiled her hair at the back of her neck, and Louise arranged the hat at a fashionable angle, with the blue tulle trim artfully cascading down to her shoulders. Louise was wearing the dress that she had bought that spring for her birthday, along with a little hat perched jauntily on the side of her head. Gerald, attired in his best suit, got Papa's car started without incident, and the three drove to the Rectory. Louise saw that Harry was there ahead of them, quietly chatting with Mama, Papa, and the Rector.

Louise was to attend many weddings over the years, but she was always to think that her sister Norah's was the most romantic, in spite of its small size and simplicity. Perhaps it was the setting, in the Rector's gracious little parlor, and later in the garden at home when the photographer Harry had arranged for came and took photographs. Her mother's flowers were at their best, and the bright sunshine seemed to make the colors of everything more vivid. Or perhaps it was the company around the dining room table, the smiling faces of the Rector and his wife, Mama and Papa, Gerald, Val and Michael, with Dorcas' delicious meal and Papa's best wine; the spontaneous toasts, laughter and warm conversation. But it was probably Norah and Harry themselves who made it unforgettable for Louise. Norah

169

was beautiful; there was no doubt about it. She had always been the prettiest of the Laurier girls, but today she absolutely glowed. Harry was looking his best in his new suit, and his thin sensitive face was alive with love for his bride. Louise had never seen Jeremy look at her like that; but then, it wasn't Jeremy's way. He didn't wear his heart on his sleeve, while Harry obviously did. Louise sighed and thought it that it might be nice to adored openly by Jeremy.

It was four o'clock before Norah changed out of her wedding attire and put on a traveling suit. Gerald took them and Norah's luggage to the hotel; they would spend the night there, and take the train to Montreal the next morning where they would catch the Transcontinental. Norah had managed to change her reservation for a bedroom and sitting room—Mama and Papa had insisted on paying the difference as a wedding gift. The Ferrises and Louise would be on the same train, too, and would be with them until Winnipeg. The bride and groom would then have another three days to themselves until they reached Fort Langley. Norah had already warned Barbara in a telegram the day before: *Am being married tomorrow. Is it all right if I am your Matron of Honor?* The answer came shooting back the next morning: *Yes! All my love to you both. Looking forward to meeting Harry. It is Harry, isn't it? Love, Barbara.* Norah and Louise laughed over the reply and remarked that it was a jolly good thing it *was* Harry.

Chapter Nineteen

LOUISE 1915-1916

The second day out Norah and Harry invited Louise, Mr. and Mrs. Ferris, and Susie for drinks before dinner. They had a spacious parlor and bedroom; Norah said she felt like the Queen traveling in state. A waiter from the dining car brought cheeses and other savouries to nibble with the drinks, and then withdrew discreetly. Louise was very impressed.

"I had no idea one could travel like this," admitted Norah. "Last summer traveling to the Island was nothing like this. Remember, Louise, our seats made up into beds and we had to go along the corridor to the bathroom."

"And just curtains separating us from everyone else. You could hear people snore," added Louise.

Mr. Ferris was telling Harry about his family in Winnipeg. "My brother and I have been estranged for a long time," he was saying. "We quarreled as young men, and he has lived in Winnipeg and I in Perth for twenty-five years. I've never met his wife or son."

"And now you're going to heal the breach," Harry said.

"He's ill. I believe he is dying. His son wrote and asked us to come. Apparently my sister-in-law isn't well either. I hope this isn't just a financial plea."

"How old is the son?"

"I believe he is twenty-one or two. He told me he is an aviator."

"You mean he flies aeroplanes?" asked Harry.

"Apparently."

"It amazes me how it has caught on. Some say they'll eventually take the place of trains for traveling."

"I can't see that," scoffed Mr. Ferris.

"Nor can I."

They eventually all went out to the dining car for dinner where a special table had been made up for six.

As they dined and chatted, they watched the wilderness of northern Ontario fly by.

"We will see you at home on our way through to the Island," Norah told Louise quietly. "We'll break our journey for a few days and visit Mama and Papa. It will seem strange sharing my room with Harry." And she blushed.

"Norah, you look so happy." Louise looked at her sister questioningly. Norah smiled dreamily. "It's wonderful," she said simply. Now it was Louise's turn to blush. She thought of Jeremy, and what it might be like being married to him. She hoped she would be as happy as Norah.

It was hot and humid in Winnipeg when they arrived the following afternoon. A tall rangy young man was there to meet them with a cab he had hired.

"Uncle James? Aunt Phoebe? I'm Johnnie Ferris. Thank you for coming."

"This is my daughter Susie, and Miss Louise Laurier, my son's *fiancée.*"

Louise found herself gazing up into a face that reminded her vaguely of Jeremy's, with his shock of thick brown Ferris hair, but there the resemblance ended. Whereas on Jeremy the handsome Ferris features were strong and rugged, on his cousin they were more finely chiseled. He was taller and thinner than Jeremy, there were laughter crinkles around his eyes, and he moved gracefully. He smiled down at the girls and shook their hands firmly.

"How nice to meet you, Susie. And Louise—may I call you Louise? After all, we will be cousins one of these days, won't we."

He chatted easily to them all as he supervised the transfer of their luggage into the cab, and assisted Mrs. Ferris into the back seat. When they had all squeezed in, he directed the driver where to take them. Louise was in the front seat with him and he had to put his right arm along the seat back behind her in order to give her room. Louise could smell the soap that he used—sandalwood.

"Dad is looking forward to seeing you. He told me you quarreled years ago, and he's been anxious to make it up."

"Is he very ill, Johnnie?"

"I'm afraid so—it's his heart, and probably just a matter of time now. Mother is rather delicate, and is not coping well, I'm afraid."

"What do you do for a living, Johnnie?" Louise asked him curiously. "I'm in the building trade," he answered, "but my real love is flying. I want very much to join the Flying Corps in England, but I can't even think of it while Dad is so ill. And besides, I don't have the money for my passage. I'm afraid to join up here—I'm just as likely to be sent off with the infantry, when what I want to do is fly."

He went on to talk about his aeroplane that he was flying at the moment. "I don't really own it. But I take people up for rides. Maybe I can persuade you and Susie to take a jaunt with me."

Louise was thrilled. "It sounds absolutely exciting," she said.

Uncle John was a frail, thin man, pale and old looking, who was now confined to bed. He was pathetically glad to see his brother. They left them alone together in the bedroom.

"I was wrong to say what I said," Louise heard him say in a quavering voice, as they closed the door.

Aunt Grace was a small, thin woman, with graying hair, sad blue eyes that gazed vaguely about, and a smooth complexion like that of pale cream rose petals. Her skin fascinated Louise. There was hardly a wrinkle, and she was certainly older than Mama. Susie also remarked on it as they were getting ready for bed in the room they were sharing.

"Aunt Grace is pretty, isn't she. Her skin is so smooth, though she is pale. Didn't Johnnie say she wasn't well?"

"Your mother said so, too. She mentioned to me that we would have to keep our own rooms tidy, and help with the meals. There's no maid or anything."

Susie jumped into bed. "Isn't my cousin Johnnie nice? He looks a bit like Jeremy, doesn't he."

"He's very good to his parents," nodded Louise. She had observed how thoughtful he was to his mother, helping her in the kitchen, pulling out her chair for her at the table, and encouraging her in their conversation.

"Do you think she's, well, a little vague? I don't think she was quite sure who we all were at first."

Louise had noticed how Johnnie had covered up her little lapses. How sad it was!

The next morning Susie and Louise visited with Uncle John in his room. "He has quite a red mark at the base of his spine," said Johnnie worriedly to Louise. "Dad, will you roll over and let Louise see your back? She's a nurse, you know."

"Well, not quite yet," murmured Louise, as she bent to examine the sick man's back. It was the beginnings of a bedsore, she thought. "Do you have rubbing alcohol and talcum? His back needs to be rubbed frequently to encourage circulation of the blood, or the skin breaks down and bed sores form."

Johnnie brought her what she wanted, and she proceeded to give Uncle John a back rub. It was something she always liked to do for her patients, and her patient's reaction now was very satisfying.

"That felt wonderful!" he sighed, as he rolled back onto his back. Louise fluffed up the pillows and made him more comfortable, then filled up a small jug with fresh water and brought a drinking glass.

"Drinking fluids helps healing, too," she told him. "Just take some sips whenever you think of it. Are you in pain?"

He smiled at her. "No, I'm quite comfortable. Thank you, my dear." He smiled at Susie. "I haven't seen your father for over twenty years," he said. "Your brother was just a little boy. You weren't even born yet. I think James told me he has two sons?"

174

"Yes," replied Susie. "Michael is thirteen. He's back home staying with Louise's parents. Louise has a brother about the same age as Michael, and they're good friends."

"I'll rest awhile now, before James comes in for another visit. Will you come back tonight and rub my back before I go to sleep?" he said to Louise. She smiled at him and nodded.

"Of course I will."

And so a pattern emerged over the next week. Louise and Susie both helped Johnnie look after his father in the morning and in the evenings. A few times Louise sat with him while he had a light meal. Once he felt well enough to get up for lunch with the family. Aunt Grace brightened up considerably when her husband was present; she smiled and chattered with Susie's mother, and even made a little joke. One afternoon Louise encouraged Aunt Grace to read to her husband, while they all went out for a walk.

"You are so good to help with Dad," Johnnie said humbly as they walked down to the river, which wasn't far away. "And here you're supposed to be on vacation."

"I think we're all here to help," Louise responded quietly. "Mr. Ferris is arranging with the doctor for the district nurse to come in regularly. And Johnnie, if you need help in the night, don't hesitate to wake me up. I like your father—he's a dear."

"Thank you, Louise," he said, his voice breaking a little.

They walked in silence for a while, then Johnnie said, "Susie was telling me that your sister just got married, and that you were all actually on the same train."

"Yes. I teased her that we were on her honeymoon with her." Louise found herself telling Johnnie how she and Norah had met Harry a year ago, and about the case of mistaken identities. "He was rude and miserable to her, and she gave him back as much—Norah wouldn't take anything sitting down—and then they proceeded to fall in love with each other. I thought she was crazy, actually, because I didn't like him at all at first!"

"You like him now?"

"Oh, yes, Johnnie! He just worships the ground she walks on, and she's just as nutty about him, and his two children. They're on their way to Fort Langley, British Columbia."

"What a peculiar destination for a honeymoon."

"Oh, Norah was going out to be a bridesmaid for her friend who's getting married next week. I honestly think Harry came roaring out from PEI because he thought she might disappear on him. You should have seen them, holding hands and stealing kisses when they thought no one noticed." And she laughed at the memory.

"And you're nicely engaged to my cousin Jeremy. Did you not consider getting married before he went overseas?"

Louise blushed. "I would have," she confessed shyly, "if I hadn't been in nurse's training. But Jeremy thought it wouldn't be fair." She held up her left hand. "I have his ring, and he writes long letters, and I can hardly wait until he comes home." They both admired the little hoop of pearls. "I wear it on a chain around my neck when I'm in uniform," she went on.

"Well, I can tell that you're a born nurse," he declared, taking her hand and tucking it into his arm. "Dad thinks you're wonderful."

That night he took her at his word and woke her up around two o'clock in the morning. She threw on her dressing gown and went into Uncle John's room, where the sick man was moaning with pain.

"The doctor gave me a hypo and showed me how to use it," he said. "Frankly, Louise, I'm frightened to give it to him. Can you do it?"

Louise nodded and went into the bathroom and washed her hands. She rather admired Johnnie for admitting his weakness. She hadn't given many hypos, and only under supervision, but she knew she had to help Johnnie and his father. She found that it was easy. She relaxed and tried to remember what Miss Love had said, and then she pinched the skin and gave the injection. She and Johnnie made him comfortable, and she said she'd sit with him for a while until he went to sleep. The drug made him wander a little in his mind, and he kept saying how wonderful it was that she would be marrying Johnnie.

"We'll have a lovely nurse in the family who can look after Grace after I've gone. I'm so worried about leaving her, Louise," he went on in his quavering voice. "She's not quite right, you know, my dear. I expect you've noticed. She forgets things and sometimes she doesn't know what day it is." He took her hand and clutched it. "Promise me you'll look after Grace." Louise didn't know what to say. He would be so upset if she told him that he was confused, that she was to marry his nephew, not his son. Finally she said, "Put it out of your mind, Uncle John. Johnnie and Susie and I will all look after Aunt Grace."

He was satisfied with her answer, and soon fell asleep. She went out to the kitchen where Johnnie had made tea. He hadn't turned on the light, just lit candles, and he was sitting at the table with his hands around a mug of tea in the pool of light. He turned when he heard her come into the room. Silently he poured tea into another cup and invited her to sit down. It was a curiously intimate experience sitting with him in the darkened kitchen lit only by two candles.

"I expect you think I'm a poor sort of fellow who can't even give his dying father an injection," he muttered.

Full of sympathy, Louise reached out and put her hand over his.

"It takes great courage to admit you're afraid," she said softly. "You've been going through a terrible time. It took me ages to feel comfortable even holding a hypodermic." She sipped her tea. "Johnnie, he's very worried about your mother."

"So am I," he replied, putting his face in his hands. "You must have noticed how confused she is sometimes. I'm afraid she's going to need someone to look after her all the time. Dad was doing that, you know. I believe it brought on his heart condition, or else made it worse." He gazed at her. "You see why I can't even think of joining up. I mean I do think of it, and it makes me feel guilty that I want to run away."

"Oh, Johnnie, don't feel guilty! You can't leave your parents! They come first, don't they, even before your country. My brother Gerald and Norah's husband both tried to enlist, and they were found to be medically unfit. They were devastated! Just think of yourself as unfit in another way. Perhaps you can get your mother into a nursing home . . ."

"There are no places for her. She's well physically, maybe a little frail, but it's her mind . . . ." He put his head into his hands again. "I won't put her in an asylum."

Louise drank her tea, and then got up. She said to him in a kindly way, "Go back to bed, Johnnie. Things always seem the worse at three o'clock in the morning."

He nodded, managed a smile, and blew out the candles, plunging them into darkness. He stood up and took her arm.

"Let me show you the way to your room. I'll look in on Dad, and then go to bed. Thank you, Louise, for your help." She felt him squeeze her hand, and then he was gone.

It was two mornings later that Louise came out of the bathroom at six o'clock and saw Johnnie standing outside his father's bedroom.

"I slept all night! He didn't wake me up—" He pushed open the door and they both went in. Louise heard his intake of breath. "Oh, no . . ." Uncle John was lying there in his bed, the morning sun shining through the oak trees outside the window making flickering shadows on his face.

Louise saw at once that he had died.

"Oh, if only I had wakened up. What if he was calling me?"

She put her hand on his arm and said gently, "Johnnie, stop and look. See how peaceful he is. I think his heart just stopped beating and he passed away in his sleep."

They went over to the bed together and gazed down upon the old man. Louise, from force of habit, took his arm and felt for a pulse, but of course there was none. She laid his hand down gently and looked up at Johnnie.

"He's gone. Very peacefully."

She saw the tears forming in Johnnie's eyes and watched them spill over onto his cheeks. Without thinking she put her arms around him, pressing her cheek against his chest. She just held him and murmured comforting sounds, they way you would comfort a child. His arms wrapped around her and he wept silently on her shoulder.

Presently he straightened up, fumbling for a handkerchief.

"Would you like me to leave you with him? I could call the doctor, if you like."

"Thank you, that would be a big help." His voice was a little stiff, but Louise understood that his tears had embarrassed him. She gave his arm a little squeeze, and went out to the telephone.

There was so much to do. Mr. Ferris and Johnnie spent the next few days going through his papers, seeing his solicitor, and making funeral arrangements. Johnnie sent a telegram to his aunt and uncle in Halifax.

"Uncle Stan is mother's brother," he explained. "They were out here two or three years ago visiting, and I got to know them quite well. Aunt Mabel is very nice, and was awfully good to mother. I certainly don't expect them to come to the funeral, but I'm sure they would want to know what has happened."

The funeral was held in the Roman Catholic church, as Uncle John had become a Catholic when he married Grace. Father Lapierre was very kind, the church was full of parishioners and friends who brought food to the house and expressed their condolences.

In the short time they had been there, Mrs. Ferris had become very attached to her sister-in-law.

"We can't go home without finding someone to come and look after her." she said to her husband. "It's not right that Johnnie should be completely responsible. The poor young man, he's completely exhausted."

"I think you young people should go out and have a good time," she told Louise and Susie. "Johnnie needs to relax for a change."

Louise agreed, but she wondered if Johnnie would agree. To her surprise he suggested his taking the two girls out to a dance at Winnipeg Beach. There was a dance pavilion there, he said, perfectly respectable. He knew some of the band members, because his father had once played the drums and xylophone with them. There was a train that went out in the morning, and returned at midnight. People took a picnic lunch with them, they swam and sunbathed, then went to the dance later on. There was always a buffet supper and it was reasonably priced. Were they interested?

To Louise and Susie it sounded like heaven.

"You met Peter MacLean at the funeral, my friend with the red hair, do you remember? He would go with us, I am sure, and he's amusing to be with."

They had a wonderful time. It was a hot day, and the water was cool and refreshing. They enjoyed the lunch the girls had packed, and afterwards the four went for a long walk on the footpath along the lake edge. It was pleasant in the woods, but, Johnnie warned them, at dusk the mosquitoes appeared, so it would be better to be back at the pier by then and get changed for the dance. There were change huts on the beach, and Louise and Susie replaced their bathing togs for pretty summer dresses and comfortable dancing shoes. Lights were being lit along the path up to the hall, and torches on the big deck outside the dancing area. In another room the buffet was laid out, and would be available all evening. The orchestra was warming up, and men and women of all ages were streaming to the hall. Some of the young men were in uniform; there was much chatter and laughter.

"If you ever come again you should come in winter, and go skating with me," said Johnnie, as he found a table. "Yes, do join us," he said to another couple who were also looking for a place to sit. "Or we could go to a ladies' hockey game. The telephone company has a league whose teams compete with each other. There's this one girl, well woman, really, she's a few years older than I am—she's a fantastic player. I think her team has scarcely ever lost. She comes dancing here, too, you might meet her."

Louise found that Johnnie was an excellent dancer. The music was fast and rhythmic, and he led most expertly. When she complimented him on his talent, all he said was, "The only thing I like better than dancing is flying," he smiled, as he took her hand. "When will you come up with me?"

Louise decided to be reckless. "Anytime you want." She slept most of the way back on the train. "She's very tired," Susie remarked to her cousin.

"She was wonderful with Dad," Johnnie said. "What a sport! She's agreed to go up with me in my flying machine. How about it, Susie?"

Susie shook her head. "You'd never catch me. Have you gone up, Peter?" The redheaded young man shook his head. "Not my idea of a good time," he said. "Say, Johnnie, are you joining up soon? I've decided to."

"Not until I get someone to look after Mother full time. I can't leave her."

Peter shook his head gravely. "I'm sorry she isn't well. How is she taking your dad's death?"

"She's lost without him," said Johnnie sadly. "It's great that Susie's parents are here. I think they'll stay for another week, what do you say, Susie?"

"Mother said she wouldn't leave Aunt Grace until you find someone to look after her."

Johnnie glanced down at the sleeping Louise, and his eyes softened.

"Good," was all he said.

October, 1915

I met your cousin Johnnie this summer, Louise wrote to Jeremy. *He's a very nice person—you'd like him. He was quite broken up by his father's death. Your parents decided to stay until they found someone to care for his mother. Aunt Grace isn't at all well, and needs someone with her.*

I had my first flight, Jeremy! It was so exciting, and I'll never forget it. I had to put on a helmet and goggles and leather jacket—it was cold up there! We were only up about fifteen minutes, but I could have stayed all day. The buildings on the ground were like toys. It got rather bumpy. Johnnie said that was the warm air rising off the ground. He landed us as gentle as can be—just a little bump, and we were on the ground. He hopes to get to England next year and join the Flying Corps. He's saving for his passage overseas. Your father offered him the money, but he refused. He said we'd done enough for him by coming to Winnipeg and staying for four weeks. Susie and I went dancing with him several times.

Louise pause in her letter writing. She would never forget her flight with Johnnie. She remembered how he glanced back at her (her seat was behind him) and she could see his smiling eyes behind his goggles. And it seemed quite natural for him to take her hand as

181

he helped out of the machine, and hold it all the way to the car. They were just good pals—but would Jeremy understand?

I missed Norah and Harry by several days when they passed through Ottawa on their way back to the Island. Mama and Papa said they had a wonderful visit with them. They like Harry very much. It's hard not to like him when you see how much he loves Norah. And she is just as crazy about him. I have a standing invitation to go to the Island, and now with Gerald next door at Aunt Bernice's, Mama and Papa may make the trip—perhaps at Christmas. We could all go! Norah writes that the twins are fine and she loves being a mother. I wonder when they will have a family of their own. She is going to teach at the local school until a substitute can be found, because the teacher has enlisted in the army.

Nursing is going well. My first year will be over at Christmas. Speaking of Christmas, there will be a parcel on the way to both you and Frankie. Do you ever see Frankie? Or are you all tied up with whatever you're tied up with? Your job sounds very mysterious. Frankie wrote from France yesterday. He sounded cheerful, and just impatient to get the dirty job done and to come home.

Christmas came, and the Laurier family, save for Gladdie, went to Fairlea for the holiday. Louise stayed with Norah and Harry. She was astonished how much the twins had grown in a year and a half. They were 'going on eight' now, and feeling quite grown up. They were also delighted to have their stepmother as their teacher, though they found it very difficult to call her 'Mrs. Kidd'. It was a merry time, there was lots of snow, and Louise played with Sarah and Ben every day. She enjoyed renewing her acquaintance with Mary and Pierre, and even Jed seemed pleased to see her. He grumbled about his sciatica, but he managed to remark to Louise that 'your sister did seem to be making Mr. Kidd happy'. The twins adored her. Even Ben was calling her 'Mama' now, as his sister had done from the start.

Norah was happy and fulfilled; she was teaching, bringing up two fine children, content in her relationship with her husband. Louise could see that she and Harry were also friends—sharing their thoughts, problems and celebrations with each other. When Louise shyly asked her about children of their own, Norah replied serenely that she was looking forward to babies whenever they happened.

Chapter Twenty

LOUISE 1916

Louise and Susie began their second year of nurse's training in January, and fifteen new students joined them. Louise felt quite mature and experienced as she watched the new recruits on their orientation gazing about with round eyes as they toured the wards. Miss Ramage, the new Director of Nurses, who had begun her work at the beginning of the year, escorted them. Miss Love was preparing to leave her interim position, and there was talk that she would be going back to England to take up a post there. The girls in Louise's class had a meeting one day in mid-January, and decided to hold a farewell tea for her, for during their first year they had become quite attached to her. Louise talked to the cook in the hospital kitchen and arranged for tea, bread and butter, and fruitcake to be served in the lounge one day the following week. Miss Love was very touched by the gesture, and she chatted to them all in quite a human manner.

"The new students will look up to you all, you know," she said finally, "so you have a reputation to maintain. I am quite sure you will do your job very well. I have enjoyed this year with you."

"Are you going back to England?" asked one curiously.

"Yes, there is a position waiting for me. There is such a shortage of nurses with this dreadful war on. I'll be leaving in three weeks."

"I can't let you go without thanking you for your interest and urging me to enroll," Louise said to her in a low voice, as Miss Love was getting ready to leave. "I love nursing. I'm so glad you gave me that gentle push."

Miss Love smiled. "You're most welcome, Miss Laurier. I'm positive that you'll make a fine nurse. Keep up the good work."

Louise felt that she was losing a friend. And to think she had called her a dragon at first!

That year passed quickly for Louise. While the war raged in Europe, Louise emptied bedpans, bathed and massaged patients, made beds, carried trays, tidied wards, measured mixtures, and counted pills. She saw her first birth, wide-eyed and disbelieving, and shed unashamed tears as she regarded the new young mother gazing rapturously at her tiny infant. While millions were dying in muddy trenches she was soothing a sick child crying for its mother, or spooning warm broth into an elderly patient. The war seemed far away to her. She was too tired after her shifts to even read the newspaper, so any knowledge of the conflict was second hand from Susie or her parents. The infrequent letters from overseas told her very little; only that at the time of writing Frankie and Jeremy were all right.

Johnnie had become a constant correspondent. He had begun to write her in the fall, and at least twice a month a long newsy letter arrived relating his activities, his mother's health, amusing anecdotes of the local folk, some of whom she had met the previous summer. News that his friend Peter MacLean had enlisted she relayed to Susie; Susie, with a smile and a blush, owned up that she already knew. She had received a long letter from Peter who was now in England waiting to be sent over to the Continent. Aunt Grace's health was slowly but surely deteriorating.

I can't leave her, Johnnie wrote one day in early spring of 1916. *She still knows me, and depends on me. The lady who looks after her during the day, Mrs. Arnott, is wonderful, but Mother asks for me the evenings I am not home, and cries when I don't appear. She asks about my father, too. She has forgotten he has died. Mrs. Arnott says Mother will*

184

need a proper nurse sometime in the next few months. Sometimes Mother wanders, and one day she walked all the way down to the Hastings' homestead. Mr. Hastings was so kind and gentle to her, and drove her home in his buggy. I feel guilty that here am I, a healthy twenty-three year old, with a talent the war effort needs, and not able to contribute. I keep hearing your voice in my head telling me that parents come first, and it soothes me some. I enjoy your letters, Louise, and I hope you'll continue to write. Give my love to Cousin Susie.

Louise had been amused when Johnnie first began to write her. He announced he was a one man SPNEM. He explained that was 'The Society for the Prevention of Nurses' Empty Mailboxes'. He always signed his name with a heart shaped dot over the 'i', and a little flourish.

Louise's nineteenth birthday was celebrated during an unseasonable heat wave. Flowers arrived at the Nurse's Residence—a huge sheaf of blooms that had obviously been grown in a hothouse and must have cost the earth to order.

"From Jeremy?" queried Susie in amazement.

"No, from Johnnie. I wonder how he knew when my birthday was." She glanced at her friend. "I suppose you told him."

"He wrote me at Christmas and asked me then," Susie said. "I hope you don't mind."

"Of course not. Johnnie's a chum, like Frankie. But he really oughtn't to have. He's supposed to be saving his money for going overseas."

"They're gorgeous, Lou. Nobody sent me flowers for my nineteenth." Susie's birthday was close to Christmas and sometimes got lost in the shuffle. "Where will you put them?"

Louise considered. "I think right here in the lounge where everyone can enjoy them."

"And envy Miss Laurier," said Susie slyly.

"That too." And Louise grinned.

Summer came, but Louise was scheduled to work nights until the last week in August, and then would have her vacation in September. Susie had the first half of July off, and fled the heat of

185

Ottawa to Ottey Lake with her parents and brother. It was during a quiet night on the ward that one of the first year students came to her with a worried expression on her face. She hemmed and she hawed, and then asked Louise outright if she knew how to get rid of a baby.

Louise was shocked. "Whatever do you mean, Miss McBride?" she asked. It seemed that Miss McBride was in the family way. Louise's first thought was to be amazed that so unprepossessing a girl as she had caught the attention of a man. Lucy was rather plain and lumpy and had teeth that protruded when she smiled. She was not the brightest of young ladies, either, Louise having had to explain a procedure several times before the younger girl caught on. "Oh, Lucy! Are you sure?" she asked her, still shocked and disbelieving. Miss McBride was fairly sure. She thought, seeing that Miss Laurier was a year older, and was engaged to be married, that she might know some things . . .

Louise assured her she knew nothing about that sort of thing. "But what about your young man? Have you told him? Will he marry you?"

"But then I'd have to quit nursing," protested Lucy. "I've tried jumping off a chair, and last weekend I went to my uncle's in the country and rode all day. Nothing happened."

"Oh, Lucy, what a fix you're in! You can't keep it a secret forever. You'll be asked to leave."

"I don't know even if he'll marry me," she confessed in a low voice. "I thought he was fond of me, and you know, with this war, who knows whether or not he'll be coming back...I didn't think once could do any harm . . ." Louise gazed at her, speechless. Lucy didn't even seem ashamed of what had happened.

"It was just the once. It don't seem fair."

"What about your parents?"

"Pa will skin me alive when he finds out. That's why I wanted to find out if there was anything I could do to get rid of it."

"But Lucy, that's wicked! You must tell the young man, and get married right away!"

"I dunno, I don't think I want to marry him, or anyone," Lucy said. Louise didn't know what to say, and was greatly relieved when a

186

patient rang a bell for attention. She went about her work thinking about Lucy McBride and her problem. Maybe the uncle out on the farm would take her in. Poor Lucy! But she had gotten herself into this mess. She has made her bed and now she must lie upon it, she thought, a little self-righteously.

Up until now Louise hadn't thought much about sex. She had known ever since she was five that babies grew inside their mothers, but not being farm bred, her ideas had been rather hazy as to how the babies got there. Having studied anatomy and physiology over the last year, she had become a bit more knowledgeable, and considered the process to be probably messy and awkward. She supposed, if it was your husband, and you were in love, it would be different. She had no doubt what Norah had been referring to when she told her dreamily that 'it' was wonderful. And it sounded as if Lucy had enjoyed herself. Well, she would trust Jeremy to be her guide once they were married. She dismissed Lucy and her problem from her mind, and concentrated on her studies.

When she returned from her two weeks' vacation she wasn't surprised to hear that Lucy McBride had left, with much whispering and gossip following her.

"No great loss," Susie remarked to Louise scornfully. "The school must have been hard up to accept her in the first place."

The students were discouraged from visiting each other in their rooms, so Louise and Susie were gossiping over tea and biscuits in the little kitchenette in the basement. Louise privately agreed with Susie's assessment of Lucy, but she said nothing, because she had felt sorry for her.

Susie dismissed the unfortunate Lucy with a toss of her head. "Enough of her. How was your vacation on the Island?"

Louise smiled happily. "It was lovely. The weather was perfect, and it was wonderful seeing Norah and the twins, and Harry, of course!"

"You didn't care for him at first, did you."

"Not one bit. I couldn't figure out why Norah was interested in him—a cranky, bad-tempered old man. Though I guess he isn't so

187

old, maybe five or six years older than Gerald. He's really quite nice, and he worships Norah."

"Well, he must be all right then," grinned Susie, knowing how Louise felt about her sister. "And how is Gerald? Does he like the life of a farmer?"

"Gerald is thriving. He says it is the best thing he's ever done. He says Rhoda did him a favor, throwing him over. He loves the island, and he and Harry are the greatest friends, which makes Norah exceedingly happy."

"And the twins—what are their names again?"

"Sarah and Ben. They are absolute dears, Susie. Norah couldn't love them any more if they were her own children. And they love her, too. Both of them call her 'Mama'. I had a great time playing with them. And bright, and talented—you should see Sarah's drawings. She's sure to be an artist when she grows up."

"I was sorry our vacations didn't coincide. It was nice up at the cottage, though the flies were bad this year. Do you hear from Jeremy much?"

"Not often, and then it's all cut up by the censor. I have a feeling that he's doing hush-hush stuff."

"That's what Dad thinks, too. What about Frankie?"

"Mama and Papa got a letter just yesterday—she telephoned me last night, all excited. Of course we don't know where he is—'somewhere in France', I guess."

Susie poured another cup of tea. "It's gotten too strong. You could stand a spoon up in it," she declared, peering at the dark liquid.

Louise giggled. "This is how Dorcas likes it. Anything weaker and it's for babies, she says. Of course she adds lashings of cream and sugar—or did, before the war. Another biscuit?"

Susie shook her head. "I'm getting much too fat. I don't know why, because the food is terrible."

Louise regarded her friend's compact figure. "You never gain weight."

Susie sighed. "I've had to let my waistband out at least an inch. And I'm short. Five pounds and I can tell the way my clothes fit.

Speaking of letters, though, Louise, do you hear from Johnnie? He hasn't written me for ages."

For some reason Louise blushed. "Yes, I got a letter when I was down in PEI, but I haven't heard from him since then."

"Mother is wondering how Aunt Grace is."

"Well, she seems to be getting worse. Johnnie is quite concerned. He's been working on the house, fixing it up inside and out. I expect he's too tired at the end of the day to write many letters."

"She's still at home?"

"Oh, yes. The woman your mother arranged to look after her still comes every day. She stays overnight when Johnnie is away, and cleans the house once a week. The District Nurse comes by most days in case Mrs. Arnott needs help. Johnnie won't put his mother in an asylum. He doesn't say much about not being able to enlist, but I know he is fretting about it."

"Aren't we lucky our parents are well!"

"I remember her in my prayers every night."

"Poor Aunt Grace!"

"Do you still hear from Peter MacLean?"

"Yes I do. He writes short little letters and begs me to write back. I think the boys over there are so homesick."

"I rather hoped that you and Frankie would make a match of it, and then we'd truly be sisters."

"Ah, I don't think we could be anything other than chums, Louise. I'm fond of Frankie, but not that way."

"I haven't told you the best news of all," said Louise suddenly.

Susie looked at her friend expectantly.

"Norah's going to have a baby!"

"How wonderful!"

"They are both thrilled with the news. She hasn't told anybody else (except Mama and Papa, of course, and Harry's mother,) but I know she won't mind my telling you."

"I won't say a word until you say I may. When is it due?"

"Middle of April—sometime around my birthday."

"What about the twins?"

"They haven't been told yet, simply because they couldn't help broadcasting it to the whole county. I think she wants to wait until she's sure everything is all right before it becomes general knowledge. She's feeling fine, she says. She looks even more beautiful, if that were possible. Harry treats her as though she were made of porcelain."

"Aunt Louise! It sounds nice."

"Sarah and Ben already call me Auntie, so it won't feel odd at all."

"You have such a nice family! I envy you your sisters. By the way, you haven't spoken of Gladdie. Is she still with that old lady?"

"Yes. The family doesn't see too much of her these days. She always seems to be off on a trip. Or organizing something. But that's her job."

Susie looked keenly at her friend. "Was she upset about you and Jeremy?"

Louise looked surprised. "How on earth did you guess that?"

"Well, I always knew she was fond of Jeremy. Sisters often notice these things about their brother! And I noticed that she didn't congratulate you two when you got engaged at your birthday party. In fact, she disappeared."

"Well, I think she was, well, surprised. Norah spoke to her. I haven't seen much of her at all this last year."

"I'm sorry, Lou. I didn't mean to probe. I can see that I've upset you." She got up and yawned, displaying a set of even, white teeth. "Well, time for bed."

Louise had pushed aside thoughts of Gladdie many times. Norah hadn't discussed Gladdie with her at all when she was staying with her. It was almost if we didn't have another sister, thought Louise guiltily, as she followed Susie upstairs.

Louise awoke, bathed in perspiration. She had been dreaming about Frankie. He was in the operating room and she was the nurse. She was standing looking down at her brother on the table and then she noticed in her hand there was a scalpel. *She had to do the operation.* "Begin, Miss Laurier, you must begin." Miss Love was there, looking over her shoulder. She had no idea what to do. And then she woke up.

The dream stayed with her all day. That evening she wrote to Johnnie.

It was the most awful dream, Johnnie. The feeling of helplessness and knowing that I was the only one who could save him. I suppose it's because I'm worried about him and also about going into the operating theatre. I start my rotation there next week, and finish at Christmas. But this will be an important part of my training if I'm to work in an army hospital.

We've had a lovely autumn here, really warm during the day with chilly nights that have put the most beautiful colors in the maples. They are pure scarlet and the contrast of them against the bright blue sky is breathtaking.

She didn't tell anyone else about the dream, nor the one she had the following night. This time as she looked into her brother's face it changed, and it was Johnnie's. In her dream she shrieked that she couldn't do it, but Miss Love was right there telling her to begin. She awoke, flat on her back, her heart hammering.

She went home for a rare weekend off on Friday and was met by a grim-faced Dorcas in the front hall. She had a telegram in her hand.

"Your Mama is lying down and your Papa has gone for a walk," she said tersely.

Somehow she wasn't at all surprised to discover that Frankie had been wounded in action. There were no details; just that he was recovering in an English hospital.

"His injuries must have been grave for them to send him back to England," she said dully.

"Where there's life there's hope," Dorcas said.

"Perhaps they'll send him home," she said hopefully, folding up the telegram. "Which way did Papa go? I'll go out and meet him."

A week later there was a telegram. *Am recovering very well from arm broken in two places and smashed leg. Will be out dancing soon. Love, Frankie.*

Mama telephoned joyfully to Louise at the residence that Frankie would be all right. That night Louise and Susie celebrated with huge dishes of ice cream smuggled up from the kitchen.

"You can't keep that Frankie down," Susie remarked, licking her spoon twice.

To her surprise Louise enjoyed the operating room. It was so different from the wards where the student nurses were the lowliest of the lows, and a doctor scarcely looked their way, let alone spoke with them. Here she was treated almost as an equal. The supervisor who taught them the technique was patient, and had a sense of humor. The surgeons, she found, conversed about everything, it seemed, except the matter at hand. Once she contaminated an instrument by inadvertently hitting it against the head of the surgeon who was bending over the operative area. She froze in horror, not knowing what to do. The doctor straightened up, looked her fiercely in the eye, grabbed the forceps out of her hand, and flung them up against the wall, where they clattered down to the floor. There was complete silence in the room for a few moments, and then he continued his task. Louise continued to hand instruments calmly. The circulating nurse, who had retrieved the offending forceps from where it reposed on the floor, came up behind her and quietly asked what had been the matter with it.

"I hit him on the head with it," Louise whispered back. She felt, rather than saw, the nurse's shoulders shaking with laughter. It was Miss Palmer, whom she knew quite well. She lived in the residence with the other graduate nurses.

"Nurse," the surgeon said to her later after the operation was over, "I did that to make a point. If you ever contaminate an instrument, you drop it immediately on the floor. Immediately. You understand?"

Louise nodded solemnly.

A cheerful letter came from Frankie in early December, not in his handwriting.

Because my right arm in completely encased in plaster a very beautiful nurse is writing this at my dictation. She is blushing, but I am

192

making her write down every word I say. They say I am doing very well, and the leg is healing. The field hospital must have done all the right things, because the doctors here say I should have lost my leg. But they saved it for me, and it's also encased in plaster. I'll be up walking in no time after my arm gets out of this cast, when I'll be able to use crutches. In the meantime Miss Carson wheels me in a pushchair, though there's no use in going outside. It's been raining for days, and it's cold.

Louise will be very interested to hear that her nemesis Miss Love works at this hospital. She came to see me soon after I was admitted, and asked me if I remembered meeting her. She introduced herself as Sister Love and said she had been your Director at the School of Nursing! I remember vaguely when Jeremy and I came to pick you up for your birthday party that a nurse directed us to the residence. I guess I didn't realize she was the head nurse there. Anyway, she runs this ward with an iron hand, but the care is excellent. All the nurses are scared to death of her, but I told Miss Carson here that Louise had her eating out of her hand.

Don't worry about me; I will be up and out of here in no time.

It was signed 'Frank', and there was a postscript: *I am doing my best to keep Corporal Laurier from trying to do too much. He is almost too optimistic, if that's possible. He keeps the whole ward amused. We are all very fond of him and are taking the best care of him.* And it was signed 'Sybil Carson'.

When Louise read this, she wiped a tear from her eye. It sounded just like Frankie. She was glad he was out of it now. Surely he wouldn't be fit enough to go back into the fighting.

They celebrated Christmas with a letter from Frank, this time in his own hand. There was a photograph enclosed, showing Frank standing with the aid of crutches. Beside him was a nurse who was smiling into the camera.

As you can see, my arm has healed nicely, and I am getting around on crutches. Sybil invited me to her aunt and uncle's home for Christmas, and we had an old-fashioned celebration with roast goose and plum pudding. Sybil's parents died when she was a child, and her aunt and uncle have brought her up. They are childless, rather elderly, and very staid. Sybil said once that sometimes she felt she was just a 'duty' to them, and she feels guilty for not being able to love them. However, Mrs. Penny made a rattling good bird for Christmas dinner, and there was a present for me under the tree.

Gladdie came home for Christmas. She was in good spirits, and chattered incessantly. Mama fussed over her because she had lost a good deal of weight, but she pooh-poohed her concern saying she felt fine. It was true, she had unusually high colored cheeks, and Louise overheard Dorcas asking her if she was using rouge. Gladdie took umbrage, and sounded like her old self when she gave Dorcas short shrift for suggesting such a thing. She treated Louise as though nothing had happened between them. Sometimes Louise thought she must have dreamed the ruined red coat.

Chapter Twenty-One

LOUISE 1917

Louise sat in the window seat of her room and watched the snow swirling by outside. The senior students had been given their choice of rooms for the final year, and Louise had asked for the large bed-sitting room recently vacated by one of the graduate nurses. It overlooked the quadrangle and was opposite the office that Miss Love had once occupied. Louise could see that there was a light on, meaning that the Director of Nurses was working late.

The room was furnished with a double bed, a large wardrobe, and in the sitting area a desk and chair, and a low table between two upholstered armchairs. Susie sat curled up in one of them reading the letter that Louise had just received from Johnnie.

"He's even more worried about Aunt Grace, isn't he," she remarked. "It sounds as though she should be locked up, poor thing."

"She tends to wander, especially at night. What a burden for him!" Susie folded up the letter and regarded her friend. "What do you hear from Jeremy?"

Louise moved restlessly. "I haven't heard from him since Christmas. Have you?"

Susie yawned and shook her head. "Not a word. How's Frankie?"

"I've had two letters from Sybil since Christmas. He's mending nicely.

195

You know, I think those two are serious about each other—at least she is. I wonder if I will have an English sister-in-law."

"Are you still thinking of going overseas after graduation next year? You'll be able to meet her if you do."

"If the war is still on I shall," said Louise decisively. "And speaking of graduation, we shall never make it if we don't study for that examination next week, and I haven't yet done my surgical project."

After Susie had left, Louise, instead of getting to work, continued to gaze out the window. Susie hadn't asked after Gladdie, (which wasn't surprising, because Louise's friend didn't care very much for her sister), so Louise had not volunteered her concern. She had been home quite often, which was a contrast from her behavior since Louise's eighteenth birthday party. Gladdie had lost more weight, and she had a cough. Mama had asked her to see the doctor about it, but Gladdie shrugged and said it was just a cold.

Louise didn't think it was just a cold, but she hesitated to confront Gladdie because their relationship was now fairly pleasant, in that Gladdie actually spoke to her without being spoken to first. She chattered about inconsequential things, but then that had always been Gladdie's way. The subjects of Jeremy Ferris or the red coat were never raised. Louise had never asked Norah what she had said to Dorcas that day when she showed her the ruined coat. She hadn't the nerve to ask Dorcas if she had said anything to Gladdie about it. It was as though the coat had never existed. This past weekend Louise had been home and Gladdie announced that she and Mrs. Marchbanks were going to spend the rest of the winter in Arizona.

"She wants the dry warmth," Gladdie said. "She says it will be good for her lungs."

It was a long trip to the southwest United States, but Gladdie was looking forward to it.

"I believe that the States will enter the war soon," Papa remarked. "Good. That means there'll be masses of handsome boys in uniform," Gladdie remarked airily.

"Have you seen the doctor about that cough?" Louise asked.

"Oh, for heaven's sake, don't fuss. You're as bad as Dorcas," grumbled Gladdie. "It's just bronchitis or something. Arizona will soon cure me."

"I hope Mrs. Marchbanks isn't working you too much," said Mama anxiously, and then bit her lip as Gladdie glowered at her. "I'm sorry, dear, am I fussing, too?"

Louise shook her head, remembering this conversation. Gladdie didn't look well. She sighed, got up, and took her books over to the desk. She had better get down to an evening of study, or she'd be failing the exam next week.

The events of April 1917 were to color Louise's life from then on. In spite of the war, life early that year had been smooth and serene. Exams had been written and passed; there had been satisfying work on the wards. She had received happy letters from Norah looking forward to the arrival of their first child; excited letters from Frankie and Sybil, who now were officially engaged. Louise wrote to her sister-in-law-to-be wishing her all the luck and happiness in the world, and to Frankie her warm congratulations. It had been three months since he had been wounded, and he was now walking every day, with just the use of a cane. He had seen Jeremy, and reported that his brother-in-law-to-be was in fine form. *He's very close mouthed as to what he's really doing,* Frankie wrote. *Do you think he's a spy or something? I hadn't realized that he's a major now. Sybil's family is very impressed.* Their letters simply bubbled over with happiness.

The only sadness was the death of Aunt Grace in late February, though in a way it was a release for her, and for Johnnie as well. He could now make firm plans for heading over to England and joining the Royal Flying Corps. *You probably have heard the news already,* he wrote, *as I have sent a cable to Uncle James and Aunt Phoebe. She wandered away that night,* and *actually froze to death. It was twenty below zero. I was away overnight, and when I returned they were searching for her, eventually finding her down by the river. The doctor told me it was a peaceful death. She would have just gone to sleep and not woken up. Poor Mrs. Arnott! She was frantic with worry and just wild with grief when they found Mother. I comforted her as best I*

197

could, and I suppose I will always feel a pang of guilt for not being there and preventing it. Or could I have prevented it, Louise? If not, I would be feeling even guiltier. I have instructed the lawyer to sell the house and furniture and put the money in the bank for when I return. There are several weeks of work for me to wind everything up, then I will be traveling to Halifax where I will stay with Aunt Mabel and Uncle Stan for a few days before leaving for England. I will make stops in Perth and Ottawa, of course! I'm not sure exactly when I shall see you, but see you I shall. Perhaps the middle of April—to wish you a happy birthday.

There were no dreams this time. No warning, no presentiment. The country had been holding its collective breath over the battle for an obscure piece of French real estate called Vimy Ridge, and when the Canadians won it, and held it, there was much rejoicing.

Louise and Susie were on their way to Perth for the weekend. They would be celebrating Louise's twentieth birthday the next day even though April 16 fell on the following Tuesday. Louise was excited and happy. She had just received a letter from Frankie, who was back in uniform, writing humorously that Sybil had nursed him too well! The army said he was fit, but he didn't know when he was being sent back to the front. Johnnie had arrived and was staying with the Ferrises in Perth; Susie had talked to her cousin on the telephone, and she said he sounded fine, and was looking forward to seeing "his two best girls."

"He's planning to stay overnight in Ottawa on Monday," she told Louise, "then taking the early morning train to Montreal."

Everyone was talking about the latest battle of three days before. "But at what price?" Louise wondered out loud to her friend as the train slid into the Perth station. "But, gosh, Susie, doesn't it make you proud to be a Canadian?" The girls picked up their overnight bags and climbed down to the platform.

"There's Johnnie!" Susie said, waving at the tall young man striding toward them. "Louise, he's grown a beard!"

Sure enough, Johnnie was sporting a small, soft brown beard. It made him look older, Louise thought idly, suddenly aware of pure happiness bubbling up inside her. Johnnie hugged Susie, and then clasped Louise in a warm embrace, kissing her on both cheeks.

"I'm practicing kissing Continental style," he announced.

"How many girls have you kissed?" asked Louise slyly. "Gosh, but it's good to see you, Johnnie!"

He put an arm around each of them and smiled down at their upturned faces, rosy in the chilly afternoon.

"My two favorite girls," he said. "Uncle James lent me the car so we'll go home in style. You know," he added, looking around him as the three walked out of the station, "I think it might snow."

"We always get an April snowstorm," Louise remarked, as they found the car and got inside.

It had, in fact, been an unusually mild first half of April, but the old timers shook their heads wisely and remarked gloomily that spring hadn't come yet. It looked as though they were right. The temperature had dropped considerably since they had left Ottawa, and the sky was a leaden color. A wind had picked up, and Louise shivered as she settled herself in the car.

"A good evening to be inside," she remarked.

The Ferrises lived outside of town on the way to Ottey Lake, and by the time Johnnie and the girls had reached the house, a few flakes were beginning to fall. Mr. and Mrs. Ferris were waiting for them and both rose from where they were sitting when the trio came in, laughing and chattering happily. Susie went to them quickly and kissed them both. Mrs. Ferris' smile came and went and she looked at Louise with a sad expression her face.

"Louise, your parents just telephoned to us."

Louise, arrested by her hostess' expression and grave tone of voice, stood still and gazed at her questioningly.

"Come and sit down, Louise." The older woman bit her lip. "My dear, you must be brave."

"What has happened?" Coldness settled in her midsection. Norah's baby! "Is it Norah? Has the baby come? What has happened?"

"No, dear, not Norah. I'm afraid there's been a telegram from overseas. It's Frank, my dear. Frank's been killed at Vimy Ridge."

Louise was aware of Susie's eyes, large and startled. She felt, rather than saw, Johnnie come to her side. She took a step toward Mr. and Mrs. Ferris.

"Frankie? It can't be. I just got a letter from him. He's only just gotten back into uniform. He said . . ." She shook her head in bewilderment. "There must be some mistake."

"Your letter must be over a month old," Mr Ferris said quietly. "We're so sorry, Louise. The War Office doesn't usually make mistakes."

"No! It can't be!" Louise wailed, and collapsed in a crumpled heap.

Johnnie caught her as she went down.

When Louise came to herself, she was lying on the big sofa in the Ferris' parlor. Johnnie had drawn up a chair, and was holding her hand, gazing anxiously at her.

"Did I faint?" she asked. "Is it really true?"

He nodded. "Louise, I am so sorry! What can I do to help?"

Louise sat up and gave him a wan smile. "Don't leave me, Johnnie." His hand tightened around hers. "The others have had supper. Do you feel like something to eat?"

Louise wasn't a bit hungry. "I must go home," she said firmly. "Mama and Papa will need me."

Mrs. Ferris came into the room in time to overhear Louise's statement. "Your father said to stay for the weekend as you planned," she began. Louise got to her feet. Johnnie took her arm. "Oh, Mrs. Ferris, I don't want to sound ungrateful, but I must go home."

"But the last train has left," Mrs. Ferris said. "It's nearly seven o'clock." Afterwards, Louise couldn't explain her desperation. She just knew that she had to go home.

Susie understood. "If it were Jeremy, I'd want to be with Mother and Dad," she said.

"If Uncle James will lend me the car, I'll drive her to Ottawa," Johnnie offered.

"It's at least a four hour drive!" exclaimed his aunt.

"I'm sure the Lauriers will put me up," he said, glancing at Louise, who brightened a little and nodded.

"I'll bring the car back first thing in the morning."

The snow was beginning in earnest as Louise and Johnnie started out. Mrs. Ferris gazed anxiously at the sky. Johnnie's uncle told him to drive slowly and stay in the center of the road, and they'd have no trouble. Louise had tried to telephone her parents, but had been unable to get through. The telephone system was still unpredictable in the country, she told Johnnie, as they prepared to leave.

She was huddled in the front seat beside Johnnie, a thick blanket around her, bundled up in her warmest clothes, as she gazed out at the swirling snow reflected crazily in the headlamps. She was beginning to have a few misgivings about her determination to go home. At one point she asked Johnnie hesitantly if perhaps they should turn around. After all, her parents weren't expecting her, and the snow was making the road very slippery.

"We'll manage, Louise," he said. He glanced at her, seeing her pale cheeks and tense expression. He reached over and squeezed her hand.

She began to talk about her brother, and the good times they had had growing up together.

"We're chums. We always have been," she explained. "There's only a year between us. Oh, Johnnie, he could hardly wait to go off to war, especially when Gerald was refused. It as though it was his sacred duty!" She glanced at him, her face stiff with misery. "I suppose you'll go off and get killed now."

Johnnie shook his head firmly. "I don't intend to. I'm a good pilot, you know. There's a dirty job to be done, and I plan on doing it and coming home." He took her hand briefly. "I understand your wanting to go home. You want to see that telegram. You can't quite believe it, can you."

Louise closed her eyes and shook her head. "One minute I do, and the next minute I don't." She peered out the window. "Where on earth are we? I'm afraid I haven't been paying attention. How long is it since we left?"

"Over an hour, I should think."

"I think we should have reached the junction by now," she said, biting her lip. "We have to make a right turn on to the main highway."

They drove a little further, the snowflakes dancing in the headlights. "I think we've missed the turn," Louise said worriedly. "Can you turn around, Johnnie?"

A quarter of a mile up the road Johnnie spotted a mailbox, slowed down, and turned into a narrow, rutted lane that was now drifting with snow. He reversed the car, and to his chagrin it stalled. He climbed out, cranked the engine, and got it started again, but as he backed up, it slid part way into the ditch, and stopped with a bump. Try as he might he couldn't get the car to move forward. The wheels spun madly, and with a wheeze, the engine died again. This time they both got out into the snow and attempted to push the car forward, but to no avail. The contemplated each other helplessly in the light of the headlamps.

"This lane must lead to a house," said Johnnie. "Perhaps there's someone there who can help us."

He left the headlamps burning and it lit their way as they trudged up the lane. Sure enough, around the corner, they could make out in the gathering darkness a farmhouse standing amidst a small grove of trees. There were no lights on inside. They knocked firmly on the front door.

"No one's home!" declared Louise. "Now what?" She tried the door, but it was locked.

"Perhaps someone's around the back," suggested Johnnie. He took her hand and they started around the side of the house. "What's that noise?" he asked.

"It sounds like a cow bawling. Look, there's a barn and a chicken house. I'll go and see."

Louise turned toward the barn, and Johnnie stepped on to the porch. He tried the back door, and it opened.

"Hello! Anybody home?" he called.

On a hook next to the door was a large kerosene lantern with a box of matches in a small niche next to it. He lit the lantern and cautiously made his way inside. He found himself in a large kitchen, still fairly warm, and filled with a savory aroma. There was a big, shiny, black kitchen range in the corner, with a large pot simmering at the back, and a round table in the middle of the room, set for a meal. He set down the lantern and went over to the stove. The fire had been banked up nicely, and it was still smoldering. He found wood in a basket next to the stove and fed the fire. It flared up well and began to crackle. Replacing the lid, he took the lantern and went into the next room, which was a small sitting room with a pot-bellied stove standing between the two windows. The fire in it had also not gone out, and he soon had it roaring away again. The door led out into a front hall and opposite the sitting room was a formal parlor, but it was cold and uninviting. He ventured up the stair; calling out as he went, but he knew there was nobody home. The state of the fires had told him that, but the kitchen table and the soup on the stove also told him that the occupants were expecting to be home tonight. On his way back to the kitchen he lit an old-fashioned oil lamp that stood on the table next to the sofa. He paused and admired the multicolored glass shade that scattered rainbow shards across the ceiling. He sighed sadly. His mother had one like it in her bedroom once. Further exploration of the kitchen revealed a little scullery with a sink and a pump.

"No electricity, no hot and cold running water," he muttered to himself. "No doubt there's no indoor plumbing, either."

Presently he wondered what Louise was doing, so he took the lantern and went out on to the back porch. Light was spilling out from the barn door, making colorful sparkles in the snow. He hung the lantern on its hook and started across the yard. Whatever animal had been making the noise had stopped, and he paused at the barn door and contemplated the scene within. Louise was seated on a small stool, and she was milking a large black and white cow. He admired the curve of her cheek in the light of the lamp she had lit, and the stray tendrils of hair that had escaped her hat and curled around her ear. Her capable hands with their long slender fingers squeezed away, and the only sounds were the splash of milk in the pail and her soft voice murmuring to the animal. His heart filled up and flowed over with love for her.

He didn't realize it at that moment, but he would take that picture with him into battle months hence, and it would become the symbol of what he was fighting for. It was a simple, homely task, but it seemed to him as he stood there and silently watched her, that it represented the things that mattered most in life: food, home, and love.

He must have made a sound, for Louise looked around and smiled, making his heart turn over within him.

"Johnnie! You must have been wondering where I had gotten to. Poor creature," she went on, "she was so desperate to be milked that she didn't mind a novice like me doing it. Did you, old dear?" she added to the cow, who turned her head and gazed at Louise with brown, long-lashed eyes, as though she understood every word the girl had said.

To cover his emotion, he said in a teasing voice, "I didn't know your talents included milking,"

"Didn't I tell you Norah and I milked Aunt Bernice's cows in PEI? I'll never forget that first time. I thought I'd die, my hands and back were so stiff." She gave the cow's teats one last squeeze. "There! We're done. My hands will probably be stiff tomorrow, though," she added ruefully. "Johnnie, whoever lives here almost certainly expected to be back by evening. They wouldn't leave their cow and chickens like this."

"I agree. There's a table set for supper, and a huge pot of soup on the kitchen stove."

"We should feed the chickens, too. They've been squawking for their meal ever since I looked in on them a while back. See that bag marked chick feed? We'll give them some of that."

She got up and stretched, patted the cow's flanks affectionately, and checked to make sure that she had lots of hay in the stall.

"Would you mind putting the milk pail on the porch? I should find something to cover it."

Johnnie picked up the pail cheerfully. "There must be tea towels in the kitchen. I'll find one. Also, I've just remembered I left the car's headlamps on. I'd better go down to the road and turn them off."

He returned five minutes later and saw Louise in the hen house, scattering feed for the chickens.

"Two eggs, too!" she announced gaily. "Do you suppose they'd mind if we ate them? I'm very hungry all of a sudden."

"That's because you didn't have any of Aunt Phoebe's delicious supper. I don't suppose the people would mind if we helped ourselves to a bowl of soup. There are gallons."

"Look—it's stopped snowing and the moon is coming out." Louise lifted her face to the night sky and took a deep breath of fresh air. Johnnie looked down at her and thought that she was the loveliest creature he'd ever known. He remembered the precise moment that he had fallen in love with her. It was two summers ago when he'd first met her, when she had traveled out to Winnipeg with his aunt and uncle and cousin Susie. His father had been dying, and Louise had gotten up in the middle of the night to give him an injection, because he, Johnnie, hadn't the nerve to do it himself. He had despised himself for his cowardice, but she had made him feel better about himself. What had she said to him? He only remembered how she'd reached across the table where they were having a cup of tea and touched his hand. In that instant he was hers forever. Why couldn't they have met sooner, before his cousin Jeremy proposed to her? He would have made her care for him. He sighed and followed her into the house.

They had a bowl of soup and bread that they found in the larder, Louise washing the dishes carefully and Johnnie wiping them and putting them back in the dresser.

"We'll have to sleep here. There's a little spare bedroom upstairs, I'm sure they wouldn't mind if you slept there. I'll be quite comfortable on the sofa in the sitting room."

"Oh, no, Johnnie! I don't want to be upstairs all by myself! Can't we just camp in the sitting room? What if they come back in the middle of the night?" So they settled themselves in the sitting room, Louise on the sofa with a large thick quilt Johnnie retrieved from the spare room bed, and Johnnie in the big chair by the stove. It seemed quite natural for him to stoop and kiss her goodnight on the cheek, though what he really wanted to do was take her in his arms.

Louise slept until morning without waking. She had been dreaming about Johnnie, so it seemed quite natural for her to find him waking her gently at first light.

"Louise. I've got the car turned around. I thought we could drive to your parents, then I'll turn around and go straight back. Nobody need know that we had to spend the night here. Your family will just think we got away very early." He took her hand. "Are you awake, Louise?' he asked softly. "We have your reputation to think about, you know."

"Johnnie. I was dreaming about you." She looked up at him and smiled. "At this moment, my reputation can go hang."

And she reached up and touched his face.

Johnnie never knew quite how it happened, but suddenly he found himself kissing her on the lips. He felt her hands steal around his neck, and she was kissing him urgently in response.

"Louise," he whispered, and stretched out beside her on the sofa. He gazed down into her lovely face, and then continued to kiss her— her mouth, her cheeks, her eyes. She was making little murmuring sounds in her throat. He drew away for a moment and her hands went to her neck, and she began to undo the buttons of her blouse.

"Louise?" he muttered, and bent to her throat and to where the swell of her bosom had been revealed.

"What's this?" he asked, as his lips touched a hard object. It was Jeremy's ring, still on its chain around her neck. He drew back and sat up.

"Louise, we mustn't! Oh God, Louise, I want you, but it wouldn't be right." He stood up. "I'll wait for you outside." And he fled.

Louise lay there, the blood slowly rising to suffuse her cheeks. With trembling fingers she buttoned her blouse up to the top and then slowly got up from the sofa from the sofa. What Johnnie must think of her, throwing herself at him like that! What had come over her? She didn't know quite what might have happened, but she had wanted it to happen. Oh, heavens above, where was the bathroom? An outdoor privy, no doubt. She found the toilet, and five minutes later she was in the scullery washing her face and hands in icy cold water at the pump. For the next few minutes she busied herself

206

making sure the house was the way they had found it. She saw that Johnnie had left a note for the owners to find, and then she went out and closed the door. She looked into the barn, and the cow gazed back at her. Well, she had done one thing right, she thought to herself as she walked down the lane to the car. A steady drizzle of rain was now falling, and the snow was melting. Johnnie sprang out of the car at her approach and opened the door for her. She got in without meeting his eyes, and sat miserably while he maneuvered the car out of the lane on to the highway. They drove a long time without speaking, each deep in their own thoughts.

I'm as bad as Lucy McBride, she thought to herself. Did I actually say my reputation could go hang? Johnnie is probably despising me right this moment. He'll never want to see me again, he'll never write another line. He'll go off to Europe and I'll never see him again.

Her face was burning again. If she had been alone she would have burst into tears.

Johnnie, also, was suffering.

Why didn't I explain how I feel about her? And why I couldn't make love to her? He asked himself over and over. I just ran away like a frightened rabbit! What a fool she must think I am!

Louise roused herself from her misery to tell him to turn at the next road, and then she fell silent again, biting her lip as her troubled thoughts tumbled one over the other.

I made myself cheap back there, she thought. That's what I thought of Lucy. Cheap and easy. My brother has been killed and I'm promised to another man, and all I can think about is Johnnie and—sex. There. She'd actually thought it. She turned and looked unseeingly out the window, tears trickling down her cheeks. Fumbling in her bag she found a handkerchief and under guise of blowing her nose, she angrily dashed them away. She hoped Johnnie would think she was just being sad about Frank. That's awful, she mused, aghast at where her thoughts were leading. 'Just being sad?' Of course I'm sad about Frankie. Aren't I? But how can I be sad about something I don't really believe yet?

The rain had stopped and the sun was coming out at they reached the outskirts of the city. It was nearly eight thirty, and Louise's stomach was growling with hunger, which served to embarrass her even more.

"Louise," Johnnie began tentatively, "I'm sorry for what happened back there . . ."

"It was my fault, Johnnie," replied Louise bravely. "I don't know what you must think . . ."

"You wanted comfort, and I couldn't give it to you. You see, I have these crazy scruples. You're engaged to Jeremy . . . ." He looked at her helplessly.

She turned away. "I'm so ashamed of myself," she muttered.

Johnnie slowed down, and carefully pulled over and stopped. There was no traffic in sight, except a milk wagon going on its rounds. He could hear the clop of the horse's hooves and see its steamy breath. The milkman tipped his hat at them as he went by and turned up a street.

"Louise, look at me."

Louise turned and gazed tragically at him. He took a deep breath. "Louise, don't you know that I'm deeply in love with you? Don't you know that as far as I'm concerned, nothing you could do—nothing—could be shameful? My precious darling—(and I haven't even the right to call you that)—there's so much I want to say to you, but this isn't the right time or the right place. Look, I'll be coming back to Ottawa Monday night, and I'll be staying at the Grand Hotel downtown. Can you come for tea or supper on Tuesday? I'll be taking the night train to Montreal that night, and I must see you again before I leave."

At his first words Louise's face changed, and it was as though the sun had come out. Her eyes shone, and she gave a little gasp of joy. Johnnie thought his heart would leap out of his chest. Then her expression sobered, and her eyes were wide and serious as she contemplated his request.

"Oh, Johnnie, I don't know whether I should . . ."

"Please," he said urgently, taking her hand.

Still she hesitated.

"Say 'I promise to meet Johnnie on Tuesday for supper at five o'clock.' You can come at five, can't you?"

Louise smiled happily and said, "Yes, I can. We only work eight hour shifts in the Operating Room, and so I'll be off duty at four."

"Will you come, then, Louise?"

She nodded gravely. "I promise, Johnnie."

He was suddenly joyously happy. "Let's get you home to your family, then."

Chapter Twenty-Two

LOUISE 1917-1918

Tuesday afternoon Louise entered the rather splendid lobby of the Grand Hotel, and looked around nervously. To her relief, Johnnie's tall, lean figure rose from a large, overstuffed chair by the fireplace and he strode across the carpeted floor to meet her. His smile, had she known it, was also one of relief. He hadn't been sure whether she might change her mind and not come.

"Hallo, Louise!" he said happily, and tucked her arm into his. "I've reserved a nice table in the Palm Room where we can eat and talk."

He led her into a large, glass domed room filled with tropical plants. It reminded her of Mama's solarium. Where Jeremy had proposed. The butterflies in her stomach began to flap furiously once more. The waiter at the door took her coat silently and hung it in a cupboard, then led them to a table by a corner window which overlooked the garden, now patched with brown grass and melting snow. They were well surrounded by lots of greenery, which served to muffle the conversations of the occupants of the other tables. It was early, and there were a few other couples finishing their afternoon tea.

"Do you like curry?" he asked her. "One of the chefs here is from India, and the curry is very fine indeed."

"I don't think I've ever had it," Louise told him, glad of a safe topic like food.

The waiter hovered.

"We'll have the lamb curry," Johnnie said briskly, "and your daily soup to start."

"May I bring madam and sir something to drink?"

"I'll have a dark ale with the curry. Shall we have tea now, Louise?"

"Oh, yes please, that would be lovely," said Louise, and took a sip of the ice water that the waiter had poured into the crystal goblets.

The waiter went silently away, and Johnnie smiled encouragingly at Louise.

"Now, tell me, how are your parents bearing up? And you, also?"

"They can't quite believe it, either, that Frankie won't be coming home. Reverend Wentworth visited on Saturday. I was so glad I had gone home, and they were glad to see me. Nobody even questioned our early arrival."

The tea arrived at that moment, and the waiter put the silver service down on a small folding table next to Louise.

"Will madam pour out?" he murmured, and discreetly withdrew. Louise took a few moments to deal with the tea and milk, and to pass the savory biscuits to Johnnie.

"There's to be a memorial service next week," she went on. "Papa's put notices in the paper. Reverend Wentworth said Frankie's commanding officer would probably be writing to us. I wrote to Sybil—she and Frankie were engaged, you know. She is the nurse that looked after him in the hospital. If I go over to England after I graduate, I shall make sure I look her up."

"Good. I'll see you then, too."

Louise broke off and gazed at Johnnie, who was regarding her with a tender expression.

"Johnnie—"

"Shall we talk about us, Louise? Am I right, there could be—'us'?"

At that moment the waiter brought the soup, and placed it deftly before them.

"Blast," said Johnnie. "Maybe a meal wasn't such a good idea. I hadn't thought about all these interruptions."

211

Louise took a sip of soup and regarded him over her spoon. "Let's talk after supper," she suggested. "I'm hungry."

"You can tell me more about your family while we eat, then."

"And you can tell me what your plans are," responded Louise, relieved that potentially dangerous conversation was being put off.

"You first. You have an older sister, don't you? She was married the summer we met."

"I have two sisters. Norah's my eldest sister, and she and Harry are expecting a child any day now."

"By George, I just remembered it's your birthday today, isn't it! What a forgetful fool I am! I should have ordered wine."

Louise dimpled. "You know, I had forgotten too!" She looked around. "But this is a lovely present, supper with you in this beautiful dining room."

He put down his soupspoon and smiled back at her. "You do have a way of making a chap feel good about himself. How do you do it?"

Louise felt her cheeks grow warm. The conversation was getting dangerous again. "You told me you were leaving tonight. Are you going straight overseas?"

"No, I will be sailing from Halifax next Monday morning. But I will be spending a day in Montreal, then two days on the train to Halifax, and the weekend with my aunt and uncle. I told you about them, didn't I? My mother's brother Stanley, and his wife Mabel. Their last name is Carruthers. They wrote me the loveliest note when Father died, and they sent a beautiful wreath to Mother's funeral. I envy you your brothers and sisters, Louise. Except for two sets of aunts and uncles, I'm alone in the world."

"Yes, growing up in a large family is rather nice, and I have wonderful parents, too."

"Tell me more about your family. Norah is married and living in Prince Edward Island, and what of your other sister? Is she older or younger?"

"Gladdie. Well her name is really Gladys, but she's always been Gladdie." Louise sobered a little, thinking about Gladdie, then found herself telling Johnnie all about the problems between the two of them. She'd never told anyone else besides Norah, but somehow it was easy to talk to Johnnie.

"Poor girl, I feel sorry for her. She must be so unhappy to have acted the way she did." He touched her hand briefly. "Don't blame yourself because Jeremy chose you. I can quite understand."

Louise blushed and quickly went on to tell him about Gerald and Val. The main course arrived, and she was fascinated by the condiments served in the little silver dishes.

"There's chutney, chopped boiled eggs, nuts, raisins, and coconut," explained Johnnie. "I usually just sprinkle 'em on. Except the coconut. I don't like coconut. When I was a little shaver I was sick in the hospital, and the nurse made me eat the coconut pudding, and I threw up all over the bed. Was she mad at me, because of course she had to change all the linens. Say, I guess that's not a good topic over dinner, is it."

Louise dimpled at him again. "I'm a nurse, remember? You should hear what we discuss over meals sometimes." She tasted the curry. "This is delicious. Lovely and spicy."

"Not too spicy, is it?" he asked anxiously.

"No—I like it very much."

"Good." Johnnie was very pleased that his choice was a success. "I was going to add," he went on with a smile, "that you should never force children to eat something they don't like. Your patients, or your own children. You won't, will you, with our children?"

Louise decided to pretend she didn't hear the last remark.

She changed the subject hastily.

"Did you always want to fly, Johnnie?"

"I remember reading 'Eight Weeks in a Balloon' by Jules Verne. Have you ever read any of his novels?" Louise shook her head. "Oh, he's a marvelous read! I immediately wanted to go up in a hot air balloon. When I read about the Wright brothers and their flight at Kitty Hawk—I was just a kid, still—then I wanted to fly aeroplanes. And you heard about Mr. McCurdy flying the *Silver Dart* eight years ago at Baddeck, Nova Scotia? A first in the British Empire, if you please. I was so proud! I wrote to him, you know, and he wrote to me back, a really nice letter, kindly encouraging me to take up flying. What a fine fellow he is!"

Johnnie's face was pink with enthusiasm. Louise beamed at him, caught up in his enthusiasm.

"When did you learn to fly?"

"The summer I was seventeen my parents sent me out to Nova Scotia to stay with Uncle Stan and Aunt Mabel, and I looked Mr. McCurdy up. What cheek I had when I think of it now," said Johnnie, with a rueful smile. "But he was kindness itself, and showed me the actual craft he flew in three years before, and what they were doing then, and the new designs. He even introduced me to Alexander Graham Bell! What a fine old gentleman he is! So I took lessons from one of his colleagues, and I was absolutely hooked on flying. You enjoyed it, didn't you when I took you up two years ago?"

Louise's eyes shone at the memory. "Oh, yes, Johnnie! It was marvelous!" The waiter was there, taking their plates, murmuring about dessert. "Oh no, thank-you," Louise said politely. "Everything was delicious, and I'm quite satisfied."

"May we take our coffee into the small lounge?" asked Johnnie. "And may I add the bill to my room? I'll be checking out later on this evening." Presently they found themselves sitting side by side in front of a crackling fire in a cozy room. The waiter had followed them in, bringing a tray of coffee and setting it on the low table beside them. Johnnie discreetly handed him a tip, and as he seated himself beside Louise the waiter said quietly,

"I hope I am not being forward, but I hope, madam and sir, that you will both be very happy together."

And he went silently away.

There was silence between them for a moment while Louise poured the coffee with trembling hands.

"He thinks we are engaged," exclaimed Johnnie. "I guess he can see that I'm madly in love." He took the coffee cup from her and smiled at her blushes. "He must have thought you were, too."

"Oh, Johnnie … ."

"Are you?"

"Johnnie, I'm so confused! How can I be feeling the way I do about you and still be fond of Jeremy? I've been composing letters to him in my head every night before going to sleep, but I haven't had the courage to put my thoughts down on paper to him." She paused; trying to express what was in her heart. "I am still fond of Jeremy, I know I am; but you make me feel— utterly complete, somehow. I have this incredible rush of happiness when I think of you, or see you."

Johnnie put down his coffee cup, and took both her hands in his. His voice was hoarse with emotion. "I told you I had scruples, Louise, so I shouldn't be holding your hand and telling you words of love when you're engaged to my cousin. I don't want to put pressure on you, darling, you have enough problems on your plate without adding me to them. Look, I've thought a great deal about us since Saturday morning." He lowered his voice. "I was utterly touched that you would want me to make love to you, and the only reason I ran away (I did, Louise, darling!) was because I was so taken by surprise. I knew you liked me, but I never even hoped in my wildest dreams that you would feel more than that. It wouldn't have been right for me to take advantage of you. Here I am, going off to the war. What if—" He broke off. "Well, you know what I mean. I could ruin you, when what I really want to do is take you away and look after you forever."

He reached up and traced the line of her cheek with his fingers. Louise caught her breath. She started to speak, but he touched her mouth with his fingers.

"Let me finish, darling. You can't get married until you graduate, can you?" She shook her head. "So I don't think you should write to Jeremy and tell him about us. It's not right that I should steal you from him when he is fighting this dreadful war. And soon he and I will be comrades in arms. I just wouldn't feel right about it. Who knows, his feelings might change toward you, though I doubt it, how could they? I know mine won't, unless I get shot up and am no use to you—"

"Don't even think that, Johnnie!" she interrupted, and her voice broke. "I couldn't bear it if you got hurt horribly and were crippled and couldn't fly—"

"Yes, I'd rather be dead! But it's not going to happen! I will come home, Louise, so I want you to promise me only one thing. Will you?"

"If I can."

"Will you promise to wait for me and not marry Jeremy until I come home? Wait for both of us, then you will know for sure what you want to do."

"I will, Johnnie, I promise."

"Will you keep this until I come home? Then if you decide to marry Jeremy, you can give it back. It's Mother's wedding ring, and it was the only thing that I could think of to give you. I think it will fit on your little finger. Mother had such tiny hands."

He handed her a narrow gold ring, worn with the years of wearing. Louise slipped it on the fifth finger of her right hand. Nobody would question it, and she would take it off when she was in uniform. What could she give him? She reached into her purse and brought out an embroidered handkerchief. It was just a wisp of silk, certainly not meant for anything except perhaps dabbing a tear at the corner of the eye.

"I embroidered it myself," she said, handing it to him. "My grandmother sat with me when I was ten and taught me needlework. I spent hours on this."

He examined it carefully. "It's beautiful, Louise! Are you sure?"

"Of course. The lady always gives her knight in shining armor something to take into battle."

He laughed, rather hysterically if truth be told, and put it in his breast pocket. "I'll look after it well," he said. "Now, let's get you home. Wait here until I get your coat."

He returned a few minutes later and helped her on with her coat. "They've called a cab for us. Are you going back to the hospital?"

"I start night shift tomorrow night, so they've given me leave to go home and spend tonight and tomorrow with Mama and Papa.

Because of Frankie, you see, as I don't have to be on duty until seven o'clock in the evening."

They sat close together in the back seat of the cab, holding hands and wondering when they would see each other again, unable to bear the thought of saying goodbye to each other. When they reached Louise's home, Johnnie suggested he go in with her and offer his condolences to her parents. He asked the cabby to wait, and Louise led the way indoors.

"Mama, Papa, this is Jeremy's cousin Johnnie Ferris," she said simply. Mama and Papa shook hands with him, murmuring their thanks for his kind thoughts. Papa drew him aside, saying that hadn't Louise told them that he was joining the Flying Corps, and Mama announced that Dorcas had baked a birthday cake for Louise, and could he stay for a slice and a cup of coffee? Johnnie glanced at his watch and nodded and told them there was time, as his train didn't leave until eleven o'clock.

Dorcas and Val appeared and were introduced, while Louise escaped to the kitchen saying she would help Dorcas serve the cake.

Dorcas followed Louise into the kitchen, and regarded Louise fiercely. "Louise, that young man is fond of you."

How does she know these things? she thought. Said Louise, choosing to misinterpret Dorcas' statement, "Yes, we're good friends,"

"Does he know you're engaged?"

Louise turned wide, surprised eyes to the older woman. "Well, of course he does! I met him when I went to Winnipeg with Jeremy's parents two summers ago. You knew that."

"Why didn't you ask him to supper here?"

Louise could say honestly that she hadn't thought about it.

"I don't hold with young unmarried ladies having meals in public without a chaperon."

"For heaven's sake, Dorcas, this is the twentieth century! Johnnie is a perfect gentleman," she added truthfully, "and would be insulted if he could hear you." She wanted to ask Dorcas if she would have preferred her young unmarried lady to be having a private supper with Johnnie in his hotel room, but she knew Dorcas would be shocked and probably not speak to her all evening.

217

When they brought the trays of coffee and birthday cake to the small front sitting room, Mama was telling Johnnie that she had known his aunt and uncle for year and years, and that she had been aware of the estrangement between the brothers.

"I think your Uncle James has regretted it always," she remarked. "We were so sorry to hear of your parents' deaths, especially your mother's so recently. Louise has told us how you've stayed home and cared for her, instead of enlisting. That must have been difficult, seeing your friends go away, one by one."

Johnnie was grateful to Mrs. Laurier for her understanding.

"Sometimes I felt I was shirking my duty to my country," he admitted. "Here I was, young and able-bodied, and not in uniform."

"Ah, but your filial duty outweighs your patriotic duty," declared Louise's mother, with conviction. "Though perhaps because I'm a mother I am biased." She looked up at Dorcas and Louise hovering with trays of cake and coffee. "Val, where are your manners? Help your sister hand round the coffee." Val had been sitting next to Johnnie, hanging on to every word as he told them of his flying career.

"I'm going to join up as soon as I am able," he declared stoutly, getting to his feet and taking the tray from Louise.

Mama's eyes filled with tears. "Frank is gone from us, will you also go and be killed, my son?"

Johnnie took the coffee cup and handed it to his hostess. "I am convinced the war will be over before Val is old enough to enlist," he said in a low voice to her. "Do take heart, Mrs. Laurier."

"You're very kind, Mr. Ferris," said Mama, wiping her eyes. "I shouldn't be weeping on Louise's birthday. Perhaps this time next year, we'll have something to celebrate. Louise will be twenty-one, and surely the war will be over as you say."

Louise didn't voice the thought that at this time next year she would likely be in England nursing the wounded. She would see Jeremy and would explain how she and Johnnie had fallen in love, and Jeremy would smile and say that he had met a charming Scottish lass and hadn't been able to say anything because he already was engaged to be married. Louise would say that she hadn't wanted to tell him by letter because Johnnie felt it wouldn't be right, when he

218

was fighting for King and country. They would wish each other the very best, and would kiss goodbye affectionately. Then Louise and Johnnie, on one of his leaves, would be married quietly in a registry office, and spend a few stolen nights together before he had to fly off again and she go on duty. Perhaps they might even start a family immediately. Louise blushed at the thought, and she looked up to see Johnnie regarding her quizzically over his coffee cup.

"A penny for them," he said teasingly.

Louise blushed even more deeply, and was rescued by Mama, who said, "A letter came from Gladdie today, Louise; you can read it later, though there's not much in it."

"I guess she didn't know about Frankie yet."

"I wasn't able to telephone her, the place they're staying is not yet on the telephone. So our letters have crossed in the mail."

"Is she well?"

"She says so; though Mrs. Marchbanks is not so well, and they're going to the mountains where it is cooler. It seems strange to think that they're sweltering in the heat, and we still have snow on the ground. She's been having a gay time, I gather, at parties and such, for the young men in uniform."

"I hope she's not overdoing it. I was worried about her last year."

Mama sighed. "She's a woman grown. I can't influence her any longer."

Johnnie arose, apologies for leaving on his lips, when the telephone bell jangled in the hall. Dorcas was there to answer it, and a moment later came into the room smiling broadly.

"It's Mr. Harry, Ma'am, telephoning from Fairlea. I think you're a grandmother at last." She hurried away, wiping her eyes, muttering, "The Lord giveth and the Lord taketh away, blessed be His name."

Mama jumped up like a young girl and rushed to the telephone. They could hear her voice, both excited and anxious, as she talked to her son-in-law. A few minutes later she called Louise to the telephone, and Louise found herself talking to the excited new father.

"It's a lovely girl, Louise," he said. "And they're both just fine," he added quickly, forestalling the inevitable question. "We're naming her Frances Louise, after all, you and she will be sharing a birthday,

219

and calling her Frances. Norah says to tell you there will be a Frankie in the family again."

Louise was suddenly crying—with relief and happiness and sadness all mixed together.

"It's wonderful news, Harry. Give her my very dearest love, and to you and the twins, too, of course."

"Do come and see us as soon as you can, Louise," he said. "And I've been sending loving thoughts to you all since we heard the news about Frank. You know how sorry we all are here. I'm so proud of Norah—she's held up well, and Gerald has been a tower of strength to us both."

"Oh, Harry, I love you all. And congratulations, of course, to becoming a father once more. This must seem like old hat to you, though."

"Not a bit, Louise. I am so excited—well, you of all people know how I feel about your sister."

Louise paused. "I know, Harry, and I wish you all the very best."

She rang off and came back into the sitting room where the new grandfather was pouring wine and shortly they were drinking a toast to the newest member of the family and her parents. Mama was just sparkling with excitement, and Louise thought that this was the very thing to divert her thoughts from Frankie, and her worries about Gladdie.

"Now I really must be off," Johnnie declared regretfully, putting down the wine glass, and shaking hands with his host and hostess. "What a wonderful way to end the evening, with such good news."

"Has the cab been waiting all this time?" asked Louise as she accompanied him to the door. "Won't it be expensive?"

"It doesn't matter," he replied. "Your mother wrapped up a piece of cake for me to take away; perhaps I'll offer it to the cabby in hopes he'll take pity on me and not charge me the earth." He was laughing as he made these remarks, and he looked down at Louise and saw that her tears were spilling over again. He reached into his breast pocket and brought out the silk handkerchief. "I didn't dare do this earlier," he whispered, and, looking around and seeing the empty hall, he gently wiped her eyes. "There. I'll be carrying away your tears with me."

"Oh, Johnnie," she whispered brokenly.

Johnnie opened the door, and drew her outside on to the unlit porch. In the darkness that now had completely fallen, he took her in his arms and kissed her tenderly.

"Keep smiling, my darling. I'll be home in no time."

Louise stood and watched him stride back to the car, and it seemed to her that he was going out of her life forever. She wrapped her arms around herself, still shivering with ecstasy over his kiss, not feeling the chilly April evening at all. When the sound of the cab had died completely away she came in and slowly went upstairs. That night before going to sleep she prayed very earnestly for Johnnie's safety, and for her sisters, both so far away; one who was likely glowing with happiness at the moment, and the other, very likely unhappy and lonely, in spite of parties and masses of boys in uniform.

Chapter Twenty-Three

LOUISE AND GLADDIE
1917-1918

Summer in Arizona is swelteringly hot, except in the mountains. On the desert floor where the air is dry and healthy, the temperature rises to over a hundred degrees before noon. The native people make their homes from adobe—mud bricks—which insulates them somewhat from the heat, but it was always their custom to go up into the mountains when the hot weather came, where there are springs of water, and cooling vegetation. So it was that Gladys Laurier and Mrs. Marchbanks moved from the resort near Phoenix to a sanatorium high in the hills twenty miles away. Gladdie had seen the doctor shaking his head over her employer as he left her bedroom the other day, and he had wanted to examine Gladdie, too. Gladdie stoutly said she was feeling fine, and was quite capable of looking after Mrs. Marchbanks. The doctor had sighed, and told her to rest whenever she could, and to think seriously about taking the sick woman home as soon as the weather improved in Ontario. She settled Mrs. Marchbanks in her new room overlooking a view of desert and mountains. It was an isolated spot, but every morning and every evening a truck climbed the winding gravel road from Phoenix, bringing mail and the newspapers. Electricity and hot and cold running water was laid on, but there was no telephone to disturb the guests, who were really patients. Each room had its own large bathroom and lavatory. Gladdie felt like royalty as she soaked in the huge marble tub, and breathed in the scented oils she had added to the water. Being a companion to a rich old lady had its compensations, she thought as she dried herself off with thick thirsty towels. She sat on the low seat in front of the long mirror and stroked cream onto her body. She had lost weight, and thought she was looking well. In her opinion, she had always been too plump, though she was proud of her large breasts, and shapely legs. She hated her freckles, and spent hours bleaching them with lemon juice. Peter had admired them, though. He was the young man who was shortly being shipped out to Europe, and whom Gladdie had met at a party in Phoenix a few weeks ago. He had promised to come up to the hotel to see her before he left. Gladdie always called it a hotel in her mind, and not a sanatorium, though it certainly was more like a resort than a hospital. The staff, some of whom were nurses, did not wear the conventional white uniforms and caps, but pastel colored pinafore-like garments over white dresses.

Gladdie thought that Mrs. Marchbanks was quite ill. She had a cough, which produced thick sputum, and the nurse had shown Gladdie how she must dispose of the handkerchiefs she coughed into. They were cheap cotton, and they eventually got burned. The elderly lady's color was high, with two bright spots of red in the middle of her cheeks. The thought of taking her back to Ottawa made Gladdie shiver. It was a long journey, and soon it would be hot and humid in that part of the world. Switzerland would be the ideal place, cool and dry and healthy. However, with the war going on, that thought was impossible.

Gladdie stood nude in front of the mirror, and admired herself. She ran her hands down over hips and across her belly. No need for laced corsets stiff with whalebone for her anymore! Then she slowly dressed, trying to decide what she would wear for her date with Peter.

"Is your young man coming to see you?" asked Mrs. Marchbanks, when Gladdie went in to give the older woman her four o'clock medication.

"Yes, he is," she answered. "I don't know what to wear, though."

223

"How about that pretty pale green dress? You always look like a breath of spring to me in that." And Mrs. Marchbanks looked affectionately at the young woman.

Gladdie, flattered, agreed to wear the dress the old lady suggested, and promised to come in and show it off to her before she met her friend. They were going to have dinner together in the dining room, and then walk in the gardens. Peter was getting a ride with the evening mail, and then planned to hitchhike back down to the town. There was often any number of people coming and going, and Gladdie had told him that with his uniform on, no one would pass him by. He had written her a note, saying that he would be there on Saturday afternoon. Monday morning his troops were catching the train to New York City.

Gladdie brought in the supper tray to her employer, and read to her in her quiet voice while the old lady picked away at her food. She was allowed a small glass of sherry before her meal to stimulate her appetite, but she'd only taken a sip of it. Gladdie finished it off, and poured herself a second when Mrs. Marchbanks wasn't looking. She took the tray away, and then helped the elderly lady to the lavatory. In the bathroom she helped her wash her face and hands, and then settled her for the evening.

She's so thin, thought Gladdie. Nothing but skin and bones. She's going to die soon. What will happen to me? she thought with a shiver.

She rubbed Mrs. Marchbanks' back and helped her into a clean nightgown. The effort of getting up had sent the sick woman into a coughing fit, and when she brought up the sputum, it was streaked with bright red. Gladdie disposed of it as she had been taught, and washed her hands thoroughly in the bathroom. She then went next door to the adjoining room she occupied, and dressed herself carefully in the green dress and matching shoes. She brushed her hair, but she could never get it to shine like her sisters did theirs. The natural curls were rather limp, but she tied them back with a green ribbon, made her face up meticulously, and went next door to say goodnight to Mrs. Marchbanks.

"You look very pretty, my dear, do have a lovely time, and bring the young man to meet me after you have your dinner. I'm sure I'll still be awake."

Gladdie said she would, though she added that she wouldn't wake her if she were asleep. She went down the hall to the lobby to wait for Peter. As she passed the office where the nurse had her desk, she put her head in the door and reported that she was off for the evening.

"Thanks, Miss Laurier," the nurse smiled. "I'll be looking in on her later on. She has her calling bell close at hand?"

"Yes, of course," Gladdie sniffed and continued on. What did that nurse take her for anyway? Gladdie figured she was just as good a nurse as any of them, especially her sister Louise. Louise would hate what she was doing, looking after a sick old woman, supporting her while she coughed her lungs out, and holding her up while she sat on the toilet. Gladdie wished she knew exactly what Mrs. Marchbanks had written in her will. The old lady had hinted that she'd be leaving Gladdie something, but she had never shown her the document. She carried it around in her little case that was with her all the time.

Oh well, she was out for a good time tonight. Peter was an attractive young man who seemed to be smitten by her. It didn't seem to worry him that she was more that four years older than he; in fact he said he was flattered that she would be interested in someone so young. He was barely twenty-one.

As she went by reception the clerk on duty called her over to say there was a letter for her. She glanced at it, saw that it was from her parents, and slipped it in her pocket as she looked around the foyer for Peter. She smiled triumphantly when she saw him standing over by the window, anxiously watching for her. She smoothed her curls, moistened her lips with her small pink tongue, and sauntered over to him. It wouldn't do to appear too eager.

"Hallo, Peter! Fancy seeing you here," she said coyly, as he started eagerly toward her.

"Gladys! You look absolutely marvelous!"

"You're looking fairly handsome, too," she responded, taking his outstretched hand. In fact, he looked magnificent in his khaki uniform. He was tall, broad-shouldered, with dark hair and eyes. His face was clean-shaven, and when he smiled his teeth were white and even.

They went into the little guest dining room, where patients could bring their relatives or other guests. She chose a table on the patio, with a view of the gardens and the pine trees beyond. After their meal Gladdie took him along to Mrs. Marchbanks' room, where the sick woman was awake and restlessly waiting for them. Peter stood awkwardly while Gladdie fussed around her patient and settled her once more. Then they went out and down the hall to the glass doors at the end that led out on to a smooth expanse of green lawn where croquet was played. She took him down a winding path to the springs where they sat side by side in silence. Gladdie thought she'd scream if he didn't try to kiss her. The moon was coming up through the trees, and it was a romantic sight.

Peter finally cleared his throat. "Well, I leave on Monday," he said.

"I shall be devastated," Gladdie declared, edging closer to him. She found his hand and gave it a squeeze.

"Oh, Gladys, you're so beautiful, how can you like an uninteresting fellow like me?"

"You're very attractive, don't you know that? Whatever is wrong with the girls you know?"

"I don't know very many girls," he confessed. "I went to a boys' school, and from there into the army. There never was time for girls."

Gladdie thought that he would be in for a shock when he got to England. She had heard that English girls were very forward and bold. They would be around him like flies to a honey pot. She sighed. She would have to be forward and bold if they were to get anywhere tonight.

"Come on, let's walk some more. There's a lovely fountain in the gardens outside our rooms. People throw coins in it and make wishes."

She took his hand, and drew him to his feet, and led him back along the path where the Sanatorium building loomed against the sky. Lights winked from the windows. Mrs. Marchbanks' window was dark, but a faint light glowed next door. Gladdie had left her bedside lamp burning.

The fountain was very pretty in the moonlight. The sound of the water falling was soothing.

"Look," she said, "if there was music, we could dance." And she hummed a little tune and did a pirouette on the smooth paving stones around the fountain.

He laughed, following her mood, and took her in his arms as though to dance a waltz.

"One two three, one two three," hummed Gladdie, as they whirled around the cascading water. "What's this?" she asked, as her hands, which had slid down his back, came into contact with something smooth and hard in his back pocket.

"Oh," he said, in an embarrassed tone. "Just a flask of whisky ... I didn't know whether we could get a drink. I don't drink much, but all the fellows have flasks."

"I have glasses in my room," said Gladdie, thinking, now, we're getting somewhere. "I'll just go in and get a couple."

"But it's mile around to the door and through the hallway," he objected. "No, it's not. Every room has a door on to the patio. My room is right here." In a moment she had gone up the stairs, across the patio, and through the door into her room. Two minutes later she returned with two glasses, clinking with ice cubes, and a bottle of water.

"Come on," she giggled, let's sit over there in the shadows. It wouldn't do to have Matron spot us from her room."

Peter followed her over to the bench under three large hemlock trees, and he brought out his flask and poured generous shots into Gladdie's glasses. He took a large swallow and nearly choked.

"Sip it, for heaven's sake," whispered Gladdie. She added water and took a small drink. He did the same, and before they knew it, half the whisky was gone. "Now you must learn to drink carefully," Gladdie instructed him solemnly. "It wouldn't do to get drunk, now would it."

227

"I'll have to have some more in order for you to teach me," he whispered cheerfully. He leaned back to take a swig straight from the bottle, lost his balance and fell off the bench.

"Watch it! You'll lose the whisky!"

Peter was sitting on the ground, triumphantly holding the flask in his hand. "Lookit—never spilled a drop."

Gladdie tried to take it from him, but he held it out of her reach.

"Say," he said, "are you more worried about my booze than me?"

"Of course," she giggled, and before he realized it she was down on the grass beside him, grabbing the flask and taking a drink straight from it as he had. A good-natured tussle took place, with Gladdie naturally winding up underneath. He looked down at her, deliberately took the flask from her and set it on the bench. Then he lowered himself beside her, bent and kissed her. Gladdie's arms went around his neck and she kissed him in return.

"Gladys! Oh what you do to me!" he muttered, and kissed her again. Gladdie rolled out from under him, and got to her knees. "I don't want grass stains on my dress," she said lightly. "Why not come inside?" she suggested, as though she had just thought of it. "Wouldn't you like to see my room?" He got up, smoothed his uniform, picked up the flask and glasses, and followed her across the lawn and up the stairs to the patio that led into her room. They tiptoed in, Gladdie conspiratorially putting her finger to her lips, eyes dancing with excitement.

"Mrs. Marchbanks is next door, but once she goes to sleep, she never stirs until morning. I'll just go and check her."

Gladdie quietly opened the communicating doors and stole in to the next room. Mrs. Marchbanks was sound asleep. Peter was emerging form the lavatory when she returned.

"All's quiet," she said in a low voice, and locked the door behind her. Peter was standing awkwardly, trying vainly to ignore Gladdie's big bed, with its counterpane turned down invitingly, exposing a soft white pillow with the wisp of silky nightgown peeking out from underneath. Gladdie went over to the mirror, and peered at her reflection over her shoulder.

"Can you see any grass stains, Peter?"

"I don't think so."

"I shall have to take it off to see," she said, and disappeared into the bathroom, reappearing in a gaily-flowered wrapper, dress over her arm. "No, it's all right,"' she said, hanging it up in the closet. "Sit down, Peter, you do take up a lot of space."

Peter took a deep breath, took her hand, and drew her to him. "No, I think I shall kiss you again." And he did so very thoroughly, leaving Gladdie altogether breathless.

"Peter, take off your jacket—you'll be more comfortable," Gladdie whispered, and began to unbutton it.

He obeyed, folded it up neatly and placed it over the back of the chair.

Then he kissed her again.

"And you say you've had no experience with girls," she whispered.

He was aware that she had nothing on at all underneath the wrapper.

"Gladdie," he whispered, "I've never done this before."

"Neither have I," she lied. "We'll have fun figuring out what to do."

She slipped under the covers and watched with amusement as he took off his ties and blouse, folding them precisely and placing them on the chair. Under the blouse was a singlet, which he removed and placed on top of the blouse. Then he sat down and took off his shoes and socks, which he placed side by side under the chair.

"Are you always this neat?" she asked him, as finally his trousers came down and were also folded neatly with the creases together and hung over the chair back.

"You have to be, in the army," he said simply, and slipped under the covers as she held them up for him.

"Take off those skivvies," she ordered. "They'll get in the way." Once more he obeyed, but that garment landed in a heap on the floor. "Can we turn off the light?" he asked nervously.

She shook her head, and raised herself up on one elbow, smiling down at him as he lay uneasily beside her. "No. I want to see you. Don't you want to see me?" She traced his jaw line with a manicured nail. "Relax, Peter," she added lightly. "Let's just enjoy each other."

229

Much later as Peter drowsed beside her, she remembered the letter in her dress pocket. She stole quietly out of bed, tying the wrapper snugly around her, and retrieved the envelope from the closet. She sat down in the other chair, and watched his sleeping figure for a few moments. For someone who had never been with a woman before, Peter was certainly a fast learner! She smiled to herself. Though he had questioned her claim of virginity immediately.

"Are you sure you've never done this before?" he asked as she lay in his arms after the first time. "You seem to know what you want. Not that I'm complaining," he added.

She contrived to look distressed. "I-I'd hoped you wouldn't guess, Peter. I really don't want to talk about it."

He looked concerned. "Was it a terrible experience? You can tell me," he coaxed.

"I was really young. My schoolteacher fancied me, and one day he got me alone and forced me—well you can guess. He said no one would believe me if I told. So I never did."

"You poor kid! How long did it go on?"

"Oh, months," she answered carelessly, "until I just wouldn't anymore."

"The cad!" exclaimed Peter.

The fact of the schoolteacher was true enough, except what Gladdie hadn't bothered to tell Peter was that it was she who had initiated the relationship in the first place. The precocious fourteen year old found that she possessed something for which men would return again and again, and because of this she wielded a kind of power. About this time the family moved into the city, and Gladdie had to cast about for another victim. She seemed to sense who would be most damaged by exposure, and pursued them discreetly but purposefully. No one ever suspected what transpired during piano lessons with middle aged Mr. Bennett, or with Mr. Smith, who was tutoring her in Latin.

Jeremy Ferris she had known most of her life. He was her brother's best friend, and he often visited in the Laurier home. He flirted mildly with both her and Norah, and the four often went about together, frequently joined by two or more friends. Nobody actually paired off. She knew that to Norah he was just another older brother like Gerald, so there was no rivalry there. He attracted her mainly because he seemed oblivious to her sexual charms. She was subtle at first, but then pursued him overtly. During the time she spent in Montreal with Mrs. Marchbanks she saw much of Jeremy, and it was one of the first times that she had him to herself without the presence of her brother and sister. They met at parties, and suppers, and for the first time in her life it was Gladdie who was in thrall.

He never actually rejected her advances; he just ignored them. He kissed her a few times, but never where or when there was opportunity to go further. Gladdie was frustrated and puzzled by him. When they were back in Ottawa he called often, and she remembered how annoyed she was when he admired Louise in the red coat and hat Gladdie had so carelessly given to her younger sister. She got great pleasure out of snatching it away from under her nose. She pursued him at Louise's eighteenth birthday party, flirted with him, and flattered him, still convinced he would eventually succumb to her charms, and was given the shock of her life when he announced his and Louise's engagement! She didn't care to think about that. She had never been so angry in all her life, and she hated Jeremy for rejecting her, and Louise for being the girl he chose instead of her. She knew when to accept defeat, however, but expressed her outraged feelings when she cut up her red coat and deposited it on Louise's bed. That must have given her something to think about!

She smiled spitefully at the memory, and looked at the letter she held in her hands. She wondered what her parents wanted. It couldn't be an answer to her last letter to them; she had mailed it only a few days ago just before they moved up to the sanatorium. The paper crackled as she opened the envelope, and Peter turned over and opened his eyes.

"What are you doing?"

"I just remembered I had a letter from my parents," she replied, as she unfolded the sheet.

My dear Gladdie, It is with great sadness that your Papa and I write to you today . . .

She read it silently, Peter watching her.

231

"It's not bad news, is it?"

"Well, actually, it is," she answered. "My brother's been killed overseas."

He sat up, filled with distress for her.

"You poor girl! I'm so sorry! How old was he?"

"Frankie? Same age as you, I guess, twenty-one."

She went to him and he held her tenderly. "It's such a shock. You must be numb, poor darling."

Louise would be dreadfully upset. She and Frankie had been thick as thieves since they were little kids. Deep down Gladdie had always envied their friendship. She pressed her lips together. It served Louise right. She hoped that Jeremy wouldn't come back, either.

"What are you thinking, darling?"

"Of my sister Louise," she said truthfully. "She'll be devastated. She and Frankie were always great chums."

He bent and kissed the top of her head. "You'll want to go home, won't you."

"I can't leave Mrs. Marchbanks."

"Surely she'll get good care here."

"Her daughter would have to come." Gladdie had no intention of going home.

She turned in his arms and smiled up at him provocatively. "Well, there's nothing I can do at the moment, is there. Life must go on, and here we are together."

He glanced at her bedside clock. "It's awfully late. There'll be no rides down the mountain at this time of night."

"I thought you said you didn't have to be back until noon tomorrow."

"I don't, but I can't stay here, can I?"

"Why not? You can sneak out before daybreak and get a ride with the night watchman. He starts home at about seven o'clock. He'll never say anything."

"You sure? I don't think you should be alone at a time like this."

"You are so thoughtful, Peter. I could stand some more comfort," she added meaningly.

"We'll comfort each other," he said, and reached for her.

232

Spring came with a rush to the Ottawa Valley. The trees leafed, the bulbs sprouted and the early flowers bloomed profusely. On the twenty-fourth of May weekend Papa put in his vegetable garden, which was his hobby. There was a walled kitchen garden at the side of the house, and a small greenhouse where he started his seedlings: lettuce, tomatoes, and some bedding plants. He appreciated Mama's tropical plants in the conservatory, but never failed to smugly remark that one could never eat orchids! He planted his carrots and beans and beets, and spent happy hours weeding and thinning. His radish crop was always the first to be ready for the table. Louise liked to eat them straight from the garden, rinsed off with the garden hose. They were sweet and crisp and tasted like nothing on this earth. Also in the kitchen garden were several fruit trees pruned to grow flat against the wall, and the south facing wall which received the most sunshine was covered with grapevines, which produce a variety of small, sweet, purple table grapes. Louise thought they were best straight from the vine, still warm from the sun.

Louise and Susie had asked for the same holiday time in July, and Louise planned a trip to Prince Edward Island for the two of them in order to visit Norah and Harry. Aunt Bernice and Gerald were next door, of course, and they would split their time at each house, not wanting to hurt any feelings. Susie was quite excited, for she had never been to the Island, and had heard Louise's rapturous descriptions. Louise could hardly wait to see her little niece Frances, who was now two and a half months old.

Mama and Papa had heard from Frankie's commanding officer, who wrote a fine letter, kind, sympathetic, with much praise for the young man. Sybil also wrote in May, and to their astonishment, she told them that she and Frankie had been married just before he went into battle. They had had such a short time together, she said, but the memories would remain precious. She was continuing with her nursing, and hoped that Louise would come to England when she graduated. Louise had mentioned this as a possibility some time ago. Was she still thinking about it? Major Ferris had come to visit her last week, she said. What a wonderful person he was, so handsome, and he thought the world of Louise. If Louise came, as soon as they were able, she would make arrangements for them to go to Flanders and visit Frank's grave.

Louise and Susie left for the Island the first week in July. Ottawa was hot and humid, and they were glad to be going to the seaside. They planned to travel all the way into Charlottetown and stay with Aunt Mercy and Uncle Rob for a few days. Harry would come into town to collect them and his mother at the same time, for she had not yet seen her newest grandchild. In her letter Mercy told them about all these arrangements, and that she and Robert would be not be visiting Fairlea until the autumn.

There will be enough people for dear Norah to cope with, she wrote, *even though you will probably be staying with my sister Bernice for part of the time. Have I mentioned how well your brother Gerald has fitted in? Bernice is so pleased that he likes the Island life, and that the local folk have accepted him at once.*

Louise had Sibyl's letter with her and gave it to Susie to read, and they discussed their after graduation plans. It seemed hard to believe they had less than six months to go in their training. Susie planned to stay at the hospital and work with the sick children—she seemed to have a real talent for dealing with babies and toddlers who were fretful and ill.

"Do you have a picture of your sister-in-law?" Susie asked, when she put the letter down.

"Just this one of her in her nurse's uniform. It was taken last fall, before she met Frankie. There's one of them both when Frankie was still in hospital, but Mama has it framed in her room at home."

Susie studied the photograph. "She's pretty, isn't she? Were you really shocked to find that they were married?"

"Not really. They were properly engaged, you know, but just hadn't set a date. I think Sibyl thought that Frankie wouldn't be sent back to the front, that his injuries were too grave. So I guess when he got his orders they got married right away. I don't blame them. They'd want some time together, no matter how short."

"And it turns out that it was all they would have," said Susie with a sigh.

234

"Poor Frankie." She gazed sadly out the window at the passing scenery.

"It will be wonderful meeting her," Louise mused. "I think we're going to be good friends."

"I was surprised to hear of my brother visiting her. He didn't mention it in his last letter to me."

"Jeremy? It's hard to think of him as Major Ferris. Sounds altogether too grand."

"You're not jealous, are you?"

"Of Jeremy visiting Sibyl? Heavens, no. It seems perfectly logical to me. Jeremy probably feels as though she's his sister-in-law." Louise's tone was light.

"Jeremy should introduce cousin Johnnie to her," Susie suggested, "then she could still be in the family. Sort of."

At Johnnie's name Louise's pulse quickened. He had written to her only once since he had landed in England nearly three months ago. The letter was much the same as his had always been, friendly and amusing; she could picture him before her chatting away. However, there was a subtle intimacy that had not been present before. She doubted if anyone reading it would notice, but in any case she had put the letter lovingly away, only taking it out and rereading it when she was alone. She'd also take his mother's ring and put it on while she read it. She knew she was being foolish, but she couldn't help it.

"By the way, I've been meaning to ask you, did you and Johnnie quarrel that time?"

"Quarrel? What do you mean?" asked Louise. "When?"

"When he drove you back to Ottawa from Perth. You remember, when we first heard about Frankie. When he got back the next day he was very quiet. He said he was tired, that he'd started off early, but I wondered if you two had words, or something."

"Not a bit of it!" replied Louise truthfully. "I actually saw him before he left for Montreal and points east. He invited me to supper."

"Oh, that's all right then. You haven't mentioned him much at all lately and I wondered if there was something wrong."

Nothing wrong that I can tell you, Louise thought guiltily. This was the first important secret she had kept from her best friend. She couldn't tell Susie she had fallen madly in love with Johnnie, and that she was planning to break her engagement to Susie's brother Jeremy. Nor that she and Johnnie had spent Friday night together alone in a farmhouse, and that they had almost made love together. Susie would be shocked and hurt. Louise would leave things as they were as Johnnie had suggested, and wait for the boys to come home from the war. Then and only then would she tell Jeremy. She knew there would be no choice for her. She might be promised to Jeremy, but she belonged to Johnnie heart and soul. I wish it could have been body as well, she thought then blushed deeply. The only thing she regretted that she would be hurting Jeremy.

Maybe, she thought, as the train rattled its way along the river to Montreal, Jeremy and Sibyl could fall in love. That would be the solution. Never mind fixing up Johnnie with Sibyl—that would never do! She smiled to herself. Susie was watching her curiously, but said nothing.

It was cool and rainy when they reached Charlottetown a day and a half later. Rob and Mercy were at the station to meet them, broad welcoming smiles on their faces.

"It's so lovely to see you again, Louise," Mercy declared, folding her in a warm embrace. "We all have been thinking about you so much since we heard the news of Frankie. I know your sister wanted to be there with you, but of course it was impossible."

"We talked on the telephone several times. I don't know what it cost Harry," said Louise. "And Gerald would have rushed home, too, but Papa said for him to stay and help Harry support Norah."

"And he did, too, I understand," Mercy said.

"Yes. When Harry called us to say the baby had arrived he remarked to me how much he appreciated Gerald being there."

Louise then introduced Susie to them.

"Welcome, my dear. You and Frankie were friends, weren't you. You must also be worried about your brother."

"I don't know what Jeremy is doing over there," admitted Susie. "Nobody does. It sounds cloak and dagger. Who knows, he may be a spy behind enemy lines. We never hear from him for months on end, then bang, everybody gets a letter."

"Good gracious," said Mercy. "You don't say! I had no idea."

Louise and Susie spent three days with Mercy and Robert, seeing the small but charming city, and partaking of its social life. They went to a musical concert in the park, and ate a picnic supper on the grass; toured the government buildings, and saw where the Fathers of Confederation had met to create a new country; had tea with Mrs. Kidd, Norah's mother-in-law, who praised Norah to the skies. Harry finally came to collect his mother and Susie and Louise on Friday, and they enjoyed the drive down to the south shore. The weather had turned fine, the cornfields were high and green, and on the grapevines, pear and apple trees, fruit was beginning to form. They sang songs, Susie and Louise harmonizing, and Harry singing bass in quite a passable voice. Even Mrs. Kidd joined in with a rather quavery but true soprano. Harry told them stories about his twins and their exploits, and how the baby was beginning to smile and make sounds. He took a longer, but more scenic route through Summerside, and he pointed out various places of interest as they drove by. Soon they had whisked through Fairlea village, and were on the dusty red road that led to the farms.

"There are the twins," Mrs. Kidd said, as two small figures darted out of the gate to Aunt Bernice's farm, waving madly.

Harry turned into the driveway, and went very slowly, the children running alongside the car.

"Auntie Louise, Auntie Louise, you're here at last," they were shouting. Gerald and Bernice were there to meet them, and Louise found herself enfolded with hugs by the twins, her brother and her aunt.

"You're all coming for supper at our house," Sarah told them breathlessly.

"We're going to eat under the trees outside," continued Ben.

"Mama and Mrs. Hastie have been cooking all day!"

"Aunt Bernice is bringing stuff, too."

"Have Mary and Bernice been cooking all day, too?" asked Louise mischievously.

"Yes, indeed," smiled Bernice. "It will be a feast. The doctor and his wife are invited, as well."

"When are you coming to see the baby?" asked Sarah, her arm twined around Louise's.

"As soon as we get unpacked," Louise promised.

Aunt Bernice was shaking hands with Susie, and Harry was getting back into the car, beckoning to the twins.

"Hop in, you two rapscallions, it's time to go home and help Mama get the supper organized."

Sarah squeezed Louise. "Hurry over as soon as you can, Auntie Louise," she said.

"Gosh, Louise, what an evening!" exclaimed Susie as they snuggled down under the covers at Bernice's several hours later.

It had been a wonderful evening. As soon as they were able, Susie and Louise had rushed over to Arbutus Farm to see Norah and the baby. Louise showed Susie the footpath and the stile that served as a shortcut between the two homes. Norah greeted them rapturously, and took them into the bedroom where wee Frances was just waking up. She had the bluest of blue eyes ("Her father's," said Norah proudly) and gave her thrilled aunt the sunniest of smiles. Louise picked her up, cuddled her, and then handed her over to her mother.

"I think she's hungry."

Norah sat down in her rocking chair, and with an apologetic glance at the girls, unbuttoned her bodice and put the baby to breast. Louise thought that she'd never seen anything so beautiful as her sister feeding her child. Norah's face glowed with a dreamy expression as she bent her head forward, watching her baby suckle. Louise thought of a painting she'd once seen of the Madonna and Child.

Sarah and Ben came in as Norah changed and settled Frances in her cradle.

"I get to help Mama bathe Frances," Sarah told Louise proudly. "When she gets bigger, I'm going to teach her to walk," announced Ben, as they both hung over the cradle, admiring their little sister.

Supper was a merry affair, spread out on the big table under the trees on the side lawn. There was cold turkey and ham, potato salad, fresh tomatoes, still warm from the sun, pickled beets, devilled eggs, and vegetable salad. The doctor's wife brought a large tureen filled with cold cream of potato soup, and Aunt Bernice provided pies and fresh fruit. Even Mary and Pierre were invited, and Mrs. Hastie sat down with them, as soon as she had finished ladling the soup. There was fresh buttermilk for the children, and ice-cold lemonade for the ladies, and chilled beer for the men. Later, after their meal had settled, Louise and Susie played hide and seek with the twins, then went in and admired the baby once more. The sun was setting when they said goodnight, and Bernice, Gerald, Louise and Susie went home over the stile, Mary and Pierre drove home in their horse and buggy, and Harry chased his twins to bed.

"No story tonight," he told them. "It's long past your bedtime."

"It was a special occasion, though, wasn't it, Daddy."

Louise and Susie went up to bed, and avidly discussed the day's events. "Yes, it was quite the day," agreed Louise. "Isn't the baby beautiful?"

"Norah looks wonderful."

"Yes, she's very happy," sighed Louise, wondering when it would happen to her.

"Louise, I don't know why you called Harry a cranky old man, he's full of fun and doesn't seem any older than Gerald."

"I know, Susie, he's changed. Maybe I have, too," she added quickly, "but he really is a different man since the first time I met him. Though it was an awkward occasion to be sure; I told you, didn't I, how I mistook his cow for Aunt Bernice's Clover, and he rushed over to stop us trying to take it back to our side of the fence."

"Yes," giggled Susie, "then you said he and Norah had an almighty row and commenced to fall in love!"

"I wasn't there when they had words, and Mary never told me what was said. It was because Norah had to tell Sarah that her mother was dead—Harry had never talked to them properly about how their mother had died. It must have been a terrible time for him, poor man," she added, forgetting how critical she'd been at the time.

"You said you didn't like him at all."

"Well, at first I didn't. But I changed my mind. And he loves Norah dearly."

"And it's plain to be seen that Norah is deliriously happy. I'm glad for her. I've always admired her. When I was little I had her all lined up to marry Jeremy—they were always great friends. Little did I know it would be you that he'd fall in love with. Gladdie I've never had any use for," she went on frankly. "It would have been awful if Jeremy had been taken in by her."

Louise was silent.

"I know she's your sister too, but you must admit, she's always been a little different."

Yes, it was true. Gladdie marched to her own drummer. Susie went on. "She didn't come home for Frankie's service."

"No. Mrs. Marchbanks isn't at all well, apparently, so Gladdie stayed in Arizona."

Susie glanced at Louise, and seeing her somber expression, said gaily, "Well, she's a long way away, and I'm sorry I brought her up. The rest of your family is perfect, and I am so glad I came with you!"

She snuggled down underneath the covers, and was soon asleep. Louise lay awake for a long time, thinking of Jeremy, Johnnie, and her sister Gladdie.

Chapter Twenty-Four

SIBYL

The next week was spent lazily on the beach and taking walks with the twins, and at other times helping Norah with the baby. Louise even pitched in and helped to milk the cows from time to time, much to Susie's surprise. Susie said she wasn't interested in learning how.

"You're very knacky," Harry observed, "and you haven't done this since last year."

Just once, thought Louise, and paused, recalling the evening—the snow falling, she in the barn milking by lantern light, and Johnnie standing in the doorway watching her.

"You make a fetching dairy maid," Harry continued, teasingly.

Louise looked up and grinned. "You couldn't afford me," she said impishly.

He started to speak, hesitated for a moment, then said in a low voice, "It's all right now, Louise isn't it? I mean, you have changed your mind about me."

Louise blushed. "Was I that transparent?"

"Well, it was obvious at first you didn't much like me, but then, I guess I wasn't very lovable three years ago. And I felt that you were going along with my marrying your sister for her sake."

241

"Oh, no, Harry, I had changed my mind about you by the time you two got married!" she protested. "And I like you twice as much now as I did then."

"I'll take that as a compliment," he said, smiling a little, as Louise got to her feet from the milking stool and carried the pail into the dairy shed. She said, over her shoulder,

"Norah and you love each other. That's all I know."

"Yes, we do. I am glad, now, that the army wouldn't accept me. I would have missed the most wonderful thing in my life had I gone away at that time." His voice broke a little with emotion and Louise saw his eyes fill before he turned and stumped away.

A few days later, Louise and Norah were sitting in the sun, Norah rocking the baby's cradle, which they had brought out and set up under the tree in the fresh air. Little Frances was slumbering peacefully. Susie had taken the twins off with the ponies, and from the Kidds' kitchen where Mrs. Hastie was baking issued the delicious aroma of new bread. The sisters had been discussing their sister Gladdie.

"She hasn't written a line since a very short note to Mama and Papa acknowledging the letter they wrote to her breaking the news about Frankie," Louise said. "We didn't expect her to come home for the service in his memory, but she didn't even send a bouquet."

Harry had driven into Charlottetown and ordered a beautiful wreath from himself and Norah, and another from Gerald and Aunt Bernice. Mercy and Robert had sent a splendid bouquet for the house, and even Mrs. Kidd wrote a lovely letter of condolence to Mama and Papa.

"Gladdie was never a great letter writer," observed Norah. "And she and Frankie were never close. In fact they fought a lot when they were both in their teens."

"But still, he was her brother."

"I think she was jealous of you and Frankie being such close friends."

"She never tried to be friends with him."

"I know," sighed Norah. "Sometimes there's one in a family that doesn't fit in. Gladdie goes her own way."

"Susie was saying the same thing the other day. She doesn't like Gladdie one little bit."

"You should write to her and try to mend the differences," Norah advised. "I know she's been horrid to you, but she's not a happy person."

Louise made a face, and made no commitment. Instead she said, "Did you know that Harry has been worried that I didn't like him?"

Norah smiled. "I told him there was no problem. Sometimes men have the strangest notions."

"We were both mistaken about him, but so was he about us."

"Remember him striding through the cornfield to rescue his cow from those awful women next door?" giggled Norah.

"I was so sure it was Aunt Bernice's cow, too!"

"And you were so sure he was the hired man!"

"Don't remind me! I felt such a fool when you told me he was Mr. Kidd."

"Not as foolish as I felt when I found out." Norah laughed quietly at the memory, and then her thoughts went on to their courtship, marriage, and honeymoon. How happy she was! And now her darling wee Frances to complete their love for each other!

"Oh, Louise, I am so blessed! My prayer for you is that you and Jeremy will be as happy as we are." And she reached for her sister's hand.

Louise opened her mouth to confide in Norah about Johnnie, and then closed it again. She'd have to swear Norah to secrecy, even from Harry, and her secret would be a burden on Norah. Norah would worry about her, and wonder. No, better she keep her own counsel. She squeezed Norah's hand in response and changed the subject again.

"You knew Mama and Papa went up to Ottey Lake to spend some time with the Ferrises."

"Are they there now?"

"They were hoping to leave a few days after Susie and I left for here. Val has been up there since school ended, of course. He and Michael are delivering newspapers as a summer job. Dorcas was planning on cleaning the house from cellar to attic since she would

243

be home all by herself. She said she'd already called Mrs. Scott, who comes into help sometimes. Those two will have a great gossip and the house will be absolutely shining when Mama and Papa return." She looked up as a car turned into the long driveway from the road. "Look, here's Harry back already."

Harry had taken his mother to Summerside where she was going to visit an old friend before going home.

"Letter for you, Louise! The hospital forwarded it. It's from England." Louise reached for it eagerly. Was it from Johnnie?

Harry greeted his wife with a kiss, and bent over his sleeping daughter, brushing her forehead with his lips. He then flung himself down beside Norah, and handed her the mail. "Nothing interesting for us. A bill and a circular, and your magazine." He looked questioningly at Louise, who was reading avidly, and had made a stifled exclamation.

"It's from Sibyl! How extraordinary! How utterly marvelous! Goodness, whatever is the date today, Norah?"

"For heaven's sake, Louise, what on earth has happened? Please don't keep us in suspense."

"Why don't you read it to us?' suggested Harry quietly.

Louise's cheeks were pink with excitement. "It's dated June twentieth."

Dear Louise, she read, *I will be writing your parents, too, but I wanted you to be one of the first to know my news, since you were Frank's favorite sister. I am to have a child sometime between Christmas and New Years'! I didn't know when I last wrote you, but I have been sure now for some time. I wanted to wait until I felt all was well before telling anybody. Dr Webster, my physician, reports that as far as he can see, everything is fine, and that I am healthy.*

However, there are complications. You know that I have lived with my aunt and uncle since my parents died when I was twelve. They are rather elderly, never had any children, and I am sure they took me in out of duty. Sometimes I have felt guilty that I could never love them. I had to break my news to them, of course, as I will be resigning my job in the hospital. They have flatly refused to have me live with them after the

244

baby is born! Too disruptive, they say, and besides, how will I pay them my room and board if I am not working?

I had a long talk with Sister Love, as she knows you and has met your parents. Frank would want his child to be born in Canada, I know. We were going to come home to Canada as soon as the war was over and he could be demobbed. Now, here is the second bit of news. Sister and I have found passage on a ship that sails on July tenth, and stops in Halifax on its way to Boston. She suggested that it would be easier traveling now than with a baby later on. She's given me marvelous references for when I can go back to work, and has been very kind about things happening at such short notice.

Dear Louise, of course there isn't time for me to write and for you to answer me before the tenth, but I know you will be as kind as she, and I hope your parents will be too. They are the only parents I have now, of course. Will you break the news to them gently and say that I will write them in a few days?

My ship, the 'Morgana V' docks in Halifax July sixteenth. I will find out about trains to Ottawa when I get there. I think I am a good sailor, because I have traveled across to France in the past with no trouble, and the English Channel can be very rough.

I hope to see you in a few weeks! I can hardly believe it, as the last time I wrote I was thinking about your coming over here next spring and making plans for us.

Dear Louise, I hope this isn't too much of a shock.

Your loving sister, Sibyl Laurier.

Louise looked up at Norah and Harry, her eyes shining. "That's only a few days away!" she exclaimed.

"And her letter to Mama and Papa is probably sitting on the hall table waiting for them when they get back from the lake," added Norah.

"So they don't even know she's coming. What shall we do?"

"Someone will have to go to Halifax and fetch her," Harry said calmly.

Norah was looking at her husband affectionately. "And bring her here to us?"

245

Harry smiled. "Of course."

"Oh, Norah, it's the very thing! And she can travel back to Ottawa with Susie and me."

"Perhaps we can prevail upon Gerald to go," suggested Norah.

"And I'll go with him," decided Louise firmly.

"I'll telephone over to Gerald and Bernice, and ask them to come over after dinner this afternoon for a family conference," Norah said, getting to her feet. "Can you help me with Frances' cradle?" she asked Harry, and between the two of them they carried the sleeping infant inside where Mrs. Hastie was putting the meal on the table.

Susie and the twins appeared at that moment.

"Just wait until you hear the latest news!" Louise told her friend.

The young woman had waited for over two hours in the hot, stuffy immigration building before an officer first saw her. She had handed over her precious papers, and now was waiting once more. She was thirsty, pale with fatigue, and felt ill. Perspiration trickled down the side of her face; she could feel stickiness between her thighs and under her arms. At that moment heaven would be a drink of water and a cool bath, in that order. A uniformed woman approached her.

"Mrs. Sybil Laurier?"

Sybil nodded.

"Come this way, please."

Sybil struggled to her feet and followed the woman across the waiting room and into a small office. She was ushered in and asked to sit down and wait.

More waiting! Sybil thought she would scream. However, the window was open and a breeze came through, fanning her hot face.

"Why don't you take your jacket off, Mrs. Laurier," the woman suggested in a kindly voice. "It's very warm today."

Gratefully, Sybil removed her suit jacket. It was creased from days of wear. Her white blouse, which at one time was crisp and starched, was now stained and crumpled. She had not taken it off for the last three days. Her unfashionably long skirt was dusty and wrinkled. She felt like a frump.

Looking up, she saw the inner door open and a man enter and sit down behind the desk. He had a sheaf of papers that Sibyl recognized as hers. When she had given them up earlier in the afternoon, she had had visions of never seeing them again. They were her only proof of who she was: her baptismal certificate, her marriage lines, the notice of her husband's death, the letter from his superior officer, and letters from her husband's family, which she had kept. There was a doctor's certificate commenting on her state of health, and a letter of recommendation from Sister Love 'to whom it may concern'.

"Well, Mrs. Laurier, everything seems to be in order." He replaced her papers in the large envelope in which she had carried them, and pushed them across the desk.

He asked her a few more questions, then rose and put out a hand. Sybil took it gratefully. "We are most sorry for your loss, madam," he went on. "I'm sure we're proud of all the young men that fought at Vimy Ridge, Corporal Laurier included. Welcome to Canada, Mrs. Laurier."

"You mean it's all right? I can stay?"

The officer's eyes twinkled, and he looked quite human. "Yes. This form you can keep with your papers. It says you are a landed immigrant, and it will be just a formality to grant you full citizenship." He looked at her closely as she closed her eyes. "Are you feeling unwell, madam?"

Sybil opened her eyes and smiled. "Yes, a little, but I feel a whole lot better now. I have to find out about trains to Ottawa. Could you tell me where I should go?"

She put the papers in her large bag, and hesitated at the door.

"Miss Ramsay will direct you," he said, as the woman who had shown her in approached again.

"Are you feeling all right, Mrs. Laurier?" Miss Ramsay asked, and took the younger woman's arm.

Sybil nodded. "I shall be fine when I can have a drink of water and a bath," she said.

"There are people waiting for you."

Sybil looked surprised. "There are?"

247

She followed Miss Ramsay across the waiting room and into the large anteroom, which was thronged with people waiting to be seen by an immigration officer. A young man and a young woman rose to their feet where they had been sitting and started across the room toward her.

"Sybil!"

The young woman coming toward her suddenly smiled her dead husband's smile, and her companion swept off his cap with a familiar gesture. Sybil stood stock still in amazement.

"Sybil, I'm Louise!"

Sybil couldn't believe her eyes or her ears. She had been imagining Louise (not even knowing what she looked like) in Ottawa, at the hospital, and here she was in Halifax!

"And this is my brother Gerald," Louise went on.

"Oh! I can't believe it!" And Sybil burst into tears of relief and joy. Louise swept her into her arms and held her tightly. Louise was not a tall girl, but she was taller than Sybil. The young English girl felt like a bird in her arms, so thin and light was she, as she shook with sobs.

"You must be exhausted," Louise went on. "Come on, let's find your luggage and we'll get you to the hotel for the night."

Two hours later, Sibyl was tucked up in bed after a long soak in the big bathtub and a light meal that they ate in the hotel room. Gerald was next door, and Louise would share the room with her sister-in-law.

"Now," said Louise sensibly, "we can talk tomorrow. You need your rest, so I'm going to leave you to go to sleep. I'll just be next door with Gerald for a while if you need me. Is that all right?"

Sibyl nodded. She hadn't even asked them how they came to be in Halifax meeting her. It was enough that they were there, and she didn't have to worry about what to do next. Louise opened the window, and the sounds of rain came to Sybil's ears. The weather had broken at last. Perhaps it would be cooler tomorrow. Both Louise and Gerald seemed so familiar to her, but of course it was because they were Frank's brother and sister. Her last thought was of Frank's smile on Louise's face. She said a prayer of thanks in her mind, and slept.

Sybil and Louise talked nonstop from Halifax to Charlottetown, or so Gerald said dryly to Mercy and Robert, who met them at the train station with their big touring car. A good night's sleep, another bath, a complete change of clothing, and a hearty breakfast, and the young widow felt like a new woman. She remarked to Louise that she'd like to burn the outfit that she had been wearing.

"I stayed up on the deck most of the time," she said. "My roommates were seasick, and in spite of being a nurse, I've always had trouble handling nausea and vomiting," she said with a shudder. "I'd make them comfortable, then escape into the fresh air. It was very rough the last two days, and I slept in the lounge, and just went below to visit the loo." She giggled. "They all thought they were going to die, and I told them, no, they'd recover. It really wasn't funny at all at the time," she added. "It was a nightmare!"

"But you weren't sick at all!"

"As long as I was up on deck in the fresh air I was fine. It's not the motion that makes me nauseated," she added meaningly.

"I know what you mean," Louise laughed.

"Do you two nurses want to discuss something more pleasant?" Gerald suggested. He was sitting opposite them, his head back and his eyes closed. "I may lose my dinner, and the other passengers will complain."

"Tell me about you and Frankie," said Louise. "You were his nurse in the hospital, weren't you."

Sybil's face softened. "He always had a smile and a nice word for the nurses. He didn't exactly flirt, but he was so appealing with all those freckles. He was in a lot of discomfort at times, but he didn't complain. I had to scold him for not letting us know so we could give him something for the pain. I invited him home for Christmas because I felt sorry for him being alone and all crocked up. Little did I know I'd fall in love with him! My friends told me I was robbing the cradle, but he didn't seem to mind that I was older than he. I'm twenty-four," she added.

"Did you decide to get married all of a sudden?"

"I thought he would be sent home," she said sadly, "so when he wasn't, and he knew he'd be going back over to France, he said, 'Let's

249

get married right now.' We got a special license, and spent three days in Scotland. That's where I went to school, you know, in a town just out of Edinburgh."

"Are you Scottish? I thought your accent was different."

"No, I'm English, but I was sent to school there after my parents died. I don't think my aunt and uncle knew what to do with a twelve year old. Sometimes I didn't even come home for holidays. A couple of times I went to stay with friends."

"No brothers or sisters?"

Sybil shook her head. "I'm all alone in the world."

"Not now," whispered Louise. "You have a big family here."

Sybil smiled and squeezed Louise's hand. "Frank told me to get in touch with you if anything happened to him. Of course I didn't believe anything would. He seemed so ... so indestructible, the way he recovered from his injuries." Tears filled her eyes, and she brushed them away impatiently. "At least I have something of his to hang on to," she added, patting her stomach.

Louise thought that Sybil must have had a lonely childhood, and said so. "When I was growing up in the countryside of North England, I was happy. My father was a doctor, and my mother taught piano in our home. It was awful after they died."

"What happened?"

"They were killed in a train wreck in France when they were on holiday."

"You weren't with them, then?"

"No, I was still at school, and I was going to join them the following week."

"How simply ghastly."

"Yes, it was. I had to leave my school and go to the city to live with my aunt and uncle, whom I hardly knew, and then when they couldn't stand having me around, they packed me off to boarding school in Scotland. Actually," she said, reflectively, "they did me a favor. I liked Saint Brenda's, and I was reasonably happy there."

Louise thought of herself growing up in her large, active family, with two loving parents, and considered that she had been indeed fortunate.

"I was just thinking how we take things for granted," she said. "We've been lucky to be born into such a nice family, haven't we, Gerald."

"I'm the eldest. It's always toughest on the eldest," said Gerald in mock sorrow. "You younger ones got spoiled. Once I complained to my mother," he said, turning to Sybil, "that she let them get away with all sorts of things that we could never do, and she just said that it didn't work with us, so why bother with the younger ones?"

Sybil laughed, and Louise gave Gerald a playful slap. "You never! What a story! Mama hasn't spoiled us."

Gerald grinned. "It's true as I am sitting here."

As the train neared Charlottetown, Louise explained her relatives to Sybil. "Mercy is Papa's youngest sister, and she is married to Robert Lesley and lives in Charlottetown. They don't have any children. Aunt Bernice has a small farm in Fairlea, next to my sister Norah and her husband Harry. They have three children, Ben and Sarah, Harry's eight-year-old twins, and the new baby Frances. Named after Frankie. Gerald lives with Aunt Bernice and is running the farm. Fairlea is just a tiny village with a few shops, a church and some homes. The doctor that looks after the area lives in the village—both he and his wife are very nice indeed. Dr McPhee, isn't it, Gerald?"

A merry-faced, brown-eyed woman hugged Sybil and said, "I'm Mercy, welcome, Sybil! This is Robert. How happy we are to meet our new niece!" With the help of two porters they were able to load Sybil's entire luggage on to the car, except for the big steamer trunk, which Robert arranged to have taken separately to Fairlea. The porters went away happily, well tipped, and the five squeezed themselves into the Lesleys' vehicle, and Robert drove them home.

"Robert and I plan to drive you to Fairlea tomorrow," announced Mercy. "Gerald left his car with us, but he couldn't possibly put you two and the luggage into it. So we'll all go down. We haven't seen the baby yet. We were going to wait until all Norah's company left, but this seems to be an opportunity. We won't stay long, just overnight. When do you and Susie go back, Louise?"

"In only ten days. We thought Sybil could come with us, if that's what she wants. Mama and Papa will be glad to have her stay with them, don't you think?"

"I think the telephone lines between here and Ottawa have been buzzing since you and Gerald left for Halifax," smiled Mercy. "Rose said Sybil must decide where she wants to stay. She's thrilled that you've come home to us,"

Mercy added, turning to Sybil. "And so pleased about a new grandchild."

"Louise told me that they are on holidays at a lake," Sybil said doubtfully. "I hope they haven't cut their time short because of me."

"No, William had to come back to the office—he found your letter, Sybil, and telephoned to Bernice straightway."

"I can't believe how wonderful everyone is being. Did Louise tell you I burst into tears when she introduced herself and Gerald to me?"

Mercy smiled. "I'm sure you were completely exhausted. Come, I'll show you to your rooms. Do you mind sharing with Louise? The big guest room has twin beds, and Gerald can have the back bedroom. I expect you'll want to stay with Norah when you go to Fairlea. Norah's very congenial. You wouldn't want to stay with an maiden aunt and a crusty old bachelor, now, would you."

"Do you mean Gerald? I don't think he's crusty," Sybil said shyly, following her up the stairs.

"A diplomat!" Mercy cried gaily, and her laughter rippled back down to her niece and nephew.

Sybil fell in love with Prince Edward Island the next day as they drove down to Fairlea. She loved the red roads, the windswept headlands, and the views of the ocean at unexpected turns. She was enchanted with the rolling green meadows and the wooded hillsides, the orchards and the fields of corn and potatoes. They lunched in Summerside and reached the farm by three o'clock. She insisted on staying with Bernice and Gerald at first, so as not to interrupt Louise's visit with her sister. As the afternoon advanced Bernice saw her guest fading a little and suggested she have a supper tray in her room.

"You won't have to make polite conversation," she said, "and you can go to bed any time you want. Don't even think of unpacking until tomorrow. The bathroom is just down the corridor, and the lavatory is next door."

Mary brought her the supper tray and whispered that it was quite normal to be suddenly tired in the late afternoon. "It's happening to me, too," she added quietly.

Sybil, who had taken to Mary immediately, brightened up at her words. "You, too? Oh, Mary, how lovely. When?"

"Sometime after Christmas. And you?"

"Around that time, too. Won't it be perfectly marvelous? They'll be playmates, along with Norah's little girl."

It occurred to Sybil later that without any conscious thought she had made the decision to stay in Fairlea.

Chapter Twenty-Five

GLADDIE

Louise was disappointed, though not surprised, when Sybil announced that she would not go to Ottawa.

"I'm sure I'll be happier in the country," the English girl said, "and I'll be able to help Aunt Bernice and Norah, too. Also, it'll be nice for the children to be together. Mary's expecting around the same time, did you know?"

Louise hadn't known.

"I hope your parents won't be disappointed. They were the ones I was worried about."

"Mama loves the Island," Louise told her. "They'll be down for a visit this fall, I am sure."

As she and Susie traveled back on the train they discussed the events of the last few weeks.

"You certainly met your sister-in-law sooner than you expected! Are you still planning to go to England next spring?"

"If the war is still on, and both Harry and Gerald think it will be," replied Louise. She was feeling flat, and not quite sure why. She had had a lovely visit with her sister, enjoyed the baby; they had toured the Island a bit and seen Charlottetown, and had been invited to several social events. Moreover, she and her brother had made an unexpected trip to Halifax and rescued Frankie's widow. Louise had envisaged using her nursing skills caring for Sybil, and maybe, even maybe assisting the delivery of the baby at home! In later years, looking back, she realized of course that she had been jealous. Jealous that Sybil must have preferred her sister's company to hers, and life in the backwater of Fairlea, PEI, to the more exciting existence in the national capital. She perhaps misjudged Sybil a little, because the young Englishwoman would have liked being nearer to Frank's favorite sister, but she immediately had felt at home at Fairlea, and knew at once that this was the place to bring up her child.

In the ensuing weeks Louise received regular letters from her sister-in-law, relating Island life, family incidents, and reports on her condition. They were so warm and affectionate that Louise's heart melted, and she felt much better about Sybil's decision to stay on in Fairlea. Little Frannie, as they were calling Norah's baby, was sitting up and taking bright-eyed notice of her world, the twins celebrated their ninth birthday on November 1. ("All Saints' Day," Sybil had remarked—"All Devils' Day, you mean," Gerald had snorted after one of their exploits. "They're not bad, just mischievous," protested their new aunt. "They ask questions because they want to know things.") Sybil had baked a huge birthday cake and taken it next door for their birthday supper that the whole family shared. It seemed that Sybil had taken over the cooking chores that Bernice and Mary once had shared. Mary still worked in the dairy, and had taught Sybil how to milk a cow! Louise smiled at this, and remembered herself and Norah learning that same skill that first time they had visited the island before the war nearly three and a half years ago. Sybil was also a trifle worried about Aunt Bernice, and hoped she wasn't speaking out of turn, as it were. "I spoke to Norah about it a few days ago, and she tactfully inquired of your aunt how she was feeling. Aunt Bernice said she felt fine. I suppose she is getting on in years, but I am concerned that her color isn't good. However, she obviously doesn't want us to fuss."

Louise worked out that Aunt Bernice, who was only five years Papa's senior, would be sixty-six on her next birthday. That was getting on, but surely not ancient! Aunt Bernice ill? She hoped Sybil was wrong.

Louise's thoughts and energy were now taken up on her last two months of training. The final examinations, both written and practical, would occur before Christmas, to allow the students to enjoy the festive season. The graduation ceremonies would take place on January 8th, following the examination results. Louise and Susie spent most of their waking hours after being on duty studying, quizzing each other, and wondering what they would have to do for the practical tests.

While Louise and her classmates wrote their final examinations on a snowy December day, tiny Carson Francis Laurier was being ushered into the world in Aunt Bernice's big spare room bed. As a smiling nurse placed the red-faced, howling infant in his mother's arms, the anxious uncle and great-aunt waiting downstairs heaved a sigh of relief.

"You have a healthy nephew, Bernice, Gerald," Dr McPhee announced, coming downstairs. Mary and Pierre were hovering at the kitchen door, Pierre holding a large tray of tea things. "Thank you, I wouldn't mind a cup of tea, Bernice. Pierre, you take that wife of yours home with you. I don't want to have to come up tonight in this weather!"

Mary, whose confinement shouldn't be for at least another two weeks, smiled and said she was feeling fine. Gerald rushed to the telephone and called his sister next door with the news, and then telephoned long distance to Ottawa to inform his parents of their first grandson. Miss Daisy Connolly, at the local telephone exchange, listened in on the conversation regarding the new arrival, then promptly informed the local folk that Miss Bernice's nephew's widow had given birth to a son, and wasn't that a lovely Christmas present for the family?

William Laurier, meanwhile, thanked his son for getting the news to them so promptly.

"Louise will be thrilled. She said to send her love to Sybil if we heard anything today. She's writing her final examinations at the hospital this afternoon, and plans to be home later on. How is Bernice?"

"She says she's fine, but I'm inclined to agree with Sybil that she's unwell. However, if she won't tell us anything, I don't want to intrude."

"She always tended to keep her own counsel," Bernice's brother remarked. He paused, and then added in a serious voice, "We received a rather disquieting telegram from your sister Gladdie today, Gerald. I'm not quite sure what is happening out there in Arizona, but I think I may have to travel out there."

"What! Right before Christmas?"

"We'll have to see. It seems that Mrs. Marchbanks has died, and there are complications."

"Let me know if there's anything I can do, Father. Shall I keep this to myself?"

"For the time being, yes, probably it's a good idea. No point in upsetting the girls, is there. Give our love to Sybil," he added, and then rang off abruptly.

Gladdie was lonely and frightened. She had been lonely and frightened for several weeks as Mrs. Marchbanks lay dying at the Desert Sanatorium. Although Gladdie's expenses were being covered by Mrs. Marchbanks' account at the sanatorium, her salary had not been paid for two months. She also was beginning to feel quite unwell, and Dr Morgan told her solemnly that she had contracted the same disease that was killing her employer. Gladdie did not believe him; her lungs had always been delicate.

The doctor had also contacted Mrs. Marchbanks' family in Ottawa and Montreal, and her son and daughter-in-law came out on the first train. When Gladdie told Mrs. Marchbanks that they were on their way to see her, the sick woman said weakly,

"That wife of his is just interested in my money, you know. She thinks I'm going to peg out, but she'll be disappointed."

Gladdie decided to mention her lack of salary, but the old lady waved her remarks aside impatiently.

"You'll be looked after in the will," she said. "Mr. Thorpe looked after all that just the other day."

Mr. Thorpe was her lawyer in Ottawa.

"Isn't Mr. Thorpe in Ottawa?" Gladdie asked, frowning in perplexity.

"I mean Mr. er, er, the young man who visited me the other day."

"Oh, Mr. Latimer, you mean. Was he a lawyer?" Gladdie had been quite taken by Mr. Latimer. He was tall and good-looking, with a shock of fair hair and very dark brown eyes. She had flirted mildly with him when she saw him out after his visit, and had been curious as to who he was. She hadn't remembered meeting him when they were staying down in Phoenix. She also wondered why he wasn't in uniform. The American army seemed to now be a presence in Europe, and the papers were full of the war.

Mrs. Marchbanks closed her eyes, and then opened them again. "Get me my jewel case from the safe," she instructed. "You know the combination, don't you?"

Gladdie went to the big wardrobe and brought the jewel case. She helped Mrs. Marchbanks sit up a little, and the old lady brought out a diamond brooch.

"I want you to have this one," she said, pressing it into Gladdie's hands.

"Oh, no, Mrs. Marchbanks, I couldn't," she began quickly, and hesitated.

"No, dear, it's yours."

"Are none of these things in the will? I mean, won't your son—"

"My jewelry is mine to give away as I please," she said testily, with surprising strength in her voice.

Gladdie thanked her sweetly, and took it away into her room. She would have preferred the sapphire necklace, but she expected that it was the most costly of her employer's things. In any case, this would fetch a good price when she got home. You wouldn't catch her wearing an old-fashioned thing like this. She looked at the piece of jewelry thoughtfully before she put it away, and then went back into Mrs. Marchbanks' room.

"Perhaps you should write down that you gave me the brooch," she suggested to the old lady. "I wouldn't want there to be a misunderstanding." Mrs. Marchbanks nodded, and reached for the writing tablet that was on her bedside table.

"Give me my pen."

She struggled to a half sitting position again, and took the pen and paper.

She started to write, but all she could manage was a scrawl.

"You write it down. I'll sign it."

Gladdie wrote the date, then 'I have given Gladys Laurier my diamond brooch.' She handed the tablet to Mrs. Marchbanks, and the sick woman scrawled her signature beneath the statement. It tailed off on an angle, finishing with a large inkblot. There was a large gap between the statement and the signature. Gladdie tore the sheet of paper off the writing pad and folded it up when the ink had dried.

"Shall I keep it?"

Mrs. Marchbanks nodded and closed her eyes, coughing weakly. Gladdie helped her to lie back, then closed the jewel case and put back where she had found it in the safe. She glanced back at her employer, but the sick woman's eyes were closed. Impulsively she opened the case as she was putting it away and picked up the sapphire necklace. It sparkled with dim blue fire. Gladdie gave a great sigh and slipped it into her pocket. She then put the case away and closed the safe. Back at the bedside, she looked down at her patient.

"I think it's time for your bath," she said. "Nurse and I will help you."

"I don't want a bath," the old lady said querulously. "I just want to be left in peace."

Gladdie turned and went into her room, closing the door. She took the necklace out of her pocket and holding it, stared at it for a long time. Perhaps she should put it back. Nobody would believe that Mrs. Marchbanks would give that away to her lowly companion. It was beautiful, though. Gladdie sighed again and put it back in her pocket. It seemed very heavy.

That night she sat at her desk and looked at the piece of paper with her employer's signature on it. She took Mrs. Marchbanks' pen and carefully continued the statement: '. . . and my sapphire necklace.' There. The die was cast.

By the time Mr. and Mrs. Jason Marchbanks arrived several days later, Mrs. Marchbanks was semi-comatose, and only responded when her son spoke to her. Coughing weakly, she clutched at his hand. The doctor was present, and Gladdie heard the young woman say anxiously to him, "Is she infectious?"

"Yes, but if we take precautions, there shouldn't be a problem."

"I'm not going near her," she said with a shudder.

Gladdie's lip curled. Doctors and nurses and paid companions could, though. Young Mrs. Marchbanks was slim and dark, her hair a smooth, gleaming cap. She crossed one leg over the other and lit a tiny cigarette. Gladdie was shocked. She'd never seen a respectable woman smoke in public before.

It was one thing to smoke in the privacy of your own home, but in the very public lobby of a sanatorium? Gladdie thought she probably also went to cocktail lounges and wore bathing costumes on the beach without a robe.

Mrs. Marchbanks died two days after her son and daughter-in-law arrived, and immediately the son was making arrangements for transferring his mother's remains back to Ottawa. She left them to go through his mother's possessions, and went down to speak to the manager of the sanatorium.

"How do I get in touch with that Mr. Latimer that came to see Mrs. Marchbanks about a week or so ago?" she asked.

"Surely Mrs. Marchbanks had his address, Miss Laurier?" Mr. Newmann looked at her coldly. "By the way, you realize that now Mrs. Marchbanks has died, you will be responsible for your own expenses from now on?"

Gladdie paled. "But I don't have much money. She hadn't paid my salary since we came up here. When I asked about it, she said it was all fixed up in her will. That's why I want to get in touch with Mr. Latimer. He came to see her as her lawyer."

There was a commotion outside the manger's office, and one of the clerks knocked on the door and murmured that Mrs. Jason Marchbanks wanted to see Miss Laurier. Without waiting to be shown in, the young woman stormed past the clerk and confronted Gladdie. Her eyes and cheeks were bright with anger.

"My mother-in-law had some valuable pieces of jewelry, and there are two missing," she announced in loud, furious tones. "I want to know what you've done with them!"

Gladdie looked at her contemptuously. "Mrs. Marchbanks gave two pieces to me," she said. "What do you think of that?"

"I don't believe you!" She turned to Mr. Newmann. "My husband intends to hold this establishment responsible as well!"

"I'm sure this can be cleared up immediately," he said smoothly. "Do you have proof of this, Miss Laurier?"

"Yes! She signed a piece of paper when she gave them to me." Well, it's half true, thought Gladdie. Thank goodness I thought of having her write it down. "I'll show it to Mr. Latimer," she added with sudden cunning.

"Who on earth is Mr. Latimer?"

"He's a lawyer she consulted not two weeks ago," replied Gladdie triumphantly, "and I wouldn't be surprised if you had been cut out of her will!"

"You're making this up!" exclaimed Mrs. Jason in alarm.

The manager looked distastefully from one to the other. "It's true she had a visitor on two occasions." He murmured an aside to his clerk, and the woman quietly vanished, then reappeared a minute later with a ledger.

The manager looked through the pages. "A Mr. Latimer came to see her on November 25, and then again on December 5," he said. "I do not know this man. Perhaps Dr Morgan referred her to him. Calm down, er, ladies, we will clear this up."

"I demand she give those pieces back!"

"They're mine, she gave them to me," muttered Gladdie sullenly.

"They're part of her estate, you little baggage! Just hand them over, or I'll have the police on you!"

Gladdie started a sudden fit of coughing that left her weak and perspiring. Young Mrs Marchbanks regarded her with alarm. The manager said smoothly to the clerk, "Conduct Miss Laurier to her room, and we'll have Dr Morgan drop by. In the meantime, we'll get in touch with this Mr. Latimer and find out what has been happening."

Mr. Latimer arrived the next morning and met with Jason and Sonia Marchbanks, Gladdie, along with Mr. Newmann in his office. He showed them a copy of Mrs. Marchbanks' will, whose contents, unfortunately, were not to the younger Marchbanks' liking. She had directed that Gladdie be paid her salary, and a legacy of $5,000; a substantial sum; and her jewelry went to her daughter in Montreal; the Ottawa house to her son; the rest of her assets to her favorite charity.

Her son was speechless; her daughter-in-law quite the opposite. She ranted and raved that Gladdie had undue influence over the old woman; her mother-in-law had promised that the jewelry would be divided between her and her sister-in-law; who wanted that moldy old house anyway.

"You got my mother-in-law to sign something," she said furiously to Gladdie. "Taking advantage of a senile old lady!"

Mr. Latimer hadn't considered that his client had been senile; he pointed out that the big beneficiary was the charity, depending on what these other assets were worth. Jason Marchbanks protested that his mother had bank accounts and investments everywhere, and what about the jewelry? The lawyer frowned, and asked Gladdie to show him what Mrs. Marchbanks had signed. Gladdie gave him the folded piece of paper, and watched him study it. Then he handed it to Jason Marchbanks. His wife looked over his shoulder.

"Why, it's not even in her handwriting!" she exclaimed. "You wrote that yourself," she accused Gladdie.

"She tried to write at first," protested Gladdie. "See that scrawl there. She was weak, so she asked me to write it, and she signed it."

"No witness?" asked Mr Latimer quietly.

"No."

"Anybody could imitate a sick old lady's signature," Mrs. Jason said.

"She signed it," muttered Gladdie.

"I want the police to investigate," began Sonia.

"There's no need of that," Mr. Newmann said hastily, looking alarmed. "I'm sure Mr., er, Latimer is capable of deciding whether or not that's your mother's signature."

"We shall contest the will," stated Jason firmly.

"I am sorry, I attempted to persuade your mother to be fair in her legacies, especially between her two children, but she wouldn't listen to me."

"It proves she was senile!" exclaimed Sonia.

Mr. Latimer ignored the younger Mrs. Marchbanks' remarks. "You will have to swear that Mrs. Marchbanks signed this, Miss Laurier," he said.

"I can swear to that, because it's true," said Gladdie confidently.

"All the jewelry should be appraised," he continued. "When I asked her if she had jewelry she wanted to mention, she said they were just baubles."

"My father gave her that sapphire necklace. I happen to know he paid a lot of money for it."

Mr. Latimer sighed. He had known there would be trouble. Why couldn't the old lady had gone home and died there? He took Gladdie's piece of paper, assuring her it would be returned, and then went to Mrs. Marchbanks' room to look at her possessions.

Gladdie waited for him, and on his way out he found her waiting for him. "Mr. Latimer, I don't have a lot of money, and the Sanatorium is going to charge me personally for all my expenses, now that Mrs. Marchbanks has died. Would you send a telegram for me?"

He agreed, and as he went out to his vehicle, glanced at the notepaper that she had given him. It was addressed to Mr. William Laurier of Ottawa, Ontario.

Mrs. Marchbanks has died, and I need to pay my expenses at the Sanatorium. Her son and his wife are making trouble because I am mentioned in the will. Please help. Gladdie

He glanced back at her for a moment. She was looking very lonely and quite frightened.

Louise came home from writing her exams in high spirits. She was relieved to have them over, and was happy because she was sure

263

she had done well. Her clinical exam was on Friday, and she had been told it would be on the medical ward. It would have pleased her more to be on the surgical ward, as she enjoyed nursing those patients that had had operations, but she decided to review several procedures that she might be asked to do. She was greeted with the news about Sybil's baby, and the family sat down to a celebration supper. Papa served wine, unusual in the middle of the week, and they all toasted Carson Francis.

"Do you suppose she'll call him Frank?" Val wondered.

"It'll be confusing having a Frannie and a Frankie in the same family," Mama remarked. "Carson is a fine name, and Sybil's maiden name, of course." Mama and Papa were fairly quiet, however, and after supper was over and the table cleared, Dorcas shooed Louise away, and said that Val could help with the dishes. Papa and Mama arose from the table and suggested they go into the sitting room.

"I have some not so good news, my dear," Papa explained. "We haven't discussed this with Val yet, until we decide what to do."

Louise looked at them questioningly as they went into the small front room and closed the door. Papa handed her the telegram. Louise read it, a frown furrowing her brow.

"Gladdie asking for help! It's not like her, is it?"

"Another arrived late this afternoon, from Mrs. Marchbanks' Phoenix lawyer, presumably the one who wrote up the last will. He says the family is contesting the will, which freezes Mrs. Marchbanks' assets. Gladdie is in need of money to pay the sanatorium bills. When the will is proved, and the funds released, these will be paid back, because it is a debt on the estate. She also owed Gladdie several months' salary, so it is no wonder she is short of money. Tomorrow I'll have my bank wire funds to a bank in Phoenix, but I think I shall have to travel out there. Someone will have to accompany her back. I have a feeling she is not well."

"Oh, Papa! When?"

"I think as soon as I can get away."

"But Papa, it'll be Christmas in less than two weeks!"

Mama intervened. "Gladdie has asked for help. We can't deny her that."

"Can you wait until Saturday? I will come with you," decided Louise firmly. "If Gladdie is sick, she'll need a nurse. And besides, you can't have Christmas all by yourself in another country amongst strangers."

"It'll probably take that much time to make arrangements," Papa said. He was pleased that Louise had offered to accompany him, and he didn't try to dissuade her. "We have been in touch with the Ferrises, and they have kindly asked you, your mama and Val to go to Perth while I'm away. Dorcas' friend Mrs. Scott will be spending her first Christmas without her husband, and is overjoyed that Dorcas can come to her."

"You've been doing some planning already, I see."

"If you are sure you want to go, Papa would be grateful," said Mama. "I'll tell Phoebe that it will be just Val and me."

"Now put this all out of your mind until your clinicals are finished," said Papa.

"Easy for you to say!" laughed Louise, whose spirits had only been slightly dampened by the news of her sister. "However, there's nothing I can do about it, so I will take your advice." She kissed her parents, and went up to her room to study. She found it was not so easy to put this latest news out of her mind, and she found herself wondering how Gladdie was, and how long she and Papa would be away. Should she move out of the residence before she left, or wait until her return? No, there'd be no time to do it before Saturday. Oh bother, she should be thinking about Friday's exam, and not worrying about a situation she couldn't change from this long distance away. She'd pray for Gladdie tonight—that's what she would do—it would do them both good.

Chapter Twenty-Six

ARIZONA

William Laurier and his daughter arrived in the desert town of Phoenix on a mild December day, even for Arizona. It had been a long trip. Louise and her father did not leave until Monday morning for Toronto, stayed overnight there, and caught the early morning train to Chicago, where they changed trains and began to steam west across the Great Plains. The train's ultimate destination was Los Angeles, but they would be stopping long before that, of course.

Louise had had no idea how flat the middle of the continent was. The furthest west she had been was, of course, Winnipeg. It had been flat there, too, but she hadn't realized the vastness of the country. She remembered going up in Johnnie's little airplane and seeing the fields like a patchwork quilt, and the myriad of lakes sparkling in the sun. Where was he now? she wondered. Perhaps he was at this moment preparing to make a flight over enemy territory. *Keep him safe*, she prayed silently, then felt guilty about her feelings, and prayed for Jeremy as well.

The desert was a fascinating experience for her.

"Cactus, Papa! Palm trees!" Louise's nose was glued to the window as they neared their destination.

They had shed their winter coats and Louise unbuttoned her suit jacket when they got off the train. It was three days before Christmas, and compared to Ottawa, Toronto, and Chicago, it was balmy. A tall young man in his thirties strode up to them as they disembarked.

"Mr. William Laurier? Miss Laurier? I'm Nathan Latimer." He stretched out a friendly hand and Louise's father took it. "My mother and I wish to tell you that you are most welcome to stay with us while you're here. She says you mustn't go to a hotel for Christmas."

Papa looked at Louise. "Such trouble to have strangers in your home at Christmas time," he demurred.

"Don't you have family with you?" asked Louise, shaking his hand. Nathan Latimer shook his head. "I'm a bachelor, and my mother and I share her home on the edge of town. We have a guesthouse that normally would house my sister, her husband and her two boys, but unfortunately the little beggars came down with the measles last week, and she's canceled her visit. It's private, and I can make a car available for you to go up to the sanatorium to visit your sister."

"How is Gladdie?" asked Louise anxiously.

"Much better, knowing that you are here," smiled Mr. Latimer. "Let's get your luggage. Do I take it that you will honor us with your stay? If you prefer the hotel I won't cancel the booking."

"You and your mother are most kind," said Papa. "It will be our pleasure to be your guests."

Louise luxuriated in a bath when they were settled in the little cottage some way from the main house, then changed and the two walked through the trees to see Mr. Latimer.

"They must be very wealthy," whispered Louise as she took in tennis courts, a swimming pool, and a bowling green. "Just think of maintaining all this."

Mrs. Latimer was tall like her son, had masses of hair upswept in elegant fashion, and wore the latest style in clothing. She welcomed them warmly, directed her maid to bring the silver tea service into her son's study, poured out for them, then discreetly left them to talk business.

Nathan handed Mr. Laurier a copy of Mrs. Marchbanks' will, which only took a few minutes to read, and then showed them Gladdie's paper that had been signed by Mrs. Marchbanks.

267

"My handwriting expert says that this is very likely Mrs. Marchbanks' signature. Oh, yes, Mr. Jason Marchbanks, or rather his wife, accused Miss Gladys of forgery," he interjected, as Louise's father frowned.

"My man says it's actually very difficult to imitate a weak signature and make it look authentic. Now, see after the word *brooch,* there seems to have been a period. *'and my sapphire necklace'* was probably added on afterwards. Now Mrs. Marchbanks could easily have said, 'Have the necklace, too,' and Gladys would naturally have added it to the statement. However, she doesn't say it happened that way, just that Mrs. Marchbanks asked her to choose two items."

Louise exchanged glances with her father. "Gladdie always tended to embroider the truth," she admitted.

The lawyer continued. "And the thing is, I've had her jewelry appraised by an expert, and those two pieces are the only genuine ones of the lot. The rest are paste—replicas!"

"Hmm," said Papa. "The daughter is not going to be amused."

"Nor the daughter-in-law."

"Do you think Gladdie stole the necklace?" asked Louise.

"I think she may have seen an opportunity, and jumped at it. I'm sorry to say this about your daughter."

"Thank you for being open with us. I don't know whether I can get the truth out of her. She can be very stubborn." Papa sat back and considered the problem. "What about the will? Can you probate it?"

"Not at this juncture. The young Marchbanks will have to go to the Probate Court and make a statement as to why they think the will is invalid. They have obtained a lawyer of their own, of course. Meanwhile, the sanatorium wants their money. They've had to pay their mother's debts, but refuse to pay for your daughter, even though that was the arrangement while she was in their mother's employ."

Louise could tell he was not impressed with the young Marchbanks. "The money you wired looked after most of it," he went on. "When the will is proved, you will be repaid."

"What if it's deemed invalid?" asked Papa.

"I don't know what the terms of her previous will were, but there is usually a phrase directing the trustee to pay all debts, and I am sure that will be deemed a debt. No, it's the validity of this statement here that's the problem. Their lawyer is already talking about a lawsuit."

"Oh dear," said Louise.

"I'm confident that if Miss Laurier returned the necklace, that would be the end of the matter, but she insists Mrs. Marchbanks wanted her to have it." Nathan Latimer drove Louise and her father up to the sanatorium after lunch. The turn off was perhaps fifteen miles north of the town, and it took another twenty minutes to negotiate the winding road up to the spa. Louise was enthralled with the views at every turn in the road. Palm trees gave way to pine trees, and the air was cool and dry. The sun shone brilliantly in a bright blue sky.

The Desert Sanatorium was a long, low building built of reddish brown brick, with a flat tiled roof. It was set on the side of the mountain and looked down over the valley below. A wide patio surrounded it, with lawns that were watered by a small creek that tumbled out of the hillside above. There was a cactus garden, and benches placed strategically for people to sit, and paths that wound through the trees. It was a magnificent setting. Louise sniffed the air appreciatively, and then buttoned up her coat. It was much cooler up here than it was in the valley.

The three conferred with the doctor, and he suggested that Louise go in alone to see her sister.

Gladdie was in bed, staring at the ceiling. She regarded her sister tentatively.

"I suppose you're here to take me home," she said, in a discontented voice.

"You should be outside in the fresh air and sunshine," declared Louise, ignoring Gladdie's tone. "Not in this darkened room."

"It's too cold. I should be down at the hotel in town where we were before we came up here."

"Mrs. Latimer has kindly asked us to stay in her guest house over Christmas. You are definitely included."

Gladdie frowned and shook her head. "I wouldn't go near that woman. She came to see me one day last week, smiled and smiled, and just dripped poison. She doesn't approve of me at all."

Louise was shocked. "Mrs. Latimer has been kindness and hospitality itself to us, Gladdie. How can you say such a thing?"

"Well, you are safely engaged to be married. You're no threat to her precious son."

Louise opened her mouth to say, "Well, you will flirt," then closed it again. There was no point in criticizing Gladdie. It would do no good.

"Besides," Gladdie continued, "Christmas is just another day. When are we leaving?"

"Papa has us all booked on the train that comes through the day after Christmas. Don't you want to go home?"

"This is a much better climate for me, but I certainly can't afford to stay here. I suppose you know those dreadful Marchbanks wouldn't pay my expenses? I don't blame Mrs. Marchbanks for cutting them out of her will. Mr. Latimer told me they're contesting it."

"Yes. Papa has paid your expenses."

"I knew he would. What time does the train leave on Sunday?"

"Four o'clock, I believe."

"There's time to come and get me after lunch, that day, then."

It would mean imposing on Mr. Latimer one more time, but Louise didn't say anything. Instead, she went to the window and drew the drapes back.

"Get dressed and come for a walk," she suggested. "It's just beautiful outside."

Gladdie allowed herself to be persuaded, carefully chose a becoming outfit when she heard that Nathan Latimer had come with them, and led Louise out on to the patio and down to the garden. They walked for a long time without speaking. Louise could hear Gladdie's wheezy and rattling breathing.

"I suppose you've talked to the doctor."

"He says you have tuberculosis, that you probably contracted it from Mrs. Marchbanks."

"I know what he thinks."

"He says you're younger and stronger than Mrs. Marchbanks."

Gladdie tossed her head. "And I want to spend that money Mrs. March banks left me."

They sat for a while on a bench.

"Mama wrote to you about Frankie's wife coming to Canada and about their baby?"

Gladdie nodded and shrugged. "How do you know she's who she says she is?"

"What on earth do you mean? She and I have been writing back and forth for months. I've got pictures of her and Frankie."

"How do you know the baby is Frankie's, then?"

Louise sat in shocked silence. Then she said, "Gladdie, you have a mean, suspicious mind! Why shouldn't the baby be Frankie's? They were properly married. She was devastated when he was killed!"

Gladdie shrugged. "Why did she have to rush over to Canada so fast? What's the matter with her family?"

"She has none," said Louise quietly. "Just an old aunt and uncle who aren't the least interested in her and the child. We're her only family now. She wants to bring up her child here—in Canada, I mean. Besides, Sybil is a lovely person. She isn't capable of being what you are hinting she is like."

"No need to get all in a lather about it. I suppose Mama and Papa are all excited about the kid. Have they been down to see them?"

"No, of course not. The baby was born just a few weeks ago. I think they plan to go whenever Papa can get away for a couple of weeks."

They got up and continued their walk.

"I suppose Mr. Latimer has my jewelry," said Gladdie presently. Louise didn't reply for a moment or so. "Gladdie," she said finally, "did Mrs. Marchbanks really give you the necklace?"

Gladdie turned to her sister, looking quite affronted. By now, she had convinced herself that her late employer had indeed insisted she take both pieces. She could even visualize the old woman saying, "Choose two that you like." Gladdie had written at Mrs. Marchbanks' dictation and the old woman had signed the paper.

"Of course she did! Are you accusing me of stealing?"

"It's just that the second phrase referring to the necklace seems to have been added on afterwards. Maybe she gave it to you later," Louise said hopefully.

271

Gladdie thought quickly. "She gave me the brooch, then said I could choose another, after I had written down what she said," she answered.

"Why didn't you say so at once to Mr. Latimer?"

"Didn't I? Well, I was upset. You haven't met those horrible people, her son and his wife. They were just nasty to me," she said petulantly.

Louise said no more about it, but she was not completely satisfied that her sister was telling the truth.

Gladdie began to tire then, so they turned and went back to her room. Papa was waiting for them there, and he kissed his elder daughter on the cheek and inquired as to how she was feeling.

"Tired, since Louise has dragged me around the grounds," she replied ungraciously.

She interrupted him as he began to explain their Christmas arrangements. "Louise has already told me that you are staying at the Latimers'. I prefer to stay here until we leave."

Papa looked surprised. "But Gladdie, I feel I am imposing on the Latimers already. This means we will need to use his car every day to come and see you . . ."

"Don't bother," she said. "I'll get myself ready to go on Monday. You can pick me up when you go to catch the train."

Louise took a walk around the room, ostensibly studying the decor. She could not trust herself to speak politely to her sister. She knew Papa was making allowances because she was ill, but Gladdie had not even tried to be pleasant. They had answered her request for help, but had found her seemingly not a bit grateful, or even pleased to see them. She had accused her sister-in-law of perfidy, and was quite likely concealing the true facts about the jewelry. Louise remembered the red coat hacked to pieces, and wondered if Gladdie still hated her for being the one Jeremy wanted to marry. Perhaps she resented Louise's health. But still—they had traveled halfway across the continent at considerable expense to be with her, and to accompany her back into the bosom of her family.

"Dr Morgan has given me a letter for a doctor at the TB Sanitarium over in Hull," continued Papa.

"You won't send me to the hospital?" she asked in alarm.

"The doctor says you will need nursing care, my dear."

"Louise can look after me at home, can't she? All I need is rest and good food."

"Louise is making plans to nurse overseas after her graduation," said Papa quietly.

"Overseas! Why, Louise, you never told me that! You wouldn't be so selfish to leave me when I need you!"

Louise said nothing.

Papa said, "We'll discuss all this later."

"Papa," she said later, as they were driving back down the mountainside, "why did you let Gladdie speak to you the way she did? I wanted to smack her face."

They were sitting in the rear seat, and Papa glanced at Nathan Latimer, who was driving. Louise didn't care if their host overheard her comments about her sister; he probably was very aware of her character, anyway.

"Oh, Louise, she's ill and frightened! I feel guilty that I allowed her to go away like this."

"But, Papa, she's an adult, she was working for Mrs. Marchbanks . . ."

"I know, my dear, but the way she reacted to your engagement to Jeremy, and this business about Mrs. Marchbanks' jewelry . . . did she mention it at all when you were together?"

"I actually asked her about it—she insisted that Mrs. Marchbanks offered her both pieces, though she did change her story a trifle, that it was afterwards that she gave her the necklace and she did add that bit on as Mr. Latimer suggested. I don't know whether to believe her or not. She went on and on about how awful Mrs. Marchbanks' son and daughter-in-law had been to her."

"She's always been a strange, unhappy girl. Secretive, discontented . . . you and Norah were always open and good-hearted . . . your Mama and I have always felt we failed her somehow."

Louise was silent for the rest of the drive to the Latimers' home, pondering his remarks.

273

The next day Louise asked Nathan if there were any nearby shops.

"I would like to buy your mother a Christmas gift, she's been so kind to us. Can you suggest anything?"

The young man thought a moment. "She's very fond of the poetry of Elizabeth Barrett Browning. I saw a volume in the small bookstore in the Village the other day and was going to buy it for her, but it slipped my mind and I came home without it. Would you like me to drive you there on my way to the office? It's about a twenty minute walk back."

"That would be kind of you. I need the exercise, too."

"I couldn't help but overhear your conversation yesterday on the way back from the Sanitarium," he said, as they drove along the palm-lined road.

"I am ashamed of Gladdie."

"Your father's right, she's ill and frightened, and Mr. and Mrs. Marchbanks are not the nicest people." He paused. "I understand that you're engaged to be married. I hope you'll be very happy."

"Thank you," said Louise, a trifle surprised.

"Your father was telling me about him when you and your sister were out for your walk. A major, and an engineer—you must be very proud of him." Louise thought of Johnnie, and was tempted to tell this pleasant young man about her quandary. She said nothing; however, and presently they turned into a cul-de-sac where there were perhaps a dozen shops and other businesses. There was a grocer's, a butcher shop, a hardware shop, and a bookstore sandwiched between a ladies' dry goods and a men's haberdashery.

"Do you have cinemas in Ottawa? We have a small one here. I wish you were staying longer—I'd love to take you and your father to see a motion picture show. They're lots of fun."

Louise smiled her thanks and got out.

"You won't get lost going home?" he asked anxiously. "Just turn left out of the shopping area and walk straight down Sunset Road until you get to Magnolia Boulevard. There's only one way to turn, and then it's about ten blocks to our street—Cactus Wren Close. We're Number One, of course." Louise spent an hour in the bookstore, browsing happily. She bought a slim volume of Mrs. Browning's verse for Mrs. Latimer, and found an embossed leather bookmark, which she bought for Mr. Latimer. She walked home in the December sunshine, marveling how different it was from her home, and how, in spite of Christmas decorations in the shops, that it didn't seem like Christmas at all. She was glad she had come with Papa. He would have been lonesome and miserable, especially with Gladdie's unfortunate behavior. She considered her sister's demand that she should stay home and nurse her back to health. If it hadn't been couched in such offensive terms, she might have agreed at once. If truth be told, the thought of going overseas to a strange situation was very daunting now she didn't have Sybil to be there to meet her. How she wished that Susie shared her desire to nurse the wounded soldiers! However, her friend wanted to nurse children, and already had been accepted on the Pediatric Ward of the hospital.

Perhaps, after several days of having Louise in close company on the way home, Gladdie just might change her mind. With this happy thought, Louise continued on her walk back to the Latimers'.

Chapter Twenty-Seven

LOUISE 1918

"It was rather a queer Christmas this year, without you and Papa both," remarked Val.

They had arrived home the day before and had settled Gladdie in her room at the top of the stairs. Mama had been very upset to see how thin she was. Gladdie had burst into tears borne of exhaustion and of seeing her mother at last. She allowed Mama to help her upstairs and wanted no one but her and Louise to get her ready for bed. Louise had gone out for more linen, and on her return overheard Gladdie begging her mother not to send her to the hospital.

"Louise says she is going away, Mama. What will I do? I do want to be home. I'll get well much quicker."

Mama soothed away her daughter's fears.

"There, there, my dear, no one shall put you in a hospital. Dorcas and I will manage splendidly to look after you."

Louise sighed in resignation. Either she would have to pay for a nurse herself, or give up her plans for going overseas. She would not let her mother nurse her sister. Mama wasn't strong enough, and didn't have the skills for looking after someone who was contagious. Dorcas would wind up doing the heavy work, and knowing Gladdie, she would monopolize them both. After all, the rest of the family needed looking after, too!

276

Now she smiled at her brother. How he had grown in the last year! She had been so busy she scarcely had noticed. He would be sixteen on his next birthday, and his voice was getting quite gruff.

"Yes, it was different for Papa and me as well," she said. "It was pleasant being in the Latimers' home, though, and not at a hotel."

Louise had envisaged being at the Sanatorium, and spending Christmas with Papa and Gladdie, but it had been much nicer celebrating in a family home, rather than a hotel, and in any case, Gladdie hadn't been in the mood to enjoy the festive season.

"What is it like there?" asked Val curiously. He was a little envious of Louise's travels. She had been to Winnipeg, and Prince Edward Island, and Halifax as well—why, he had never been west of Perth, Ontario!

"It's desert, Val. There are mountains, too. The train went south from Denver along the eastern side of the Rockies. It was quite splendid, and when we got to the desert, we saw cactus and all sorts of queer trees, too."

Christmas had been a pleasant day. Mrs. Latimer had been very pleased with her volume of Mrs. Browning's poetry, and her son, who had asked Papa and Louise to call him Nathan, was also surprised and pleased with the little gift that Louise had bought. The four were served a sumptuous meal of roast beef and Yorkshire pudding, horseradish sauce, and fresh vegetables, a treat for Louise and Papa at this time of year. Plum pudding with brandy sauce followed, and cups of steaming, fragrant coffee, accompanied by orange liqueur in tiny crystal glasses. Louise sat back and sighed.

"Never have I tasted better roast beef," she said. "I shall have to let out my waistbands if I keep this up."

She played carols for them on the piano after dinner.

"If Gladdie were here she'd do a much better job," she remarked, as she struggled through 'O Holy Night' and 'Adeste Fideles'. "She's a splendid pianist, and is used to entertaining company that Mrs. Marchbanks would have at her home."

Mrs. Latimer hadn't seemed overly disappointed that Gladdie had declined the invitation to spend Christmas with them. However, the next day, when they left for the Sanatorium to pick her up, she

277

wished Louise and her father well, and hoped that Gladdie would make a speedy recovery.

"With you in charge, my dear," she said, "I am sure she will soon be on her feet."

She shook hands with Papa and called him 'William' and actually kissed Louise on the cheek, saying how glad she was that they had been there to break the loneliness of Christmas without her dear daughter and grandsons. At the train station Nathan held her hand a little longer than was necessary, and Louise had the sudden notion that if Papa and Gladdie hadn't been there, he might have kissed her goodbye. She was surprised at herself for thinking it, and even more astonished when she realized that she wouldn't have minded if he had!

"I saw Mr. Latimer holding your hand and making sheep's eyes at you," said Gladdie, as Louise settled herself beside her sister in their compartment. "One beau at a time isn't enough for you, is it."

Louise ignored her sister's remarks, but she wondered at herself. Was she a fickle woman that a good-looking man should attract her so? Was she in love with Johnnie or Jeremy, and how could a man who had been an utter stranger five days ago send shivers up her spine by just gazing longingly at her? She was lonely for the companionship of an adoring young man, that was all, she decided. When she got to England, she would somehow see both Jeremy and Johnnie, and would know her heart for certain.

Now she stole a glance at her young brother and wondered if he had discovered the charms of the opposite sex yet. He was a nice looking boy, Louise decided. He had curly eyelashes, and nice teeth when he smiled. The girls probably had discovered him already!

Gladdie's health and spirits improved immensely now that she was home. Louise marveled at this, as her sister had never seemed close to her family, and for the most part had been away from them for the past three years. Louise went back to the hospital to complete a week of her experience of being a head nurse on the medical ward, and to prepare for graduation ceremonies on the eighth of January. To her surprise and pleasure, she had been voted Valedictorian, and this plus very good results on all her examinations made her feel that life was very fine indeed.

"Do I thank you for this dubious honor?" she asked her classmates, who had gathered around to congratulate her. Her cheeks were pink with pleasure and excitement. "This means I have to write a speech for the eighth!"

Perhaps Gladdie was on the road to recovery after all, and all that would be necessary would be regular visits from Dr Redmond, their family physician.

Dr Redmond, however, shook his head and called in a specialist, who poked and prodded and listened to Gladdie's chest, and explained to her parents that she should be in the tuberculosis sanatorium over in Hull. Gladdie made such a fuss about it that Mama and Papa hadn't the heart to send her away, but promised the doctors that there would be a trained nurse to look after her. Because there was so much on Louise's plate at the moment, they decided not to discuss this with her until after graduation.

Louise finished her last day on the wards on the Friday, polished her speech first thing Saturday morning, then proceeded to get dressed for the ceremonies. She and Susie admired their new white starched bibs and aprons, and the skirt that ended above the ankles, showing six inches of black stocking. Their shoes they polished until they gleamed, and each helped the other as they fastened studs and pearl buttons. They struggled with collars and cuffs, giggling all the while.

"Do you suppose we'll ever get the hang of this?"

"We'll have to have roommates in order to get to work in the morning!"

"When do you start on pediatrics, Susie?"

"A week from Monday. Mrs. Compton, the head nurse there, suggested I take a week's holiday, though where I'll go in January is a mystery."

"Are you staying here in residence?"

"For the time being—Matron said I could have your room, by the way. I guess I haven't mentioned it. When do you leave for England?"

Louise didn't answer for a moment, and concentrated on the gold studs. "I don't know. Gladdie's ill, you know. TB. She should be in the Hull San, but she worked herself into a tizzy when Dr Redmond suggested it, and Mama promised she wouldn't be sent away. She's been pretty good since we got back, and they're coping so far. I showed Dorcas how she should handle Gladdie's handkerchiefs, and I told her, wash your hands all the time!"

Susie looked at her friend speculatively. "You feel obligated."

Louise nodded, and looked around at her room, which was rather bare, as she had packed most of her things in her trunk.

"I'll think of you living here, Susie," she said, giving her friend a hug. They put on their cloaks, deep blue with a scarlet lining, with 'OMH' embroidered on the stand up collar, and went on the wards to visit some of their former patients. Then they met the rest of their class in the residence for a group photograph. Flowers arrived for both Susie and Louise from Jeremy. He had cabled his father instructing him what to buy and what to write on the card. Yellow roses for Susie with 'Congratulations, little sister,' and red ones for Louise with 'Congratulations, darling Louise' on the card.

Graduation passed in a blur. Louise gave her speech, fourteen young women received their diplomas and pins, and there was a splendid reception in the residence lounge afterwards. Later on the Ferrises and the Lauriers all went to the Grand Hotel for dinner. As they crossed the lobby, Louise remembered her supper with Johnnie, and glanced into the Palm Room where they had eaten. The staff must have reconfigured the tables and chairs, for no longer was there a cozy table for two by the corner window. Mr. Ferris had reserved a table for eight in the formal dining room, (Val and Michael were included, of course), and soon the two families were happily eating and drinking and visiting.

"How is Gladdie, Rose?" asked Mrs. Ferris as they waited between courses. "Is the new nurse working out?"

"Mama! What nurse? You didn't tell me you'd hired a nurse!"

Mama sighed. "We didn't want to worry you during these last few weeks, Louise, dear," she said. "Dr Redmond insisted on a trained nurse. He sent Nurse Phillips, but she lasted only a few days.

Nurse Halley seems to be coping all right at the moment, though Dorcas and she are constantly at loggerheads. I'm afraid Gladdie hasn't been very cooperative. Ah, here's dessert. Let's not talk about problems. I want to hear about Susie's plans." Louise didn't listen to the ensuing conversation. She picked at the pudding in front of her, and thought about her sister at home in bed, the job in England waiting for her, Johnnie flying into battle in a fighter airplane, and Jeremy doing heaven knows what. She was feeling guilty about not going home during the last two weeks to see how Gladdie was; she had telephoned once or twice, and Mama had said Gladdie was about the same. There had been no mention of nurses, of course. Louise echoed her mother's sigh.

The two families parted after dinner—the Ferrises were staying at the hotel—and the Lauriers went home. They found a grim faced Dorcas in the kitchen uncharacteristically rattling crockery and grumbling out loud.

"That nurse can't even come down for her own tea tray, Mrs. L.," she said. "And complains about the stairs. It's much quicker to use the back stairs, but oh no, my lady insists on coming down the front stairs and traipsing through the house!" And she clattered the silverware into the drawer unceremoniously.

Louise went upstairs to discover an equally grim faced nurse taking her patient's temperature, all the while lecturing her.

"You must drink more fluids, Miss Laurier," she was saying. "You're not even trying!"

Gladdie couldn't respond with a thermometer in her mouth. When she saw Louise in the doorway she took it out of her mouth and would have spoken, if Miss Halley hadn't popped it back in immediately, with an admonishing remark.

"Here's your sister home at last," she said. "Now we must be on our best behavior!"

She recorded Gladdie's temperature and pulse on the chart, and turned to Louise. "I'm Eliza Halley, Miss Laurier. Your sister's not too grand tonight, I'm afraid. Her temperature is up, and she's rather restless."

281

"I've been waiting for Louise to come home," said Gladdie crossly. "Can we be alone, if you please?"

"Why don't you go down and have your supper?" suggested Louise gently. "I'll settle Gladdie for the night, if you like."

Miss Halley went away, not really knowing whether to be pleased or sorry to have Louise take over.

"She's awful, Lou," said Gladdie, as Louise closed the bedroom door and came over and sat down beside the bed. "She either treats me like a mentally defective child, or lectures me about 'trying'. As if I didn't want to get better!"

Louise's practiced eye went over the state of the room and of the patient. Miss Halley might be indeed 'awful', but she knew how to keep a tidy room and make her patient comfortable. Everything was fresh and clean, the bed was neatly made, and there was no clutter.

"Have you had a wash and a back rub yet?"

"No. I think she was about to do that when you came."

Louise went to her room, took off her cloak and hung it in her wardrobe. She went to the bathroom and washed her hands thoroughly, then went back to Gladdie's room.

"You give a much better back rub," sighed the patient, as Louise gently massaged her back and shoulders. "She pummels me."

Louise persuaded Gladdie to drink the fruit juice that was at her bedside, then turned the light down and bade her sister goodnight.

"I'll just have to use the commode in the middle of the night," Gladdie grumbled, as she sipped the juice.

"I'm just next door, Gladdie, you know that. Try and get some sleep." Louise went downstairs where she found that Miss Halley had already gone home for the night.

"She's not sleeping here, then."

"She did at first," intervened Dorcas, still looking a bit like a thundercloud. "Gladdie was too demanding, was always ringing in the night, and wanting attention. I said I'd see to her at night, but oh no, my lady wouldn't have it. Finally, she decided to sleep at home. Her cat needed her, if you please!"

Louise sighed and glanced at her parents, who were drinking tea silently. "What do you think of her, Mama?"

"I think she's a good nurse," was all Mama said.

"Is she very expensive?"

"That doesn't matter, dear," said Papa.

Louise repressed another sigh. "If she's not working out, I'll take over. Gladdie doesn't like her. She grumbled on and on while I was settling her for the night."

"What about your job overseas?" asked Mama.

"That can be put off, or canceled, if needs be. Miss Love will understand."

"Isn't Jeremy expecting you?"

"Yes, but who knows how much I'd see him, anyway? I'm sure he'll understand. He and Gladdie were friends for a long time." Johnnie, too, would understand completely. He had been in the same situation.

The next day was a mild day for January in Ottawa. The thermometer shot above the freezing mark and by the afternoon water was running in the streets from the melting snow. Miss Halley had walked from the streetcar, and came in pink cheeked and smiling.

"Do you think it's warm enough for Gladdie to take a turn in the back garden?" Louise asked the older nurse tactfully. "The fresh air would be good for her."

"Oh, much too cold for her, I wouldn't want to expose her to the chill," declared Miss Halley at once.

"Even if we bundled her up well with a scarf over her mouth? The sun looks so nice."

Gladdie interrupted Miss Halley's response.

"I wish you two wouldn't talk about me as though I wasn't here," she said crossly. "I for one would like a change of scene. I've been stuck up here in my bedroom for three weeks, ever since we got back from Arizona. It's been very tiresome."

"Now, Miss Laurier, we don't want to get a chill, do we?"

A mulish expression came over Gladdie's face, and Louise realized she had made a mistake in bringing up the subject in front of her sister.

"I want to go outside," she said. "Louise, help me get dressed."

Miss Halley shrugged. "You asked my advice," she said huffily.

283

"I didn't," snapped Gladdie. "I'm perfectly capable of going for a short walk. Louise, where's my grey skirt and coat?"

There was nothing to do but to help Gladdie get dressed and take her downstairs. She was flushed with excitement as she put on her warm coat, gloves and hat. Louise wrapped the scarf around her throat and mouth, and they ventured forth out the solarium door into the back garden.

"Miss Halley worries too much," she grumbled. "Is there snow on the canal path? Let's watch the skaters for a while."

However, she soon was tired and short of breath, and was ready to come back inside. She was flushed and perspiring.

"This is awful, Louise," she said. "I'm not improving at all." "You mustn't be impatient, Gladdie. These things take time."

Gladdie took a long time to climb the front stairs to her room, and Louise was concerned that she had overtaxed her patient. Miss Halley didn't say 'I told you so,' but looked it, as she fussed around her patient, and settled her back into her bed. She threw reproachful glances at the retreating Louise, who went downstairs thoughtfully and joined her parents in the morning room where they were drinking their midmorning coffee before getting ready for church.

"Papa," she said, "do you think it possible that we might turn one of the downstairs rooms into a sick room for Gladdie? I think she feels really confined upstairs. It took her a long time to get back upstairs just now."

"I have been considering that very thing, Louise," answered her father, putting down his coffee cup. "What room do you have in mind?"

"What about the front sitting room? We could use the drawing room instead, and the sitting room is such a nice bright room looking out at the garden and the street. It would be more interesting for Gladdie than being cooped up in her bedroom upstairs. The only thing is a lavatory. Or lack thereof."

"Did you know James Ferris has recently installed a lavatory on the main floor of his house? They are finding it exceedingly convenient."

"Could we do it, Papa? Wouldn't it cost a lot of money?"

Papa looked at his daughter's bright eyes, and smiled. "I think we could do it, my dear. We'd have to call in a builder and a plumber...."

"Dorcas has suggested this room," Mama put in. "Then she would be close by at night."

Louise was a trifle disappointed that it hadn't been she that had had the bright idea first.

"I think the sitting room is a better idea, Rose," said Papa. "The big closet under the stair across the front hall is a possibility to turn into a small lavatory—"

"Or what about the closet in the sitting room?" asked Louise excitedly. "You can walk right into that one, too. And it's nothing but a catch-all for all the Laurier junk."

"Let's get ready for church, and we can discuss it properly at lunch," suggested Mama. "Louise, will you rout Val out of his room when you go upstairs?"

They returned from church to find Nurse Halley, coat and hat on, waiting for them in the front hall.

"I cannot remain on this job, Mrs Laurier," she said grimly. "I can deal with a difficult patient, but I need support from all the household. Your daughter is ill and needs good care. I find I cannot give it in this situation."

"Miss Halley, what on earth has happened?" demanded Mama.

"Suffice it to say I shall want my paycheck immediately. Miss Laurier," she continued, looking at Louise, "if you need advice, don't hesitate to call me. I am on the telephone of course. Here is the patient's chart. I have left a note for Dr Redmond." She stood, waiting, while Papa went to his study, and returned with a check. "I hope you will give me a good reference if I call upon you to do so," she said stiffly to Mama as she sailed out the door. "I do regret this action, I assure you." The door swung to with a snap behind her, leaving a chill in the hall caused by more than just the weather outside.

Mama marched into the kitchen to tackle Dorcas, Louise right behind her.

285

Dorcas was looking equally as grim standing over the stove, briskly stirring a pot of soup.

"She questioned my integrity, Mrs L.," Dorcas stated. "I soon told her what I thought of her. Gladdie was in such a state!"

Louise said nothing, but turned and went quickly up the back stairs, and down the hall to Gladdie's room. Her sister was in bed, seemingly peacefully asleep, but Louise thought she was feigning. Louise sighed. There was no point in questioning Gladdie at this moment. Eventually they would find out exactly what had happened. She sat down and quietly read through the chart, studying the doctor's orders, and attempting to get a picture of Gladdie over the past few weeks. Then, making certain her patient was comfortable, she went slowly downstairs.

"It looks as though my decision is made for me," she told her parents over lunch.

Papa looked distressed. "I am sorry, Louise," he said. "However, we will pay you the same as we were paying Miss Halley." And he named a fee.

"That's far too much, Papa!" she protested. "After all, I will be getting room and board."

"I have a feeling you will be busy around the clock, if you're not careful. You must take regular hours off. We don't want you getting sick." He paused. "I think we must move Gladdie downstairs. That way Dorcas will be nearby at night." Dorcas' bedroom was on the ground floor at the foot of the back stairs. "The first thing tomorrow I will call Harold Benny. He's the builder who designed your Mama's solarium."

Louise wrote to Miss Love, explaining the situation. *I was looking forward to coming to England next month, but I fear I cannot. My sister needs me, and I believe it is my duty to stay and nurse her. If you can give me any advice in nursing consumptive patients, I would be glad of it. I shall try to get the loan of a hospital bed from Memorial Hospital and set up a proper sick room either in the morning room or the front sitting room. Papa is determined to install a bathroom and lavatory on the main floor, so things won't be easy for the next few weeks while that is being done.*

To Jeremy she wrote, *Unless the war drags on for another year, I won't see you now until you come home. It's good to be needed, Jeremy. I have my work cut out for me. Mama hasn't said anything, but I know she's relieved that I shall be staying home.*

To Johnnie she poured out her frustration and disappointment. *I had so hoped to see both you and Jeremy and resolve the situation between us. Now we must wait and see. I wouldn't put it past Gladdie to have orchestrated the whole blowup between Dorcas and Miss Halley. She refuses to tell me exactly what happened, but I suppose it really doesn't matter now. I have a job to do, and will need all the patience and good humor I possess to do it properly. Take care of yourself, my dear.*

Miss Love wrote back immediately encouraging her and naming a good book to read on tuberculosis. *You are brave to tackle such a difficult situation. Get lots of rest, good nourishing food, and fresh air. Take all precautions managing your patient—remember this is a contagious disease.*

I had a delightful letter from your sister-in-law, Mrs Sybil Laurier. She and the child are apparently well, and thriving down in the country. She says she has never felt more at home than with your family. How sad that your brother never knew that he was to be a father. This war is hell.

She heard from Johnnie soon after. *I seem to remember your telling me that my duty to my parents came before my duty to my country. I understand how you feel, and I am also disappointed that we won't see each other. Has Jeremy written that we've met at last? He's a fine chap, and I can understand why you admire him so. He's quiet, isn't he. He didn't say much about you, but when your name was mentioned his eyes lit up and he smiled the most tender of smiles. I am jealous that he has known you for so long, and remembers you from childhood. You will remember your promise to me, won't you? But I am so afraid you will choose him....*

Louise put his letter away and smiled over the last remark. Foolish darling! As if she could marry anyone after having met Johnnie! It wouldn't hurt him to worry a bit, though, she thought, and not start taking her for granted.

She didn't hear from Jeremy for three months, but when he wrote at last he had received her letter and was relieved that she would be safe at home. Louise remembered how he had admired his friend's sister who was nursing practically under fire in France, and could only think that he felt differently when it involved his own, especially having seen at first hand what she might have to put up with.

Papa had been lucky to find his builder between jobs and willing to start immediately. They decided on the sitting room and to enlarge the big closet at the end of the room and turn it into a small bathroom. Gladdie grumbled daily about the noise, and Dorcas shook her head over the plaster dust, but at last it was done. Louise exclaimed over the gleaming metal cabinets painted in white enamel, and the shower with a folding door. There was a large mirror over the sink and plenty of storage space for linens and medications. The sitting room had been transformed. Louise and Dorcas had taken up the carpet and removed the draperies from the windows, leaving only the blinds. The floor was of polished oak. A hospital bed and a pushchair were on loan from the hospital, with the exception of a desk, two chairs and the small sofa, all the furniture was relocated in other rooms. Gladdie's bedside table had been brought down from her room. A fire burned briskly in the hearth, and on the deep window seat a large vase of flowers stood. Louise settled her patient in the new bed, and cranked it up so she could see out the window. The garden was still covered in snow, but the hedge was bare of leaves and you could see the street and the houses beyond. Gladdie was delighted, and for the first time in weeks she smiled and complimented Louise on her planning and taste.

"You're welcome, I'm sure," replied Louise dryly, "but don't forget to thank Papa. He paid for it."

Louise's days were full of routine, planning Gladdie's meals, helping her bathe, changing her bed, giving her the medications ordered by Dr Redmond and the specialist, and keeping the room clean and tidy. Mama read to her every day, and played the piano in the drawing room across the hall. Louise took every afternoon off, changed out of her uniform, and went for a walk, or shut herself in her room and read. Once in a while she would take the streetcar to the hospital and meet Susie for lunch or afternoon tea. Sometimes Susie would come and call on her days off, and though she had never much cared for her friend's sister, she would make a duty visit, and bring flowers or fruit for the patient. Quite often on her afternoons off Louise would visit the lending library and bring home books for her patient. From five o'clock to ten o'clock she spent with her patient, and then went to bed after she had settled her for the night. Dorcas slept with her door open, and Gladdie had a bell if she needed anything, but most nights she slept through and had to be wakened by Louise in the mornings. Occasionally a friend of Gladdie's would come to visit, and she would be bright and cheerful for the rest of the day. Norah wrote often and Louise would read to Gladdie about the life of their brother and sister in Prince Edward Island, and of the rest of the family. Norah was worried about Aunt Bernice's health, and wondered if Papa could spare the time to come and visit. Sybil was still living with Aunt Bernice and Gerald, and little Carson was beginning to sit up, while small Frannie next door was almost walking.

"It's hard to believe that tiny baby is almost toddling," remarked Louise one day, after sharing a letter with Gladdie.

"Don't people talk, Sybil and Gerald being in the same house together? You'd think she'd be staying at Norah's," Gladdie said.

It had not occurred to Louise that people would think anything was wrong with the arrangement.

"Good heavens, Bernice is there, and besides, I think Sybil is very helpful, with Auntie not very well," returned Louise. Trust Gladdie to think the worst!

Spring came, and though the weather improved, Gladdie spent most of her days in bed. Louise tried to coax her out of doors for fresh air and sunshine, but Gladdie usually refused. Mama's front garden began to bloom with daffodils and tulips, and the lilac hedge, now green with new leaves, bloomed in purple and white. Louise arranged the bed close to the windows so that her patient could see outside.

"I'm so tired, Louise," she said one evening. "Just so tired. Life isn't worth living this way." She lay back on the pillows, flushed and perspiring. "Louise, I—I'm sorry about that old red coat. You've been such a brick looking after me."

289

It was the first time that incident had ever been mentioned. Louise's face paled, and then flushed, remembering what had occurred three and a half years ago. She gazed at her sister in alarm.

. "I thought you were looking so much better. You are feeling better, aren't you?"

"Oh, Louise, you know I'm going to go just like Mrs Marchbanks, don't hide your head in the sand, for heaven's sake."

"You must get better," said Louise, knowing as she said it, that Gladdie was probably right. "Look, Gladdie, you do have something to live for. I haven't told anyone this, but I'm not going to marry Jeremy after all. You were such friends, weren't you, perhaps he might—"

"Not marry Jeremy!" exclaimed Gladdie blankly. "Whatever are you talking about? Has he thrown you over?"

"Well, no, of course not . . ." Her voice trailed away as she saw the expression on her sister's face.

"And I thought you were so madly in love!" She looked at her younger sister speculatively. "That other boy you write to—is it him? Susie mentioned him the other day when she was here. Her cousin, isn't it? She said you both met him when you went out to Winnipeg that summer." A look of scorn came over Gladdie's face. "Did I say I was sorry about the red coat? Well, I've changed my mind," she said. "I hated you both for a while, you know, because I wanted Jeremy, too, and he wasn't having any! Now you're throwing him back at me! Well, I wouldn't take him if he changed his mind and wanted me! He prefers his wife to be a virgin, you know. I never fit that mold!" He eyes narrowed. "I suppose you spent the night with this fellow, and now you're both feeling guilty about it." And she smiled a not very nice smile.

Louise was stung into an answer. "Well, I suppose I have, but not in the way you mean," she retorted. "We got stranded in a snow storm last spring and had to stay in an empty farmhouse. There wasn't anything wrong between us, no matter what you think." Only because Johnnie stopped, she thought ruefully.

"So now you think you're in love with him, and Jeremy can go to hell! Fine little fiancée keeping the home fires burning you've

290

turned out to be! Serves you both right, and the cousin, too!" And she turned her face to the wall.

"You won't say anything to anybody, will you?" Louise asked anxiously, realizing her enormous error confiding in her sister.

There was a long silence. "No, but only because it would upset Mama if she found out."

That night Louise lay in bed, agonizing over the exchange she'd had with Gladdie. Somehow Gladdie had managed to make Louise's love for Johnnie seem sordid and dirty. What had she meant by herself not fitting Jeremy's mold? Did she mean she wasn't a virgin? Surely she and Jeremy hadn't . . . no of course not. She said that he 'wasn't having any'—did she mean she had asked of him, well, what she herself had almost asked of Johnnie, and Jeremy had refused Gladdie? Oh, why on earth had she ever said anything to Gladdie about Johnnie? At least she doesn't know his name, she thought. Oh, if she says anything to Susie!

"Oh, why didn't I hold my tongue!" she muttered to the ceiling.

The next day, Mr Lachance, the Laurier family solicitor, paid a call. He spoke first to Papa, who was home that day, then was taken in to see Gladdie. The lawyer was a small dapper man, who wore a *pince nez,* a smart three-piece suit, and spats. Fluently bilingual, the only sign that English was not his mother tongue was a slight thickening of his th's. He carried a brief case with him, and cautiously seated himself a short distance away from the bed. Louise cranked up the bed, started to leave, but Gladdie stopped her.

"Stay, Louise. I think this is about Mrs Marchbanks, isn't it, Mr Lachance? You remember my sister Louise. She and Papa were in Phoenix last December."

Mr Lachance rose hurriedly and bowed with a flourish. "I'm afraid I didn't recognize you all grown up and in uniform," he said, smiling. "Your father mentioned that you and he had gone out west to accompany your sister home. I have good news for Gladys today." He turned to the ill woman. "Mr Latimer in Phoenix has been in touch with me, and Mrs Marchbanks' will has been probated at last. The courts ruled that her last will was true and valid." He brought out a document from his briefcase an handed it to Gladdie. "This is your copy," he told her. "Mrs Marchbanks' estate has paid you your back salary, which was just over $300, and a cheque for $5,000 has been forwarded to me. The jewelry your employer gave you is yours." And he brought out a small package. "Mr Latimer also forwarded the two pieces to me. Will you check and see that they are as you received them?"

Gladdie, even more flushed than usual with excitement, opened the parcel and brought out the brooch and necklace. Louise hadn't seen them, so she gasped with surprise and pleasure at the gems.

"Yes, these are the pieces she gave me," Gladdie assured the lawyer.

"I think you had better make a will, Gladys," he said seriously.

This time Louise slipped out, leaving the two to discuss this. She looked into Papa's study and found her father at his desk, reading and making notes. He looked up and beckoned her to come in.

"Everything all right?" he asked.

"I left them discussing Gladdie's will."

Papa's face grew grave. "Yes, I would think that was fairly important now," he said. "Mr Lachance hinted that she had a substantial legacy."

"Papa, five thousand dollars and that wonderful jewelry! Gladdie is well off!"

Papa raised his eyebrows.

"I hope she'll be willing to pay you back, Papa. She can afford it now."

"It doesn't matter, my dear. We just want her to get better so she can enjoy her good fortune."

Gladdie died on a hot, muggy morning in August. Louise, entering the room at six o'clock that morning, saw at once that she had gone. She went over to the bed and felt for a pulse even though she knew she would find none. Gladdie's skin was cool, her eyes were closed, and she looked quite peaceful. Louise cranked down the bed, and covered her sister's face with the sheet. Then she went slowly upstairs to her parents' room. Mama cried a little, and Louise left

Papa to comfort his wife. She went downstairs, and found Dorcas in the kitchen making tea.

"Gladdie's gone, Dorcas," she said wearily.

"Ah, you poor lamb. It's not been easy for you, has it."

"It was inevitable. I will telephone to Dr Redmond, then I'll put in a call to Norah. She can let Gerald know."

As Louise waited for Dr Redmond to arrive, she thought of the last conversation she had had with Gladdie the evening before. It was evident that Gladdie's time was short. She was wasted away, her eyes unnaturally bright, her breathing labored. She hardly had the strength to cough now, and Louise could hear the rales in her chest, hollow, bubbling, metallic sounds of the air passing through the damaged lungs. She had written on the chart, 'cavernous rales heard.'

"Do you want me to sleep on the sofa here tonight, Gladdie?" Gladdie was silent for a moment. "Dorcas asked me that tonight, too. No, thanks, Louise, I'd rather be alone. You know, I always thought I'd be afraid to die, but it would be a relief now. To everybody."

Louise's eyes filled. "Oh, Gladdie...."

"I haven't been what you would call 'good', you know, Louise. Men have always liked me, and I've liked men." There was a glint in her eyes reminiscent of the old Gladdie. "I really am sorry about the red coat. I went a little crazy for a while when I realized that Jeremy loved you and not me. I wanted to hurt you."

"I know, Gladdie, and I forgave you ages ago."

The glint in her eyes appeared again. "And I did take the necklace, you know. I just lifted it out of Mrs Marchbanks' jewel case when she wasn't looking, and added to the paper that she had signed. But she did give me the brooch, and that's the truth."

Louise believed her.

"I've left them to you in my will. You can do what you want with them, just don't let that young Mrs Marchbanks get her claws on them. She was horrible to me."

She coughed weakly. Louise wiped her mouth for her. The handkerchief was stained bright red.

"There was this boy that came to see me up at the Sanatorium. I can't even remember his name, now. I met him at a party in Phoenix.

He was so good-looking, but naïve! He'd never been with a woman before!" Gladdie smiled. "He spent the night with me, right next door to Mrs Marchbanks! I flatter myself he had an enjoyable night."

Louise blushed. She was shocked and embarrassed, but she didn't say anything.

Gladdie put out a bony hand and clutched at Louise. "You've been good to me, Lou, when I was horrible to you. I think you're making a mistake, though, throwing over Jeremy. Do you really know this fellow you're so taken with? I quizzed Susie about him when she was here last, and she says he's a flyer. They're pretty wild, aren't they? By the way, I never said a word about you and him to anybody."

"Gladdie, you shouldn't be talking so much. You'll tire yourself." Gladdie had been leaning forward as she talked so earnestly. Now she lay back on the pillows, pale and perspiring. "I've said all I want to say. Goodnight."

Louise tidied the room, turned down the light, and went out, leaving the door ajar. Later, she checked on her patient before she went to bed herself, but she was sleeping. She could hear the labored breathing halfway up the stairs. She never spoke to Gladdie again.

Now she paced the room restlessly as she waited for Dr Redmond. Mama and Papa had spent a little while alone with their dead daughter, and Val had come in reluctantly as well. At sixteen he was as tall as Papa, but Louise thought he looked like a frightened ten year old. She took his arm and smiled up at him.

"It's a good thing to say good-bye to Gladdie, even though you weren't close, Val. It's a blessing to be able to say good-bye. We didn't have that chance with Frankie."

At the sound of his beloved brother's name Val's face worked at holding back tears. He stared down at his sister, lying so still and cold.

"It's a good thing she's gone, when she wasn't going to get better," he said. "She was so sick."

Louise squeezed his arm. "You're right," she replied. "Just last evening she herself said it would be a relief to go."

"Do you think she knew she was dying?"

"Oh, yes, she knew," Louise said, once more remembering their conversation.

Louise was standing at the window looking out into the front garden when Dr Redmond's car drove up to the house. He came in gravely, examined the body, and signed the death certificate.

"Well, it's over, my dear," he said to Louise, covering Gladdie's face again.

He looked at her keenly. "I want to see you in my office first thing tomorrow. Will you come in, please?" And he smiled in a kindly manner.

Louise felt the tears welling in her eyes. "I am tired."

"You need a long, rest, Louise, but first I want to check you over completely. I'll be in my surgery at eight o'clock tomorrow morning. I'll let my nurse know you'll be in then." Without waiting for an answer, he turned and stumped out.

Chapter Twenty-Eight

LOUISE 1918

True to her word, Gladdie had left the jewelry to Louise in her will, along with the sum of a hundred dollars. There was a small sum to Dorcas, and one hundred each to Gerald, Norah, Val and Sybil. The rest she left to Mama and Papa, which made up for the renovations and Louise's salary many times over. Louise was pleased that Gladdie's last gesture had been a generous one, and that she had thought kindly of Frankie's wife at the end, treating her as one of the family. Louise took the necklace and the brooch out of their cases and wondered what she would do with them. She thought about it for a long time.

Dr Redmond had duly examined her the day after Gladdie died, pounded and pummeled her, listened to her chest, harrumphed and muttered to himself, and finally pronounced her fit.

"A long rest, Louise," he told her firmly. "Your lungs are sound, but there's no way of telling if you may be harboring the infection somewhere else in your body. I'm worried about this influenza that is going around. Go and visit your sister. A few months in the country will do you a world of good. Drink fresh milk, eat fresh fruits and vegetables and get lots of sea air. Stay away from crowds and the city. You'll be right as rain and able to take up your nursing again. You did a fine job with Gladdie, my dear. She was a difficult patient in many ways."

296

So it was that two weeks or so after the service for Gladdie, Louise took the train to Montreal. It was her intention to call on Mrs. Marchbanks' daughter, whose name was Charlotte Fairbairn, and return the necklace to her. Louise had read the old lady's will again, and it definitely stated that her jewelry should go to her daughter. It would have been easy for Louise to instruct Mr. Lachance to get in touch with Mrs. Fairbairn and have him hand over the jewelry to her, but somehow Louise felt the need to see the woman in person and apologize for Gladdie's behavior. She had written a letter to her and explained how the necklace had come into her possession, and her intention of returning it to the rightful owner.

I will be in Montreal on September the fourth, she had written, *and will call upon you in the afternoon at about four o'clock. Will you please let me know if this is convenient? I will be catching the eastbound train the next morning.*

Mama and Papa objected to Louise's traveling out to Prince Edward Island on her own, but Louise flatly refused any sort of companionship, packed a large suitcase, and made her plans accordingly. Susie tried to persuade her to go and stay with her parents out at the lake, but Louise shook her head and kissed her friend goodbye.

"I have yet to see my little nephew, and I also just want to get away!" Papa also objected to her carrying a valuable piece of jewelry with her, when it would be much simpler and safer to have their lawyer take charge of it. "And you are under no obligation to return it to her, you know, my dear," he said. "The court ruled that Mrs. Marchbanks had indeed given it to Gladdie."

"I know, Papa, and I wouldn't be doing do this if Gladdie hadn't told me that she had taken it without Mrs. Marchbanks' knowledge. I feel obligated to make restitution. I don't want the thing."

"Sell it, and give the money to charity, then."

Louise hesitated, but in the end she wrote to Mrs. Fairbairn, and the die was cast.

A week later she received a short letter from Mrs. Fairbairn, who expressed surprise and pleasure that Louise was planning to give her the necklace.

She wrote, *I have taken the liberty of booking you a room at the Duke of Gloucester Hotel, where I hope you will stay as my guest. It is within walking distance of the train station, and is a very respectable establishment. I will be in touch with you when you arrive.*

"It's very queer," Mama commented. "I wonder why she doesn't ask you to stay at her home. I believe it is very beautiful. I am sure that is where Gladdie stayed with Mrs. Marchbanks that time she was in Montreal for Christmas. I remember how she raved about the place." She thought a moment. "At least let me contact Cousin Muriel Marsh. She would put you up for the night."

Louise reread the letter, and had to agree with her mother. She was, however, intrigued by Mrs. Fairbairn's letter and not being overly fond of Cousin Muriel, she decided to follow the instructions. At least the hotel was near the station.

It was a very warm September day when she arrived in the big city. She asked a porter for directions to the hotel, and he informed her that it was at the end of the block on the right, and just around the corner. She left her big suitcase at the station, carrying only an overnight case with her, and her handbag. When she checked in the clerk handed her an envelope, saying there was a message for her. She went upstairs to her room, took off her traveling things, washed her face and hands, and sat down to read the note. The message was very brief.

I have taken a room here also, and I have ordered a tea tray at four o'clock. Please join me in room 25, which is just down the hall from your room. Sincerely, Charlotte Fairbairn.

She had been uneasy and nervous when she entered the hotel, almost regretting that she was not safely in Cousin Muriel's little house in nearby Outremont. She recalled how she had felt two years ago when she had met Johnnie at the hotel in Ottawa. Here she was staying unchaperoned in a strange hotel in a big city, and traveling alone. A young woman would not have done this before the war!

Louise checked the time, and it was just after three o'clock. She took off her outer clothes and lay on the bed, thinking what she might say to the woman when she met her. She dozed off for thirty minutes and awoke surprisingly refreshed. She put her coat and skirt on, took the small jewel box out of her overnight case and put it in her handbag. Then she let herself out of her room, carefully locking the door behind her, and walked down the hall, peering at the room numbers on the door. She tapped lightly on the door of Room 25, and a moment later the door opened, revealing a small dark-haired woman in perhaps her early forties standing there.

"I'm Louise Laurier."

"And I'm Lottie Fairbairn. Do please come in, Miss Laurier."

The room was similar to Louise's, but done in a different color scheme. A trolley stood nearby covered with a long white cloth on which was a large tray of tea things. Mrs. Fairbairn led the way and indicated Louise to sit in one of the comfortable armchairs by the window.

"They just delivered the tea tray. May I pour you a cup? How do you take it?"

"With lemon, if there is some," Louise said politely.

She hadn't really known what Mrs. Marchbanks' daughter would be like, but certainly had not expected this mousy little woman who looked like a governess rather than the daughter of the tall, elegant, and sometimes-flamboyant woman for whom Gladdie had worked. Mrs. Fairbairn poured out two cups of tea, handed one to Louise, and sat down in the opposite chair. She passed a plate of bread and butter, and Louise discovered that she was hungry.

They sipped tea, and a rather awkward silence ensued. Presently Mrs. Fairbairn put down her teacup and reached for some papers that had been lying on the table between them.

"I brought your letter with me, and a copy of the will. I didn't want there to be any question as to my identity, when you would be handing something valuable over to a perfect stranger," she said, with a glimmer of a smile.

Louise glanced at the letter she had written to Mrs. Fairbairn, and recognized the will as a copy of the one that she had read after Gladdie had died.

"Of course I believe you when you say you are Mrs. Fairbairn," she answered.

"I'm actually registered here as Lottie Cannings," Mrs. Fairbairn said. "That was my mother's name. I've always been called Lottie, except by my husband." She paused. "Thank you for coming, Miss Laurier. You didn't need to do this, you know. The necklace really did belong to your sister."

"I know that. My father pointed it out to me, and my response was that I didn't want it since I knew that Gladdie had come by it dishonestly. You see, I was sure she had taken it without your mother's permission, but Gladdie always denied it. It wasn't until the night before she died that she told me she had done so. She thought it was a great joke. She said she had left the jewelry to me in her will, and I could do anything I liked with it as long as Sonia Marchbanks didn't get a hold of it."

Mrs. Fairbairn smiled sadly. "I understand my brother and his wife were very hard on your sister. I remember Gladys very well. She came with my mother one Christmas a few years ago. I'll have to admit I didn't care very much for her, but we obviously had a mutual dislike of my sister-in-law. My brother and his wife tried to recover the necklace at first, but gave it up when they realized that your sister had the only two good pieces of jewelry that Mother owned, and if it didn't belong to her, it would belong to me." She gave a little mirthless laugh. "I guess it was my good fortune that Jason and Mother quarreled just before she went out West. I was always afraid she'd leave everything to him, because she might feel I didn't need it. My husband is very well off, you know."

Louise was rather taken aback at these comments. She couldn't imagine quarreling over money with her brothers and sisters.

Presently Louise recalled what she had come to do, and reached into her handbag for the little jewel case.

"Here are my ill-gotten gains," she said, with a smile.

Mrs. Fairbairn opened the case and took out the necklace. She sighed as she held it up.

"It's very valuable, you know," she commented calmly. "This will enable me to leave my husband and set up a small business for myself."

Louise was shocked. "You're going to leave your husband? Where will you go, Mrs. Fairbairn?"

"Please call me Lottie. May I call you Louise? I'm sure you have been wondering about all this subterfuge, registering under another name, meeting you here instead of at my home. The fact is, Louise, my husband would be furious if he knew what I was planning to do. He was very angry when I wouldn't hand over to him my legacy from my mother, and doubly so when the jewelry was appraised and they were found to be all replicas—worth maybe a hundred dollars, no more. I told him I wanted a little money of my own. He gives me an allowance and I have to account for every penny I spend. He's been away on business for some weeks now, and when your letter came I knew that this was the chance I'd been waiting for. The butler Wilkins scrutinizes the mail when my husband is absent, but he wouldn't dare open it. I told him your letter was one of condolence from an old Ottawa acquaintance, and that seemed to satisfy him. Luckily you hadn't put your name with the return address, so unless he made a note of the address, they wouldn't know where to start looking for me."

"Looking for you?" repeated Louise faintly.

Mrs. Fairbairn gazed at her, a determined expression on her face. "Yes. My husband wouldn't let me leave him—he might lose face in front of his friends."

"Where will you go, Lottie?" repeated Louise.

"I'm catching your train tomorrow morning and will go to Halifax. I have an old nanny who retired to her hometown in Cape Breton Island, and I plan to go to her for the time being. She's Scots, and a delightful person. I can always remember her saying, 'I'm Scots, Lottie, not Scotch. That, I believe, is an ill tasting beverage from the Highlands.' And she would roll her R's with a vengeance and wrinkle her nose."

Lottie wrinkled her face up and Louise could hardly refrain from laughing. She could visualize Lottie the child, and imagine a teetotaler Nanny shaking an admonishing finger at her little charge.

"Is your husband—unkind to you?"

"In a word—yes. Oh, he's never left any marks on me, or anywhere they'd show," replied Lottie. "He flaunts his affairs in my face—flirts with young women—your sister was one of them, by the way. But I don't think he got very far with her that Christmas—she was too focused on pursuing a young man in uniform." She looked apologetic. "I'm sorry I said that."

Louise waved her hand in dismissal. She had known what her sister was like, and she could guess who the young man in uniform was!

Lottie went on, "It's mostly that I feel I can't call my soul my own. I'm a very good seamstress, you know, and I think I could make my living at it. My husband thinks it's shameful that I would want to work for people, though I consider I would be providing a service. You are helping me to escape."

"From the gilded cage."

"Yes. From the gilded cage."

"What will the butler think when you don't come home tonight?"

"I told the servants that I was going up to Ottawa to see my brother about my mother's estate. Wilkins actually drove me to the station yesterday afternoon, and I had to pretend I was boarding the train. I waited for an hour before I ventured out of the station and came here. I had made these reservations last week when I wrote to you."

Suddenly Louise felt that she was a co-conspirator in an adventure. She had discovered that she liked Lottie, and was very glad that her gesture was going to help her. She found herself telling the older woman about her family, Frankie's untimely death, Gladdie's illness, even about her confusion over Johnnie and Jeremy.

"He gave me his mother's ring," she told Lottie, "and made me promise not to marry Jeremy until he also came home, and then I would choose between them. The trouble is, I am fond of Jeremy as well, and I shall hate to hurt him."

"You'll know what to do when they both come home," said Lottie. "My grandmother used to say that the best kind of love starts out as friendship and grows from there."

"I don't know why I've told you all this."

"Sometimes it's easier to confide in a stranger than someone close to you, and you know I'm safe because I don't know any of the people you're telling me about."

"But it's very queer, you don't feel the least bit like a stranger," declared Louise.

Lottie smiled. "Thank you, my dear. Have you noticed the time? Let's go down to the dining room for supper. Remember, you are my guest, and that we have an early start tomorrow."

Louise sat in the dappled sunshine with Norah, Sybil and the children. The day was warm and summery. Norah had spread a large blanket on the grass under the apple trees, and brought out a jug of lemonade on a tray. Sarah and Ben were in school, six-month old Carson was slumbering peacefully in his basket nearby, while little Frannie sat in the sun examining her handful of autumn wildflowers. Norah had put on a little weight, Louise noted, but Sybil was slim and lovely. They had listened avidly to her account of her adventures in Montreal assisting Lottie Fairbairn to 'escape' from her husband.

"She said she wrote Nanny and just said she was coming, so I hope everything is all right," Louise said, pouring another glass of lemonade. "I would love to go and visit her, and see how she is doing. She gave me her address in Nova Scotia; here it is: care of Miss Dora Morrison, Middle Harbour, Cape Breton, Nova Scotia."

"Why don't you? You're this far," observed Sybil.

"You don't have go home by a certain date, do you?" asked Norah. "I'm trying to persuade Papa to bring Mama and Val down for Christmas. The whole family would be together at last."

"Gerald and I are worried about Bernice," added Sybil.

"I don't think she looks well at all," said Louise. "It's been some months that she's been ill, hasn't it."

"We're are afraid—"

"That she's dying?"

"Yes."

The baby woke up at that moment, and Sybil reached for him.

"Do you mind if I feed him right here? Nobody's about," she said, unbuttoning her dress.

"This will be a signal for Miss Gorton to call," laughed Norah, as she took the handful of wild flowers Frannie handed her. "Thank you, my pet, come here for a cuddle with Mama," and the toddler tumbled into her mother's arms with a gurgling laugh.

"Who's Miss Gorton?" Louise asked.

"Just the village busybody," Sybil said, as she put her baby to her breast. Louise thought once again what a lovely sight it was to see a mother nursing her infant.

"Nursing a baby would offend her?"

"Oh," said Norah, with a smile. "If she saw me take Harry's hand it would offend her. 'There are some things you don't do in public,'" she quoted, in a prunes and prisms voice. "Did I tell you what she said to me the other day, Sybil? 'I do hope you aren't planning to bring another child into this world of woe.' I just looked at her and said that for me, children were the hope of the world, if we can only bring them up to see that war isn't an answer for everything."

"Norah!" exclaimed Louise, examining her older sister with new eyes, "are you—expecting?"

Norah smiled and patted her stomach. "We haven't made an announcement yet, but we are hoping that in the spring—"

"That's lovely!" Louise eyes sparkled as she reached over and kissed her sister on the cheek. "I won't say a word to Miss Gorton!"

The three young women laughed, Norah propping herself against a tree with a cushion, Frannie cuddled in under her arm. Louise stretched out on the blanket, her hands tucked underneath her head. She had been at her sister's for a week, and was thoroughly dug in. Ottawa and nursing Gladdie seemed miles and miles and years and years away. She listened to the voices of her sister and sister-in-law discussing things purely maternal and domestic, Norah's rich contralto and Sybil's light English tones, and her thoughts drifted. It was lovely here. She was glad that Sybil and Norah were such good friends. How could she have been so jealous of them last year? Perhaps she had grown up a bit in the meantime. Lottie Fairbairn had been good company on their trip east. Louise had been surprisingly reluctant to leave her to cross over to the Island. The last thing Lottie said was that she would keep in touch, and would she consider a trip to Cape Breton? It was too bad she didn't have wings and could just fly across the water to visit her new friend. If Johnnie were here, he'd fly her there. She opened her eyes as she felt a small hand tentatively exploring her face, and found Frannie's smiling countenance two inches from hers.

"Auntie Lou-Lou," she said.

"Not Lulu, darling, Louise. Loo-eeze," she repeated slowly.

"Weeze?"

Louise grinned. "Why are there no nice diminutives for my name?"

"Don't bother Auntie Louise, Frannie," said Norah.

"Ah, my beautiful niece could never bother me," said Louise with a smile. "A hug for auntie?" And she put her arms around the toddler and held her lightly on top of her. Frannie gurgled and tucked her head underneath Louise's chin.

"Weeze," she said firmly.

Louise closed her eyes again. As she held the warm little body that was Frannie, aware of the small heart beating lightly against hers, she thought what a lovely child she was: sweet natured and always smiling. Maybe someday she'd have a little girl just like her, only with Johnnie's brown wavy hair and sparkling eyes. Warmth spread through her as she pictured Johnnie as she'd seen him for the last time. She had stood in the circle of his arms, and though it had been a brief embrace, she could still feel the strength of his arms around her. Oh, if only this war was over, and the boys home again! There was a pang in the region of her heart as she remembered that some would never return. Her darling Frankie, with whom she'd played and fought and made up all through her childhood—they'd been such pals! She remembered him bent over the dining room table studying the map of the Balkans at the outbreak of the war, his eyes squinting in concentration, a finger tracing the border around the country in question. She saw him rushing into the house, eyes alight with the excitement of his first real job, Frankie in uniform smiling at her and wishing her happy birthday. Tears filled her eyes, and she shut

305

them even more tightly. Remember the good times; cherish those memories, she told herself. Her arms tightened around Frannie who lay so quietly on her breast. Norah was right, she decided. Children were the world's future.

Presently Frannie wriggled free and crawled away, and Louise was lulled into a light sleep. She dreamed she was flying with Johnnie, the wind rushing by her with terrific speed, the sun bright in a blue sky. Then, to her horror, the earth began rushing toward them and she knew they were going to crash. She looked at the pilot's seat, and it was empty. Where was Johnnie? She tried to scream, couldn't, and awoke with a jerk.

"You were asleep," remarked Norah.

"I dreamed—it turned into a nightmare . . ."

"Louise! Don't be so upset. It was only a dream."

"I know, but it was so real . . ."

Voices distracted them, and Sybil said, "Here are the twins and Gerald."

Ben and Sarah were arguing vigorously but good-naturedly about something.

"There's mail! A big envelope for Aunt Louise!" Sarah called as they crossed the backyard.

"I want to give it to her!" complained Ben.

"If you're going to argue, I shall hand it to her," Gerald said to his niece and nephew severely. "Hallo, girls, I see you're being sensible and enjoying this lovely day outside."

He smiled down at them, and Louise was surprised to see that Sybil continued to nurse Carson, smiling calmly back at Gerald. Gerald flung himself down on the blanket beside her and tossed an envelope to his sister.

"Letter from home, I think. It's very fat. Just circulars for you and Harry," he told Norah, "and a letter for Bernice from Mercy and Robert."

"How's Bernice today?" asked Norah. "Sarah, why don't you and Ben take Frannie and help her on the swing?"

The twins obediently took Frannie by the hand and led her to the swing that their father had hung under the oak tree.

"Bernice is having one of her good days," Gerald said. He glanced at Louise who was reading her letter. "Momentous news from the parents?"

Sybil had put the baby down on the blanket in front of her, and was buttoning up her bodice. "I should be thinking about supper, Gerald, will you bring Carson's basket with you when you come home?"

"Sure. Why don't you take Bernice's letter to her—I'll be along shortly." They smiled at each other; Sybil got to her feet, picked up the baby, and started across the yard to the house next door.

"It's just a short note from Mama," said Louise. "They enclosed a letter for me, who can it be from?" She handed the note to Gerald and turned to the other envelope. "Carruthers—in Halifax. Why does that ring a bell?" Ripping it open she began to read. "Oh, of course, Johnnie's aunt and uncle—" She broke off, the color receding from her cheeks. "No, no, no … it's not true, it can't be true . . ." her voice ending in a wail, the letter falling to the blanket on which Louise was sitting. She buried her face in her hands.

"Louise, what has happened?" Norah asked.

Louise looked up at her, dry-eyed and stony faced. "It's Johnnie. They received a telegram. His plane crashed and burned. He's dead. I don't believe it."

"May I read the letter, Louise?" asked Gerald gently. Louise handed it to him. Norah got up and came around, looking over her brother's shoulder.

> *Dear Miss Laurier,*
>
> *We haven't met, but I am Johnnie Ferris' Uncle Stanley. Johnnie named us as his next of kin. I don't know why he chose us over his father's brother, perhaps because he has known us longer. He told us about you, and asked us if anything should happen to him, that we should let you know.*
>
> *My dear Miss Laurier, I have the misfortune to pass on to you the saddest of all news. On September 4th, Johnnie's airplane crashed and burned, and he was killed. I have no other details as yet. I am so*

307

*sorry to have to tell you this. I know he was very
fond of you. I expect another letter soon from his
commanding officer, and I will write to you again.
Believe me, I am*

*Yours most sincerely,
Stanley Carruthers*

Norah and Gerald gazed at her pale, grim face sympathetically.

"Life's so unfair, isn't it!" Norah said, moving over and putting her arms around her sister. "Losing friends is so ghastly."

Louise began to shiver uncontrollably. Norah gazed over her sister's shoulder at her brother with a concerned look on her face.

"Louise, let's go inside and I'll make you a cup of tea. Come on, now. Gerald, will you ask the twins to watch Frannie until I come back out?"

Norah led Louise into the kitchen where Mrs. Hastie was preparing supper.

"Ah, the poor lamb," exclaimed that worthy woman when Norah explained that Louise had just received some very bad news. "I'll make the tea, Miss Norah, you tend to your baby. Send the twins in to lay the table for me, will you?"

Norah went back outside and collected Frannie. Gerald had been playing with the three children, and after Norah had sent Sarah and Ben indoors, he said, "She's taking it very hard. Had you met this fellow?"

"No. Mama said in a letter that he brought Louise home on her birthday two years ago and he came in to give his condolences about Frankie. I think he was there when Harry telephoned the news of Frannie's birth. Jeremy's cousin, she said. Remember, she went out to Winnipeg with Susie and her parents? They were on the same train as Harry and I on our way to British Columbia."

Gerald nodded. "I guess I had better get on home. I'll tell Sybil and Bernice about it. Poor Louise! What next?"

The next day Louise wrote a note to Mr. and Mrs. Carruthers, asking them to write her at Fairlea, PEI. She sealed it in an envelope, and then sat quietly, thinking. Presently she wrote another letter, this one to addressed to Lottie Cannings, care of Dora Morrison in Middle Harbour, Nova Scotia, then walked to the village to post them. She walked back, and on the way turned off and took the road that led to the beach. It was a windy autumn day, clear and sunny and cool. She walked up and down the beach, listening to the waves crash on the shore. *Break, break, break on thy cold grey stones, O sea.* It was nearly dark before she came back to Norah and Harry's.

Norah opened her mouth to reproach her sister for being out so long, but closed it when she saw the misery on Louise's face.

"I'm not particularly hungry," Louise said, when Norah called her for supper.

A day or two later Norah sought out her sister, who after coming in from a long walk had closeted herself in her bedroom. The room was dim in the waning light. Louise sat on the corner window seat in the shadow of the drapes.

"Louise, can we talk?"

Louise turned her face and gazed out the window. Evening was drawing in. Through the trees on the ridge the last pale rays of the setting sun glimmered.

"Louise, I understand that you've lost a friend, but you can't go on like this. When you're not out walking for hours you're brooding all alone in your room. Ben and Sarah are convinced they've upset you in some way. We've said, no, Auntie Louise is sad because her friend has died. Louise, dear, was he more than a friend?"

Louise turned slowly and faced her sister. "You're going to think I'm a terrible person," she said in a low voice. "Here I am, engaged to Jeremy, and I've fallen in love with his cousin. And now they say he's dead! Oh, Norah, what shall I do?" The tears began to slowly trickle down her cheeks.

Norah gathered the girl into her arms and made soothing, shushing noises. "My darling sister, nothing you ever did would make me think you're terrible! Sometimes we can't help what our hearts do."

She continued to hold Louise in her arms and soothe her as she would had Frannie fallen and skinned her knee. The only sound was

309

Louise's heart-broken sobs, muffled on Norah's shoulder. Gradually the sobs subsided, and Louise straightened up.

"I'm being very selfish, aren't I, only thinking about my own feelings? I'm sorry, Norah!"

"I had no idea that you felt that way about this young man. I remember Mama said he brought you home from the hospital on your birthday. She thought him a very nice person."

Louise swallowed. "We never meant to fall in love. I mean, I admired him for how wonderfully he treated his parents when they were both so ill. He took Susie and me about when we were in Winnipeg—he took me up for a flight in an airplane—Norah, it was marvelous! We were just friends one minute, and the next minute we—just belonged together. He asked me to wait and not marry Jeremy until he came home from the war—now he's never coming home!" Her hands twisted a handkerchief in her hands. "I wrote his aunt and uncle in Halifax and asked them if I could come and visit them. Johnnie stayed with them before he went overseas. Should I go if they invite me?"

Norah pondered only a moment. "I think you should—perhaps it will help you grieve if you can talk to someone who knew him also. Does anyone else know about your feelings for him?"

"I confided in Mrs. Fairbairn—she was so sympathetic and it was a relief to talk about Johnnie to someone. I could go and visit her, too. I wrote her the other day as well."

"I'll keep your secret, dear, even from Harry if you want me to."

"I don't mind Harry knowing."

"Do you think you could come and eat some supper?"

Louise forced a wan smile. "I'd better wash my face, hadn't I." She hugged Norah. "Thank you for being so understanding."

Chapter Twenty-Nine

NOVA SCOTIA

It was two weeks later that Louise stepped off the train in Halifax. The platform was out in the open, and a fine mist was falling. As she gathered her things together, a middle-aged man approached her. He was short and thin, rather yellow of complexion, but with brown twinkling eyes and graying hair. He carried an enormous umbrella.

"Miss Louise Laurier? It is Miss Laurier?"

Louise looked up and nodded. Her eyes were almost on a level with hers, so short was he.

"I'm Louise Laurier. Are you Mr. Carruthers?"

"I am indeed. Welcome to Halifax, Miss Laurier. Let me get your luggage."

"I just brought the one—I borrowed my brother Gerald's Gladstone bag," said Louise, indicating the brown bag at her feet.

Mr. Carruthers picked it up, indicated Louise to come in under his umbrella, and they proceeded down the platform and into the terminal.

"Summer seems to have deserted us," she commented, shivering, as they came out into the street.

"It seems colder because it is so damp. After all, it is October. I brought my car—it's parked not far away."

311

"You are so kind to meet me and have me as your guest," said Louise, as she settled herself beside him in his car. "Perhaps it was forward of me to write and invite myself. I apologize if I have inconvenienced you."

Mr. Carruthers guided the car out into the street before answering. "Miss Laurier, Mabel and I were very flattered that you wrote and wanted to come and visit us. We have no children of our own, and Johnnie we considered our son after his parents died. We are glad you are here."

Tears pricked Louise's eyes.

"We are also holding a letter for you from a Miss or Mrs. Cannings."

"Oh, thank you!" Louise said. "I hope you didn't mind—I asked her to send it to your address because I didn't know when I was leaving Fairlea. She lives in Middle Harbour, on Cape Breton Island, and I thought I'd like to go and see her while I was here. Are there trains?"

"I know Middle Harbour. We have friends living not far from there, in a small inland town. Yes, there is a branch line that goes to the Cape. You have to change trains at Windsor." He broke off, and was silent for a while.

Johnnie's aunt and uncle lived in a modest bungalow in a quiet residential part of the city. There was a lawn at the front, split in half by a sidewalk that led to the front door. The driveway led to a small garage at the back of the house where there was a garden, and a few fruit trees. Mrs. Carruthers greeted them at the kitchen door where she gently scolded her husband for not bringing their guest in through the front. The room was filled with the aroma of coffee and newly made bread.

"Welcome, my dear! May we call you Louise?" When Louise nodded her assent, she went on, "and you must call us Mabel and Stan! Do come in. Stan and I have coffee every afternoon at about this time. Can you tell I made bread this morning? Isn't it a lovely smell? Stan, do take Louise's bag to the spare room, and bring the tray into the dining room for me, please?"

Mabel Carruthers was a tiny woman, bright-eyed and gregarious. She reminded Louise of a little grey squirrel, darting about, doing this and that, all the while chattering away.

"I expect Stan has told you there's a letter for you. I've put it on the dresser in your room."

"She lives in Middle Harbour, Mabel," Stan informed his wife. "We've been meaning to visit Bill and Laura for a long time, haven't we."

Mabel smiled brightly. "We have indeed, and one must practically go through Middle Harbour in order to get to Glencannon, mustn't one."

Husband and wife exchanged understanding glances, and then Mabel busied herself pouring coffee.

"How do you take your coffee, dear?" she asked Louise.

"Milk and sugar, please. You know, the hospital coffee was so bad that the only way I could drink it was to have it one third hot water, one-third milk and one-third coffee with lots of sugar. I still put milk and sugar in, though I suppose I really shouldn't."

As they drank their coffee and ate Mabel's fresh bread and butter, her hosts begged her to tell them about her family on the Island.

"My oldest sister Norah married a farmer, a widower with two children," she explained. "They now have one of their own, a little girl who's a year and a half old. The adjacent farm belongs to my Aunt Bernice, my father's elder sister. It's how Norah and Harry met—we were visiting our aunt just when the war broke out. My older brother Gerald now lives with Aunt Bernice and runs the farm for her. She's not very well. Then there's Sybil, my sister-in-law."

"Gerald's wife?"

"Oh, no! Gerald is a confirmed bachelor, I think. He was engaged to a girl named Rhoda before the war, but she threw him over. I was glad. I didn't think she was good enough for Gerald." She took another sip of coffee and sighed. "You make good coffee, Mrs. Carruthers—Mabel. No, my brother Frank married an English nurse just before he was—killed." Louise swallowed. She still wasn't used to the idea that Frankie was gone forever. "She wrote to us that she was expecting a child, and could she come to us? She and Frankie had planned to come home to Canada, of course, after the war. Her

313

parents are both dead, and she was sort of brought up by an elderly aunt and uncle. Can you believe, they said she couldn't go on living with them after the baby was born! What was the poor girl to do?" Louise grew indignant all over again, thinking of Sybil's heartless relatives.

"So she came to Canada?" asked Mabel, leaning forward with interest. "Yes—a year ago this past summer. My friend Susie and I were down visiting at the time, so Gerald and I took the train to Halifax and met her. She was exhausted, poor thing, and was so glad to see us. We took her to Fairlea, and I expected that she would come back to Ottawa with us, but she stayed with Bernice and Gerald, and just loves it on the island. She has a dear little baby boy now, who's just over nine months old."

"What sort of farming do they do?" asked Stan.

"I guess you'd say mixed farming. Both Bernice and Harry have small dairy herds. Actually, I think Gerald and Harry are running the farms together. They grow hay and corn, and Harry planted fruit trees last year, too. Fairlea is just a small village, but it's not too far from Summerside, about an hour's drive in an automobile. Nice people there, too. I forgot to tell you about Mary and Pierre—they work for Bernice, Mary in the dairy and Pierre on the farm—they've been married for about three years, I guess, and have a baby girl of eight months. They don't actually live on the farm, but come every day during the week. Mary's awfully nice, and is really a friend more than an employee. Sybil said she's been very good to her, and when Mary isn't busy milking or making butter she helps Sybil in the house. Her mother works as housekeeper at my sister Norah's. She came to look after the house and the twins when Harry's first wife died, and has stayed ever since."

"It sounds like a wonderful family. You must miss them when you're home in Ottawa."

"Oh, we all do! Our house is big and empty now, without Frankie and Gerald. Norah taught away from home for five years before she got married, and Gladdie was sort of in and out."

"Gladdie is the sister you've been nursing?"

"Yes. She died in August." Louise moved uneasily. "Gladdie was—well, an unhappy person. We didn't always get on."

"Johnnie wrote that you were planning to go to England and nurse wounded soldiers."

"Yes. I graduated last January, but I had to cancel my plans, because of Gladdie. She was ill, but I didn't realize how ill at the time. The doctors wanted her to go to the sanitarium over in Hull, but she wouldn't agree. I couldn't let Mama look after her, it would have been too much for her...."

"So you nursed her at home. How brave and kind of you!" Mabel said, smiling at her.

Louise was embarrassed. She hadn't thought she'd been either brave or kind.

"Tell us how you met Johnnie," suggested Stan.

Louise was happy to talk about him, so she related how she had gone out to Winnipeg with the Ferrises to visit Jeremy's uncle who was then very ill, and of their time there. Her excitement of flying with Johnnie, the sadness of his father's death, and her admiring observation of what a good son he was.

"Johnnie told us about you," Mabel said, getting up from the table. "He said that his cousin and her friend who was engaged to her brother were just wonderful girls. He didn't let on what his feelings for you really were until he was with us just before he sailed for England. 'I didn't really have the right to, but I asked her to wait until both Jeremy and I came home.' I remember how his eyes lit up when he said, 'And she said she would.' Come into the parlor, dear, I want to show you something."

On the piano in the parlor, draped in black, was a photograph of Johnnie in uniform. Beside it was a box. Mabel opened the box and said, "His commanding officer sent this to us. It arrived only yesterday."

It was an identification bracelet. Louise held it, and looked at the name engraved on it: Johnnie's full name, rank and number. She looked at the photograph, then at the bracelet, and sat down on the piano bench.

"It's true, then," she muttered. "I didn't really believe it, you know."

"The letter gave us some more details. They're not very nice," warned Stanley.

Louise just looked at him steadily. "Tell me, please."

"His airplane crashed a few minutes after takeoff. It landed in a wood about two miles from the aerodrome. Apparently there was quite a fire—it could be seen for miles. The aeroplane burned up completely, and there was no way to identify him except by his ID bracelet. I'm sorry, Louise."

So that was the way Johnnie's life had ended—two miles from home. He hadn't even had a chance to go after the enemy. It seemed very ironic. Please God, he hadn't suffered. It would have been quick, wouldn't it?

"His commander said he had shot down ten enemy aeroplanes, and that he was a fine officer. He offered his condolences and added that we must be proud of the sacrifice he and many of our boys have made. We were going to adopt him formally, you know," he added.

"You never know, you might have become our daughter-in-law," said Mabel sadly. "Come, dear, I'll show you to your room."

Louise opened Lottie's letter a little while later. It was full of sympathy for the loss of her friend, and she urged her to come for a visit anytime. There followed instructions as to how to get to Middle Harbour. *Don't worry about letting us know, just come,* she wrote. *We're not on the telephone here. Nanny has a lovely guest room that is always available.*

"Do you think you could drive me to the train?" she asked her host later at the supper table.

"We can do better than that," replied Stan. "We'll drive you there on our way to visit our friends in Glencannon."

"Oh, you mustn't do that for me!"

"We've been meaning to visit our friends for a long time. It's a great opportunity. Here, dear, do take another helping of chicken."

"Oh, but Mabel, would you be going all that way if it weren't for me?"

"Probably not, dear, so we have you to thank for getting us there. Bill and Laura will be so pleased to see us."

Louise had no answer for that one. "Lottie says not to bother letting them know, but I hate to come unannounced, and they have no telephone. What if it's inconvenient for Miss Morrison?"

"We'll send a telegram," decided Mabel. "Shall we go the day after tomorrow? We always go to the symphony concerts, and there's one tomorrow night. When we knew you'd be here, I bought an extra ticket. I hope you'll come as our guest."

Louise would have rather stayed home and talked about Johnnie, but she managed to sound enthusiastic as she said, "How nice! I haven't been to a concert in months." And then she thought of Dr Redmond telling her to stay away from crowds. However, it seemed churlish to refuse.

"Some of the proceeds are going to the war effort, I believe." Mabel poured the tea, and passed the biscuits and cheese. "We'll send a telegram tomorrow and tell them we'll be there late Friday afternoon. Stan can hand it in at the telegraph office, can't you, dear."

Stan's mouth was full of biscuits and cheese, so all he could do was nod in assent, crumbs tumbling down his shirtfront to the linen napkin on his lap.

Louise smiled at them both, her heart full. "You both are so good and kind," was all she could say.

Chapter Thirty

LOUISE 1918 CONTINUED

Middle Harbour was a small fishing village on the east side of Cape Breton. Most of the shops and cottages were built on the hillside that fell steeply to the sea, but there were some on the cliff top. One of these was Miss Dora Morrison's house, prosaically named 'Seaview'. Across the road was the Presbyterian Church and the Manse with the churchyard behind dotted with headstones. Next door was the doctor's house and surgery. The townsfolk laughingly commented that if you wanted to see the doctor you had to be well enough to climb the hill to his office, but if you were well enough to do that, why did you want to see him in the first place?

Miss Morrison and Lottie had greeted Stan, Mabel, and Louise enthusiastically. She asked Stan and Mabel to stay for supper and the night, but Mr. and Mrs. Carruthers regretfully declined, saying that Bill and Laura were expecting them for the evening meal. Miss Morrison pointed out that the road to the village continued beyond, wound up the hillside several miles past Middle Harbour where it joined the highway just before it turned steeply inland on the way to Glencannon.

"That's our market town," she said. "It's about a forty-five minute ride in my little Ford car. In horse and buggy days, it was a day's excursion. We children would pile into the wagon and Mother would pack a lunch. We always looked forward to the last Saturday of the month."

"Nanny drives there nearly every week," said Lottie. "Isn't that amazing?"

Stan and Mabel made amazed sounds, and then Mabel asked, "Perhaps you know our friends, then? Bill and Laura Johnstone. That's Johnstone with a 't' and an 'e' on the end. They haven't lived there long, though. Laura's aunt died a few years back and left her the house. Their friends were astonished when they decided to retire to the wilds of Cape Breton, but Laura writes that they love it there, and that they've made some very good friends. Her aunt had lived there for many years, so I suppose that helped them become established."

"I don't know any Johnstones in Glencannon. Do you remember the aunt's name? I might have been acquainted with her."

Mabel shook her head doubtfully. "No, I don't. But I'll ask Laura tonight. How long will you be staying, dear?" she asked, turning to Louise.

"As long as she wants," Miss Morrison answered for her.

"As long as you are staying with the Johnstones," Louise said to Stan and Mabel. "They're going to put me on the train at Windsor on their way back to Halifax," she explained to her hostess.

"I expect Laura and Bill will be glad to see us leave after three or four days," chuckled Mabel. "Shall we say Tuesday morning? Then that gives us time to drive to Windsor and catch the afternoon train."

They smiled kindly at Louise, turned and went down the path to the car. Miss Morrison picked up Louise's bag briskly.

"Come away in, then," she said. "I'll show you to your room, and then we'll have a nice hot cup of tea in the sitting room."

Louise always remembered that weekend as a restful hiatus before getting back to the business of ordinary life. Miss Morrison, who soon became 'Nanny' to her, was as plump and motherly as one of Aunt Bernice's hens, and Louise immediately found herself tucked under her wing. She discovered that Lottie had sold the necklace in Halifax, and was making plans to start a business. She was hoping that there would be enough customers in Middle Harbour to support a dressmaking business; she liked the village and its inhabitants, and

319

was pleased to be able to live with Nanny. Miss Morrison had one permanent tenant, who was the local primary schoolteacher, but she hoped to attract a clientele that would come during the summer months to enjoy the seaside. A path from the back garden led down the hillside to a sandy cove, which during the warm weather was quite suitable for sun bathing and swimming, and there were several walking trails in the vicinity. A family from New Brunswick had stayed with her in July, and Nanny hoped that the word would spread that Middle Harbour was a pleasant place in which to stay.

"Word of mouth is the very best advertising," she said later, as they had their tea in the sitting room. Nanny had a delightful accent. Her R's rolled richly out of her smiling mouth, and she had an infectious laugh that began with a low chuckle deep inside, then rose to a hearty laugh of merriment. You couldn't stop smiling around Nanny when she was in good humor.

Later on Lottie took Louise up to the second floor where she was preparing a workroom for herself. A young man was busily building cupboards and a closet where she would store materials and hang clothes. It was a bright room facing the morning sun, with a view of the village.

"I'll make curtains for the windows as soon as my sewing machine arrives." It seemed that one of Lottie's first purchases was a brand new Singer sewing machine, which she had ordered in Halifax. "But I've been knitting. Come on down to my bedroom and I'll show you what I've done. I won't be able to use this room until young Mr. Hobbs is finished. Too much dust, and the smell of varnish is rather unpleasant." So saying, she led the way downstairs. "There are two babies expected this winter, and I've already had a request for sweaters and booties and such," she said, bringing out some tissue wrapped garments, and laying them out on her bed.

"Lottie, they're beautiful! Are they all spoken for, or may I buy two or three sets? This dress would fit little Frannie perfectly! And Carson needs a set like this. Such dear little leggings and a matching sweater! I wish I could knit like this. My grandmother tried to teach me, but I was hopeless. Mind you, I did some embroidery, that's far more difficult, isn't it. I wonder why I didn't like to knit?"

Lottie said that the outfits were available, and cautiously mentioned a price. Louise admired them again, and Lottie wrapped them up carefully.

"Oh, I can't bring back gifts for the babies and not the twins! I don't suppose you have anything suitable for eight-year olds, do you?"

Lottie suggested she knit something for them for Christmas, and the next little while was spent looking at pattern books. Louise finally selected a cheerfully striped sweater and stocking cap for Ben and a twin set for Sarah in a soft robin's egg blue.

"I almost forgot about Mary's baby!" she exclaimed, as Lottie was folding the garments and putting them away. "Mary is Aunt Bernice's dairy maid and housemaid, and she and Pierre (who is Bernice's hired man) are practically family. She and Pierre had a baby girl a month after Carson was born. The white sweater would fit her."

Lottie smiled and wrapped up the white sweater. It was trimmed with white satin ribbon and there was a bonnet to match.

"I hope my subsequent customers are as generous as you," she remarked as they settled accounts a little later. She glanced at her watch and remarked that it was nearly suppertime. "Let's go down. I like to ask Nanny if I can help, though she always refuses. Isn't she a pet?"

Lottie led the way down the stairs to the main floor. "I hope you won't be bored here with a couple of old ladies like Nanny and me," she said, over her shoulder.

Louise shook her head. "Don't worry. I came to see how you were doing. I feel responsible, somehow."

"Middle Harbour is such a small place, and there's not much for a city girl like you."

"It's a beautiful spot, and I like Nanny's house—it's warm and friendly. Besides, I will enjoy just sitting and not doing much. Mabel and Stan trotted me all over Halifax, when all I really wanted to do was hear about Johnnie. Don't mistake me—I'm not ungrateful. Mabel's a good, kind creature, though she does chatter so."

A steady rain was falling several days later when Louise returned to the Island and was met by her brother Gerald at the ferry terminus. He was smiling cheerfully in spite of the gloomy weather, and uncharacteristically gave Louise an affectionate hug.

"It seems like ages since you left," he declared, putting the Gladstone bag in the boot, and opening the passenger door for her.

"It seems like a long time to me, too," she admitted.

Gerald cranked the engine, wiped the rain off his face, and climbed into the driver's seat. "How was the visit?" he asked cautiously, as he guided the automobile out into the traffic.

"Mabel and Stan Carruthers—they're Johnnie's aunt and uncle—are good people. They were very fond of Johnnie; in fact they talked about formally adopting him when he came home. They showed me the letter from his commanding officer, and his identification tag that he wore."

In a faltering voice, Louise told Gerald how Johnnie had died. Gerald took one hand off the wheel and put it on her shoulder sympathetically.

"It's awful when you lose a friend, isn't, old girl," he said gruffly. "Norah hinted that you were pretty fond of him."

"Yes, I was. But that's over now," she said resolutely. "I had a lovely stay with Lottie Fairbairn in Middle Harbour. Though she goes by the name of Cannings, now. That was her mother's maiden name. She's in hiding from her husband, but she's happy as can be. She's not at all worried about him. She wrote him a letter and said he could divorce her for desertion. Is that grounds in Canada?"

"I don't know."

"And Nanny—Miss Morrison—has to be seen to be believed. She's plump and jolly and kind hearted and has a chuckle that makes you want to laugh right along with her. She owns this big old house on the cliff above the village. The local schoolteacher boards with her. There's just the primary school in the village. The high school children catch a bus that takes them into Glencannon, about fifteen or twenty miles away inland. Miss Stone (that's the teacher) told me, in the winter, the roads are sometimes blocked with snow and the bus can't get through, so she has to give the older children lessons along with the little ones. They are quite in awe of the 'big ones', she says. Sunday we all went across the road to church. Lottie has already been recruited to sing in the choir, and she's been there scarcely a month. Now, tell me, Gerald, how's everyone? What about Bernice?"

"Bernice is amazing the way she carries on. She's looking forward to Christmas. Mother and Father are coming with Dorcas and Val, too, of course."

Louise clapped her hands. "How marvelous that Papa can get the time off!"

"He says he thinks the war will be over before Christmas."

"That's what they said in 1914," Louise said skeptically. She sighed. "But wouldn't it be wonderful."

"He seems to be pretty positive. Apparently there are negotiations going on."

Louise was silent. "A pity it's too late for Johnnie and Frank," she said bitterly after a moment.

"We're not the only family that has lost loved ones," Gerald reminded her gently.

Louise felt a little ashamed of herself. It was true. So many young men had died—a whole generation, in fact. There were so many widows, so many young women who might never marry now. She sighed again.

"If you need me to help look after Aunt Bernice, I'll stay as long as necessary."

"Oh, Lou, you've just had such a session with Gladdie. Norah said you're supposed to be resting and recovering."

"I feel fine. If you need me, I'll stay on," she said firmly.

"Thank you," he said gruffly. "Sybil will have her hands full with Carson." He paused. "I want to tell you something, Lou." He turned and smiled suddenly at her. "I'm the happiest man in the world—Sybil has agreed to marry me!"

Louise was thunderstruck. "Gerald! I had no idea! And here I was telling Mabel and Stan that you were a confirmed old bachelor." She smiled at him. "Congratulations!"

"When you and I met her last year in Halifax, I knew at once that she was the girl for me," he said solemnly, "but I waited until

323

this summer before I said anything to her. The night before last she finally said she'd marry me."

"When will you be married?"

"I think at Christmas, when the family is all here. Mercy and Robert will spend Christmas with us, and Father is going to get in touch with Uncle Simon and try and persuade him to come down with them. It quite possibly will be Bernice's last, though you would never know it by her attitude."

Louise was silent. "I don't believe I remember Uncle Simon at all."

"He has visited us once or twice. He's so much younger than Father that I don't think they have much in common. Mercy says she'll write him and beg him to come. She says he's always been a loner."

After a while Gerald said hesitantly, "I think Sybil is wondering how you'll react to our news. She knows how close you and Frankie were, and hopes you won't think she is being disloyal to his memory."

"It's crossed my mind once or twice whether Sybil would ever remarry," admitted Louise, "but I never thought of you, Gerald! Gosh, she and Frankie hardly had time to get to know one another, and you both deserve happiness. Carson needs a papa, too. I think it's absolutely perfect!"

Gerald took his eyes off the road a moment to smile at his sister gratefully. "Will you tell her that, please?"

Louise nodded, her eyes shining. "War over or not," she declared, "we're going to have a wonderful Christmas!"

The day of armistice arrived, and for the family and especially Louise, it was bittersweet celebration. Later on Mama told her that in Ottawa a huge crowd gathered in front of the Parliament Buildings, many holding flags, both the Union Jack and the Tri-color. When the signal came that the war was over, there were tears and cheers and dancing in the streets. Mama said that Dorcas got down on her knees in the middle of the kitchen floor and gave thanks, and wept for Frankie all over again.

The family gathered for Christmas in Fairlea and managed a wonderful celebration. It was the first time that Papa's whole family had been together for many years, for Uncle Simon came after all, albeit reluctantly, got acquainted with his nephews and nieces, and then went reluctantly home shaking his head, wondering why he had taken so long to make a visit. Bernice rallied, and sat at the head of the table for Christmas dinner. Seventeen in all, including Frannie and Carson in their high chairs, crowded around the big dining room table in which all its leaves had been placed. After the meal Mama played carols on the piano and everyone sang. Mercy and Louise worked up a skit with the twins, and they performed for everyone.

Susie telephoned long distance from Perth to say they'd had a cable from Jeremy. He was well, but would be tied up in England for several months.

"Peter has written me," she added. "Do you remember Johnnie's friend, Louise?"

Louise remembered the two of them dancing together at the lake, and later, her blushes when she revealed that they had been corresponding.

"He'll be home in about a month," she said, "and has asked if he can call on me."

"Ah ha! I smell romance!"

"Oh, Louise, I'm not sure about anything. When are you coming home?"

"I don't know, Susie. I told you Aunt Bernice is not well." She lowered her voice, glancing at the family gathered in the big parlor. No one was paying any attention to her. "I think I will stay and look after her. I don't know how long she has."

"Oh, Louise. You seem to have inherited patients to nurse, haven't you? I say, have there been any cases of influenza down your way?"

"Not so far, touch wood. Johnnie's uncle wrote to say that Mabel was sick, but I haven't heard how she's doing. Dr Redmond was worried last August."

"There seems to be an epidemic happening. It's probably a good thing that you're away in the country."

"Look, Susie, don't you get sick. Get lots of rest." She hung up, vaguely worried.

Gerald and Sybil were married quietly in the village church, with all the family there—even Bernice got dressed in her best outfit and went with Mama and Papa. Harry was Gerald's best man, and Louise was bridesmaid. Sybil had wanted Norah as well, but Norah was shy about standing up in public obviously pregnant. The church was beautiful with the Christmas decorations still in place, and after a stand-up buffet lunch at Norah and Harry's the young couple drove to the hotel in Summerside for the weekend. Eleven-month-old Carson fussed a bit when Norah offered him a bottle, but all in all he was a good baby. After all, it was the first time he had been separated from his mother, though there were plenty of substitutes—his grandmother, two aunts, and his doting twin cousins.

The newlyweds arrived back on Monday, flushed and smiling. Louise thought that Gerald had never looked so pleased with himself. Sybil absolutely glowed. Norah came over from next door with Carson, who, of course had stayed with the family for the weekend.

"Here's Mummy back from Summerside!" she said gaily, striding in with Carson on her hip. He was becoming quite a sturdy little boy, and he smiled at his mother who clasped him affectionately in her arms.

"Who's my big boy, then?" Sybil crooned, hugging him with delight. Carson caught sight of Gerald standing behind his mother, and he waved his fists and chuckled out loud.

"Da-da!" he said firmly, in his baby voice.

Louise took one look at Gerald's face as Sybil handed Carson to him, and turned away, glancing at Norah, who was observing the tableau with interest and pleasure. Louise murmured something about getting supper organized, and the two sisters went down the stairs to the kitchen.

"I hope those two have lots of babies," remarked Norah. "Did you see Gerald's face when Carson said Dada?"

Louise's eyes were shining. "Oh, Norah, I thought he was going to weep, he was so happy!"

"I think the marriage will work out just fine, don't you think?"

"They're perfect for each other."

"I agree. I'm glad you feel that way. I'm so fond of Sybil."

"They both deserve to be happy, and Gerald will be a wonderful father to Carson. Frankie would be the last to want his widow being alone and unhappy bringing up his son by herself."

"They're very much in love. I can tell."

Louise twinkled at her sister. "Just like you and Harry."

Norah gave her sister a swift kiss on the cheek. "Yes," she answered firmly. "Just like Harry and me."

"I wonder . . . ." Louise broke off, as she opened the oven door and peered at the roast simmering inside.

"What do you wonder?"

"Oh, nothing."

Norah smiled understandingly at the younger woman. "You will find happiness, Lou," she said. "I know it."

Louise straightened up, closing the oven door with a snap. "I'd better set the table, and then see if Bernice feels like eating with us."

"And I'd better get along home," Norah said, pulling on her boots and shrugging into her warm coat. She peered out the window. "It's beginning to snow again. Let's all go on a sleigh ride tomorrow if it's not too cold. I'll talk to Harry. Bye, darling."

Bernice smiled weakly at Gerald and Sybil who were gazing anxiously at her. Pale January sunshine streamed in through the window in her bedroom.

"I know there's not much time left for me," she said.

"Oh, Auntie, dear, don't say that . . ." began Sybil.

"Sybil, dear, you're a nurse, and you know when a person is dying. Louise knows, too. I'm happy that you and Gerald are settled and married. The farm will be yours when I'm gone, you know."

Tears sprang to the beautiful eyes of the Englishwoman. "You are too good to us . . ."

"Not at all, my dear." Bernice's voice had some of the old bounce in it. "Gerald has worked hard, and so have you since you came to live with us. Your son will inherit this eventually, I hope." She paused. "I want you to make sure Pierre and Mary are looked after—they both have been good and faithful servants. I've left them a little legacy, but their place here is important, too, as long as they want to

327

stay." Gerald nodded. "You and Harry are friends as well as brothers-in-law, aren't you," the older woman continued. "I'm glad of that, too. Now that the war is over we can get back to living again. Louise, don't you be working forever. Jeremy will be home eventually."

Louise had been sitting by the window, gazing across the snow-covered yard toward the meadows and the sea beyond. She turned to smile at her patient.

"I think you must rest, now, Aunt Bernice," she said, and Gerald and Sybil nodded in agreement and went out.

"When are your parents returning to Ottawa?" the old woman asked, as Louise plumped up her pillow and offered her a drink of water.

"Papa, Val, and Dorcas are leaving on the fifth. It's been wonderful that he's been able to get so much time off. He's a bit worried about this influenza outbreak, and is insisting on Mama staying here. She's quite happy to stay until after Norah's baby comes, and I'm glad she's here. She hasn't been completely strong since that operation she had in 1914. Val would love to stay longer, but the winter term begins next week and he should be back in school if he wants to go to university in a year or two. Mama is so relieved the war is over, and there's no danger of Val joining the army. As for me, I shall stay as long as I am needed here."

"You're a good girl, Louise." Bernice smiled at her niece, closed her eyes and slept.

Chapter Thirty-One

LOUISE 1919-1920

Bernice died on the last day of January, quietly and peacefully. Her last days had been happy, for her family had been all around her, and Louise had kept her comfortable with small amounts of medication.

"I don't want to be doped up," she told the doctor. "I want to be aware of what's happening."

The children had kept her company, Sarah reading to her in her light, childish voice, Frannie sitting close to her while Carson crawled about on the rug by the bed. Ben delighted her and amazed Louise by reciting a poem he had composed: "How I'll Miss my Aunt Bernice." Sarah commented that she, Aunt Bernice, was lucky, because quite likely Sarah's mother would be there to meet her when she got to Heaven. "She'll probably give you a tour of the whole place."

Harry was dubious about the twins spending so much time in the sickroom, that it would likely upset them with memories of their mother, but Norah smiled and shook her head. Harry was in time to hear that remark about his late wife, and later Louise overheard him say quietly to Norah, "You're so wise, my darling. Bernice is helping them, and they're helping Bernice."

A week after the funeral Louise took the train home. She had been away for over five months, and so much had happened. In spite of all her activities she felt refreshed, and not for the first time contrasted Bernice's death and that of her sister Gladdie. What a difference! Bernice had been calm and peaceful, and in her dying had actually ministered to her family and friends. Gladdie, on the other hand, had been as fretful and discontented in her dying as she had been in her living, though at the very end she had made some semblance of peace with her sister. Louise sighed. Now it was time she applied for a job at the hospital and began to add some savings to the small legacy from Gladdie that she had carefully put away. She needed to help with the household finances, too, now that Papa was the only one bringing home a salary. The house was big and expensive to run. Perhaps it was time for Mama and Papa to think of buying a smaller place, for it would soon be just Val who was home.

Or would it? Four years ago her future had seemed assured. A short career as a nurse, then the longer career as Mrs. Jeremy Ferris. But war and circumstance had turned her world upside-down. For a while she thought that she might marry Johnnie, but how was she to break her engagement to Jeremy? Then the unthinkable happened and Johnnie was killed, and so far as she knew, Jeremy was safe. How was she to tell Jeremy that her heart had changed? He was expecting to marry her. She was therefore in two minds about Jeremy's return, whenever that might be.

Papa met her at the station with bad news.

"Phoebe Ferris is very ill with influenza," he told her gravely. "Susie has been given leave to go home and look after her mother."

"Oh, Papa! How awful!" Louise felt a vague sensation of guilt. While she had been agonizing over Jeremy's return, his mother was perhaps dying! "I shall go up to Perth as soon as I can," she said firmly, making up her mind.

"I thought you'd say that. I wish you wouldn't, dear. It's very contagious, and you've had a long bout of nursing Gladdie and my sister Bernice. I know of two chaps in my office that caught it, and both were gone in less than a week!"

"Nevertheless, I must. Susie is my best and dearest friend, and Jeremy...." What was Jeremy now? She touched his ring, still on its chain around her neck and nestled in her bosom.

"I understand, dear. Dorcas has anticipated your reaction as well, and is boiling up gallons of chicken and garlic soup."

Susie opened the door to Louise two days later. She looked drawn and tired.

"Louise! You're the second ministering angel to arrive in as many days! I thought it might be Peter. He's been calling on me, but I sent him away when Mother got sick. I told him I didn't want him to have escaped injury on the battlefield, then to come home and catch influenza." Her eyes filled.

Louise put down her luggage and hugged her friend fondly. "I just got back from the Island, and Papa told me your mother was ill. How is she?"

"About the same. Dr Fisher looks worried. She's sleeping right now, and Daddy is sitting with her." The two young women went inside, and Susie closed the door. She picked up the pail that Louise had been carrying. "What on earth's this?"

"Dorcas' chicken and garlic soup. It's her cure-all. She insisted I bring it."

"My goodness, it weighs a ton! How kind of her, and how good of you to lug it all this way. Let's get it to the kitchen. Mrs. Cooper arrived yesterday and has taken over. It's such a relief."

"Dorcas' Mrs. Cooper?"

"Yes. She just arrived on the doorstep and said that Dorcas had sent her, and where was the kitchen."

"Dorcas must have telephoned to her when she heard that your mother was sick. That's really something! She hates to use the thing, you know."

Susie smiled briefly. "You're all angels. Could you take over for me tonight? I am so tired."

Louise squeezed Susie's hand. "That's what I'm here for," she replied simply. She gazed at her friend in concern. Susie's usual pink complexion was pale, and there were large dark circles under her eyes. Louise took her firmly by the arm and led her toward the kitchen. "I'll get Mrs. Cooper to heat up some soup for you, then you're going

331

to bed at once. You look all done in. You don't want your young man to see you looking so haggard."

"I'm all right, only tired, but my back does ache so. I must have pulled a muscle, lifting mother. It's difficult, when the patient is in a low bed."

She stood over Susie until she had finished the bowl of Dorcas' soup, then followed her upstairs and supervised her getting undressed and into bed. Susie wanted to just flop down, clothes and all, but Louise insisted that she get into her nightdress and wash her face and hands before getting under the covers. Susie smiled gratefully up at her friend as Louise dimmed the lamp by her bedside.

"I feel better already," she said, and was instantly asleep.

Louise took her bag into the spare room, changed into her uniform, washed her hands thoroughly in the bathroom, and then knocked quietly on Mr. and Mrs. Ferris' bedroom door. Mr. Ferris worried face peered out at her, but broke into a smile when he saw whom it was.

"Louise, my dear!" he explained. "When did you arrive?"

"Less than an hour ago. Susie is in bed, already asleep, and Mrs. Cooper is busy making supper for you and Michael. Is Mrs. Ferris still asleep?"

"She's very restless, coughing and sighing," he said. "I've been trying to get her to take fluids, but she seems so weak... she takes a sip at a time, no more. We've cabled to Jeremy, you know."

"Have you heard from him?"

"Yes. He answered today, 'Coming home soonest'. So I gather he's got leave."

Louise wondered what he was still doing, now that the war had been over for some three months.

"You go down and have a bite to eat, then if you will bring up a cup of the soup Dorcas sent with me, I'll try and feed Mrs. Ferris. Away you go, now."

Louise was used to anxious hovering relatives, and realized that they needed something specific to do. Susie's father nodded gratefully, turned, and went downstairs. She heard the front door slam and Michael's voice asking his father how his mother was.

"About the same," she heard Mr. Ferris say wearily, and then pushed open the door and went inside to her patient.

She had her hands full all night, and by morning had two patients, for Susie woke with a raging headache and a dry harsh cough. The doctor came and tut-tutted over Susie, and examined Mrs. Ferris with a worried frown. He muttered that she should really be in hospital, but he hesitated to move her.

"I'd get you some help if there were any nurses available. Just do your best, er, Miss . . ."

"Laurier, Louise Laurier."

"Ah, aren't you engaged to be married to Jeremy?"

"Yes."

"Mr. Ferris tells me he's on his way home. I don't know, though . . ." And he shook his head. His step was slow and heavy as he went down the stairs to the front hall.

"You get some rest, too, Doctor," Louise called softly after him. He shrugged his shoulders in reply as he went out the door. Louise went back to her patients.

For three days Susie fought for life. Just as her daughter returned from the brink of death Mrs. Ferris gave up with a sigh and quietly slipped away in her sleep. Louise comforted a distraught Mr. Ferris as best she could, and then had to tell her friend that her mother had died.

"I didn't get the chance to say good-bye," Susie said sadly. Louise held her hand tightly.

"The doctor said the germ attacked her heart," she explained. "Have you heard from Jeremy?"

"Your father cabled England, but he missed him. He must be on his way home."

"I'm so glad. Do you think he'll be able to stay?"

"Well, his cable said he had been given two months' leave. That sounds as though his work isn't finished, doesn't it."

"How is Michael?"

"Doing very well. He's being an enormous help to your father. Your brother's a nice young man, Susie."

Susie smiled weakly. "Yes, he is. When can I get up and help?"

333

"Not until Sunday at least," her nurse told her firmly. "You know, I've heard of several people who got up too soon, to help nurse a relative, and so on, and then had a serious relapse. Mrs. Cooper is a treasure, she said she'd stay as long as she was needed, and Papa and Val and Dorcas are arriving on Saturday. Papa and Val are staying with the Coxes; remember, Mr. Cox was one of Papa's partners years ago in the Perth offices. He retired last year, and he and his wife are the kindest of people. They came over with flowers and food yesterday, and said that Papa had called them about your mother. Dorcas will stay with Mrs. Cooper, and they're going to houseclean."

"What does it matter if the house isn't clean," said Susie wearily. "No one will ever notice."

"Ah, but Mrs. Cooper and Dorcas are old fashioned," smiled Louise, as she began to give her patient a bed bath. "Turn over, darling, and I'll wash your back. People will be calling, so the house must be spick and span." As Susie obediently turned over, she squeezed the washcloth and began to gently soap her patient's back. "By the way, your young man has been camping practically on the doorstep. Shall I tell him that you are now in the land of the living?" She smiled at Susie's blush. "I told Mrs. Cooper not to touch your mother's room," she continued. "I'll do my best ward maid job and clean it properly, just as Miss Love taught me. Oh, Susie, that seems like a lifetime ago!"

"Yes. So much has happened in the last five years, hasn't it," murmured Susie.

Presently Louise changed the sheets deftly and made her patient comfortable.

"Now get some more sleep, dear. I'll send your father up in awhile, I know he wants to talk to you."

The next morning Louise spent two hours cleaning the sickroom. The undertakers had come and gone, of course, but there were so many items that were reminders of Mrs. Ferris. Louise could scarcely believe that she would never see Susie's mother again. Her silver backed brush and comb set lay on the dresser, and a silver framed photo of Jeremy in uniform. Louise wondered when he would be getting home. She opened a window to let fresh air in. It was still

334

chilly outside, but not as cold as it had been. She stripped the bed, bundled all the linens and took them downstairs to Mrs. Cooper.

"Hottest water possible," she told her, and then went back upstairs with mop, pail, and sponges. She dusted, swept, scrubbed, and washed down the bed with disinfectant. The floor and the walls received the same treatment. Michael helped her move furniture, suggesting that they rearrange things so that his father wouldn't be reminded of his mother all the time.

"How thoughtful, Michael," said Louise, straightening up and holding her waist, for her back was aching from the unaccustomed activity. "We should probably ask your father first, though. Perhaps it would be comforting to have it the same as it always has been."

In the end they left things as they were, Louise making up the bed with fresh linens.

"Your father and Val are picking me up after lunch," he confided. "We're going to the new cinema to see moving pictures. Do you think that's awful of me?" He regarded Louise anxiously.

"No, I don't," replied Louise firmly. "It will take your mind off things for awhile. Your mother wouldn't have minded your going out at all, I am sure." Michael looked relieved, clattered down the backstairs to the kitchen, while Louise went in to Susie's bedroom to check up on her patient. Susie was sitting up in bed, reading.

"I've been listening to you and Michael in Mother's room," she said, "and feeling badly that I can't be of any help."

"It's all done, Susie, and of course you know I wouldn't let you up, and especially to do hard work." She stretched. "Peter is downstairs and I've told him he can visit you for fifteen minutes, no longer. And no canoodling, my pet. There still may be germs about. Will you be all right if I take a nap now? I didn't get much sleep last night."

Susie looked concerned. "Now this the nurse in me talking. You go straight to bed. Perhaps Mrs. Cooper can send up a cup of tea for Peter when she brings up my lunch." She fussed with her hair. "Do I look all right?" she asked anxiously. Louise handed Susie her hairbrush and assured her patient that she looked fine. Susie went

335

on, "It was sweet of your father to invite Michael to the matinee. I've been longing to go to the moving pictures. Have you seen any?"

Louise nodded, yawning, and sat down in the chair by Susie's bed. "When I was in Charlottetown before coming home last week I went with Mercy and Robert. It was such fun. A woman played the piano to follow all the action on the screen, and such goings on there! The villain tied up the heroine and left her on the railroad tracks, and the hero rescued her, whisking her away just as the train was about to bear down on her. I could hardly stay in my seat. Mercy practically held me down!" She smiled at the memory, then added, "When you're perfectly well we shall go. It's a promise." She yawned again. "I'm off to bed. I'll send your young man up now. Wake me if you need me."

When Louise awoke it was late afternoon, and the light was fading fast. She felt refreshed, and as her uniform was crumpled and soiled, she put on a dress, brushed her hair, washed her face, and went across the hall to Susie's room. Susie smiled from her bed, where she was propped up against several pillows, reading.

"Guess what! Jeremy's home! Isn't it exciting? We wouldn't let him disturb you. Daddy went off to see the minister about the funeral a little while ago, but I don't think Jeremy went with him. He's probably in the kitchen talking to Dorcas and Mrs. Cooper."

Louise felt Susie's forehead. It was cool and dry.

"What time did he get in? How does he look?"

"It wasn't long after you went to bed. Peter was still here, so I introduced them. Dorcas looked in on you, and said you were sound asleep." She paused. "Then, to answer your second question: you go on down and see him. I'm just fine here. I'm hoping you'll let me up for supper," she added slyly.

Louise tiptoed down the stairs, her heart beating rather quickly, whether from anticipation or anxiety, she wasn't sure. The Ferris house didn't boast a formal drawing room as did the Laurier's home; instead, there was a big sitting room at the front of the house, and a cozy little parlor at the back that Mrs. Ferris had always used as her boudoir. It was to the latter that Louise went, remembering Susie's telling her once that her brother would always go there first when he came home, in order to visit with his mother. Sure enough, Jeremy was there, leaning against the fireplace, gazing out the window at the darkening sky. He was half turned away from her, and his shoulders slumped sadly. Louise caught her breath. He was so thin! He had changed out of uniform and had donned a pair of old grey flannel trousers, which hung on him loosely, as did the pale blue shirt. Her heart went out to him.

"Jeremy . . . ."

He turned and smiled eagerly, and in two strides had caught her in his arms. She pressed her cheek against his chest, feeling the smooth cotton and the smell of the freshly ironed garment.

"Jeremy, I am so sorry about your mother, so sorry . . . ."

"Oh, Louise, Susie has told me what a brick you have been, how you just came and took over from her when she got sick! The doctor has visited, and he told me that nothing in the world could have saved Mother, that her heart was affected . . . Louise, you're not blaming yourself?"

He put his hand under her chin and tipped her face to his. She shook her head.

"No, I am just so sorry you didn't get here in time to see her, Jeremy." He drew her down on to the sofa. Holding both her hands in his, he gazed at her anxiously. "You've had a bad time of it, haven't you, darling! First Frank, then Gladdie—it's hard to believe Gladdie's gone, you know. She was so full of life—and now Susie tells me you nursed your aunt in her last illness."

And Johnnie—don't forget Johnnie—though he was just a dream, wasn't he.

"Oh, darling, I'd like us to be married right away," he exclaimed. "I want to take you back with me and show you Scotland. Scotland is so beautiful, Louise! I've seen it in all seasons and weather and I love it. The city of Inverness is where I was based, and it's especially appealing." Seeing her troubled expression he paused and gave her a rueful smile. "I know it's impossible—we're both in mourning, and besides—"

"You do have to go back, then."

337

He nodded. "Yes, I do. There is an awful lot of tidying up to do, you know. I still can't really talk about what I've been doing—"

"Were you a spy?"

He smiled, bent, and kissed her on the lips. "Let's say I was in the business of gathering information," he said, and kissed her again, then put his arms around her. "Ah, Louise, it is so wonderful to see you! You're so beautiful, and sensible, and sane—you drove the horrors away, my dear, you know! I would just imagine you and me like this, and I'd know that everything would be all right."

Louise's heart was beating very quickly. How lovely it was in Jeremy's arms! How comforting to know that she didn't have to make a decision after all! She stirred uneasily, her face growing warm with shame. Just a few weeks ago she had been agonizing how to tell Jeremy that she couldn't marry him, that she loved Johnnie. With an effort, she banished her dead friend's dear, smiling face from her mind. He was only a dream. Only a dream.

Louise started guiltily as Jeremy went on, as though reading her mind. "Did I tell you I finally met my cousin John Ferris when I was in England?" Louise nodded, and then remembered that in fact it had been Johnnie that had written her of the meeting. "I could see why you and Susie had taken to him—he was a fine fellow! What a shame that his airplane crashed! I would have enjoyed getting to know him. He certainly sang the praises of you and Susie—I was almost jealous, except that I knew we were safely engaged." He kissed her again, then added, "and speaking of Gladdie, Dorcas told me an odd story of an American friend of hers coming to call last week in Ottawa."

"Somebody who didn't know she had died?"

"It seems so. She'll probably tell you herself."

At that moment, Dorcas herself put her head in at the door, no doubt having listened tactfully before doing so.

"There's coffee in the kitchen, Louise," she announced. "And Sadie Cooper's shortbread is as good as mine. Won't the both of you come along? You're not too good for your mother's kitchen, are you, Major Ferris?"

Jeremy grinned at Dorcas.

"You've always been hard on me, haven't you," he said, in mock sorrow. He got to his feet, drawing Louise up beside him. "Do you know," he said solemnly, turning to her, "that Dorcas spanked me once? She's never let me forget it."

"No!" Louise said, smiling broadly. "I don't believe it."

"It's true," said Dorcas, as she led the way down the hall to the kitchen. "And it was for teasing you, Louise. He ought to have known better, too. He was ten years old. I just smacked his bottom for him, and sent him outside. You were crying."

"I don't remember," said Louise gaily, "but I forgive him."

There was a delicious smell of coffee in the kitchen, where a short, plump little person was setting out cups and saucers. There couldn't have been a greater contrast between Dorcas and her friend. Where the Laurier housekeeper was tall, dark and thin, Mrs. Cooper seemed as broad as she was tall; Dorcas' facial expression was generally serious, while her friend's was jolly and smiling. Dorcas's voice had faint Scottish overtones, while Mrs. Cooper's voice was pure London Cockney. When Louise had first met her last week, she had been reminded of Lottie Marchbanks' old nanny, Miss Dora Morrison, in Middle Harbour. Both women seemed to be surrounded by an aura of goodness.

"Sadie, this is Major Ferris," said Dorcas.

Mrs. Cooper's round face beamed with pleasure as she shook hands with him. "I'm proud to welcome you 'ome, Major."

"You've been so kind to come and help us like this," Jeremy said, smiling. He thought a moment. "Cooper—have you lived long here in Perth?"

"Why, Cooper and I came here on our honeymoon and have lived round the corner from the Presbyterian Church ever since."

"Are you Mathilda's mother, by any chance?"

Mrs. Cooper beamed. "Why fancy you remembering our Mattie!" she exclaimed. "She'll be tickled pink when I tell her."

Jeremy turned to Louise. "Do you remember Mattie Cooper?— No, no, you're too young. She was a couple of years behind Norah and me in school, but she was with us on the debating team. She was

339

a whiz bang at it." Mrs. Cooper smiled proudly at this praise for her adored daughter. "Where is she now?"

"Bless you, she married 'Enry Spencer and lives out on the Scotch Line. Runs a chicken farm. 'Enry got discharged from the army in 1915. Lost a leg at Ypres." (She pronounced it like wipers.) "They've got two little boys, and are very 'appy. She'll be delighted that you remembered her."

Jeremy finished his coffee, and got up. "Dad will be back soon, and I promised to look up pictures of Mother for the funeral. You stay and visit with Dorcas and Mrs. Cooper, Louise."

"Begging your pardon, Major, I'd like to go home to Cooper for a couple of days. I'll be back to help with the reception after the funeral. Dorcas and I have made a fruitcake and a seed cake, and we've gone over the 'ouse."

"The house is spick and span from top to bottom," put in Louise. "They've worked like blacks for two days."

"Ah, Mrs. Cooper, you don't need my permission to go home. You have been more than kind and generous with your time and talents. My father says he doesn't know what he would have done without you."

Mrs. Cooper's beam became even brighter, if that were possible.

"It's a privilege to serve your family, sir," she said simply.

Jeremy shook hands with her again, and left them. Mrs. Cooper found her coat and hat, and said goodbye to Louise and Dorcas.

"You know what's in the h'oven for dinner, Dorcas," she said, as she went out the door. "I'll see you Tuesday morning." She nodded at Louise. "You tyke a rest, now, Miss Laurier. Dorcas can cope just fine."

Still beaming broadly, she closed the kitchen door behind her and trotted down the footpath to the lane behind the house.

Louise later that night lay sleepless in bed, her mind going over the day's events.

After Mrs. Cooper and Jeremy had left, she and Dorcas had settled down for a good gossip about family affairs. She learned that

Papa had phoned to Fairlea, PEI, to tell Mama about Mrs. Ferris, and that all was well with Norah.

"Mama isn't rushing home to the funeral, is she?"

"Your Papa forbade it, of course." She paused. "She's very worried about you, Louise. I told her you'd be fine. You'll write her, now that Susie is better."

"Yes, of course, I will." Louise felt a little guilty that she had not considered how her family would be feeling.

"I suppose Major Ferris mentioned my story of a young man coming to call for Gladdie."

Louise glanced at Dorcas, who frowned a little, but continued on. "The Major came in the kitchen while I was telling Mrs. Cooper all about it. I told him I'd be telling you."

Louise was silent. She had discovered that she didn't much like to remember Gladdie's last days.

"Your Mama would have handled it much better," Dorcas went on. "It was just that I was so taken aback."

"Tell me about it, Dorcas," said Louise finally.

"He was young, an American soldier," the older woman said. "Nice looking, still in uniform. He knocked on the door of your house and asked me if this was where Gladys Laurier lived."

"'She used to live here,' I said. I didn't quite know what to say. Then he said, 'I do want to get in touch with her. She's all right, isn't she?' I should have asked him in then and there," Dorcas said, with a troubled expression. "Your Mama would have, and given him a cup of tea or maybe something stronger, but all I did was blurt out that she had died last summer! He looked so shocked, and then he burst into tears! I didn't know what to do, Louise. He stood on the doorstep with tears rolling down his cheeks. 'I didn't know where to write her,' he said, all choked up. 'I told her I'd come back to her. What happened to her, Miss?' he asked. I told him it was the consumption, and that her sister had nursed her at home. I gave him your name, Louise; I hope you don't mind. I said you were away on a nursing case, and I wasn't sure when you'd be home. So, perhaps he'll write for details."

"Gladdie mentioned a young man that she had met in Phoenix," Louise said slowly. "She hinted that they were very close." Louise's cheeks burned as she remembered what Gladdie had said about him. "Perhaps he'll write to me. It sounds as though he was very fond of her."

Not long after that Mr. Ferris came home from his interview with the minister, and Papa with Val and Michael practically on his heels.

"Louise, dear!" exclaimed Papa, embracing her. Then he gazed at her keenly. "You are all right, aren't you?"

Louise assured her father that she was fine, and that she expected Susie to make a complete recovery. Mr. Ferris insisted that he and Val should stay for supper, so Louise allowed Susie downstairs for the meal, and they had a cheerful visit around the Ferris dining room table, the boys regaling the others about the cinema. Louise noticed that every once in a while Mr. Ferris would gaze sadly down to the other end of the table where there was an empty space. Presently he related to the others the funeral plans he had discussed with the minister, and then went on to talk about his wife.

"She was so grateful that you had survived," he said to Jeremy, "and that you were coming home. So many young men wouldn't be. She mentioned Frank, and how sorry she was for William and Rose. But she was so pleased that you and Louise would be marrying. She knew the wedding would take place without her, you know. 'I hope they won't wait too long,' she said." He glanced over at his son. "Will you be setting a date soon?" he asked.

"We're not even thinking about that until I'm home for good," answered Jeremy firmly. "I probably won't get back until late summer, and I will quite likely stay in the army for a year or two. Time enough when I get home to consider dates. Louise wants to nurse in the hospital for a while, don't you?" He smiled at her, and then glanced slyly across the table at his sister. "However, perhaps Susie and her young man will be making a match of it sooner. You were looking very flushed and excited this afternoon when I got home, sis, and I don't think it was for me!"

Susie blushed. "We haven't—he hasn't asked me yet," she stammered.

"Louise tells me he practically haunted the front porch while you were ill."

"I'm sure Louise exaggerates," said Susie, with a little more composure. Louise smiled at her friend. "He's a very nice young man. I'm sure he'll be calling again tomorrow."

"Have I met him?" asked Mr. Ferris.

"Dad, I told you, his name is Peter MacLean. Johnnie's friend. Remember him from Winnipeg?"

"He has a head of bright red hair," put in Louise.

"He and Johnnie took Louise and me to the dance at the beach."

Mr. Ferris said he vaguely remembered, then remarked that in his day a young man would first ask permission to call upon a young lady. All Susie could think to say was that it was the twentieth century now, and anyway, there had been a war on. Louise gently steered the subject to the service Tuesday, then presently, noticing Susie's flushed face, chased her patient upstairs to bed.

Later on, Louise and Jeremy went for a walk.

"That was all right, wasn't it, what I said to Father about setting a date?" he asked anxiously. "After I said it, it occurred to me that I really should have consulted you properly."

"It was perfectly all right, Jeremy. We had talked about it, and I do want to work for a while. After all, I've spent three years training, and it would be a shame to waste it."

"Will you be able to work after we get married? I mean, I don't mind, and I may be doing a fair bit of traveling. I'm going to be building things," he went on seriously. "Roads, and dams to make electricity."

Louise suddenly felt an immense pride in Jeremy. He had worked hard, had been through terrible experiences in the War, and had risen to become a major. He was a professional engineer. His future seemed assured, and so was hers. She squeezed his arm affectionately.

343

"I'll work as long as I can. It will depend upon how many nurses there are available. If we should start a family, I would resign, of course."

Jeremy stopped, and took her in his arms. "Darling!" he murmured, kissing her tenderly.

Louise tossed and turned in her bed. She thought of Johnnie and her promise to wait until he came home. It was foolish to feel guilty, of course, because of course Johnnie wouldn't be coming home. His broken body was in a grave somewhere in England—burnt and broken when his airplane crashed on the tarmac. Uncle Stan had his identification bracelet, and a letter from his commanding officer telling him what a good flier he had been. There was a photograph of Johnnie in the uniform of the Royal Flying Corps on Aunt Mabel's piano, draped in black. Johnnie was dead. She would never see him again.

Chapter Thirty-Two

LOUISE AND JEREMY

Jeremy didn't return until September of 1919, and he remained in uniform for another year and a half. They were married in June of 1920, and honeymooned in Scotland as he had promised her. Louise loved the Highlands. The wild and desolate landscape touched something in her soul. She wrote to her sister Norah, '*The coastline is wild, and unexpected vistas appear around every curve in the road. It's amazing how temperate the climate is on the West Coast. We found rhododendrons and azalea blooming in the gardens of Dunvegan Castle on the Isle of Skye, and in a garden even further north there were palm trees actually growing in a sheltered part. Norah, I love this country and the friendly people. I feel very much at home here. I mentioned to someone that Mama was born a McLeod, and immediately we were accepted as one of them. "You must go to Dunvegan Castle and register as a member of the clan," someone told me, so of course we did (I hope you got my postcard—I thought it was a beautiful photograph, and nicely colored by hand as well—the colors are quite natural, too) and we are now official members, including Jeremy, by virtue of being my husband! Which, of course, was a turn of events—he's used to thinking of me as Mrs. Jeremy Ferris. Not that I am objecting to that, of course, but you know I like to be my own woman. What about Louise McLeod Laurier Ferris? Doesn't it sound grand? We are having a wonderful time,*

Norah, but I will be happy to be home, because then I will be seeing you! Jeremy has agreed to disembark in Halifax, and we will take the train to Charlottetown. It's time he met the rest of his Island nieces and nephews, don't you think? In a few days from now we will travel south to London, and we hope to organize a trip to Flanders to see Frankie's grave. Then a week's walking tour in Cornwall, after which we sail from Southampton on the 5th. I expect we'll be in Charlottetown approximately a week from then. We plan to call on Mercy and Robert, and will telephone you from there. Hugs and kisses to all the children, and my love to you and Harry and Gerald and Sybil.'

A week later Louise and Jeremy stood on the fields of Flanders and gazed at her brother's grave. She felt a wave of sadness pass over her, and then a spurt of anger that so many young lives had been lost.

"Wasted," she said to Jeremy bitterly. "Have they solved anything, really? Be honest, Jeremy."

Jeremy put his arms around her. "I don't know, darling," he admitted. "Time will tell. But you know Vimy Ridge was an important victory for the Allies."

Louise sighed. Frankie shouldn't have even been there. He had been posted away from his men when he was sent to fight at Vimy Ridge after his injuries had healed. Perhaps he would have survived otherwise. She brushed a tear impatiently away. There was no point in moaning for what might have been. The important thing was to remember him, and make sure his son Carson knew that his father had been a hero.

The day before they left England, they stood by another grave. She took a photograph of Johnnie's headstone, which she would send to Stan and Mabel. She felt only an empty sadness as she gazed down at Johnnie's resting place. He had died doing what he loved most, which was flying.

"A nice chap," Jeremy remarked, which was high praise coming from him.

They spent a week in Prince Edward Island visiting Louise's family. Louise hadn't seen her brother and sister for over a year except at her marriage to Jeremy, and the week of the wedding had been filled with a flurry of activity, not conducive to visiting. In fact the time was all somewhat of a blur to Louise.

The children, save for the twins, who both proudly participated in the wedding ceremony, had all been left behind in the care of Mary and her mother Mrs. Hastie. So now the newlyweds relaxed in the company of Norah and Gerald and their respective families, enjoying the long summer evenings on the lawn. Louise listened to the laughter of the children at play and mused that the last time she had been in this place she had contemplated a family with Johnnie. She gazed across at her husband, who was in earnest conversation with his old friend Gerald, and decided that she was happier at this moment than she ever thought she'd be. Jeremy was a kind, loving, and thoughtful husband, an interesting companion, and a considerate lover. Johnnie had never been anything but a dream. She smiled fondly at Norah's youngest, now over a year old. Small Louisa would never be as pretty as her sister Frannie, but she had a small piquant face, sparkling green eyes, and golden curls. Both Norah and Sybil were expecting again this fall, and were literally blooming. Louise's feelings about starting a family were ambivalent.

She was enjoying her nursing career, and had been promised that her job would be available when she returned. Her eyes suddenly met those of her husband's. Jeremy looked up from his conversation with his brother-in-law and smiled at her across the lawn. He touched two fingers to his lips, which was their secret way of saying 'I love you'. Baby Louisa had crawled into her aunt's arms at that moment, and Louise smiled back at him over the child's head.

"I know you're still honeymooning, but it *is* nice to see a husband and wife making eyes at each other," said a low voice in her right ear.

She turned, coloring a little, and met the smiling eyes of her sister who, now growing heavy as she entered the last months of her pregnancy, lowered herself gingerly on to the grass beside her.

"You're happy with each other, aren't you, Louise."

"Yes, I am. I was just thinking that very thing,"

"Tell me your plans, dear, are you continuing with your nursing?" Louise leaned back on her hands. "Yes, I am, for at least a year, I hope, unless something intervenes," she said with a laugh.

347

"Where will you live?"

"We've taken a lease on a small flat near the Parliament Buildings. It's very convenient, only a fifteen-minute walk to the hospital for me, and a ten-minute walk for Jeremy to his office. It's only a few minutes to the streetcar stop, and a twenty-minute ride home to visit Mama and Papa. There's also a vista onto the river, and in the fall we'll see the maples in their gorgeous color along the far bank. Jeremy won't be leaving the Army for another six months, then he's to join a private company whose offices are fairly close to the hospital, so when I'm on day shift, we can go to work together."

"It sounds ideal. Have you chosen any furnishings yet?"

Louise clasped her hands and smiled. "No, not yet, he just moved his bed there the day before the wedding."

"He has his priorities," Norah said wickedly.

Louise ignored this sally and went on, "We'll have fun buying a few things. I've been saving like mad, and Mama has said I can take a few pieces from the house. I think they're thinking of selling the house in the not too distant future, and moving into a smaller one, with just Val at home, and he won't be there forever."

Norah nodded. "Mama hinted as much in her last letter. Will you feel bad about that? Would you and Jeremy ever want to live there?"

Louise looked surprised. She had never thought of such a thing. "You mean, they'd sell the house to us?"

"It is a wonderful family house," said Norah.

"Far to big for Jeremy and me."

"It won't be Jeremy and you forever, you know."

Louise shook her head. "We couldn't afford a house that size for years yet." Norah changed the subject. "Will Jeremy be traveling in his business?"

"I think so; the Army has had him going all over the place since he's been back home. So I'll be glad of my job to keep me occupied."

"How is his father doing, and Michael and Susie?"

"Mr. Ferris is fine. Michael and Susie miss their mother a lot. She's engaged, you know, to Peter MacLean, that she met in Winnipeg. They're to be married at Christmas, and she's asked me to be her matron of honor. It's going to be a very small, quiet wedding (unlike mine) and Mama is helping her plan it. She wants me to wear a red dress. Will I look awful?"

"Not at all—just make sure the color is a cherry red—that will be most becoming," answered her sister promptly.

Little Louisa crawled back into her mother's lap and snuggled up to her, tiny hands pulling at her bosom. "I haven't yet been able to completely wean her," Norah said ruefully in a low voice. "She still seems to need that nursing at bedtime. Come on inside with me and we can get her ready for bed. I don't like to be seen feeding her at her age, the great big lump. Aren't you, sweetheart?" she said to her little daughter. "Half an hour, Frannie," she called to her four year old, who was playing with her cousin on the swing. "Mummy will be inside getting the baby to bed."

"Yes, it's time Carson was getting to bed, too," said Sybil lazily from the lounge chair under the apple tree. The two children protested, but their mothers both repeated the half hour warning.

"I find that the children need that little bit of warning time to prepare themselves for going to bed," remarked Norah, as she and Louise headed up to the house with her youngest.

"You and Sybil are good friends, aren't you."

"Oh, yes! I can't imagine life without her. That doesn't mean I love her better than you, sister o' mine," she added quickly, tucking her hand into Louise's arm. "But Gerald and I have always been good chums, like you and Frankie were, so I am everlastingly pleased that he married such a congenial girl." She bent down to pick up Louisa, but Louise intervened.

"You shouldn't be lifting the baby now, Norah, let me carry her in." Gerald and Jeremy watched the sisters as they walked slowly toward the house.

"Thinking about a family soon, Jer?"

Jeremy shook his head. "Louise wants to work for awhile, and I will continue to be traveling somewhat, so we plan to wait a year or so. Though your mother I am sure will be looking forward to having a grandchild nearby." Harry who was sitting nearby smiled, and

349

began extolling the delights of fatherhood, and Gerald immediately chimed in.

"What delightful girls we have married," he remarked, rather fatuously. "I think we should congratulate ourselves."

"Or maybe the girls," said Harry dryly.

Louise and Jeremy lived for nearly two years in the flat near the river. Their first Christmas, with the help of Dorcas, she produced the enormous dinner of turkey and all the trimmings, inviting her parents and Val, Jeremy's father and Michael, Susie and Peter, who had just returned from their week long honeymoon of skiing the Laurentians. She and Jeremy decorated the flat with boughs of greenery and a small Christmas tree covered with tinsel and topped by a sparkling star. Jeremy had bought her a gramophone for Christmas, plus several records of Christmas music, and the strains of 'O Tannenbaum' and 'God Rest Ye Merry, Gentlemen' added to the festive flavor.

They were already looking for a house when Louise discovered she would be having a baby, and her happiness was complete when she saw how excited and thrilled Jeremy was. After all, he was thirty-three years old, and many men of his age had several children by now. Louise was twenty-five, and was glad that she was at last starting her family. She'd work for another month, and then settle down to making baby clothes and furnishing the spare room as a nursery. Jeremy was all for buying the first suitable house that came on the market, but Louise reminded him that the flat's lease wouldn't expire for six months.

"Just when our baby should be arriving," she said. "It couldn't be better timed if I had planned it that way."

So the young couple, in their spare time, began a systematic search for the perfect house in the perfect location, and eventually discovered a house for sale not very far away, on a quiet street, with a walled garden at the back, and even closer to the tram line that ran past her parents' home. There was a small park within walking distance, and some shops conveniently located just around the corner. They moved in April, two months before the baby was due. She felt well; she loved her little house with its cozy parlour, kitchen full of labor saving devices, and wide sunny nursery. Louise thought that nothing could ever mar their joy. She stood in front of her mirror, hands resting lightly on her swelling abdomen, and thought she looked almost as beautiful as her sister Norah. Twenty-four hours later would find her standing in the same spot, gazing into the same mirror, but feeling very differently.

Chapter Thirty-Three

JOHNNIE

The bomb fell the next day when the letter arrived from Halifax. It was addressed to them both, and was short and succinct. It was signed 'Stan and Mabel'.

> *My dear Louise and Jeremy:*
> *We have just received a telegram from Johnnie. He is alive! The airman who was killed in the crash was his friend Sidney Bolton. They had exchanged identification bracelets 'for luck'. Johnnie was gravely injured when his airplane ran out of fuel and he crash-landed in France. He remembers nothing after that until some months ago. Apparently a farmer found him, hid him from the Boche and nursed back to health. He didn't know his name, nor where he was from. He has lived with them since the autumn of 1918. It's a crazy story, isn't it? He is on his way home, and will spend some time with us. I expect he will be in touch.*

Jeremy read the letter out loud in a wondering voice, and then looked up as Louise got to her feet and went to the window to gaze out on the spring garden, a riot of color.

352

"Louise," he said softly. He went to her, and put his arms around her. "Isn't this the most wonderful news? It's like Enoch Arden, back from the dead."

Louise was silent. "It's such a shock," she said faintly. "I don't know what to think."

"Darling," he said anxiously, "you feel all right, don't you?"

"Don't fuss, Jeremy," she said shortly.

Two years too late! she thought, a short time later, as she stood in front of her mirror in her bedroom. *If it weren't for this...* and she put her hands on her stomach. The baby kicked hard, as if to remind her that there was no going back now.

Johnnie came to Ottawa a month later. Louise would have refused to see him, if not for the fact that Jeremy would think it most peculiar. Jeremy spoke to him on the telephone.

"Come for lunch tomorrow," he said warmly. "I have to work in the morning, but I shall be home by noon."

He calmed Louise's doubts about making lunch. "Darling, we'll just have what we would normally. There's cold roast beef leftover from dinner tonight, isn't there. Make your macaroni salad that I like so much, and there's your mother's applesauce for dessert. Why are you worrying, darling? It's not like you."

"I feel so big and awkward," she murmured. "So ugly."

"Louise! What are you saying? I think you are the most beautiful creature on earth! Who cares what my cousin thinks, anyway? Fancy changing ID with his chum! I wonder what they said to him when he reported in. I expect we'll hear a very interesting story." He kissed her. "Why don't you telephone Susie? Weren't Peter and Johnnie friends? Let's have a little party to welcome our cousin back!"

She had felt a little better talking to Susie. Her friend was delighted to be asked to lunch, and offered to bring her poppy seed cake that she had just baked.

Louise slept very little that night. What would she feel when she saw Johnnie? How would he react to her and her condition? She turned awkwardly in bed, trying to find a comfortable position. Aware of Jeremy's quiet, regular breathing beside her, she felt a small resentment that he could sleep so soundly. She thought of Johnnie again as she turned over on her back and stared at the ceiling. She had accepted his death and had gotten over him. She and Jeremy were so happy together. What right did Johnnie have to come back so unexpectedly and tear her heart out? It had been better when he was thought to be dead! She closed her eyes. How could she even think such a thing? Of course she was delighted that he was all right. Everyone was. Susie had talked of nothing for the last few weeks. Stan and Mabel had written endlessly of their happiness in their nephew's return from the grave. Mabel, who had never really picked up after her bout with the flu three years ago, had been given a new lease on life. It was Johnnie this, and Johnnie that. There had been complications, of course, regarding the young man's estate, for of course his will had been proved, and all his assets had been turned over to Stan, who was his next of kin. Johnnie had visited his solicitor, was now on his way to Winnipeg to clear things up, and was taking a side trip to Ottawa to see them. You'd think, thought Louise resentfully, that he could have allowed more than one day in order to visit, forgetting that a moment ago she had been wishing him back amongst the dead. He had arrived that day, would spend one night, and planned to catch the afternoon train back to Montreal tomorrow. She was glad, though, that Susie and Peter were coming to lunch. She hadn't wanted it to be just her and Jeremy and Johnnie. She opened her eyes again and stared at the patch of moonlight on the wall. The draperies were not drawn completely, and there was a long line of light on the wall facing her. Was she afraid? She remembered their night in the farmhouse, and their drive back to town. "Promise me you'll not marry Jeremy until I get back," he had said, and she had promised. She had broken that promise, hadn't she? But he had been declared dead. There was a photo draped in black on Mabel's piano, and an identification bracelet that had been found in the ashes of the burned aeroplane. She had mourned him, and had since got on with her life. Now he had come back. Oh, God, was she glad or sorry?

The morning sunshine and several hours' sleep chased away her middle-of-the-night horrors, and she hummed a tune as she put away the breakfast dishes. Jeremy kissed her goodbye saying he should be home by twelve o'clock, and she started to plan her day. She tidied the kitchen, and set the table for five in their sunny dining room. She checked the living room, whisking away dust here and there, and plumped up cushions on the sofa. Then she bathed, selected her outfit carefully, and tidied her hair. She chose her prettiest smock, the one that Mama had embroidered with roses and ivy leaves. It fell gracefully over her burgeoning figure down past her knees. The silk stockings Jeremy had given her for her birthday felt smooth and snug over legs that had swollen a trifle. The doctor had told her to rest every afternoon with her legs raised, but he didn't have to cook and launder and clean. Mind you, Dorcas came over once a week and cleaned house for her, which she appreciated very much. The first time, three or so months ago, Louise had offered payment, and Dorcas had refused in no uncertain terms.

"I'd be insulted to take money from you, child," she said firmly. "Don't you even think of such a thing."

She went into the kitchen, found her apron, and after putting the coffee pot on, began to slice the cold roast beef. The macaroni she had cooked the day before, so now she assembled her salad, opened jars of homemade pickled beets and horseradish preserves, and arranged devilled eggs on a pretty platter, garnishing with parsley from her herb garden. She had invited Susie to come early, so when the doorbell rang at eleven thirty, she was slightly puzzled. Susie usually let herself in by the kitchen door, always making herself at home in her brother's house. Wiping her hands on her apron, she went to the front door. Her heart leapt as she saw the tall shadow through the windows that surrounded the door. When she opened the door, there was Johnnie smiling down at her, looking practically the same as he had almost five years ago when she had said goodbye to him. He was thinner, looked older, and his hair was different, but he was the same Johnnie. She put a hand to her throat, and gazed up at him, speechless for a moment, then hurriedly untied her apron.

"Am I early?" he asked, and stepped in as she stood aside.

She closed the door and they regarded each other steadily. Then she smiled and put out her hands, the apron falling to the floor.

"Johnnie! It is so good to see you!" And it was.

He took her hands, bent and kissed her cheek.

"You are more beautiful than ever," he said gravely. Stooping, he picked up her apron and gave it to her.

"I've made coffee, would you like to have some while we wait for the others?" At his questioning glance, she added, "Susie and Peter are coming to lunch as well."

"Peter MacLean? Uncle Stan told me about you and Jeremy, but he didn't mention Susie and Peter. Are they married, then?"

"They were married six months after Jeremy and me. No family yet, Susie is still nursing at the hospital—" She broke off as she saw Johnnie's eyes resting on her swollen figure. She blushed deeply.

"Susie and old Pete! Here I was thinking that I'd look him up when I got to Winnipeg." Johnnie strode to the window and looked out. "What sort of job has he got?"

"He's working for the Ottawa Valley Dairy Company. He's been driving a milk wagon for two years now, and thinks he's got good prospects to get into management." Louise fetched the coffee from the kitchen and brought the tray with cups and saucers and cream and sugar back into the sitting room. "Do sit down, Johnnie, and tell me what happened to you."

He took the coffee, laced it liberally with cream and sugar, and sat down in the big chair by the fireplace that Jeremy always took. Louise sat down opposite him and regarded him gravely.

"I know it's been nearly four years since the war ended, but it doesn't seem that way to me, Louise. Am I being unreasonable to feel so disappointed that you didn't wait for me?"

"Wait for you! Johnnie, they said you were dead! They sent Stan your identification bracelet! I even visited your grave in England!" Louise was angry all of a sudden. "What a crazy thing to do, change identification!"

He sighed. "I know. Stan and Mabel said you came to see them, and that you were very upset."

Louise thought of the miles she had walked on the beaches at Fairlea. "I mourned you, Johnnie, and then Jeremy came home for his mother's funeral. We didn't get married until 1920."

"What if I hadn't changed ID's with Sidney?" he asked in a low voice. Louise had been afraid that he would ask her that. She hesitated, and at that moment there was the toot of a horn outside, and the crunch of wheels on the gravel driveway. She got to her feet and moved to the window.

"Here's Jeremy home," she said lightly, "and Susie and Peter are coming up the front walk."

Johnnie jumped to his feet, reached out and took her hand.

"Would you have waited if I had merely been 'missing'?" He gazed down at her intently. He touched her cheek lightly and Louise felt an electric shock go through her.

She hesitated, and opened her mouth. At that moment the back door opened and they heard the sound of Jeremy's footsteps in the kitchen, and Susie's voice as she followed her brother into the house. Louise backed away and was at the window when Susie breezed in, smiling, arms outstretched to her cousin, saying gaily what an idiot Johnnie was, and she didn't believe for one moment this story about amnesia; he'd merely found a gorgeous *mademoiselle* to make love to, and had to flee when her husband came home. She threw her arms around him and kissed him soundly, and he hugged her affectionately in return. Louise took the opportunity to escape to the kitchen. Jeremy was hanging up their coats.

"Sorry we're late, old thing," said Peter, kissing Louise's cheek. "The car wouldn't start—there wasn't a thing to do but to walk, toting Susie's cake. My, it got heavy after awhile!"

"Is there coffee, darling?" asked Jeremy. "I'm dying for a cup! We'll sit down and hear Johnnie's saga, and then have lunch. Coffee, Peter?"

Louise poured out three more cups, and brought them into the sitting room, where Susie was laughing and chattering a mile a minute. Peter shook hands warmly with his old friend, saying that he'd better have a pretty good story for them, and what about the chap's family, the one who'd had Johnnie's bracelet?

"Sidney Bolton," said Johnnie. "I went to see them when I got back to England. They had given up ever seeing their son again, and I had to tell them that he was the one buried in the grave with my name on the headstone. It was a weird feeling, looking at a grave with one's name on it." He paused. "The army put me in the hospital for

357

observation, but after a few days gave me a clean bill of health. They believed the story I told them—"

"Which was, old man?" asked Peter.

"That up until six months ago I didn't have any memory of my life before I crashed my aeroplane."

"None whatsoever?"

"Oh, a few scattered scenes in my mind, but nothing I could take hold of. I even assumed I was English, and everyone referred to me as '*L'Anglais*.'"

"Didn't you have your friend's identification?" asked Jeremy, frowning.

"No! That's a mystery that will never be solved, I think. I thought I put it on properly, but Monsieur and Madame Blanchette said they never saw it."

Blanchette had apparently found him wandering in a daze near the crash site, and took him back to the farm. They hid him from the Germans at considerable risk to themselves, he added. The local doctor examined him, but it was a few weeks before he was well enough to be up and about.

"I just settled in to life on the farm, and found I could help them. They had no help, except for their daughter Elise—"

"Ah ha! I knew there was a *mademoiselle* involved," interjected Susie. "Was she very beautiful?"

Johnnie smiled. "As a matter of fact she was, though she couldn't compare to you and Louise," he added gallantly.

"Was she a good French teacher?" persisted Susie, with a sly grin.

"*Excellent, Madame,*" he said with a Gallic flourish.

Over lunch, Johnnie continued his story. The villagers accepted him as one of the members of the Blanchette family—the parish priest even suggested that he and Elise be married. Her fiancé had been killed during the first days of the war, he told him, and Pierre and Madame needed help on the farm.

"She will inherit the property one day," he added.

Johnnie explained, that until he discovered who he was, he couldn't marry anybody. He might be married already to someone in England.

"Why didn't you go to England after the war was over?" asked Jeremy curiously. "Someone might have recognized you there."

"I don't know!" said Johnnie. "I thought of it many times, but kept putting it off. I even seriously considered marrying Elise after all and settling there permanently. I was quite happy with the Blanchettes." He put down his knife and fork and leaned back in his chair. "About six months or so ago I began to get flashes of memories. I knew my parents had died, and that I was single." He turned to Louise. "Believe it or not, the first vivid memory I had was taking you up in the aeroplane in Winnipeg all those years ago! My returning memories were disjointed—for example, I was talking to the village schoolmaster one day, and I thought, 'Miss Turner was my first schoolteacher.' And I had a clear picture of her at the front of the schoolroom writing something on the blackboard. I still have headaches from time to time, but other than that, I am quite well."

"Will you return to France?" asked Peter.

"I don't know. I was happy, as I say, but I still want to fly for my living. I shall be talking to Mr. Dandridge when I'm in Winnipeg. He owned the little aircraft I flew there," he explained.

"It's quite possible there will be a great need for pilots one of these days," said Jeremy quietly. "We were talking about that very thing the other day." The telephone rang at that moment, and Jeremy got up to answer it. He returned a few minutes later putting on his jacket.

"It was the office—a minor crisis is happening, and they want me there right away! I'm sorry, old man, I'll have to say goodbye now. I'm sorry I can't drive you to the station, maybe Peter—no, his car wouldn't start, would it."

"It's all right," Johnnie told his cousin. "I'll call a cab."

Louise served dessert and coffee, and the four chatted in a desultory way. ("Like old times, in Winnipeg," Peter remarked. Remember the dance at Winnipeg Beach?") Then Susie and Louise cleared the table and left the men to talk some more.

"Did you notice," remarked Susie, as they washed and dried the dishes in the kitchen, "that none of the fellows discuss the war—

Johnnie has mentioned it only as it affected his stay in France? What do you think of his story, Louise?"

"I find it odd that he didn't go to England as soon as he was well enough after the Armistice," said Louise. Had Johnnie been in love with Elise Blanchette? Was that why he stayed? I have no right to be jealous of her, she thought. No right at all.

Presently, with the kitchen and dining room tidied, they joined the others in the sitting room. Peter was getting ready to go.

"I must see about the car, Susie," he said. "Remember, we're supposed to pick up your father this afternoon."

"Heavens, I had forgotten all about it! It was a lovely lunch, Lou," she exclaimed, kissing her friend warmly. "Now you just rest all the afternoon. Goodbye, Johnnie, it has been absolutely ripping seeing you again after all these years. You did cause a major shock, though, you know, returning from the dead like this."

Peter was about to leave by the front door, but she stopped him.

"We must go out the way we came. It's bad luck to come in one door and out another," she declared, and disappeared into the kitchen. "Sit down, Louise, we'll let ourselves out!" They heard the back door bang, then open again.

"Just came back for my cake tin!" she called, and the door slammed again. Louise sat down and put her feet up on the stool. "I love her dearly, but she can be a whirlwind at times," she remarked. "Johnnie, please use the telephone to call a cab. It's in the hall."

Johnnie did so, then came back and sat down beside her. "It'll be a little while," he said, and suddenly there was an awkward silence between them.

"You never did answer my question," he said finally.

Louise was silent, then said,

"Please don't ask me what I might have done if events were different. I simply don't know!"

"Would you go away with me now if there wasn't to be a child?" he persisted.

"You would ask me to leave my husband?" she asked in a low tone. "Louise, I still feel the same about you! I came home, even though I feared it was too late for me." He was gazing at her earnestly.

"You know, I did have one memory of the past all along, and it was of you in a barn on snowy night, milking a cow! Sometimes I thought you might be my wife, but being on a farm didn't seem familiar to me—I tell you, I was rather confused, to say the least! Louise, my dear, are you happy?"

Louise looked him full in the eyes and nodded. "Yes, Johnnie, I am happy."

"And I have no right to be saying these things to you. I know." He stood up. "I think I had better go. I can wait outside for the taxi."

Louise got to her feet and put out her hand to him. "Goodbye, Johnnie. Good luck."

He ignored the proffered hand, but put his hands on her shoulders, drawing her gently to him. Stooping, he kissed her on the lips.

"I wish you nothing but the best," he murmured, turned, and let himself out the front door. Louise stood with her back to the closed door, heart racing. She thought about that snowy night in the farmhouse, or rather the next morning, and how Johnnie had kissed her on the sofa. She had wanted him then, hadn't she? She wanted him now. She put her hands on her abdomen again in almost a despairing gesture. The baby kicked her hard.

361

Chapter Thirty-Four

LOUISE AND LULU 1985

I lay in bed and watched the sun rise in the morning. I had remembered so much, so many people, most of them dead now. I would tell Lulu some of it, when she came to visit this afternoon, and show her more pictures of those days. I had several albums of photographs, if I could remember where I had put them. Were they in the storage closet under the stairs? Or were they in my cedar chest at the end of the bed? The April morning was cool, so I put on my warm dressing gown and went to the bathroom. Then I opened the cedar chest and retrieved the albums, marked '1912-1922'. Ten years out of my young life. It had seemed like a lifetime to me back then. I carried the albums into the kitchen, and put them on the table, then proceeded to make my morning tea. This was one of the times I missed Jeremy. He always made my morning tea and we would drink it together in the bedroom. Sometimes he would come back to bed, too. I sighed. That seemed like a long time ago. I took my tea back into my bedroom and drank it by the window and watched the day grow bright. Then I had my bath.

My granddaughter arrived at noon, with two white boxes, and a bottle of wine.

"I hope you didn't forget and make lunch, Gran," she announced, and proceeded to turn on my oven, pop in the boxes to stay warm, and set the kitchen table. My table stood by the window overlooking the back garden. The lounge chair that I had dozed in yesterday was still in the middle of the lawn, my paperback novel still open where I had carelessly left it.

"Shall I make a pot of tea as well?" I rarely took wine at midday, but I didn't want to insult Lulu by refusing her gift. But I would need my tea.

We ate our lunch of miso soup, sushi, and teriyaki chicken and rice at the table by the window; it was too chilly today to be out on the patio. For the first time I noticed that Bruce's engagement ring was absent from Lulu's finger. Had she made the decision so soon, then? As though reading my mind, she held out her left hand.

"I've taken off Bruce's ring, Gran. Not because I've decided to break our engagement, but I just didn't want to be distracted by it."

She's an interesting young woman.

I brought out the album, and over a cup of tea we studied the photos. These old pictures had never been under the plastic film of the newer types of albums, and they were still in fairly decent condition. I am told that plastic can ruin photographs. Lulu was fascinated with the people in them, and wanted to know who they were, and their relationship to me. She was enchanted by the old-fashioned attire and hairdressing styles.

"Why do they look so much older than we do?" she asked curiously. "This picture of you—you look years older than I do."

I hadn't looked in this album for years, so I studied the photograph with interest. "I remember clearly when this was taken. It was my eighteenth birthday, and Jeremy and I had just gotten engaged—"

"You were only eighteen?" she interrupted. "You think I'm too young at twenty!"

"I was amazed that he wanted to marry me," I went on with a smile, ignoring her interruption. "I had thought he was fond of my sister Gladdie."

"She was the one that died young, wasn't she."

"Yes. There she is in this group photo. It's a copy of the one in the study I have framed. It's not particularly good of her. Oh! Here's

363

one I haven't thought about in years! It's a studio portrait she had taken after she left home. She's maybe twenty-two or three."

Lulu gazed at the portrait curiously. Gladdie was wearing a smart outfit that she had bought with her earnings. I remembered it because she had bought the red coat at the same time.

"She's not beautiful like you and Aunt Norah," she said slowly, "but she's got something."

"Sex appeal," I said. "Dorcas called it 'the come hither look in her eye'. We just called it 'It'." I paused and reflected. "She always had men buzzing around her from a young age, but she wanted Jeremy."

"Did that cause problems between you?"

"You might say so," I said, remembering the red coat. I still felt a momentary shudder when I pictured the coat in heap on my bed, slashed and ripped to pieces. I think that Gladdie had been temporarily mad when she had inflicted that damage.

I began to tell Lulu of my girlhood, and my two loves. She had heard the story of Norah's first meeting Harry before, but she urged me to tell it again. I emphasized my mistake that led to the confusion, their violent quarrels, and how they then proceeded to fall madly in love with each other.

"Did I meet Aunt Norah? Was she the tall, pretty, white haired old lady at your golden wedding?"

"Fancy your remembering! Yes, it was the last time I saw Norah and Harry. He wasn't well at the time, but he insisted on traveling all the way out from PEI. Sarah came, too, with one of her granddaughters—she was about your age. Harry died later that year, and my darling Norah seemed to lose interest in life when she lost Harry. She came down with the flu that winter, it went to pneumonia, and she never recovered. I remember Sarah telephoning me. She wept as she told me my sister had died—I think she loved her stepmother better than anyone in the world! I am very fond of Sarah. I would love to see her again before I die. But we're both old now, and it's not easy traveling across the country."

"You've never said much about your wedding. You should frame this one of the whole wedding party. Wasn't Grandfather handsome!

There's Norah, is that Sarah?" indicating the pretty teenager in a long bridesmaid's dress. "And who are the other attendants?"

"That's Sybil, my sister-in-law. I'm sure I have mentioned her. She married Frankie in England, just before he was killed, and came to Canada when she found out that she was having his baby. Gerald fell madly in love with her and married her two years later. She was the only one of the wedding party that wasn't at our Golden Celebrations. She died just after the last war. Her son Carson, that was Frankie's child, had been killed in action in Italy in 1944. I think she died of a broken heart. She and Gerald had three daughters, but I think she loved Carson best. She was a nurse, like Susie and me. I was very fond of her. Susie is standing next to me. It's amazing to think that Susie and I have been friends for eighty-odd years. She writes me every month, like clockwork. I would like to see her again, too, before we both die. She's a year older than I am, but her mind is as keen as ever. Her husband Peter died a few years ago. She met him when we went out to Winnipeg with her parents to visit her aunt and uncle. That's where I met Johnnie."

"Grandfather's cousin. The one everyone thought had been killed in the war but her turned up afterwards."

I nodded.

She looked at me expectantly. "He was special, wasn't he, Gran."

"You asked about my wedding," I reminded her. "I would have liked to have been married quietly like Norah and Harry, but I knew Mama wanted a proper wedding when she brought out her own wedding dress and asked me to try it on. 'Norah is much too tall; I never considered that she could wear it,' Mama said. I tried it on, and I must say I was impressed with the result."

"It's a beautiful gown," Lulu said, studying the wedding photo more closely.

Mama hadn't said much, but I gave in without any argument. After all, there was no longer a war on! I wrote to Norah and Sybil and asked them to be my attendants along with Susie. Sarah was an afterthought, to tell the truth, and I was so glad I asked her. She was thrilled, and was so proud to be included amongst all the adults. Jeremy thought it a fine idea, so when he wrote Gerald to ask him to be his best man, he also wrote to Ben and asked him to be one of his attendants as well. The whole family came up from PEI except the little ones—Carson, Frannie, and Louisa—they were left in the loving care of Mrs. Hastie and Mrs. Kidd. Norah and Sybil's babies were only six or seven months old, and they were still feeding them, so came along with them. Mary and Pierre I also invited, but they regretfully declined. "Somebody has to stay home and mind the store," she wrote. I also wrote to Lottie Cannings, and she cheerfully traveled up to Ottawa from Nova Scotia and stayed with an old friend there. It was delightful seeing her again, though we really didn't get much of a visit in. You know what weddings are like. Jeremy and I invited everybody we could think of—there were two hundred guests, and it was a fine party. Still I harkened back to Norah's simple marriage and the luncheon in our dining room and decided that she had had the better of the two.

"Grandfather does look handsome in his uniform," she said. "Gran, who's this?"

She had turned the page of the album and found the photo of Johnnie that his Uncle Stan had sent me those many years ago. It was the one that had been framed and had stood on Mabel's piano. He was in the uniform of the Royal Flying Corps and had been perhaps twenty-three when the picture was taken.

"That's Johnnie Ferris."

I handed it to her, and began to tell her how we had met, and how our friendship had grown into love. I told her about the night stranded in the farmhouse—the first person, except for Norah, that I had ever told. Even Susie had never heard that story. I told of the agonies of knowing I was going to have to choose between him and Jeremy, and then the deep down empty pain of his death.

"How would you have chosen, Gran?" she asked.

I smiled. "I have often wondered. "You know, Lulu, I was almost angry with him for coming back and disturbing my life that was beginning to unfold so nicely. I was happy. Jeremy was a successful engineer, we owned our first little house, I was expecting my first child . . ."

I went on to tell her of his visit to us and lunch with Susie and Peter. "That old magic was there, Lulu, you had better believe it," I said with a smile. "If it hadn't been for the fact that I was hugely pregnant with Harriet...."

"You might have run off with him? Gran!"

"I don't know. I'd like to think that I wouldn't have, but the attraction was strong between us, Lulu—very strong. I never quite forgave him for not trying to find out who he was after the war was over, but just taking the easy way and staying with the family he told himself that he was obligated to. I've often thought that his amnesia might have been as much psychological as functional, and that he was ashamed, and was afraid of being called a coward, or worse, a deserter! I also think that he had been living with Elise, though he didn't admit it to me at the time. I believe he actually went back to her for a while, but eventually returned to Canada where he continued his flying career."

"Did Grandfather know?"

"No. I think he would have asked me about him if he had realized that Johnnie was in love with his wife. He never did, and I never confessed. No point in it, really, and what was there to confess? That I had been enormously attracted to his cousin and promised to wait for them both to come home and make my choice then? And that I was still attracted and still tempted? That the first time I might have done something about it if Johnnie hadn't been such a gentleman, and this time I was prevented by my child from making a fool of myself? Johnnie went out of our life, and we continued on as though he had never existed. Carrie and Sheila came along, and our family was complete (we thought), Jeremy's career advanced, we moved out to the West Coast, and there you are."

Lulu was looking at me quizzically, as if she couldn't quite believe that I had been young once with two handsome young men in love with me.

"I was lucky, I guess, that events conspired against me," I remarked. "Weren't you and Grandfather happy, Gran?"

"Yes, we were; there were ups and downs as in any marriage, of course."

I pictured in my mind's eye the dance, I heard the music, and the singer's voice: *'I'll remember April and you...'* Blue eyes looking into mine; hand firmly in the small of my back, then his lips against my cheek, and his whispering words....

"Gran, you're a million miles away. Are there more photos?"

I opened the second album. There was the infant Harriet in her christening gown, screaming her head off; here were Jeremy and Harriet and I at the cottage at the lake; here were Susie and Peter and their twins, laughing and playing with four year old Harriet; here was a sulky Harriet, balefully eyeing the infant Caroline. What a temper tantrum she had when we explained that we couldn't take the baby back to the hospital! "You can take stuff you don't want back to Eaton's," she protested. "But we want Caroline," I said sweetly. "Well, I don't!" she roared, and proceeded to turn purple with rage. You can imagine her reaction to a second sister, Sheila arriving only fourteen months later. Fortunately, by then, she was old enough to go off to school every morning, and Jeremy would drive her. She would sit on his knee and cheerfully pretend that she was the one who was driving. I used to worry about this, but luckily they came to no harm. She and her father went on to form a close relationship—she could always twist him around her little finger. As the children grew up, there were times when it was I who felt a little shut out from my children—Carrie and Sheila so very close, sharing everything each other; Harriet often distant, delighting in showing her preference for her father. That's why I was so taken aback at Harriet last night, when she accused *me* of shutting *her* out!

And when David was born so unexpectedly, a tiny miracle, a beautiful son, the light of my life...Jeremy so proud and pleased, so worried about me, so concerned and loving; the husband I thought I had lost restored to me . . .

"Gran, you're really dreaming today."

"Yes," I sighed. "So many memories...."

She turned the pages in the album, smiling at pictures of her aunts as children, teenagers, and her father a beaming infant in Jeremy's arms, a curly headed blond toddler in my lap, a little boy between his two teenaged sisters who obviously adored him.

"Daddy was a darling child, wasn't he, Gran ... ."

"He was my own special miracle," I said.

She leaned back in her chair. "You've seen a lot of changes, haven't you, Gran."

"From horse and buggy to landing on the moon. From crystal radio sets to colored television."

"And you went up in an airplane when you were, what, eighteen?"

"Yes, it was a thrilling experience I'll never forget."

"Gran," she said thoughtfully, "did you ever see Johnnie again?" I hesitated. "Yes," I said slowly. "Yes, I did. Once."

All marriages have their ups and downs, and Jeremy and I weren't immune from a bad patch here and there. If we ever had serious differences, it was usually over the handling of our eldest daughter. I thought Jeremy indulged her, and he thought I was too hard on her. When he was away on business she sulked until he returned—then greeted him with delirious joy. He always had a present for her.

Caroline and Sheila did take up a great deal of my time when they were small, the two of them so close together in age, and Harriet was jealous of them, and of me as well. She would come into our bedroom in the morning and creep in between Jeremy and me. This annoyed me no end, especially the times when I hadn't seen my husband for a few weeks, and I wanted a lock on the door. Jeremy thought it sweet that his daughter was so attentive, and refused my request. Instead, he would come home for lunch when Harriet was at school, and the babies were down for their naps, and would take me to bed in the afternoon!

There comes a time when a relationship gets stale. It's not that love dies, but somehow the magic is gone. The demands of job, housework, growing children with piano and dance lessons, all take their toll. Sex becomes predictable, even boring, and our marriage was complicated by his frequent travel. You'd think that our frequent reunions would turn out to be little honeymoons, but it didn't always work that way. He was always tired, and had started to drink a bit more than was healthy for him, I thought, and every time I

369

mentioned it he told me I was nagging him. So I closed my eyes to it, and threw myself into more volunteer jobs and pretended everything was all right.

In 1936 Jeremy came home from a trip to Japan bearing gifts for us all (mine was my silk kimono) and announced that we were moving to the West Coast. The company was opening a new office in Vancouver, and he was the one picked to get it going.

"Dad, can't you just go there for awhile and then come back?" asked Harriet, horrified that she would be leaving her friends in Ottawa forever.

"Can't be done, Sugar," Jeremy replied, kissing the top of her head. "I'll also be doing more traveling to projects around the Pacific—Japan, Korea, et cetera," he went on. "Much more convenient out of Vancouver."

Carrie and Sheila thought it would be an adventure, and immediately began to read anything they could lay their hands on regarding British Columbia. Harriet sulked.

"My sister Norah has a friend that lives out in B.C.," I said cheerfully, hiding my dismay. "Did you ever meet Barbara Windsor, Jeremy? She married a policeman twenty odd years ago. She and Norah still correspond, I believe. I'll get her address and let her know we'll be coming."

Work took Jeremy away soon after, leaving me to cope with selling the house and organizing the move. I resigned all my volunteer jobs (the only positive thing I could see about the situation) and hired cleaners and gardeners to tidy up the place. I was upset about leaving my parents, who, although not really elderly, were getting on, and Mama was not in the best of health. My brother Val, now in his early thirties, had never married, and still lived with them in the big house on the canal. Contrary to my sister Norah's expectation, my parents had not sold the house, merely took in boarders from time to time, and Val, who had a good job teaching at a local private school, contributed to its upkeep. Dorcas, at the age of sixty-eight, still ran things with an iron hand.

"I don't like to be so far away from them at this stage in their lives," I told Val seriously. "I hope Gerry and Norah make a point of traveling up here more often, now that their families are nearly grown. I'm going down to PEI next month for Sarah's wedding, house or no house. She's marrying a very nice young man, according to Norah and Sybil, and I want to be there. I thought I'd take Harriet, if she's interested. Jeremy will likely still be away."

"Where's he this time, Sis?"

"Vancouver at the moment, then he'll be points west. Indo-China and Japan again. It seems peculiar, doesn't it, to travel west to get to the Far East."

"The world is round, you know," he replied unnecessarily. "We think that way because we're Europe-centered, and we on the eastern part of North America even more so. To us China has always been in the east. Look," he added, "go to Fairlea and enjoy yourself. I'll look after things while you're away. If there's an offer on the house I'll ring you long distance."

I went alone, as it turned out. Jeremy was still away, Harriet had other fish to fry, and Caroline and Sheila were at summer camp. I insisted that she stay with Mama and Papa, but I think she spent most of the time out at the lake at the Ferris cottage. Her grandfather Ferris allowed her to invite two of her friends, and I'm sure she had much more fun than she would have had with me visiting a lot of relations that were to her almost complete strangers.

Packing up and moving to Vancouver took a lot of energy, not only physical, but mental as well, coping with Harriet's sulks and threats not to go with me. Caroline and Sheila couldn't understand her tantrums; to the nine and ten year old girls the thought of a train trip across the country to the fabulous Pacific Ocean and a house overlooking the sea was heaven itself. They had said goodbye to their friends, but because they were their own best friends, it wasn't the wrench that it was to their nearly fifteen-year-old sister. Harriet cried for the first two days out, then sulked for the rest of the way. She didn't properly unpack her things for nearly three months.

Jeremy had found the most wonderful piece of property on the North Shore, where he had to travel by ferry across the inlet to the city. There was a marvelous view of the broad bay, and Stanley Park, and on clear days the mountains of Vancouver Island. We took the family

371

over to the Island one weekend on the large ferry—to Caroline and Sheila it was a trip on an ocean liner. We had staterooms, and slept overnight, and had dinner in the dining room, with white tablecloths and napkins, and fresh flowers on the table. Victoria is the capital, of course, and in those days was a quiet little city on the Inner Harbour. We stayed at the Empress Hotel and had High Tea in the lobby.

And though all this impressed her, it wasn't enough to really mollify her. She moped in her room, refused to unpack her suitcases and take her books out of the packing cases. She would come home from school with a long face and say that the girls were laughing at her. When I asked her how she knew that she said that when she would walk by a group of teens they would stop talking, and then burst out laughing. Whether their mirth was actually directed towards her is a moot point; she perceived it as such, and continued to be desperately unhappy. Meanwhile, Caroline and Sheila, in the fourth and fifth grades respectively, were making friends, joining groups, and doing well in their studies. I urged Harriet to join the local church Young Life group, which met Sunday afternoons for social occasions. One of the girls she met attended a private school in Vancouver, and came home for weekends. Harriet immediately wanted to go to that school. They wore blazers with a gold and green crest, tartan kilts, and white shirts. She harped and harped on it, and gave me no rest until I promised to speak to her father about it when he returned from his business trip. I explained we couldn't afford the fees, and her father, I knew, would back me up. Hadn't our move cost us a great deal?

To my consternation, Jeremy agreed to send Harriet to private school! We had a serious quarrel over this issue.

"I'm sick to death of the two of you at loggerheads all the time," he said coldly. "Since I can't send you away, perhaps it would be better for us all if Harriet were somewhere else."

His words hurt me deeply, and for several nights we slept each on our own side of the bed, not even touching.

Harriet was a different girl, now that she was going to private school. She would take the bus home every Friday afternoon, and she'd actually be smiling. If her father were home, she would spend the first hour in his study talking with him about her week. She was openly triumphant that she'd got her own way, and tried to lord it over her sisters, who, of course were not impressed.

"She's a snob," I overheard Caroline tell Sheila one day.

"What's a snob?"

"It's when you think you're better than other people, only you're not," answered her sister shortly.

I must admit Harriet looked good in her uniform, and her marks were good. But we took no more trips to the Island, and Jeremy didn't mention again his idea of our getting away on our own for a week or so.

In 1938 I received a birthday card in the mail from Johnnie. I hadn't heard from him directly since he had had lunch at our house in Ottawa sixteen years before. He wrote to Susie occasionally, and she would fill me in on his activities.

I have just returned from France, he scribbled. *Elise died last month of cancer. I got there in time to say goodbye to her. Things are looking rather grim in Europe. I think I shall join the Air Force. I believe there will be another war.*

I showed his note to Jeremy.

"He's right, you know. The Germans never really disarmed. Hitler will plunge the whole continent into war, and we will have to follow."

"Not again, Jeremy!" I cried.

He put his arm around me. "I'm going to be away a lot in the next few months. Shall we spend the weekend at Harrison Hot Springs? Someone told me there's a very nice spa hotel there."

"This weekend?" I said doubtfully. "Oh, Jeremy, we can't. Sheila is in a play Saturday night, and we promised to attend."

I could see Jeremy wasn't enthused about a class of eleven year olds prancing around on the stage, but he went with reasonable grace, probably wishing the whole time that we were off in our hotel room, or sitting in a hot pool. I know I did. When I suggested another weekend, Jeremy shook his head, and said that he was snowed under with work preparing for his trip.

That year we had a splendid view of the construction of the new bridge across the First Narrows. Rumor had it that it would be opened next spring when the King and Queen visited Canada. Jeremy's company was not involved in it, but he was keenly interested in its construction, of course, as it was being touted as the finest bridge design in Canada. There was another bridge across the second narrows of the inlet, but it was old and narrow and ten or eleven miles out of the way to his office in the downtown core. He was extremely busy; when he wasn't traveling on business he was working late at the office. I suspected that he was having an affair with one of the secretaries; I had seen how one or two had flirted with him at the Christmas party, and our sex life was almost nil.

After a silence of so many years, Johnnie began to drop me the occasional note. They were merely friendly letters—anybody could have read them—but I treasured them because he seemed really interested in my life, my children, and my activities. So I wrote back to him, poured out my heart, told him my dreams, the problems I had with Harriet, but never mentioning my deteriorating relationship with Jeremy.

I think it was about then that I started a day dream in my head about Johnnie, and what my life might have been like had he come home from the war when he planned. At night in my empty bed I would let my imagination run rampant as I waited for sleep to come. Jeremy would come in late, crawl into bed without a word, and be asleep in a minute. I took long walks down the hill to the beach at Ambleside, did my shopping in the village, and then toiled up the hill again to wait for the delivery of my groceries. All the while I would be a thousand miles away in my mind with Johnnie. And though the walk was good for me, I am not so sure that my daydreams were very helpful.

Jeremy had been away for nearly a week, and was due back on Monday or Tuesday. My birthday was on the weekend, and he had forgotten it. He had been away before on my birthday, but he had always sent flowers, or a card, or left something for me to find. There was nothing this time. Harriet asked if she could borrow the car Friday night, as she was invited to her friend Ruby's for the night, and they were going to a movie the next day in town. Caroline and Sheila were at a weekend retreat with the church young people. They had rushed off after school was out with their weekend cases packed to the brim, with a hurried kiss and an apology for not being at home for my birthday the next day. Harriet didn't even mention it. I was going to be forty-two, and nobody cared. I looked in the mirror and found a gray hair, which I ruthlessly plucked out. I felt better when three cards arrived in the mail, from Norah, Mama and Susie. There was a lovely newsy letter from Norah relating all the news in her family and Gerald's. Carson had joined the army, and was being sent to Camp Borden in Ontario—Sybil was upset because everyone was talking about war and Hitler, and even though the civil war in Spain was over, she was afraid he would be sent overseas. I was rereading her letter when the telephone rang, and to my surprise Johnnie's voice came over the line. He was in Vancouver for the weekend before flying to California where he would be working for the American Air Force giving flying lessons.

"I'm being lent to the Yanks by the RCAF," he said. "How about you and Jeremy coming downtown and having dinner with me?"

I told him Jeremy was still out of town.

"You come, then, Louise. I'd love to see you."

There was no reason why I shouldn't see Johnnie, my husband's cousin, and an old friend, was there? I had no plans for the evening. I'd have to take a taxi, of course, as Harriet had the car. I told him I'd meet him in the lobby of the Hotel Vancouver at seven o'clock. I went to my closet to decide what to wear, and chose a dress of a soft maroon jersey. I was off the shoulders, and I had always thought it flattered me. The ankle length skirt flowed smoothly and swirled as I walked. I had a long bath, did my hair carefully, dressed, and called a taxi at six o'clock. The cabbie took the long way around by way of the Second Narrows Bridge, and we discussed how convenient the new bridge would be. I arrived at the hotel shortly after seven to see Johnnie in his blue uniform waiting for me.

As I said to Lulu yesterday, I may be old, but there are some things one doesn't forget: the racing pulse, that exquisite lurch in the midsection, the melting sensation in one's legs. It was exactly forty-six years ago, give or take a week, and I still remember the rush I felt when I saw him standing there, his eyes lighting up when he saw me. He took my hands in his and gazed down at me.

"Oh, Louise," he breathed.

He took me home in a taxi and we held hands all the way. I pictured us in front of the fireplace sipping a liqueur, so I whispered an invitation to come in for a while. His response was to lift my hand to his lips and kiss its palm. I could see his eyes light up in the glow of the headlights reflected back inside the cab. When we turned into the driveway, I saw to my consternation my car sitting there, and a light burning in Harriet's bedroom window upstairs.

"Harriet has come home. She was supposed to be sleeping over tonight. I guess you'd better not come in."

I was astonished at the disappointment I felt.

He cupped my face in his hands and kissed me, his mouth moving over mine. I found myself responding hungrily. Presently he got out, walked me to the door. He didn't kiss me again, just looked at me with an expression that turned my bones to water.

"I'll call you tomorrow, Louise. Goodnight, darling."

I went inside, turned on the outside light, and watched the taxi drive away with Johnnie in it. It was probably just as well, I thought. Those kisses of his might have led to who knows what!

"Where on earth have you been?" called Harriet from the top of the stairs.

"Having dinner with an old friend," I replied lightly. "I thought you were sleeping over."

Harriet wasn't really interested in where I had been and with whom, only as it related to her.

"Ruby and I quarreled," she said sulkily, "so I came home. I had to crawl in a basement window!"

"Why on earth didn't you take your key?" I asked.

"I didn't think you would be out. Do you know it's after midnight!"

I didn't comment, only went into my room to get undressed. Later I lay in bed, thinking of Johnnie, still feeling the marvelous attraction we had for each other. Perhaps it would be better if he went away without our seeing each other. I could still feel the pressure of his hand in the small of my back, and his lips moving over mine. I had wanted to open my mouth and drown in that kiss! I shivered and turned over. Oh, God, when had I last felt this way with Jeremy? And when had Jeremy last made love to me? I hadn't known how starved I was.

The next day Harriet got a telephone call, and when she hung the phone up she turned to me triumphantly.

"That was Ruby! She has apologized, and wants to go to the movies after all! Can I have the car?"

No 'please'; no 'mother, do you need the car?'

"Actually, I need to do some shopping downtown, Harriet," I said, inventing an errand. "Can't Mrs Hopewell pick you up?"

"I suppose," she answered sulkily. "I don't know why I can't have the car, though. You couldn't have had it if I hadn't come home last night."

She went out an hour later, and I went about the house tidying up needlessly, pretending that I wasn't waiting for a telephone call.

"Come for lunch," Johnnie urged me, when he called just before noon. "Please, Louise, I want to see you."

Why not, I thought. There was no harm in having lunch with Johnnie. I bathed and dressed carefully, and met him at one o'clock in the lobby. "There's a great lunch buffet on the Roof," he said. "I haven't had breakfast, only coffee, and I'm starved!"

We took the elevator to the Roof Restaurant, and sat in a corner table, and had lunch. He ordered a bottle of white wine, and we sipped slowly, hands touching under the table. I don't remember what we talked about, last night's dance, the view perhaps, the food, perhaps; he must have mentioned his comfortable room on the tenth floor, else how did I know to press the button marked ten when we got back on the elevator? His hands were trembling as he unlocked the door to his room, and a moment later we were inside, the door clicking firmly behind us. We couldn't get our clothes off fast enough, and didn't even pull the counterpane back, but made love in a tangle of arms and legs quickly and wordlessly on top of the bed. I remember that I had an orgasm very soon after he entered me, something that hadn't happened with Jeremy for a long time. He cried out my name when his climax came a moment later.

"Are you always that fast?" he asked me with a smile in his voice. We went into the bathroom and showered together, then went back to bed and made love again. This time we got under the covers. It took much longer this time, but it was sweet and pleasurable, and my body sang with wonderful sensations. His hands and lips played me beautifully until I could stand it no more and begged him to finish. He took me then, almost savagely, and we cried out passionately together at the end.

"Louise, you must come away with me." I said nothing, only held him tightly.

"I have loved you always, Louise. We were meant to be together, don't you see?"

He fell asleep soon after, and as I listened to his regular breathing, I thought long and hard about what I had just done. I was an adulteress, wasn't I? Was I to compound the sin by leaving my children and husband?

I slipped out of bed and got under the shower again, soaping myself and scrubbing as though not wanting to take anything of Johnnie home with me. I dressed silently, then sat down and wrote a note to him. I left it on the desk, and then quietly let myself out. I went to the department store and bought a pair of shoes, after which I drove home.

Was it guilt that made me welcome my husband into my bed when he returned two days later? For I made love to him as passionately as I had made love to Johnnie, and there was absolutely no pretense in it.

"Gran, you're a million miles away again. Are you thinking about Johnnie?" Lulu was gazing at me.

I told her that Johnnie had come to town in April of 1938, and that we had had dinner together and had gone dancing. He was on his way to California to start work as an instructor for the US Air Force.

She was looking at more photos, and took out one of Johnnie in uniform. "He and Grandfather looked quite a bit alike when they were young, didn't they." She looked up. "What happened?"

"He was killed in a flying accident a month or so later," I said.

"How awful! But I meant, what happened when you saw him? Did he ask you to go away with him again?"

I paused and thought for a moment. I didn't intend to tell Lulu that I had had an affair with Johnnie, brief though it was. She saw me hesitate, and I am afraid my cheeks grew warm.

"Gran, you're blushing! What happened that night?"

"Nothing," I said truthfully. "Except a kiss in the taxi." And I smiled, remembering again.

"Did you see him again?"

"Yes. The next day we had lunch together."

I am neither proud nor ashamed of what happened between us.

In my note I wrote that it would be no use for me to go away with him; my children were the most important things in my life just then. Perhaps we should go on as if this had never happened. I wasn't going to tell Jeremy— could we just remain friends?

He telephoned that evening. Harriet was at home, of course, but she wasn't interested in who was phoning me, only in as much as I was tying up the line. He begged me to reconsider, and said he'd be in touch. I received only one letter from him before the accident, and it was a friendly letter addressed to both Jeremy and me.

I know Lulu was longing to ask me if I had wanted to go away with Johnnie. To her, this was a romantic story that had really happened.

I think I left the hotel while Johnnie was still sleeping because I was afraid that he might possibly persuade me to leave Jeremy. He had made me feel young and beautiful and desirable, but surely that wasn't a valid reason for throwing nearly twenty years of marriage away! I know I would not have been able to endure the censure of family, friends, and most of all, of my husband and children. Carrie and Sheila would have been bewildered and puzzled, Jeremy deeply wounded, and Harriet despising. Or would she have been secretly pleased to have her father all to herself? My sister Norah would think

I had gone off the rails. Sarah would have been ashamed of her Aunt Louise.

But what did I really want? I thought about it all that next day, and when Johnnie telephoned I was able to send him away firmly.

I wanted my husband back, loving and close as we had been before.

I tried to convey some of this to Lulu.

"We had gone through a bad patch, Lulu, your grandfather and I, but it would have been insane to throw it all away."

"And then Daddy came along. What a surprise for everyone!" She picked up another, small, album, which she opened. "What's this one?"

I peered over her shoulder. "Why, it's an old album that Johnnie's Uncle Stan sent me after the war. Mabel had died, and he was clearing out his house. I think it's of Johnnie's parents and when he was a boy. I haven't looked at it for years and years. Yes! There's Aunt Grace. She was a sweet woman. When I first met her she was in the first stages of Alzheimer's Disease, or some kind of senile dementia. She died a couple of years later, I think I told you that . . ."

"Gran! Is this Johnnie? Why he's the spitting image of my brother Johnny! Isn't that amazing?"

It was true. The two teenaged Johns were alike as two peas. I had not seen this photograph for nearly forty years.

"An amazing coincidence, isn't it," I said. "Your brother is certainly a Ferris."

Lulu studied the photo, and I could practically hear the wheels going around. She could count nine months back from her father's January birthday. She was wondering, I knew, if it were possible that Johnnie had fathered my son David. Of course it had occurred to me. I had wondered many times, and finally came to terms with the fact that I would never know for sure, and that it really didn't matter. David had brought Jeremy and me back together, closer than before, and I thanked God continually for his existence, however he came to be.

"Your father was a miracle," I went on, ignoring the speculative glance she gave me. "Jeremy never thought he'd have a son, and was as proud as punch. I think it altered his attitude toward the war. Before David's advent it seemed to me it was a game to him, a dangerous one to be sure, but after seeing his son, I believe it became more a dirty job, to get over with as soon as possible. I didn't know until long afterwards that he had never stopped being involved in espionage. Many of his 'business' trips in those years between the wars were actually cover for his government work." I paused. "He kept a diary for thirty years, you know, and I think he always meant to write his memoirs. One day soon I will give it to you, Lulu, and you might try to do something with it."

"Really, Gran?" she asked, her eyes shining. The photograph album she closed with a snap. Johnnie was forgotten. "Grandfather was a spy? That is totally cool! When may I read it?"

I smiled. "One of these days," I promised. I became serious. "Lulu, don't ever lose faith in your husband, and don't be afraid to tell him how you feel. I nearly lost Jeremy because I was afraid to talk to him about my feelings." I smiled again. "But I don't think you and Denby will have that problem."

She blushed. "Oh, Gran, do you think...." Her voice trailed away.

I stretched out my hand and touched her face. She was so dear to me, so beautiful, and so full of love to give to the right person! "Just follow your heart, my dear," I said softly.

Chapter Thirty-Five

DENBY AND LULU

Denby Chalmers studied the photographs he had taken the previous afternoon. He had worked into the night to develop them, and this morning he framed two that he was planning to give to Lou's grandmother. He gazed at the face smiling at him from the picture, and sighed. She was so young, and he was really too old for her, but he knew that he was deeply in love with her. It amazed him that this could happen so fast after so long. When Patricia had broken their engagement nine years ago, he had sworn that he would never get involved again. To love meant to be vulnerable to hurt.

The date had been set for months, the wedding, which was to take place in his sister's garden, planned down to the last detail. Gifts were pouring in from friends and family. Two weeks before they were to be married she told him the wedding was off. He still remembered her as she stood there, her outstretched hand holding the engagement ring. She was a small slender girl, with straight blond hair falling to her waist. Her large blue eyes, fringed with curly lashes, gazed rather defiantly at him. She had met someone else, she said, and was going away with him. She was carrying his child, she went on, her voice faltering at this point, and he remembered how her hands dropped protectively to her abdomen. She was sorry to hurt him, and she hoped that he would forgive her.

382

He remembered his anger—searing, white hot anger that spewed out a stream of abuse at her. She stepped back, stricken, face ashen, lips trembling. He turned away, his hands shaking, and he told her to get out; he was disgusted with her, and he would never, ever forgive her.

He was immediately deeply ashamed of his outburst, but pride prevented his calling her back to apologize. Visions of her and the unknown young man together fueled his hurt and anger even more. He remembered telephoning his sister and pouring everything out to her.

"This must have been going on for months," he said bitterly. "Why didn't she come and tell me before now?"

"Perhaps she was afraid to, Den," said Norma. "You know, sometimes you can be a bit intimidating."

He left it to his sister to return the gifts and to cancel the arrangements; he carried on with his teaching as though nothing had happened. He would not show his hurt to the world. Someone told him later that Trish, as she was now calling herself, had moved to Salt Spring Island with the young man in question, and had 'gone back to the land'. They apparently smoked pot, she trailed around braless and barefoot, and let the child run about stark naked.

Well, she had certainly done him a favor, hadn't she? He had definitely not needed a flower child for a wife! He was no hippie; he hardly drank, had never smoked anything. How could he have had such terrible judgment?

He hadn't thought of Trish and whatever-his-name-was for a long time. As he studied Lou's picture he knew that he had never loved Trish the way he should have, and that she most certainly was better off with someone else. He had tried to change Patricia to his image of Denby Chalmer's wife; ironically now he was terrified that he wasn't the image of Lulu Ferris' husband! Moreover, he was now hoping to be 'the other man', and desiring that Lou would eventually break her engagement to Bruce! He felt a guilty compassion for the young man who was in love with Lulu, and suddenly knew that he had forgiven Patricia and her lover, and actually wished them well. Was she all right? Were they even still together? He would get in touch with the person who had told him about their moving to Salt Spring Island and find out. In the meantime, he was determined not to rush Lou.

He studied the photos again, one of Lulu that her grandmother had chosen, the other one of the two in the garden that he had taken yesterday. It was excellent of them both. They were smiling at each other, and the light behind them was very beautiful. He didn't think that Mrs Ferris would mind her wrinkles showing—he had not used a filter—for she hadn't struck him as a vain person. Lou had told him she was eighty-eight. It was hard to believe. Perhaps he would visit her this afternoon and give them to her. Would she mind his dropping in? She was an active person—she might even be out, though it wasn't as warm as it had been the day before.

He got into his car and drove across town, admiring the spring blossoms along Sixteenth Avenue. When he drew up outside Mrs Ferris' house, he sat for a few moments. He really wanted to talk to her, didn't he? He wanted to sound her out about Lou. It was hard to believe that they had met scarcely three weeks ago. He had noticed her at the Naturalists meeting before Hannah Jacobs had introduced them—he had admired her hair, shining honey colored curls that framed her face like a halo. They were natural curls that curled even more in the rain the following Sunday on the outing at Blackie Spit. The day had been dreary, wet, and chilly, but she had turned the grayness to sunshine for him. He wasn't the least insulted when she mistook his picture taking motives—in fact her split-second misunderstanding rather endeared her to him, and she had blushed so attractively.

He sighed and got out of the car, photo portfolio under his arm. He hoped Mrs Ferris didn't mind unexpected company. He didn't know why he hadn't telephoned first. As he approached the front door he could hear music from within, classical music whose volume had been turned up high. He didn't know what it was—there seemed to be bells and cannons and crashing cymbals. He was not a classical fan. In fact he had informally studied the history of popular music, and his favorite music was jazz and swing. The Beatles were a close second. As he raised his hand to knock, he realized that Mrs Ferris would not hear him, so he thought he might go around to the back. Perhaps he could rap on the window, and get her attention that way. He hoped he wouldn't startle her.

To his surprise and pleasure, he saw through the window Lou sitting beside her grandmother, eyes closed, obviously listening to the music with great pleasure. There was a crash and a boom, and the piece was over, so he took the opportunity to ring the doorbell. He heard her voice saying something to Mrs Ferris, then her light step to the door. It swung open, and her smile turned to surprise, then pleasure, color rising in her cheeks.

"Denby! I thought you were Daddy—he said he'd pick me up about now." She looked past him as if she expected to see her father bearing down on them. "Will you come in?" she asked, remembering her manners.

He stepped inside, smiling down at her. "I framed the photos, so I thought I'd just drop by—" He stopped, and took a half step backward. He had the most extraordinary desire to kiss her. They stood looking at each other rather foolishly for a moment, and then Mrs Ferris' voice came from the living room.

"Is it David, dear?"

The color in Lulu's face ebbed, then came flooding back, brighter than before.

"No! It's Denby, Gran!"

"Well, bring him in, dear."

He followed the girl into the cozy sitting room, where a fire was burning cheerfully in the grate. Mrs. Ferris was putting on another record, and a mournful jazz melody filled the room. As the first notes were sung, he said, " 'I'll Remember April'—Thelma Grayson, I think."

"Fancy your knowing that!" remarked Mrs Ferris. "Such an obscure singer, too—she never did become particularly famous. I love the song, though; it brings back such memories. Do sit down, Denby. Have you brought my photographs? How quick you are." She glanced at Lulu, who was standing in the middle of the room looking slightly bemused. "Is the coffee still hot? Do bring Denby a cup. That is, if he cares for one."

Denby seated himself beside Mrs Ferris, but smiled at her granddaughter. "A cup of coffee would be very nice. Just a little milk, please."

He handed Mrs Ferris the folder, which she opened. "You've framed them! How lovely!" She got to her feet and went over to the window, where the light was better. "Oh, I do like them! Look, Lulu, dear, what Denby has brought me."

Lulu had come into the room with a large blue mug of steaming coffee. Denby had arisen with Mrs Ferris, and now he turned and took the mug from Lulu's hands. Their fingers brushed very lightly. Lulu sat down next to her grandmother, who had resumed her seat, and Denby took the large overstuffed chair by the fireplace. He watched with pleasure the two faces bent so close, one young and beautiful, the other very old, and yes, still beautiful. She reminded him of the Queen Mother, in a way. It was the serene smile, he thought, and the bright eyes, bare of spectacles. Amazing, that she didn't need glasses.

As he sipped his coffee, they all heard the front door open, and steps across the hall.

"That must be Daddy!" exclaimed Lulu, jumping to her feet.

A middle aged man, slim, six feet tall, entered the room, and stopped in surprise, eyebrows raised, as he saw the young man uncoil himself from the chair to stand up respectfully. Lulu stood dumb.

"David, my darling, come and meet Denby Chalmers. My son David." Mrs Ferris had risen and was kissing her son on the cheek. The photographs she had laid down carelessly on the coffee table, and seemed to forget them. "Coffee, dear?" she asked vaguely.

"No thanks, Mother," he said, as he shook hands with the younger man. "Petra's parents expect us at five o'clock, and it's an hour's drive. Are you sure you won't come along? They would be delighted to see you."

"Thank you, no, dear, I have planned a simple supper and early to bed. Do give my regards to Will and Mary Anne."

Lulu had retrieved her jacket from the closet, and was waiting by the hall door, her eyes fixed on Denby. Denby gave her a slow smile, then walked over and took her hand.

"Goodbye for now," he said, and then saw that her other hand was ringless.

She saw his glance, and her face flushed scarlet, but she said nothing. Presently she followed her father out, with an anguished backward glance at Denby and her grandmother. Mrs Ferris smiled sweetly at her.

"Do call me, Lulu, dear," she said. "Goodbye."

She nodded at Denby as the front door closed. "Do sit down, and we will talk. You did come in order to talk to me, didn't you?"

Lulu got into the back seat of the car and found she had to sit between her brothers.

"Possession is nine points of the law," remarked Peter, who was long legged and sandy haired, when his sister hesitated and looked at the window seats.

"I'll sit in the middle coming home," offered Johnny, the youngest of the three. His fair hair was slicked back, and his blue eyes twinkled at his sister. Lulu squeezed in between the two boys, who were getting quite large.

"We need a bigger car," Peter grumbled.

"Or a second one," Johnny put in. "You'll be getting your license soon, won't you," he added, an envious tone in his fourteen-year-old voice.

While the boys, distracted, talked cars and sports, Lulu managed to fish Bruce's ring out of her pocket and slip it on. She didn't need awkward questions today.

"My mother does manage to collect the oddest friends," remarked David to Petra. "A strange young man was looking quite at home in Dad's chair. Had you met him before, Lulu?"

Lulu found her color rising, but it went unnoticed by her brothers. "Why, yes," she said. "He teaches at the college, and he gave a lecture at the Naturalists Club last week. I told you that he was leading the birding walk last Sunday."

"You did?" asked her mother. "What's his name?"

"Dennis Chalmers," David said. "Is that right, Lulu?"

"Denby, Dad. He's a photographer, too."

387

"What sort of photos, dear?"

"Mostly wildlife. He does people, too."

She decided to say nothing about the photographs he had taken of her grandmother and herself. Instead, she stared out the window at the passing scenery and listened to her parents' conversation.

"One day Mother is going to pick up a con man."

"Do you think so, David? Your mother is still sharp as a tack. Don't start sounding like your sister Harriet. She gets very tiresome at times."

"She was up on her soapbox last night, wasn't she. No, you're right, darling, I shouldn't worry about Mother; it's just that a dose of Harriet can be catching," he added with a chuckle.

Denby threw another log on the fire at his hostess' request, then sat back in the comfortable chair, legs outstretched, hands tucked behind his head. Mrs Ferris smiled at him encouragingly. He found himself telling her all about Patricia.

"I guess I wasn't very mature for twenty-five," he confessed.

"What was she like?"

"Fragile, sweet-tempered, childlike in some ways; she was very pretty, with long blond hair that fell almost to her waist, big blue eyes, a tinkling laugh. Come to think of it, her laugh might have gotten a trifle irritating after awhile." He shook his head. "I must have been blind not to have known there was something wrong, but I didn't notice. I was teaching full time then, and coaching little league baseball. I guess she felt neglected—she was barely out of school—Lou isn't much older than she was. Is there something the matter with me, I wonder?"

"You mean, your choice of women much younger than you."

"Mmm."

"Your reaction to her faithlessness still bothers you."

"Mrs Ferris, I am still ashamed of my outburst and it's nearly nine years ago! And not just what I said to her, but my feelings toward her. I didn't know I had those feelings in me!" He stared into the fire. "I remember wanting to put my hands around her neck and throttle her. And worse!" He looked rueful. "Not the best story to be telling Lou's grandmother is it."

"Do you lose your temper often?"

"Not really. I get annoyed about things, just like anybody, but I've never hauled off and punched someone in the nose."

"Did you ever apologize to her?"

"No. I put her completely out of my mind."

"Not completely, I gather."

"I haven't been carrying a torch," he protested. "Marriage would have been a disaster."

"My sister Norah told me how her husband, before they were married, felt very guilty about his behavior toward the parents of his best friend who had died. She persuaded him to visit and apologize to them. She said he returned a different man."

Denby smiled rather ruefully at the old woman. "I don't even know whether they're still on Salt Spring Island."

Mrs Ferris smiled, but said nothing.

"I guess I could find out, couldn't I."

"Would you like a cup of coffee?"

"No, thanks, Mrs Ferris. One cup was fine. Mrs Ferris, is it crazy to think I could fall in love so quickly with someone I've known for such a short time? I feel I do know her—she's beautiful, inside and out."

The old woman nodded. "I'm biased, of course. I've always thought there was no one good enough for my darling girl. Until perhaps now."

Denby blushed. "But you don't know anything about me."

"But I know your sister Norma."

Denby left after a short while, and drove home, deep in thought.

"I think Trish is still on Salt Spring Island, Den. I can check with her sister to make sure, if you like."

Denby had tracked down an old acquaintance to enlist his help in finding Patricia. He was feeling more and more that his relationship with her, though long over with, needed some sort of closure before he pursued a serious one with Lou Ferris. Two days later he was told that Trish was indeed still on Salt Spring Island, married to the father of her child, and raising more! He wrote a note to her inventing a visit to the island that weekend, and asking her if he could pay her a short visit while he was there. He paused as he wrote, thinking that it would be so easy to tender his long overdue apologies in the letter, ask after her health, and sign his name, sincerely yours. He shook his head.

"No," he muttered to himself, "I think I had better go and see her, if she'll let me."

If she didn't want to see him, he would reply and tell her how sorry he was for his past behavior and beg her pardon. To his surprise he received a telephone a few days later from the mutual acquaintance that had had given him her address, with a message from Patricia, asking him to come and see her on the Sunday. There were instructions how to find their farm, and she would expect him sometime in the early afternoon.

"She didn't think a letter would reach you in time," said the acquaintance, "and she didn't know your telephone number. She sounded curious as to what you wanted."

No more curious than you are, my friend, thought Denby with a little smile. Feeling he didn't have to explain his reasons to anyone, he thanked his friend sincerely for his trouble, and said goodbye. He stared at his reflection in the mirror.

"Well, the die is cast," he said aloud, and made plans for his journey.

Petra Ferris regarded her daughter in dismay.

"Darling, how long have you known this young man? Has he said anything to you about marriage? Doesn't he know you're engaged?"

Lulu tried to be calm. "Yes, he knows I'm engaged, and no, he hasn't said a word to me. I know he likes me, Mother. That's all. I just know I'd go to the ends of the earth with him if he asked me, so I can't marry Bruce or anyone feeling that way, can I?"

She clasped her hands, biting her lip. Bruce's ring lay on the table in front of her.

"I've written to him," she went on. "Do you want to read the letter before I mail it to him? Then I shall go and visit his mother and return the ring to her. I'm sorry that I won't be having her for a mother-in-law, because I really am fond of Mrs Paton. I hope this won't spoil yours and Daddy's friendship with them."

Petra sat down in the chair opposite Lulu and gazed at her helplessly. What could she say?

"I'll read it if you want me to, darling. Have you thought how he'll feel? Bruce loves you very much."

"He won't want a wife who can't stop thinking about another man, will he?" she replied sensibly.

"Can't you wait for a few weeks and see—"

"And see if I change my mind? This—thing—that has happened to me is so amazing, Mother! I'll never change my mind!"

"And what if Denby wants only friendship?" asked her mother quietly.

Lulu sat back in her chair. "I guess that will have to be enough for me. You can't see Bruce letting me be friends with another man, can you?" And she held out the one page letter she had written.

Petra took it with a small smile. "No, I can't see that," she agreed. She read the note, and said, quietly, "It's very good, my dear. If you really feel this way, I agree that you must tell Bruce at once."

Lulu took the letter back and put it in an envelope. She studied her mother, who was gazing out the window.

"Oh, Mummy, I'm sorry!" she said impulsively using the old childish diminutive.

Petra stood up and held out her arms. Lulu jumped up, and mother and daughter embraced.

"Darling, if you really love this man, I hope he feels the same. I'll kill him if he breaks your heart!"

Lulu laughed at her mother's fierce tone.

"It's all right, Mother! You'll like Denby, I know you will!"

"When will I meet him? Your father made a comment that he looked very much at home in your grandfather's chair."

"How could Denby know that was Grandfather's chair?" she asked. "By the way, Gran likes him."

391

"It's doubtful that he would have been sitting in her husband's chair if she didn't like him. I trust your grandmother's judgment, too," she added.

"Mother, am I crazy? Do people really fall in love at first sight?"

Petra drew her daughter's arm through hers, smiling reminiscently. "Well," she confided, "I believe I knew at once that your father was the one for me. He took a little persuading, but he came around."

Lulu laughed delightedly. "Really?" she asked.

Her mother nodded.

"Gran told me her life story the other day," Lulu went on. "She had two romances when she was young, did you know that? One of her young men was reported killed, so she married Grandfather. The other one turned up several years after the war was over, isn't that amazing?"

"Your father told me something about it, now that you mention it. He suffered from amnesia, so the story went. I always thought it very fishy."

"Oh, no, Mother! Apparently he carried a torch for her all his life. I think it is so romantic." Lulu turned to her mother, remembering the diary. "Gran said that Grandfather kept a diary for years and years. Did you know he was a spy, Mother?"

"Your dad did say once that he was involved in espionage for the government during the war."

"She said that perhaps I can write his memoirs one day."

"That would be a very interesting project."

"I'm going out to mail this letter to Bruce, now, and then I'll go and pay a visit to Mrs Paton."

"Do you want to take my car?"

"Thanks Mother! I won't be long!"

Denby guided the car up the narrow, rutted driveway to the farmhouse, and parked the car near the garage. It was a fine, sunny day, and he had enjoyed the ferry ride to Long Harbour. The instructions he'd been given were simple and easy to follow, and as he got out of the car, he saw Trish come out of the house and wait for him on the porch. She had gained weight, he saw. Hair was still long and fair, but it was pulled back into a ponytail and tied back with a colorful ribbon. There were two toddlers holding on to the long denim skirt she was wearing.

She smiled uncertainly at him as he ascended the steps, so he held out his hand in a friendly way.

"Hallo, Trish!" He had gotten used to the new name, so it came easily off his lips. "You're looking well."

"Too well," she responded, with a nervous laugh. "Do you want to come in?"

They went inside where she busied herself making tea. "I hope you like herbal, it's the only kind we drink," she said, as she came in with an old-fashioned brown betty teapot and two mugs. She gave the two toddlers carrot sticks, and they retired to the other sofa and chewed happily on them, all the time gazing at Denby with wide, curious eyes.

"My eldest, Summer, is in grade four," she said proudly. "You probably passed the school just before you turned up our road." She gestured to the children. "Starlight is the one on the right, and Moonglow is the other. They're just a year apart. Danny, my husband, didn't really want to meet you, and he was a little worried about me being alone here with you, but I told him if you wanted to murder me, you certainly wouldn't have written and made an appointment." She gave her nervous titter again, and sipped her tea to hide her confusion.

"I came to apologize for how I treated you when you broke off our engagement," he said.

"I guess I deserved being yelled at, but you were pretty awful," she observed. "I don't mind telling you I was scared spitless! I thought you were going to hit me."

Denby had the grace to look ashamed. "The news was a shock, but that didn't give me the right to treat you the way I did. I am sorry."

"Well, you're forgiven," she returned with the smile that Denby remembered. "Do you want to see the place?"

With the two little girls running ahead, Trish gave Denby a tour of her house. It was shabby and a trifle untidy, but it was clean. In the dining room was a large pedestal table that, with some restoration work, might be a fine piece. He duly remarked on it, but Trish merely shrugged her shoulders saying that it had been purchased with the house. The kitchen window looked out on to the meadow where their flock of sheep grazed peacefully. There were two bedrooms upstairs, and one on the main floor at the front of the house, where Trish and Danny's double bed was located. In a crib by the window a baby of five or six months was now stirring. Trish leaned over and picked the child up.

"This is Danny Boy, isn't he gorgeous? Come on girls, let's go into the front room, and I'll feed Baby. The house isn't much," she said, at bit diffidently over her shoulder to Denby. "But we like it."

"You've made it very homey," Denby replied truthfully.

She sat down in the rocking chair, unselfconsciously undid her blouse, exposing one pale plump breast. The baby suckled eagerly as she rocked gently back and forth. Denby stood by the window, not wanting to stare at her.

"You're happy, Trish, aren't you."

"Yes, I am, Danny's a good farmer, and a good father to the kids. We like it here."

Presently she put the baby to the other breast. "I hope you don't mind me doing this," she said at one point.

Denby shook his head and sat down again.

"Are you still teaching school?" she asked.

"Yes, and quite involved in the Natural History Society—I'm leading a group to the Galapagos Islands in the fall."

He saw that Trish had no idea where the Galapagos were, so he explained their unique history and why they were fascinating for those interested in natural history. She nodded.

"You were always going on about birds and things," she said. "Did you ever get married?"

He shook his head. "Just never met the right person." Until now, he thought.

After the baby had finished nursing she sat him on her lap and gazed at Denby.

"Did you get what you came for?"

Denby was a little taken aback. "I guess so," he said. "You've accepted my apology, there's no grudge between us, is there."

"We wouldn't have been very happy together, you know."

"I know," he answered, getting to his feet. "Don't get up, Trish; I'll let myself out. Thanks for letting me come."

She held out her hand and he took it gratefully. She made Danny Boy wave his fist. "Wave bye-bye to Uncle Denby," she said in a baby voice to her little son. "Say bye-bye, girls."

They chorused their good-byes as he went out the door. "Good luck, Trish," he said.

Lulu walked slowly up the front walk to the Patons' front door. It had been easy talking to her mother, but this was going to more difficult. Mr and Mrs Paton had been delighted when she and Bruce became engaged, and besides, she liked them both very much, especially his father, who was warm and funny, with bright blue eyes that twinkled when he smiled. Mrs Paton always made a fuss over Lulu. She was a little more serious than her husband, but she was kind and generous, witness the lovely ring she had given to Bruce for Lulu to wear. It was a family heirloom, and Lulu was loath to give it back, but return it she must.

Mrs Paton answered the door, and her smile died when she saw Lulu regarding her so gravely.

"Lulu, dear, do come in! Bruce has written you, then?" she asked, opening the door wide and stepping aside.

Lulu looked puzzled. "Just a postcard from Niagara Falls a week or so ago," she answered, and then found herself babbling nervously. "Is anything wrong? I came to talk to you about Bruce. Is Mr Paton at home, too? I guess I should have telephoned you first before coming over."

"I'm so upset and disappointed with my son! Richard is in the garden. He is furious! Sherry says she wonders how she'll be able to face you."

Sherry was Bruce's elder sister, and Lulu remembered her once saying that her mother had spoiled Bruce when he was a child, and she hoped that Lulu was prepared. It now flitted through Lulu's mind that Bruce was inclined to sulk when he didn't get his own way.

She followed Mrs Paton out the french doors into the back garden where Mr Paton was laying out annuals.

"Mrs Paton, what—"

"Yoo-hoo, Father! Lulu's here!"

Mr Paton got up from his knees, shedding his gloves and wiping his face with a large white handkerchief.

"Lulu, dear! We are so sorry!" he exclaimed, giving her a hug.

Lulu sat down in one of the garden chairs and regarded them both, bewildered. They were acting as if they already knew she couldn't marry Bruce. How could they possibly know about Denby? Mrs Paton began to speak again, but her husband, watching Lulu's face, held up his hand, and said quietly in the silence,

"Bruce has written you, has he not, Lulu?"

"I told Mrs Paton, just a postcard from Niagara Falls that came a week last Monday. He just said what a spectacle it was and the weather was good; that they'd been having some nice spring weather . . ." Her voice trailed off. "I came to talk to you about what has happened to me, and to bring back the ring you gave me. I just wrote to Bruce breaking our engagement." She waited for their reaction. She hadn't meant to drop a bomb, but she hadn't been able to get a word in edgewise.

"Richard, isn't that just the limit! Lulu, dear, Bruce telephoned us two weeks ago saying that he was getting married! He wanted us to break it to you, but we said he must write to you. They couldn't even wait for us to go down to Ontario. We've been so upset . . ." She stopped. "But what has made you change your mind?"

Lulu couldn't believe her ears.

"You mean to tell me that Bruce is married? That he sent me a postcard on his honeymoon?" Lulu didn't know whether to laugh or burst into angry tears. "I've been in agonies wondering how I'd tell him that I can't marry him without hurting him!" At that moment Lulu could have killed Bruce. His parents looked so contrite, however, that her heart softened. Deliberately calming herself, she said, "It's not your fault, and you were right to ask him to tell me himself." She couldn't believe he could just say nothing. She brought out the velvet pouch with her engagement ring in it. "I came mainly to explain things to you and to return your lovely ring."

Feeling relieved that at least they wouldn't have a hysterical girl on their hands; Mrs Paton sat down with a thump.

"No dear, I couldn't possibly take it back after Bruce has treated you so shabbily. It's yours, of course."

Lulu shook her head firmly. "I don't want it now, beautiful as it is. You must take it."

Mrs Paton, looking even more distressed, was silent for a moment. "I wasn't going to tell you this, but Bruce asked me if I could get the ring so he could give it to Sheila. So unless I tell him a lie that I haven't got it, I'll have to give it to him."

Lulu wondered briefly why Mrs Paton couldn't just refuse his request. "May I give it to Sherry, then? It ought to be hers, anyway."

"A dandy solution, Lulu!" exclaimed Mr Paton. "I told Margery just to refuse, but she's never been able to say no to Bruce."

Lulu's head was still spinning, but her sense of humor was coming to her rescue. She had been worried sick and feeling so guilty about falling madly in love with Denby, and she needn't have at all! She sat back and laughed a trifle hysterically. Mr and Mrs Paton exchanged relieved glances. Composing herself, she then quietly told them about meeting Denby.

"I imagine that as soon as Bruce receives your letter he'll be on the blower wondering if we'd told you about his marriage," said Mr Paton thoughtfully. "I will tell a white lie and say we haven't and that he must write to you."

"Actually, I don't care if I never hear from him again," Lulu said firmly, "so you can tell him you told me, if you want." Just a few months ago she had been tempted to give in and go to bed with him. How glad she was that she hadn't! She now wanted to leap up and yell a cheer of relief. When had she fallen out of love with Bruce? Had she just outgrown him?

"We're very sorry you won't be joining our family," said Mr Paton.

"Never mind, we'll still be friends," she replied comfortingly.

"It's bound to be awkward if Bruce and his wife are with us," Mrs Paton said with a sigh.

"I have nothing to regret," Lulu said primly. She smiled at herself as she got to her feet. "I should go."

Bruce's parents arose, and stood a trifle awkwardly. Impulsively, Lulu kissed them both on their cheeks.

"May I call you by your first names?" she asked suddenly. "Then you won't be Bruce's Mum and Dad anymore, but just friends of mine."

"You're a sweet girl, and we'd be pleased if you would," Richard Paton said. "I like to be called Richard, and Edith prefers Edie."

"She knows that, Father. After all I'm sure she's heard her parents call us that."

"I'll call Sherry myself, if you like, and I'll give her your ring. Are you sure that's all right?"

"If you feel you can't keep it, Lulu, dear, then that is perfectly all right," Edie said firmly, kissing the girl fondly. "And bring your young man over to sometime. I'd like to meet him."

Her head still in a whirl, Lulu drove home, and hurried indoors. "Mother! Dad! You'll never guess what has happened! I still don't know whether to laugh or cry!"

Denby drove along the tree-lined street toward the Ferris home. His mind still churned with thoughts of his visit with Trish, and what he meant to say to Lou when he saw her. The sight of the ornamental plums in full bloom momentarily distracted him. He slowed down a little, admiring the rows of pink froth on both sides of the street. God, they were beautiful! The sky was bright blue and the late April sun felt warm through the windows of the car. He had done a little traveling, but had never seen a more beautiful city than the one he considered his. He had been born here, not far away from this street, and had grown up on the west side of the city.

What was he to say to Lou? He still marveled at the fact of her, was amazed at his feelings for her. She was the most exquisite thing he had ever seen. His mind's eye could see her golden curls the framed her small, heart-shaped face, the thick-lashed eyes of deep blue, and the dimples that came and went in her cheeks. And her mouth! He could write a poem to that mouth. There was a kissable dent on her upper lip, and when she smiled, she showed white teeth, perfectly even except for her two front teeth, which were slightly crooked. He thought it made her smile even more endearing. He had wanted to kiss that mouth from the first, when she gazed up into his face and told him how wonderful his photographs were. They were in a crowd of people balancing coffee cups and cookies, but he had been aware of nothing except her. He wanted to pick her up, take her away and look after her forever. Though not to his bachelor digs—they were small and cramped, a Murphy bed in the sitting room, a tiny bathroom one person could hardly turn around in, and an equally minute kitchen. No, he'd have to move, whether he could afford it or not. He turned off the main street and drove by an apartment block. There was a 'For Rent' sign on the lawn which announced that there was a 'one bedroom and den' apartment available. Perfect. And it was just a few blocks from her parents' home. She could walk there whenever she wanted. Goodness knows how much it cost—probably far beyond his means. Perhaps his sister might help out financially until he got his raise at the college.

He shook his head at himself then. He was about to propose to a girl already engaged to another man, and he didn't even know how she felt about him! He must be crazy. He was rehearsing in his mind what he would say to her, when he found to his surprise that he had arrived in front of her house. He stayed in the car for a few moments gathering his courage, then got out and strode purposely up the walk to her front door.

When she opened the door, her beautiful smile illuminating her face, his carefully planned speech fled.

"Lou, you just can't marry Bruce! I won't let you!"

She held open the door and he stepped into the hall. She was giggling, and her eyes were shining with mirth.

"You're right," she replied. "It would be bigamy if I married Bruce. Besides, I am going to marry you!"

He gazed at her in astonishment.

"I've been jilted," she went on. "Practically left in the lurch at the church. Isn't it wonderful?"

And it seemed quite natural for her to step into his arms and lift her mouth to his.

It was some time before they disentangled themselves, and standing in his arms she told him how she had written to Bruce to break their engagement, and then discovered the interesting fact from his parents that he had already eloped with a girl he had met in Ontario. Denby couldn't believe anyone could be so ill mannered as to treat his fiancée like that. Not a word beforehand, not a word now! He was indignant on behalf of his beloved, while at the same time delighted with the situation.

"What a bastard," he said. "Not even one word?"

"No, he wanted his parents to break the news. And get this, he asked his mother for my ring back so he could give it to what's-her-name!"

He couldn't believe it.

"She made me keep it, so I am going to give it to his sister."

"Lou, did you really mean it when you said you wanted to marry me?"

"Absolutely!"

"Darling!"

He gathered her in his arms again, and kissed her.

When the pair came into the living room where her parents were sitting, Petra's first thought was, 'He's been kissing my baby', though why that should disturb her, she didn't know. Presumably Lulu had been kissed many times by Bruce, and maybe more than just kisses. Though she was quite sure her daughter was still a virgin. She had always felt that she would know in her heart when her beloved first born took that step.

Earlier in the day Lulu had told her mother how she felt about Denby, had written to Bruce, and then discovered that her former fiancé had gotten married! Petra had never been so angry as she had been with Bruce, but she could see now that Lulu didn't care at all. For here she was now, hand in hand with another young man whom her mother had yet to meet!

"Mother, Daddy, this is Denby."

"I think I've got you straight," David said, as he shook hands with his future son-in-law. "You're Norma Chalmers' brother, aren't you."

Denby cautiously acknowledged the relationship.

"We were both in the concert band at high school. I remember her very well, and the fact she had a very young brother. She brought him to band practice on several occasions. That was you, wasn't it?"

"I remember being dragged off to the high school when Norma was babysitting me," he replied. "I was pretty little, only three or four."

"I actually dated her once or twice in a group with Hannah Jacobs and others. Hannah was Lulu's teacher, you know."

"He knows, Daddy. Hannah introduced us at the Naturalists' Club meeting."

Denby remembered Dr Ferris' slight frown when Mrs Ferris introduced him to her son last Sunday. It was as though he wasn't comfortable seeing him in his mother's living room. It was different, now that he knew who he was.

"Denby is leading a group to the Galapagos Islands in the fall! He wants me to go with him! Isn't that wonderful?"

"As my wife, of course," he assured Lulu's parents. "I think that's the only reason she's agreed to marry me," he added, grinning at Lulu.

Lulu grinned back. "The only reason! You don't think it's for your *beaux yeux*, do you?"

Denby turned to David and Petra, and said earnestly, "I am very much in love with Lou and want to marry her. I can't afford a fancy honeymoon, but the trip to South America will be great."

Petra shook her head. "I don't know, Denby; I should think you'd want to be off by yourselves after the wedding." She thought a moment. "What about Mayne Island, Lulu?"

"Mother, what a great idea!" She turned to Denby, her eyes shining. "Mother's family have a cottage on Mayne Island. We usually go there every summer, though we have to take turns with

Aunt Ruthie and my cousins. It's nice and private, but not far from the few shops in Miner's Bay. Have you ever been on Mayne?"

Denby shook his head. Petra continued.

"We always take the month of August, get a locum for our practice, and spend it on Mayne. It's quite delightful. Very quiet, too. We keep our bicycles there, and the beach is not far away. What do you think of a couple of weeks there?"

Lulu gave her mother an affectionate hug. "That's perfect, Mother! How sweet of you to give up half your vacation time! Denby, would you mind if we went there? You'll love it, I know!"

Denby smiled. He was ready to give Lulu anything she wanted.

"Thank you both!" she went on. "Shall we go and tell Gran our plans, Denby?"

"Come back for supper, both of you," Petra called, as they headed for the door. "We've got lots to talk about!"

She watched them go out hand in hand, and thought about the cottage on Mayne. She would go with her sister soon for the annual spring-cleaning to prepare it for the summer. Before the wedding she would go over again and stock the pantry and fridge with food and wine, and leave recipes of some of Lulu's favorite dishes. She would make sure the whole place was shining, suitable for a honeymooning couple: Champagne and flowers and fresh fruit and new linens for the big bed in the master bedroom. She hoped that Denby appreciated the gift of virginity that Lulu was bringing to him. The thought of them together in the bed in which she and David always slept bothered her not a bit. She was beginning to realize that she was relieved that Lulu wasn't going to marry Bruce, in spite of her friendship with Edie and Richard. She would get in touch with them tomorrow to let them know that she wasn't blaming them for Bruce's bad manners. Well, maybe she did blame Edie somewhat, but she had always been fond of her, even if she had over-indulged Bruce now and then. It seemed unbelievable, that Bruce, who had been so possessive of Lulu, (and this fact alone had been a concern that she hadn't even shared with David) should suddenly throw her over for another woman. She was beginning to think that Lulu had made a good escape. She just prayed that she wasn't jumping from the frying pan into the fire. The fact that David had known Denby's family was no yardstick either. She had known Richard and Edie for over fifteen years, and had watched Bruce grow from a rather spoiled child into a rather pedestrian but pleasant young man. She remembered her mother-in-law once calling him 'worthy, but dull', and wondered what she would think of the whole affair.

And now, a date for the wedding had to be decided upon, and what sort of reception and where.

David watched his wife, her mind far away, pick up a pencil, and start to make a list.

Epilogue

LOUISE

As I sit at my dressing table I find I am rather pleased with life. Oh, not with the infirmities that old age brings, but there isn't much one can do about that. The image in my mirror tells me I don't look my age; I have a very satisfactory family, including Harriet whom I do love despite her failings; my life has been interesting, and the many reflections upon it in which I have lately been indulging have been an interesting exercise. It's amazing how the memories have flooded back into my mind.

A long letter came from my niece Sarah this morning. She is not well at all, and I have been thinking that if I don't go down east for a visit, I will never see her again in this life. I wonder if I have the energy to fly all that way. Perhaps Lulu would come with me. We could break the trip in Ottawa and visit Susie, then continue on to Prince Edward Island. Sarah lives in Cavendish, the town that Lucy Maud Montgomery made famous as the 'Avonlea' in *Anne of Green Gables*. I read the books to Lulu when she was a child, and she loved them. I must confess I still take them off my shelf and read them. They are still delightful to me. Lulu would enjoy seeing Cavendish, and also Fairlea. Sarah's brother Ben's son Mark and my brother Gerald's grandson jointly run the family farm there. Sarah says it hasn't changed much at all since the last war. I also would like to visit my sister's grave. We should go soon, before the wedding plans get out of hand, and Lulu gets too involved.

For of course Lulu and Denby will be married this summer. They rushed over yesterday afternoon to tell me their news. I happened to be pulling a few weeds in the front border when Denby's car stopped with a screech, and the two tumbled out. They came toward me hand in hand, faces shining. I was suddenly taken back seventy years and remembering my sister Norah and Harry coming into the house from their walk. Harry had rushed up from Fairlea when he heard that Norah was traveling out west to her friend Barbara's wedding. Norah had been in a tizzy all week wondering how she would feel about him when she saw him at last. She needn't have worried, of course. Harry was as much in love with her as Denby was with my Lulu, and the expression on their faces was eerily similar as these two in my garden yesterday: a mixture of joy, wonderment, and amazement.

I straightened up and removed my gardening gloves, and accepted my granddaughter's exuberant embrace.

"We're engaged, Gran!" she exclaimed unnecessarily.

"You surprise me," I murmured dryly.

Lulu grinned. "I guess you could tell something was up, right, Gran?" I put out my hand to Denby and offered congratulations, then invited them both in. We went around to the side door where I put my gloves away and washed my hands in the entryway sink. The entryway is a handy alcove next to the kitchen where I hang up outdoor clothes, stash rubber boots, and the smaller gardening tools. I believe they call them mudrooms these days. There is a cupboard where I keep my vases and flower arranging stuff, and shelves for pantry overflow. All in all, it is a useful little room.

I asked Denby to open the wine that he would find in the refrigerator, and Lulu to get down my best wine glasses from the top shelf. They had been wedding presents from Norah and Harry, fine, thin crystal, and I still had the whole dozen, despite their traveling more than half way across the continent, and two subsequent moves. We were just pouring the wine when the front doorbell rang, and Lulu went to answer it. I heard delighted voices in the front hall, and a moment later two more of my grandchildren, Stephanie Williams and her cousin Paul McNabb, followed Lulu into the kitchen.

"Wine!" exclaimed Stephanie. "What are we celebrating? Gran, darling, we have the most wonderful news." And she kissed my cheek.

Denby, who was reaching up into the cupboard for more wine glasses, turned around and regarded the newcomers with amazement. Stephanie was equally astonished.

"Denby! What on earth are you doing in my grandmother's kitchen?" she exclaimed.

"I wasn't aware you two were acquainted," I said.

"Acquainted! Why, Denby and I are cousins! Paul, you met him years ago when we were all kids together. Auntie Margie used to dump him on us when Norma refused to babysit him," she laughed. She accepted the glass of wine, and as I led them into the living room, Stephanie was still explaining. "At least we called her Auntie Margie, really she was Pop's first cousin. This is utterly amazing! I had no idea you knew my cousin Lulu!"

"Not only know her, but plan to marry her this summer."

"Do sit down, everybody," I said with a smile. "It seems as though we have a lot of catching up to do."

"Whatever happened to Bruce?" Stephanie asked Lulu interestedly. "I thought he gave you a ring at Christmas."

Lulu smiled and said lightly, "I am happy to say he jilted me. He eloped with some woman he met at university without so much as a by your leave. I had already written a Dear John letter to him, went over to confess all to his parents and return the ring, and found out that he was married! And I was so worried about hurting him. He obviously wasn't worried about hurting me."

"I'm not surprised," declared Stephanie. "I always thought you could do better than Bruce." She paused and smiled slyly at her cousin. "Denby is much better."

"Galling, though," Lulu went on cheerfully, "that his heart won't be broken."

"You said you had some news, Stephanie," I interjected, though I suspected what it was.

Stephanie glanced at Paul. "Shall we tell them? I don't want to upstage Denby and Lulu."

"No fear, Steph," Denby said.

"Well, folks, after years of agonizing, Paul and I are going to get married. Mum and Aunt Carrie are making disparaging noises, and Uncle Tom is having a fit. Pop is trying to calm them all down."

"Uncle Toby told me just to go and get married and make it a *fait accompli*," Paul said.

"That would have been my advice as well," I said, amazed that I should be in agreement with Toby over anything. "After all, how old are you two? Thirty-five? Well past the age of consent, anyway."

"I won't be thirty-five until November," Stephanie said, "and my biological clock is ticking furiously away. I want babies now."

It was odd that Carrie and Sheila hadn't been on the phone to me straightaway as soon as Stephanie and Paul had announced their intentions. Perhaps they knew what I would say.

"Are you still photographing everything in sight?" she was saying to Denby. Turning to Lulu, she added, "He had this camera when he was about ten and he followed us all around snapping photos. He was mowing lawns to save up for a proper camera with a telephoto lens, if I remember correctly."

"He takes wonderful photos!" Lulu exclaimed. "Look at these!" And she jumped up and retrieved the photographs Denby had framed for me. Stephanie and Paul admired the photographs.

Stephanie looked up at Denby and said quietly, "You are wasting your time teaching biology, Denby. Will you take some photos of Paul and me when we tie the knot?"

I saw Denby flush with pleasure and smile affectionately at his cousin. "I would love to. Congratulations to you both, by the way."

"And to you, too," said Paul. He looked from Denby to Lulu. "How long have you known each other?"

"Three weeks ago I didn't know she existed." Stephanie blinked. "Love at first sight, huh? As I said before, you couldn't do better, Lulu. I've known this guy forever, and he's perfect, except he's got a bit of a temper. I guess I haven't seen you, Denby, since your mom's funeral, and that was two years ago."

"Nearly three."

"Oh, golly, is it that long? I told myself I would keep in touch. I'm sorry, Den. How's your dad?"

"He's well, and coping beautifully. He's away on a cruise with a lady friend at the moment."

Lulu said, a bit shyly, "Does it seem odd that we should get engaged after such a short acquaintance?"

Stephanie leaned back. "Not at all. Paul and I have known forever that we would eventually marry."

Denby laughed. "I remember you introducing Paul to me the first time I came to stay with you and Aunt Sheila. You said, 'This is my cousin Paul, and we're getting married when we grow up.' You were about ten."

Meanwhile, Paul was chatting quietly to Lulu about each other's plans. No longer concentrating, I listened to the scraps of conversation drifting by me.

"Denby will take fabulous photos of you and Stephanie. It's a shame Aunt Carrie and Aunt Sheila don't approve."

"They'll come around."

"Honeymooning on Mayne Island! I always envied Petra and David that cottage. We went over there a few times when Lulu and her brothers were little. You'll love it, Den!"

"We've got the license, done the blood tests, Steph just has to set a date."

"Just tell the family when and where you're doing it, and go ahead."

This was Lulu's advice, wise for so young a girl.

"Where will you two live?" Stephanie asked Denby. "You're not still in that little hole near City Hall, are you?"

"As a matter of fact, I am," he replied, and turning to Lulu, he added, "You haven't seen my bachelor pad, Lou. The bedroom is my dark room—and I sleep in a Murphy bed in the living room." He looked at me for permission, eyebrows raised, and reached for the bottle of wine to replenish the glasses when I nodded to him. "We'll definitely have to look for a bigger apartment, Lou," he went on. "We'll have to rent for a while, I guess."

I suddenly came awake with a bright idea in my mind.

"What about the apartment downstairs?" I asked.

"Gosh, Gran, I'd forgotten about the suite," Stephanie said. "Have you been down there, Lulu?"

Lulu shook her head and commented that she hadn't even realized that there was one. I told them about the 'mother-in-law suite' that had already been there when Jeremy and I had bought the house, and our efforts at some renovations downstairs when we redid my kitchen soon after. My cleaning lady Holly went down there once a month or so and whisked through it.

"It may have possibilities," I said, "though I haven't been down there for a couple of years. Harriet made me promise not to use the stairs in case of a fall."

"Gran, are you serious? Denby, what do you think?"

"I think it would get your Aunt Harriet off your grandmother's case," he remarked. "Didn't you say she was wanting your grandmother to move in with her? If we were nearby . . ."

"It's perfect!" exclaimed Lulu.

"Let's go down and see. Paul, you can be the consultant. After all, you are in the business."

And they all rose, taking their wine with them, and trooped down the basement stairs. I had temporarily forgotten that Paul worked for a kitchen and bathroom renovation company. He would be very useful, I thought. Their clatter on the stairs made me decide that carpeting would certainly be in order. I smiled and leaned back in my chair. It would be fun for Lulu and Denby and me to go about together and choose materials and colors. I listened to their voices, muffled by the floor, doors opening and closing, and footsteps to and fro as they inspected the premises.

It is a nice little suite, with a separate outside door that opens into the garden at the back, the house being built on the slope of the hill. There is a small kitchen and sitting room that faces the garden, so there is plenty of light for the living area of the apartment. The bathroom is rather small, but there are two good-sized bedrooms, and a smaller room off in the corner. It takes up rather more than half the basement area of the house. In the other part of the basement are the furnace room, a storage room, a cold room, and a tool room.

The four young people returned with enthusiastic smiles on their faces. "It's perfect!" Lulu repeated, coming over and kissing me affectionately. "It needs some work," said Stephanie critically. "Paul and Denby say they can do it in their spare time."

"The little room at the back will be ideal for my darkroom, and we can make a study out of one of the bedrooms for Lulu to write in."

"New carpeting," I said firmly. "And drapes. Not necessarily for privacy, but to make it cozy. What do you think?"

"I like those blinds you have on the kitchen windows," Lulu said. "They're the same as in your kitchen up here."

"Roman shades," I said. "Yes. We put in new countertops and floor tile down there as well when we redid the kitchen. How does it look?"

"It's just fine, Gran," Paul replied. "Paint the walls, build some cupboards and shelves in the spare room, some new light fixtures, and Bob's your uncle."

"New carpets in the sitting room and up the stairs," I repeated. "Denby, it'll be fab," Lulu said, taking his arm. "When can we go and choose colors?"

"I'll be paying for all this," I added firmly. "It'll be a tax deductible expense, you know. Now, darlings, sit back down. I've got some other ideas I want you to consider."

Then I suggested that Stephanie and Paul be married in my garden whenever they wanted, instead of in an office in City Hall. Did they think their parents would agree to that? Carrie and Toby's apartment was rather small to hold a wedding, and besides, it was easier for them to come into town rather than I make my way out the valley. To tell the truth, I didn't relish an hour and a half's drive with Harriet, after her outburst the other night. We hadn't talked since then, and I was feeling a little guilty about it.

A great discussion ensued, Stephanie objecting to something that might thrust me in the middle of a family dispute. I pointed out that it was neutral territory, so to speak, and that it would be

411

simple—just sandwiches and wine and wedding cake. Did they have a minister in mind?

"We have a great friend who's a Justice of the Peace," said Stephanie. "She said she'd make herself available—just tell her where and when." She gazed seriously at Paul. "What do you think, Paul, shall we do it here? Just tell everyone to come, say, next Sunday at two o'clock?"

"Whatever you want, Love," he said. "Shall I telephone Sophie and ask her, or do you want to?"

Stephanie sat back and smiled at Paul. "Go ahead, Paul, and see what she says." She glanced over at me. "Is Sunday afternoon all right, Gran?"

I nodded. "Perfectly all right."

Paul got up and went into the kitchen. I could hear his deep voice, but not what he was saying. Finally, I heard him say, "Thanks, Sophie, see you then!" He strolled back into the sitting room and said, "Sunday at two it is.

Now you can't change your mind, Steph!"

Stephanie jumped to her feet and kissed him briefly. I caught a glimpse of Paul's face as he caught her around the waist. He smiled at me affectionately. "Thanks, Gran! What do you want us to do?"

I sat back and considered. "You two look after the cake and flowers. Lulu and I will plan the rest. Let me know the numbers later in the week. Just sandwiches and wine, my dears. We'll keep it very simple."

Both Carrie and Sheila telephoned me later that evening, both sounding resigned at their children's plans. Carrie was a little reproachful.

"You always did encourage them, Mother."

"They know their own minds, dear."

"Did you talk to David and Harriet?"

"Yes. Harriet agrees with me for once—and I understand so does Toby. Amazing things can happen, can't they."

"Mother, you're too hard on Toby," Carrie grumbled. "I'll make four dozen tea sandwiches, and Sheila will bring a crudités tray. Stephanie said it's going to be simple. Do you need me to do anything else? Dishes or wineglasses?"

"Petra has said that she will bring a dozen glasses. I have lots, dear. But I could use your big coffee maker." We chatted for a while about plans, and then she rang off. Today I got in touch with Holly and Barry, her husband, and they'll both be here on Saturday to spruce up the house and garden. Holly insisted that she come on Sunday and serve. "I don't want you getting all tired out, Mrs Ferris," she said sternly.

I shall talk to Lulu and Denby when they drop over tomorrow about the trip back east, early July, perhaps? Possibly Denby would stay in the house—he and Paul would want to work on the suite, anyway.

I smile again into the mirror. Oh, it will be splendid to see Susie, who will turn ninety while I am there, and my dear Sarah! She has a granddaughter around Lulu's age, so Lulu will have someone to go about with while I visit my dear sister's stepdaughter. I shall write her tomorrow after I have discussed it with Lulu, and also to Susie. Perhaps I shall just phone Susie. It's been ages since I've talked to her.

Yes, it is good to have things to look forward to. The little wedding in the garden on Sunday, the renovation of the suite downstairs and shopping for furnishings, a trip to Ontario and Prince Edward Island in July, Lulu and Denby's wedding, and then their return from their honeymoon and later their trip to the Galapagos. How can I not stay young?

Finis

413